THE
SHAAR
PRESS

THE JUDAICA IMPRINT
FOR THOUGHTFUL PEOPLE

The Gordian

A novel by
Yair Weinstock

translated by
Sheindel Weinbach

edited by
Miriam Zakon

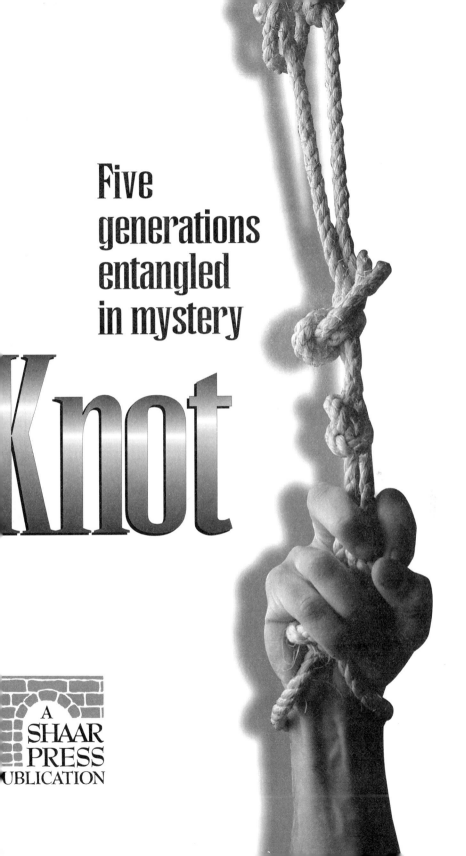

Five
generations
entangled
in mystery

Knot

A
SHAAR
PRESS
PUBLICATION

Published by **SHAAR PRESS**
Distributed by MESORAH PUBLICATIONS, LTD.
4401 Second Avenue / Brooklyn, New York 11232 / (718) 921-9000

Distributed in Israel by SIFRIATI / A. GITLER BOOKS
10 Hashomer Street / Bnei Brak 51361

Distributed in Europe by J. LEHMANN HEBREW BOOKSELLERS
20 Cambridge Terrace / Gateshead, Tyne and Wear / England NE8 1RP

Distributed in Australia and New Zealand by GOLDS BOOK & GIFT SHOP
36 William Street / Balaclava 3183, Vic., Australia

Distributed in South Africa by KOLLEL BOOKSHOP
Shop 8A Norwood Hypermarket / Norwood 2196 / Johannesburg, South Africa

ISBN: 0-89906-285-7 Hard Cover
ISBN: 0-89906-286-5 Paperback

Printed in the United States of America by Noble Book Press Corp.
Custom bound by Sefercraft, Inc. / 4401 Second Avenue / Brooklyn, N.Y. 11232

Do not judge your fellow

until you have reached his place.

— Chapters of the Fathers

The
Gordian
Knot

Т

he mass of people streamed down the streets of Jerusalem towards the Old City. The large fleet of buses could not contain even a fraction of this pulsating flood of humanity. Thousands made their way in private cars, despite the strictures of security forces to refrain from doing so. Traffic on Jaffa Street came to a standstill as myriads of pedestrians headed for Jaffa Gate. At the same time, a huge throng of walkers swarmed the streets of Meah Shearim in the direction of Damascus Gate.

The snow began falling from early evening.

For two days stormy winds had howled through the streets of Lublin. On the third day, the sound grew even more frightful, almost human. If you had no compelling reason to be outside, you stayed home. Only the brave dared face the chill wind and freezing temperatures.

Towards evening, black clouds spread across the city skies. At the edge of the horizon even thicker, heavier clouds could be seen approaching. Suddenly the wind died down, its demonic shrieking stilled, giving way to snowflakes rare in their enormity. Within a very short time Lublin was covered with a fleecy feather-quilt. Store shutters were quickly drawn and bolted as both shopkeepers and customers prepared to dash homeward before the mighty snowstorm trapped them outdoors, far from the cozy warmth of their homes. The hustle of the market turned to stillness; the big city grew silent.

The sound of footsteps echoed in the quiet street. The snow piled up on the dry, frozen ground with dizzying rapidity. With each step the man's shoes sank deeper and deeper into the soft whiteness, leaving behind them a trail of footsteps swiftly disappearing in the clean fresh snow.

The French flag flew proudly over the gateway. The man knocked quietly, hesitantly, on the door. No answer. He intensified his knocking to a thunderous drumming.

"Ye-es!" a familiar voice sang out slowly, as footsteps thumped down the stairway and the door opened.

A warm vapor escaped through the narrow crack and a pair of suspicious eyes peered out, scanning his face.

"Oh, it's you, *Rabbiner.* Come in. Don't stand outside in this terrible cold!"

"Is the Consul at home?" He was impatient. Lublin had not known such freezing weather for many years. The journey home still lay before him, through deep, overpowering snowdrifts, with nothing more than a pair of worn shoes to protect his feet.

"The Consul will return from Warsaw in two days' time, the weather permitting, to be sure. But the postal carriage has already come today. Wait a moment while I go up to check the mail pouch."

Another moment passed. The man returned with a long grey envelope in his hand. "Yes, there's a letter for you. You are lucky, *Rabbiner,* that you did not come all this way in vain!"

He studied the envelope with its familiar seal. In the past two years he'd had many such as this, but none as critically fateful. Had he received a satisfactory reply? Were his questions answered?

"Thank you!" Even in the stress of the moment he did not forget the dictates of aristocratic courtesy. He turned around and began the long trek back home.

Closing and bolting the door to his house, the hunched figure pulled out the letter and read avidly, fervently. Again and again he stared at the large sheets, lest he miss a precious word or even a single letter which might have some unknown significance.

Yes, everything was understood. The message was clear. The words had never been so transparent. It was not the intense cold that caused his hands to tremble. He lit another candle and sat down by the table to write.

All through the night the quill scratched across the thick paper. It was of the finest quality: It would need to stand the test of the many coming years. Occasionally he would halt and dip his quill into the small inkwell. Then he continued writing with infinite diligence.

Dawn rose on snow-covered Lublin as he transcribed his last lines:

> "... and therefore I hereby command my family: After I depart this world, open only the first part of this will. The second part, which I have entitled 'A Secret Scroll' and have duly enclosed within a sealed wooden tube, shall not be opened under any circumstances! It must be transmitted from son to son, generation after generation.
>
> "I beg you, guard this scroll as your most precious possession, and may the Guardian of Israel protect you from all sorrow and harm. Do not lose it and do not let it out of your possession. One hundred years after my death it is to be opened by my descendants and its contents read most carefully by them. I repeat and beg of you with all my heart: Please, transmit to the coming generations my command that you open the scroll on the one hundredth anniversary of my death. This will prevent a great calamity from befalling the Jewish people, G-d forbid, collectively and individually."

The quill was dipped into the black inkwell for one last time. He affixed his signature with a sure hand, spread the sheets of paper by the stove, and when the ink had dried, rolled up the thick papers and bound them together with coarse string. He slipped the roll of paper into a wooden tube and sealed it over with wax, a seal within a seal, and laid it away in his closet.

He stood lost in his thoughts for a long time. He finally shook himself out of his reverie, got up and left the house in silence. Bright white feathers of snow floated about in the freezing air above, circling dizzyingly before sinking slowly to the ground.

That day he did not go out to work.

After the morning roll call he slipped off to his barracks, waiting for the last of the stragglers to leave.

When he was finally alone, he leaped off the shockingly narrow bunks and sped to the rear of his room. His long fingers rummaged feverishly in a hidden niche, finally drawing out a ring of shining nickel keys.

He hid behind the barracks for an eternity, his shaved head peering out from time to time. Finally, he found the opportune moment; no one was about. This was his chance!

He sprang out with lightning speed, shooting frightened glances over his shoulders in all directions to see if anyone was watching.

The key almost slipped through his fingers while he was working to turn it in the keyhole. The brilliant idea of hiding his treasure deep inside the very lion's den, in the administrative barracks, had been entirely his.

Each morning after roll call, the officers went off to the dining hall. While they were busy gorging themselves, he would enter their room and make himself at home.

But this morning he was gripped by a paralyzing fear. He had a sinking premonition of evil and had to force himself to overcome his terror. Completely illogical, he told himself. The strict rule of order made no allowance for officers to be found in this particular part of the camp at this hour. It was thanks to these punctilious regulations that he had never yet been caught.

He entered, promising himself that today he would take his 'package' with him and hide it someplace else, anywhere, so long as it would spare him setting foot in this room ever again.

He quickly wound the straps around his arm, arranged the *tefillin* on his head, hastily murmuring broken phrases of the blessings and verses and covering his eyes with his hand...

Sometimes a person gets the feeling that his heart has stopped beating. He suddenly felt that his heart had, indeed, grown silent and dead within him.

His ears had not deceived him. He had heard the clicking of keys outside. The door opened. He froze in place, like a pillar of salt.

"W-what?" the roar shook the walls of the barracks, activating shock waves that bounced off every item in the room. "Here? In my very room!"

There was no point in trying to explain. A hail of blows pelted down on his head, his back, upon every square inch of his tortured body.

"What else are you hiding here?" the officer forced him to get up. He rose laboriously, weaving on his legs, awaiting the approaching end. He pointed helplessly to a hiding place.

The officer's thick arm drew out a long wooden tube. "What's this?" he wondered, trying futilely to open the sealed cover. "Never mind. Nothing will happen if I let this ride until tonight. When I've finished my shift I'll deal with your treasures," he hissed between his teeth.

Crushed and broken, he lay on the concrete floor, his body burning like fire. He lost count of the hours and had no idea if it was day or night. It didn't really matter; he was indifferent to everything and didn't know whether to be thankful for his life, or to be sorry that he had not forfeited it at the mercy of the whip's lashes.

Everything had drained from him and lost all meaning. Until now, the scroll had been his possession; he'd held onto it as a lifeline, extracting drops of encouragement and comfort from it in his most difficult hours. Now he had betrayed his trust; it had been wrenched from him cruelly and was gone! Would it ever be returned to him?

The Weizmann Institute — Rechovot 5755 (1995)

The microscopic creatures writhed in the liquid as if delirious. They danced and gyrated in all directions. He scrutinized them through the lens of his electronic microscope and compared the result with a previous picture, a satisfied murmur accompanying the examination.

"The power of change!" he chuckled.

PART ONE
DAVID AND BUKI

Moshav "Yetzivim"
5713-5720 (1953-1960)

1

The ringing of the alarm clock rent the stillness of the night. A hand shot out from under the warm cover to silence the raucous sound before it awakened the whole family.

David peeked at his wristwatch with sleep-webbed eyes. The phosphorescent hands indicated the number four.

His bed beckoned to him in the darkness, calling him back to its cozy warmth, bidding him to lie down and place his weary bones upon the straw mattress. A brief battle took place. David wanted so badly to go back to bed, to curl up under the thick, warm woolen blanket and drift back into sleep…

"A waste of time," he scolded himself, somewhat annoyed over the battle that repeated itself each morning. "Dina and Chedva are waiting for me."

He slipped quickly into a shirt whose original color had long since faded, and into wide, dirt-encrusted trousers which had known better days. He drew on his high boots and slipped silently out of the house.

When he emerged into the bracing air he was glad that he had not succumbed to the urge to sleep. This was his favorite time of day. A blessed silence reigned. The black sky was strewn with thousands of stars and even the east showed no sign yet of the approaching dawn.

A chill wind caressed his face as he strode energetically along the dirt path. He suddenly shivered, whether from the sudden cold or from something else, he wasn't sure. A dull, intangible sensation struck him and he felt he was not alone. There was some other presence here besides him; was someone watching him this very moment, studying and surveying his steps?

"Nonsense." He quickly dismissed the thought. "Winter has sprung upon us and it's become cold, that's all!"

Nevertheless, he hastened his pace and strode quickly towards the cowshed to make sure that everything was all right, that nothing had been stolen and no damage wrought.

When he reached the shed he felt reassured. This was his domain; here he was intimately familiar with every square centimeter.

He could already hear the impatient lowing of the cows.

"Patience!" he shouted at the locked door. "Don't you realize I'm already here?" He quickly bent down to the bottom of the water barrel and took the key out of its hiding place. He turned it twice in the lock and swung the door wide open. The rusty hinges creaked their protest. The sound was the steady accompaniment to each morning's ritual and had become an inseparable part of milking time, but this morning it evoked a hidden fear in his heart, as if it were a tolling alarm bell.

"What's the matter with me this morning? Why am I so frightened by every little rustling?" David turned the light on in the barn. Chedva and Dina stood silently side by side, gazing at him with their large eyes. "See, it pays to be patient," he scolded them affectionately as he stood the rinsed pail in its place and began milking.

If there is anything good in this world, it is this. You hitch yourself comfortably down on a stool and squeeze. The warm milk squirts in a thin stream into the big pail, releasing a bubbly froth. The cow stands content, casting her head back from time to time and glancing at her master, as if reading his mind. If he was not mistaken, he thought he could spot an occasional gleam of affection in those big animal eyes. Sometimes it seemed to him that a human soul was hiding inside that huge body. If there is any rapport, any connection between man and animal, this is where it was woven, between the coarse concrete wall and the manure-laden floor. What others considered an offensive smell which could not be borne for even a short spell was for him a heavenly aroma, the embodiment of nature.

David would not have traded the predawn milking hour for anything in the world. He didn't care if Odelia took on the evening shift. But the early morning was his hour of communion, his connection with the little bit of good in the world which he could call his own.

He would sit and chat with the cows, at ease, the pails filling up with frothy, steaming milk. Sometimes a cow might turn mischievous and kick the bucket over with her foot and the precious liquid would spill over and spray his face with a mighty splash, whitening his long dark beard. How many scoldings had he already directed at the misbehaving cows over the damage they caused...

Alas, *parnassah, parnassah*. A man had to make a living, didn't he? A pity he had to sell the precious milk. He would gladly have gulped it down to the last drop, but he was paid for it, a good price at that. How would he be able to feed his family if he squandered his treasures?

By the time he left the barn carrying the metal jugs, the east had already turned rosy. Dark clouds were rapidly approaching from the west, mercilessly covering the delicate orb which had just risen out of the darkness to shed its golden rays. Darkness returned to cover the *moshav*. A cold wind began whistling. Soon the first rain would whip him with its large drops.

He turned the key quietly in the keyhole and tiptoed into the room.

"David..." Odelia was already in the kitchen. The small kettle was standing on the smoky paraffin stove and she poured him a cup of hot tea. The smell of mint, *naanah*, filled the kitchen and David inhaled it deeply into his lungs with pleasure. "You don't have to tiptoe; the children are fast asleep and I'm already up."

David carefully sipped the scalding tea, taking tiny sips lest he burn his tongue.

"D'you know, something strange happened on my way to the barn. I had this eerie feeling that I wasn't alone, that someone else was wandering about outside."

Odelia glanced at him with suspicion. It was beginning again…

"You have nothing to fear," she said in a quiet voice. "Maybe it's because of the robbery at Shikma…"

The words were hardly out of her mouth when she wished she could take them back. David looked at her, his eyes dilating with terror.

"No, I didn't hear a thing about that," he whispered. "Are they beginning to get closer? Oh, no!"

It was too late for regrets. She'd have to tell him everything. "Yesterday in the early dawn infiltrators entered Moshav Shikma. They stole three cows and two calves from Shmulik Bodenheimer's barn. His wife, Rivka, heard strange noises around two in the morning but was too afraid to get out of bed. They only discovered their loss this morning."

"Why didn't you tell me? We've got to arrange a night patrol, starting this very evening. Oh, it's very late already." He glanced at his watch. "I've got to run off to *shul*." He hastily grabbed his *tallis* and *tefillin* from the dresser and slipped into the children's room to kiss the sleeping tots who lay enthralled in their sweet childhood dreams.

His prayers that morning were troubled and filled with thoughts that had nothing to do with the text, thoughts generated by the present situation. To his surprise, he discovered that he was not the only one. Everyone seemed upset and overwrought. What was the matter? Had a single theft in Shikma disturbed people to such a degree?

"What do you say about the Bodenheimer robbery?" he asked Hillel Weiss after prayers. "I'm telling you, the chutzpah of these Arabs knows no bounds. And we keep quiet and do nothing. I heard about it only this morning…"

"What are you talking about?" Hillel looked at him in surprise. "Is that your only concern? Your own people come first!"

"What do you mean?"

"What? You haven't heard? Last night we also had the honor of a similar 'visit.' Five sheep stolen from Mazuz' sheepfold."

Now he understood why his fellow *moshavniks* had looked so upset. This time the plague had struck them. They suddenly felt helpless, exposed to danger.

His feeling that someone had been near him that morning had been correct... An alarm began ringing loudly inside his head. Was there any single island of safe, solid ground? His hands and feet began trembling, dark spots danced crazily before his eyes and everything whirled in a dizzy circle about him.

"David, what's the matter?" Hillel bent over him, holding a washing cup filled with water. "Why did you fall down? We thought you fainted!"

He lay on the cold floor, stunned. For a moment he looked about, not understanding what was going on around him. What had happened? What did they want from him?

"It's nothing, really. Just a spell of dizziness that will soon pass," he whispered. A strange thought crossed his mind: This scene could almost have been funny. His position accorded him an unusual angle of vision; Hillel and Sheike's rounded eyes, Kobi and Mordoch's heavy-set chins, Moishe's reddish beard. He had never noticed it was that long...

"*Chevra*, move aside, I'm getting up," he announced, leaping lightly to his feet.

"You're okay?" Hillel ran after him, the washing cup still poised in his hand, just in case.

"Maybe you'll be kind enough to remove the water?" David said in a tone that mixed reproach with warmth.

"Look at him, the big hero," chuckled Mordoch. "First you stretch out on the ground without any warning and a moment later you're angry that people rush to help you."

David looked at him, his expression inscrutable. The spark that had been ignited in his eyes for a fraction of a second died out, with the same suddenness it had appeared.

"Friends," he announced coldly, "we are being targeted, and if we don't stop the infiltrators now, our *moshav* will become a free-for-all to any petty thief from Gaza. We've got to set up rotating shifts to stand guard, starting tonight."

A babble of voices cut his words short; everyone was talking at once, as if seeking to shake off the tension. First of all, several *moshavniks* said, David should be exempt from duty; he wasn't feeling well. Everyone had seen how he had fallen and fainted. Secondly, they couldn't make decisions about night patrol on their own. They would have to discuss it, plan their strategy and coordinate it with the security forces.

"Oh, sure! They'll protect us just like they helped Shikma and like they prevented the big robbery in Moshav Tvua, when the huge barn was emptied out. Fifteen cows they shlepped off to Rafiach, and we're expected to sit, arms folded, waiting for someone to do the work for us?" This was David's longest speech since the establishment of the *moshav*. He spoke with bitter cynicism and suddenly felt his knees buckling under. He eased himself down on the bench.

It was finally decided to wait another day or so. Until now the infiltrators had not struck twice in one place, at least not in the same week. Meanwhile, they would reinforce the barbed-wire fence that surrounded the *moshav*. They already knew where the thieves had entered the past night. It was a breach near the Morali home at the northeastern end. Today they would repair the damage. Two men would keep watch that night. Woe to the Arab who dared attempt to steal anything...

"Tell me, David, what really happened to you?" Hillel walked by his side on their way home from prayers.

David was very fond of Hillel, but he kept those feelings under wraps. Hillel sensed it, however, in his own way. The two were like night and day. Hillel was an inveterate chatterbox, optimistic and good natured. David was chronically taciturn, a pessimist, his eyes dull with futility. Even in their outward appearance the contrast was marked. David was tall, thin and long legged. Hillel resembled a bouncing ball. He had virtually no neck; the outline of his chin slipped straight down to his enormous paunch. He rolled from place to place on a pair of thick legs.

In one area people were of a unanimous opinion: Hillel was one of the best. He overflowed with magnanimity and goodness. He could not stand distress, especially in a close friend, such as David for example.

"How about coming in for a hot cup of tea with *naanah*?" David suggested, evading his question. Hillel declined. They parted with a nod.

Hillel was filled with disturbing thoughts. What was the matter with David? Why was he always so distant and reserved?

Breakfast was waiting for David on the table. Buki jumped on him with glee. "Abba, come see what I did yesterday!" Little Baruch — Buki — pulled him towards the yard with his small hand and pointed to a small channel no more than a centimeter wide, running around the base of the apple tree. "I dug it all by myself! It's got to be irrigated with water, right?"

David stood speechless. A three-year-old with such initiative and such articulate speech. The words rolled from his lips like polished jewels, his childlike enunciation filled with warmth and charm. Without a word, David encircled the small figure and drew him up to his chest, hugging the child fiercely. "Have you drunk your cocoa yet?"

"No, but Yigal hasn't eaten his cereal yet either. So what?"

David trundled the child off to the kitchen and made sure he drank the cocoa, sweetened with brown sugar which the father had obtained through the black market with considerable effort. He couldn't understand how someone could leave cocoa on the table without drinking it.

The sun's rays had broken through the clouds when he sat down with Odelia in their small kitchen. A gentle light penetrated the snowy-white lace curtains. A beam of light penetrated his heart and flooded it with hope.

He quietly told her the news while they ate bread and salad and his own home-made cheese. Yigal sat on her lap and Buki by her side in a highchair. The young mother fed her children quickly and efficiently.

"Who's going on patrol first?"

David cleared his throat. "Mordoch and Shukrun," he answered quickly, ashamed to tell her that he had been disqualified because of the stupid incident in *shul*.

She asked no superfluous questions. She had always known how to handle him: no pressure, and avoid stepping on his toes. That was her special skill, the essence of their marriage.

By the time he went out to the field, the clouds had already dispersed. The strong wind had driven them southward to release their stored water upon the heads of their enemies. Perhaps it was for the best. Let them keep busy in their fields. Let the Arabs be preoccupied in productive work and leave them alone.

For the first time in a long while, he stood and looked at the horizon, anxiously studying the border fence. He felt fear sending its cold, clammy fingers to clasp his heart with a painful pinch. The border was so close! If they wanted, they could cross over with nothing to stop them and…

He shook his head to banish these disturbing thoughts and fell upon the vegetable rows with zest, spade in hand. Weeds had suddenly sprung up between the tomato plants. He had probably been slack in his weeding during the summer and now had to suffer the consequences. There were no two ways about it; the rules of life were hard and fast. If you didn't sow with tears and sweat, you didn't reap with gladness.

The smell of the first rain wafted up from the damp ground. The earth had drunk up the isolated drops thirstily after the summer dryness. He broke off a clod of earth and inhaled its smell with pleasure. The light drizzle had not sufficed to turn the dry ground into messy mud, but had given the earth that primal smell of the first rains, the *yoreh*.

He continued working for many hours, back bent, investing all of his strength to remove every suspicious-looking stalk. In the summer, when the sun had beat down upon his head and his body had been bathed with rivulets of sweat, he had been unable to make the effort, and had worked superficially. Today, that laziness was taking its harsh toll. Now, with the sun partially hiding between the clouds, peeking out now and then for a moment, the work was not as arduous.

Something unusual aroused his sudden attention. Footprints.

The rake fell from his grasp. He studied the marks with intense concentration. There was no doubt about it; two pairs of footprints led from the outside to the interior of the *moshav*. But these were not the prints of bare feet, as had been discovered that morning near Mazuz' barn. These were footprints he was familiar with — high, hobnailed boots! They snaked their way through his field into the *moshav*.

His forehead became covered with a cold sweat. His mouth opened wide in shock, but only a dry cough emerged from his throat. A silent scream echoed into space.

2

The figure raced over the fields of the *moshav,* over the furrows and rows of vegetables, looking to the eyes of the *moshavniks* like some kind of vengeful ghost. When the figure approached they were barely able to identify David's cadaverous face, so stamped was it with horrified panic. "What happened, David?" they asked, attempting to pull some explanation from him. He waved his hands wildly in the direction of the fields, blurting unintelligible staccato syllables. He then resumed his headlong flight towards Yoni's house to report to the *moshav* secretary.

Yoni's heart skipped a beat or two at the sight of his unexpected guest. David's face was completely bloodless; he looked like a figure fresh out of the grave.

"Mr. Eliad…" Yoni was taken aback. "What has happened?"

David tried to say something but his tongue refused to obey. He tried again and again but not a syllable came out. Yoni took out a bottle of shnaps from the wooden cabinet on the side and poured a shot for David. David downed it in one gulp and felt his throat scalded by its sharpness. He heard himself saying: "A terrible calamity is about to happen; I'm telling you, something horrible!"

Yoni stared at him, not comprehending. "What are you talking about?"

The words stuck in David's throat. The footprints! He wanted to tell about the footprints he had discovered in his fields, about the hobnailed boots that led into the interior of the *moshav,* but his tongue betrayed him. All he succeeded in blurting out was: "A terrible calamity." The words repeated themselves again and again, like a broken record.

Yoni looked at him and shook his head. *From the very first moment, I was against accepting him.*

David shook himself, the warmth of the cheap whiskey surging in his veins, melting his momentary panic. "Come with me, quick." The urgency in his voice convinced the *moshav* secretary. He ran after David to the field to examine the fearful evidence.

A few minutes was enough to convince him. Yoni raced back to his house. He threw his army jacket over his shoulders, a souvenir from his soldiering days, and raced to the tarpaulin-covered jeep parked in his yard.

With a roar the jeep sped to the nearby Bedouin camp.

A dense cloud of fear had descended upon Moshav Yetzivim. Half the *moshav* streamed towards David's field to see with their own eyes and be convinced; the other half did not get the chance because someone reminded them that it would be a foolish thing to do. With so many footprints, they would obliterate the evidence!

Everyone awaited Yoni's return with bated breath. The teenagers rushed out to be the first ones to catch sight of the jeep and the two experienced trackers he'd set out to bring.

The rains made their second appearance that day. A strong wind brought a sheaf of clouds in its wake. The skies darkened with the same rapidity in which they had cleared before. This time it was a generous rain that swamped the entire area and sent the crowd scurrying for shelter.

Yoni did not arrive until afternoon. The Bedouin tracker Salaah had gone shopping in Beersheba and Yoni had awaited his return to the camp. After an hour Yoni had understood that time was working against him. He dragged Salaah's comrade Monir along with him and the two arrived drenched to the bone.

"There's no point in going out to the field." Monir got out of the jeep shivering. Water ran down from him, gathering in puddles at his feet. "The rain has wiped out all the tracks, you can be sure."

Nevertheless, Yoni and Monir went to inspect the evidence. The Bedouin did the best he could. He spread himself out on the ground, full length, getting himself filthy with mud. With infinite determination, he examined every centimeter of ground as if looking for precious diamonds. He sniffed at the mud and finally said, hopelessly: "There's nothing here. Everything has been wiped out. No footsteps, no odor, nothing."

That night no one closed their eyes. The terrible thought of murderous infiltrators hiding in the area banished all sleep from the members of the *moshav*. The endless night was prefaced by many hours of thorough, intensive searching from house to house, chicken coop to chicken coop, barn to barn.

"I don't want you to overlook a single building." Yoni gathered all the members to the playground near the *moshav* store and handed out orders in his strong voice. "Remember, check every storage shed, every haystack. At least two infiltrators have slipped into our *moshav*. What they are capable of doing, I have no need to tell you…"

Yetzivim was searched thoroughly that night. After hours of searching, the members returned home with mixed emotions. They bolted their doors carefully, drew the shutters on every window and… trembled with fear. The frightening knowledge that the intruders had not been found paralyzed the entire *moshav*.

The following morning they emerged from their houses red eyed. The terrible night was over.

"*Nu*, David. How did you pass the night? Did you stand by the door with a broomstick?"

David froze. From the first day the *moshav* had been established, that voice had never addressed him. He looked at Meir Tzuriel with glassy eyes.

"Leave me be." he begged plaintively. Meir continued on to the *beis knesses*, half walking, half skipping. He had accomplished what he set out to do.

"And I tell you there were footprints there." Yoni stood by the long washbasin with its many faucets, surrounded by the worshipers of the first *minyan*. They demanded an explanation. Some (the disappointed ones who had not made it to the field) even went so far as to claim that it had all been a figment of David's imagination and there were no prints at all.

"Of course there were!" Yoni argued heatedly. "If not for the rain, we would have tracked them down already last night. But never mind. Let those mice sit in their hole for another day or two. We'll find them yet!"

"But I'm so scared," peeped a childish treble. Everyone burst into laughter. Moshe, the *moshav* clown, always managed to break the tension at the most difficult moments with his bubbling humor.

Two days passed and the tension dissipated. It had been a mistake, or perhaps the infiltrators had fled. Perhaps they had been frightened away by the high state-of-alert. Life returned to its normal routine.

And then everything exploded...

As he walked towards the barn before dawn, David felt an unaccustomed serenity. Thank G-d, the nightmare had passed. He drank in the cold night air and looked with pleasure at the homes of the slumbering *moshavniks*.

Something suddenly caught his attention. It was nebulous, indefinite; more a premonition than anything visual. Wait. Stefansky's windows. Why were they open wide at such an hour? In this intense cold?

He approached with hesitant steps, drew out a flashlight from his pocket and flashed its beam inside the room. Pools of dark blood spread on the floor tiles, next to the children's beds. And the beds themselves...

A long moment of eternity passed. He stood petrified, his blood frozen in his veins. What was this? The mad thought flickered through his numbed brain: *Had he gotten this far, the wretched Roman Spiegel?*

A dreadful scream finally emerged from his paralyzed throat. The cry reverberated in the air, suspended for a moment above his head, only to come crashing down in thousands of smithereens, echoing again and again between the houses.

"He-ee-elp!"

"He's coming to."

"Give him another dose, please, Nurse. Let him sleep for at least two days. He mustn't be allowed to wake up so soon; his nerves are shot."

Voices, sounds hovering very close, touching but not touching. Who was talking there in the background? Everything was so vague and hazy. *They've stuffed my head up with cotton wool until it feels about to burst. Why can't I see anything?*

A needleprick in his arm and everything began going black again. The order he had tried to impose upon his brain cells was being demolished, his mind was in a turmoil. The vestiges of his thoughts melted down and ran off as the bittersweet intoxication took over. The voices receded, disintegrating into absolute nothingness. Quiet. Blessed silence. *Now I can float off upon the wings of dreams to wherever I like.*

Dreams or memories?

He felt himself returning to Latrun.

3

Latrun — 5708 (1948)

Machine guns exploded all at once in staccato bursts. The soldiers threw themselves onto the loose earth without cover, without any protection whatsoever.

The soldiers of the Seventh Brigade had failed in their previous attempt. The Arab Legion fully controlled Latrun, and it had proven its superiority over and over.

"Do they think that we have any chance of capturing such a fortified building in this idiotic way?"

David glanced to the side toward the rebellious whisper which echoed the thoughts that had been racing about inside his head for the past three days.

"Tell me," continued the stubborn whisper, proving that it was not coming from his own heart, "how can we possibly succeed: an unorganized force, untrained, against well-disciplined and experienced Legionnaires like theirs, eh?"

"Who are you?"

"I'm lying to your right. I dug myself a small ditch so that you can't see me without raising yourself. Hey, don't do that! Are you crazy? Do you want a bullet in your head?"

After night fell he was able to make the acquaintance of his entrenched neighbor. "Shai Matzliach," he introduced himself. "I'm from Battalion Two in the Alexander Brigade. I arrived last night with the group sent to help capture the Latrun Fortress. But due to faulty planning, we arrived late and became exposed to the Arab Legionnaires at sunrise. They massacred us. And you?"

"David Eliad. I was in the Givati until a week ago. Now I'm in the Seventh Brigade."

Under cover of darkness, the fighters retreated again. The attacking force returned to lick its wounds in Kibbutz Hulda.

The soldiers bit their lips in pain. The defeat was too bitter to face. The attack upon the proud fortress had ended in a complete failure. Tens of fallen and wounded soldiers lay on the ground.

"And all this a hopeless exercise. Our blood is being drained just because our commanders didn't do their homework!" Shai was bitter. This time he spoke aloud.

"Open your eyes, you fools!" he ranted. "What kind of attack did we launch today? No training, no preparation. They stick a rifle from the days of the Turks into your hand, with thirty bullets, and order you to storm the hill. That's all. It's a wonder any of us are still alive."

"Who's talking there?" Gidi, commander of the platoon, demanded, afire with rage. He had heard every word and felt, with his sharpened instinct, that this ordinary soldier, with his Oriental accent, was right in every word he uttered. The soldier was no fool. On the other hand, he was liable to start the entire platoon thinking, and that was something very unhealthy. A thinking soldier was capable of rebelling.

"Shai. When we get settled I want to see you in my tent. And that's an order." Shai was silenced. David, sitting nearby, thought he would burst. If a person said the truth, he deserved a punishment?

The members of the kibbutz watched their return from their windows. The men's faces said it all; there was no need to add a thing. The expression of frustration and despair sat upon the returnees like a dark cloud. The wounded were immediately transferred to a makeshift hospital. The treatment of the dead took place far from a seeing eye. In victory, one quickly forgets the victims. They have, after all, paid the price of winning. But in the case of defeat, every additional corpse turns into an accusing finger pointed at the decision makers. Everything is done to hide the dead, to obliterate everything...

Shai emerged from the command tent, having gotten off easily: guard duty until morning.

"I'm with you," said David, wanting to protest the punishment in his own way. He had no trouble getting permission to join Shai for his night-long vigil.

The two sat at the entrance of the camp, chatting. This was a get-acquainted talk, the initial overture of what was to become a fast and hard friendship, one, they both felt, that would not fade quickly. Shai talked a lot that night, while David was silent. A feeling deep inside told him to listen to every single word, to preserve everything in his heart.

Shai told him how he and his twin sister had fled from the Tunisian island, Djerba, immediately after the Second World War, arriving in *Eretz Yisrael* via France with forged documents. He spoke of the ancient heritage of Tunisian Jewry. David, fascinated, drank in every word. It was his first introduction to something foreign, unknown to his own world. It was as if someone had pushed aside a curtain and opened his eyes to the world and its fullness as it existed beyond his own small room.

"And where do you live now, you and your sister?"

Shai sighed with pain. "You know, we came here as green as cucumbers. The Jewish Agency officials sent us to Kibbutz Maayan Daniel. We hate it there. The members look at us as if we were relics of the Stone Age. They can't stand anyone who thinks differently. After the war, the first thing I intend doing is to take her to live in Jerusalem or to some Torah-observant settlement."

Towards dawn, David finally opened up. He proceeded cautiously, moving slowly in very wide circles, careful not to get too close. *He's hiding something,* Shai felt. David talked mainly about his most recent life, since he had gone to live in the Chalissa neighborhood in Haifa, and up to the point when he had been drafted into Givati.

"Do you have anyone here in the country?" Shai inquired delicately, careful not to tread too crudely. You never knew where something painful might be hiding, especially during these times.

"I have no one! No one!" David didn't shout the words, they screamed themselves from the chambers of his bleeding heart, bursting from his throat, shattering the stillness. His gaze suddenly clouded over. Shai felt the end of a thread slipping out of his grasp. He tried to catch hold of it before he lost it altogether. His hand reached out in the darkness, groping for David's. He patted it warmly. "I'm with you, David. I'm with you."

David was silent, removed, disconnected. Suddenly he leaped to his feet, pressed Shai's outstretched hand and whispered, "Thanks."

Shai watched as David walked back to his tent, alone. Suddenly a thought struck him: a blinding light. A daring idea began taking shape, fermenting in his subconscious. He would not yet speak: His thoughts had not yet crystallized enough to assume the shape of words. Tomorrow. Tomorrow he would surely find the way to convey his idea to David.

At dawn, a group of sleep-robbed men stood at the top of the hill, daydreaming, longing for the warmth of their sleeping bags, their eyes focused on the stubborn hill that rose opposite them.

"I hope that you all understand the strategic significance of the Latrun fortress." The commanding officer had learned the lessons of the previous battle well. He would prepare his soldiers for action, at least let them know what they would be fighting for.

They listened to his briefing in silence, learning the tremendous strategic importance of the area.

"Because of its particular location, the Latrun Fortress commands our most strategic crossroad. As you all know, Jerusalem is besieged; it has no water or food. Our convoys can't break through with supplies of food and equipment.

"It is our aim to recapture the fortress, to wrest it away from the Arab Legionnaires in order to remove the suffocating ring around Jerusalem and from the other settlements of the plains as well. When we finish all of our preparations here, we will set out again for Latrun!"

David did not say a word. His gaze was fixed upon some faraway, indefinite point along the horizon. When the briefing was over, he moved away with heavy steps.

David and Shai sat upon overturned wooden crates. David stared at the sandy ground, his head bent. He drew circles in the loose dirt with a thin branch. Suddenly he turned to his comrade.

"What's bothering you, Shai?" he asked.

Shai gave him a look both astonished and impressed. He'd only met Eliad yesterday, and yet the man knew him, sensed his feelings of outrage and anger.

There was something very deep about David, something you couldn't pinpoint. A great deal of pain; depths of agony were reflected in his clear blue eyes. Two souls, if not more, reposed in his body, or so it seemed. Sometimes he was pleasant and calm, his gaze sharp and piercing. He conversed comfortably on all kinds of subjects (except for the forbidden topic of himself!). Then suddenly, without warning, his eyes would grow murky and a mysterious film passed over them. In one moment, everything would be changed. He would clam up inside and metamorphose from a likable, quiet fellow to an angry, curled-up porcupine poised for battle; a porcupine ready to fire one of its spiky quills upon the slightest provocation.

"You know what, why don't you step outside and see for yourself?" Shai finally answered. "Go to the big tent behind the orchard and talk with the new recruits who arrived last night. You'll be able to communicate far better with them than I can. After all, you know Yiddish. I had to break my teeth talking to them last night."

"When did they come?"

"Right after guard duty last night. I heard the engines of a few trucks. I strained my eyes and saw group after group getting off. I waited until they finished getting organized in their barracks and at five in the morning, I paid them a visit. They spoke a very broken Hebrew. '*Lushen koidesh*,' they called it." It sounded very funny on his Oriental lips. "But I understood them. The heart understands every language. I still can't get over it."

"All soldiers are to report to the parade ground at once," blared the loudspeaker, echoing through the camp and interrupting their conversation. "Prepare for action."

4

The commanding officer again enjoyed the limelight, surrounded by hundreds of excited, anxious men. It was clear that they were about to charge the stubborn fortress of Latrun once again.

"A few days ago we received an urgent telegram from the commander of the Harel Brigade. The situation in Jerusalem is very serious. There's hardly any water. The civilians and soldiers barely receive a ration of two slices of bread per day. If we cannot break the siege, the capital will fall!"

"Jerusalem shall not fall," declared a trembling voice.

"Who spoke?" a junior officer said angrily. "You're interrupting the colonel."

"*ViYehudah l'olom teisheiv, Yerushalayim ledor vodor,*" the voice said in its Ashkenazi intonation. Jerusalem, the prophet had promised, would endure forever.

All eyes turned towards him. "He's one of the new guys," Shai whispered to David, "I spoke to him yesterday. He's from Poland. He's been through the Holocaust, poor fellow."

Leibel, a young dark-haired Polish Jew, stood in the last row, two long curly *peyos* dangling down the sides of his head. The uniform hung like a sack on his emaciated frame. His hands waved dramatically, slicing the air with vigorous gestures. He spoke in *lashon kodesh* mixed with Yiddish and seemed slightly unbalanced.

"When I was still there, *in der laagers*, the camps, by the accursed Germans, *yimach shmam, die Deitschen*, we knew that in the exile, we were in evil hands. But here, in *Eretz Yisruel*?? *Uv'har Zion tihiyeh pleitah, Yerushalayim Ir Hakoidesh* will not fall!"

Giggles began to be heard here and there, increasing into a mighty roar. The top-notch soldiers, the kibbutzniks, couldn't contain their laughter. Here stood this little raisin of a man with a big black *kipah* on his head, speaking pathetically about *'Yerushalayim'*... Who cared where he came from or what he had gone through...

Leibel stood there, abashed and insulted, not understanding what was so funny. Didn't they all know about the Divine promise? Weren't they Jews like him?

"And this *nebich* and hundreds like him who perhaps arrived yesterday or the day before... he was sent straight from the ship in Haifa to the front lines, to fight against the Arab Legionnaires," Shai whispered again. "They haven't even managed to register him in any government office. They have no documents for him, not a single official paper. They don't even know his name, or that of any of these trainees. What if something happens to them?"

David stood there, frozen, like a block of ice. Shai could see two tears slipping down his cheeks.

⤳⤖

The Ben Nun Campaign, Stage Two, was postponed in the end for several days and rescheduled for Sunday, the twenty-first of Iyar.

"'If you walk in My statutes...'" quoted Shai from the previous day's Torah reading. "Who knows? Perhaps we will be granted the fulfillment of the Divine promise of 'pursuing our enemies and seeing them fall before us'," he whispered in a hopeful voice into David's ear as they marched down the path. They were part of an offensive force that had been divided in two. The infantry was supposed to reach Shaar Hagai and attack from the east, while the armored force, in which Shai and David had been placed, were ordered to attack Latrun from the west.

A cool breeze blew. A sudden heat wave that had almost choked them these past few days had subsided and given way to this cool, refreshing breeze.

The armored vehicles camped in the nearby woods, carefully hidden among the trees by a camouflage expert under brown-and-green blotched coverings that obscured their sharp outlines and made them blend perfectly into their surroundings.

Shai stood, fascinated. He looked at the spring blossoming and was breathtaken. The meadows all around the kibbutz were lush in greenery, dotted with yellows, reds and all the colors of the rainbow. Wild poppies, jasmines in bloom wafted an intoxicatingly sweet aroma. The chirping of the birds blended in with the cadenced humming of the bees and the dragonflies, lending an aura of serenity to the air. A strange silence reigned, as if no one dared interfere with nature's symphony of thousands of magic notes.

Shai drew his small *Tehillim* to his lips and kissed it warmly.

"*Hashem yishmor tzeiseinu...* Hashem shall watch our going and our coming," he murmured, and David hastened to answer a fervent 'Amen.'

The motor revved into life, coughed and sputtered, alternately roared and went limp before warming up into a steady loud rattle. The armored truck began moving, its wheels spraying clouds of dirt and torn-up flowers on all sides.

For a few minutes, the fighters sat in silence. They were coiled, tense, knowing what lay in store for them. The previous battle had been child's play compared to what lay ahead... But the heart has a language of its own, and a wave of emotion can defy cold logic and infuse calm even into a brain petrified with fear. One can forget. One can sing...

And they sang... They sang with an inexplicable loftiness of spirit, with *dveikus*.

"*ViYehudah l'oilom teisheiv...*" Leibel, the Holocaust survivor, began haltingly. To his great surprise, he was joined by none other than the very soldiers who had ridiculed him a few days earlier, for those same words.

The song began quietly, but soon swelled in strength and volume. The small line of armored vehicles traveled to Latrun. The *moshavniks,* sabras who had never tasted Shabbos or seen a Chassidic figure outside of caricatures, were swept along in the fervent singing of the new recruits, and sang the old-time favorites with hoarse voices. *"Yismechu bemalchuscha shomrei Shabbos..."*

Beneath the noise of the singing, Shai and David found time for a last talk before battle.

David opened up slowly, like an onion shedding its layers. At first he told one revealing fact, then another. Finally he almost swamped Shai with the flow of his memories.

Shai looked at him, mesmerized.

"You know, David," he said hesitantly, "I always felt that deep down you were different from what you seemed, from what you projected. I even thought of something for you. On that night that we first talked together, I was struck by a crazy idea for you."

"What is it?"

"I'm embarrassed; you might laugh at me."

"Men — quiet!" The order was whispered from ear to ear. The singing and humming stopped abruptly, as if cut by a knife. Absolute silence enveloped the advancing line of vehicles.

They halted about two kilometers away from the fortress. Orders were again given to move on and the motors suddenly came to life again.

If the Bin Nun Campaign No. 1 was a failure, the Bin Nun Campaign No. 2 was a disaster.

Due to a lack of coordination, the armored division didn't know that the infantry coming from the east had encountered strong fire. They had succeeded in passing through Shaar Hagai and capturing Dir Ayub without opposition, but when they went up the Yalu on their way to attack Latrun, they were met by a murderous rain of bullets. The soldiers, mainly new men who had just arrived in Israel from the D.P. camps, were not trained for battle. They retreated towards Shaar Hagai, suffering heavy losses. Dozens, perhaps hundreds of men who had succeeded in hanging on to life by the skin of their teeth, surviving the Nazi hell and finally reaching the Promised Land, became cannon fodder. Many were killed before they even had a chance to register their names.

Meanwhile, the armored force succeeded in battling their way into the police courtyard, certain that the infantry would reinforce them from the other side. And then they came under murderous fire...

"I've been hit!" Shai groaned, blood spurting down his back. David lost no time. He threw him to the ground in a quick motion and tried to stem the flow of blood with a makeshift tourniquet.

In vain. Shai grew weaker before his eyes. Shai's life was draining away, together with the blood spilling out of him. David looked on, helpless. Hell had broken loose all about him. The battle's outcome was a foregone conclusion. His best friends were cut down like stalks under the sickle. The efficient fire of the Jordanian Legion shot them down mercilessly.

"David, I want to tell you something."

Shai beckoned with a finger and murmured a few words. David bent over him, ignoring the bullets whistling ceaselessly all around.

"David, I know who you are. I always knew..." He coughed and spit up blood. "D'you know what I've been trying to tell you all the time? There in the armored truck... I wanted... After this war is over, I want you to go to Maayan Daniel. Go to my twin sister, Odelia, and explain who you are. Tell her that I said that you are her destined match, that I sent you."

David cried like a baby. Shai gurgled thickly. Every word he uttered came with superhuman effort.

"Remember your grandfather, David! Remember *Sabba*!"

He gave one last grunt and was silent. His glassy eyes looked heavenward with a hollow gaze.

Time stopped. The world stopped. David bent over his friend's body, oblivious to the battle raging on all sides: The devil's dance seemed to be taking place on a different planet. His retreating friends finally grabbed him and pulled him forcibly away. He got up from Shai's limp body, lifeless as his own. But those last words had ignited an extinguished wick.

"Remember *Sabba*!"

5

"**A**nd therefore we ask of You, our Father, Our King, to have mercy upon us and on our babes and children who were killed and massacred *al kiddush Hashem.*"

The elderly R' Shraga Feivel Goldberg finished his words in a shaky voice. Silent sobbing accompanied his long eulogy like a melancholy background motif.

The huge crowd stood on the hillside, in Yetzivim's small cemetery. Three white stone slabs, frightfully small, marked the only graves in this cemetery, a mute testimony to the terrible massacre that had taken place six years before. A cold wind penetrated the thick layers of winter clothing and people shivered in the frigid air.

Six years had passed since that day, but the wound was still fresh, as if Yetzivim had just laid to eternal rest the three tender children who had been murdered in their sleep.

Yitzchak Stefansky, the bereaved father, wanted to say *Kaddish.* He looked into the *siddur* glassy eyed, opened his mouth and collapsed and fell to the ground.

"Water! Water!" voices cried on all sides. "He's fainted."

"Why do they let him come here?" complained Yoni. "He can't take it."

This scene repeated itself every year, a permanent ritual. Yitzchak Stefansky would faint each time at the *yahrzeit* of his three children. Sometimes it happened before the *Kaddish*, sometimes as soon as he finished. Six such occasions had taken place, and six times cold water had to be dashed upon his head.

Six years had passed since that night when the Arab infiltrators had murdered Yitzchak and Sonia's three children. The place where they had concealed themselves for three days inside Yetzivim still remained a mystery. Only a pair of fresh footprints that recrossed through David Eliad's field showed the direction of the murderers' flight towards the Gaza Strip. But the events of that black day were still fresh in the collective memory of the members of the moshav; it seemed to have taken place that very day.

It had been David, again the harbinger of doom, who stood by Stefansky's open windows and screamed, over and over, in an unnatural voice, repeating a single word:

"He-elp! He-elp! He-elp!"

The sight was too much to bear. The two daughters of Yitzchak and Sonia Stefansky, founding members of Yetzivim, eight-year-old Leah'le and five-year-old Chagit, had been found stabbed to death in their beds. Their baby brother, one-year-old Nechemya, lay in his crib, lifeless like his sisters. Only Chaim Nachman had been spared. It had been his luck to be born half a year later. When his bereaved parents sought to give him a name that would befit what had befallen them, the name 'Chaim Nachman' seemed the only choice.

David had managed to summon the security forces and the emergency services of Magen David Adom during the commotion that ensued. He had even held Yitzchak Stefansky up, since the latter was only semi-conscious, and walked him into the ambulance.

The ambulance left with a wailing siren, awakening thousands of alarms from their slumber in David's memory. The sound of the siren sent him back into the past...

He stood watching the disappearing ambulance with shock-filled eyes.

And then a frightful scream burst from his mouth, *"Watch out! Roman Spiegel is coming!"*

Before anyone had the chance to catch any other words, David slumped to the ground, unconscious.

For two weeks David lay in the hospital. He regained consciousness after two days, but the doctors pumped him up with sedatives. Odelia did not leave his bedside throughout the time. She tried to catch his unintelligible mutterings. During the first days, David muttered in a foreign tongue. Odelia rushed through all the departments, looking for someone who could understand him.

"He's speaking Polish," an elderly nurse finally said after listening for a long time.

"Can you understand what he's saying?" she asked with a worried face.

"Of course I understand," she said. "I haven't spoken the language for thirty years, but it was my mother tongue."

"Well, then, tell me what he's saying," Odelia begged. The nurse bent an ear. Her brow wrinkled up with the concentrated effort of joining one word with the next.

"He's saying something like 'Don't hit me,'" she finally stammered. "Could it be? Did anyone hit him?"

The nurse bent over the patient again and stayed there for several moments, hunched and listening.

"Now he's talking Yiddish. He says he wants to sing…"

"What?" Odelia was shocked. "I don't understand."

"If you don't understand, how do you expect me to?" she said sharply. "A speedy recovery, madam. I'm busy. Why don't you continue listening, yourself? He might say something that makes sense to you, something in Hebrew… Don't you know your own husband?" she finally blurted, leaving Odelia embarrassed, alone and helpless by the bedside of her delirious husband.

"Don't you know your own husband?" The sentence the nurse had thrown at her over her shoulder as she went down the corridor evoked a wave of thought. After five years of marriage! *Of course I know my own husband. I've been living by his side day after day, hour after hour. I share all of his experiences...*

And yet... Perhaps there is some truth in the nurse's words after all. The disturbing thought gnawed at her. *Here you are, married to a man for five years, and suddenly you find yourself peeking into a closed room, from behind a curtain that has been moved aside for a moment.*

How many closed rooms was David hiding in his soul?

Yes, he had told her something of his past on that day in Maayan Daniel. But she suspected that he was revealing little and concealing twice as much. Even then she had followed her intuition; her instinct had never steered her wrong. (Was that true? She was beginning to doubt it now.) She had listened to an inner voice whispering from deep inside her: "He is a good man. He is honest, through and through. You can trust him."

But how had he succeeded in concealing such basic details as the simple fact that he spoke Polish? He had never uttered a word in that language.

What else had he said? "I want to sing."

A sad smile crossed her lips. If it were not so sad, it would almost be funny. David and music? Two worlds apart! He had never opened his mouth in song. She had not heard him sing a single song in all their five years of marriage. Not even a solitary tune. He gave the impression that he didn't even know what singing was. He was as dry as a bone, completely devoid of the slightest inclination to music. Every Friday night, when all of the houses in the *moshav* resounded with beautiful singing, each family with its traditions, each with the tunes remembered from youth and home, David sat and recited the *zemiros* as if under duress, in a semimonotone.

Perhaps that was the reason: precisely because he was so tone deaf, so far removed from the world of song, that he longed to be able to sing. Perhaps he had been hiding this all the while. But now that he was not in control of himself, he was not his own master, he was revealing what lay hidden in his heart!

She looked at David wonderingly. Certain dark memories floated to the surface. Memories of their first meeting, under such very tragic circumstances…

≈)⊆

She had been sitting in her room in Maayan Daniel, engrossed in a pleasant conversation with her friend, when she heard the knocking.

Her friend went to open the door and drew back in confusion. "Two army officers and a nurse would like to speak with you."

The three entered. The nurse was carrying a medical kit. She took out a clumsy-looking hypodermic needle, broke the head of a thin ampule and inserted the needle into the tube. With an extended motion, she drew the transparent liquid up, to the surprised look of the two young girls.

"Are you Miss Odelia Matzliach?" she asked, approaching with her poised needle. "I am supposed to give you this injection."

"Who are you?" she asked in alarm. "Why must I get an injection? I'm not ill."

"Let's first get it over with, then you can ask questions," said the nurse, trying to sound reassuring as she drew closer.

Her face ashen, Odelia retreated to a corner of the room. "What do you want from me?" she shouted, her eyes full of fear. "Why did you come here?"

"Jacky, I can't work like this. Do something!" the nurse said, irritated.

The officer named Jacky approached. It was clear that he would have preferred to be anywhere else. This assignment was not a pleasant one, even if he had already performed it dozens of times in the past. Each such encounter wounded his soul as if it were the first. "I am an authorized military doctor. My name is Jacky. This is my friend, David Eliad," he motioned towards his comrade, a tall man standing by the door, almost overcome by embarrassment. "Don't be afraid of us. We've come to help you. David will explain everything."

She wanted to protest, but before she could say a word, the needle was thrust into her arm, and everything whirled around. A pleasant lassitude settled upon her.

She shook her head to free the thick cobwebs from her mind. A feeling of fear mingled together with the sweet intoxication of her senses. She had heard about the 'black delegations' that visited the families of dead soldiers, sowing mourning and misery wherever they went. And here, three strangers had barged in on her. She suddenly understood.

"What happened to my Shai?" she screamed hysterically. "Tell me the truth!"

"Odelia, sit down," her friend begged, a premonition of evil welling up in her heart. The bright and cheerful Odelia was about to become a creature of misery.

Jacky drew near. "Do you only have one brother?"

Odelia nodded stonily.

"Where are your parents?"

"They remained in Djerba, Tunisia," the friend offered. Even Odelia did not yet know the full bitter truth. Her parents had been murdered a year before by Arab rioters. She would only learn about it in two years' time.

Jacky shook his head mournfully. "David, tell her what happened in Latrun."

David told her.

He remained in Maayan Daniel. Jacky and the nurse left immediately after calming down the hysterical girl. The nurse said that physically, Odelia would be able to take the terrible tragedy. Her heart was strong.

But what about her soul? asked David. You took a cheerful, happy young girl and made her wretched in one moment with the dreadful news that her twin brother had been killed. All alone in a strange land. Not a single soul in her world! How could he rush away and leave her there to handle this terrible calamity alone?

David remained in Maayan Daniel for a week. Odelia wanted to sit *shivah* for her brother, but she was not sure how to go about it. David ran back and forth between R' Goldberg, the rabbi of a nearby settlement, and the bereaved girl. He felt a growing admiration for the heroic spirit the young girl showed, for the sublime serenity with which she stood in prayer three times a day in face of the ridiculing stares of the kibbutz members, for how she adhered so scrupulously to every detail of the complex laws of mourning.

Whole chunks of his life which had sunk into the depths of his soul and drowned long since in the abyss of agony, memories of entire chapters of his past which he had tried to erase from his life, which he thought had already died for good, suddenly sprang back to life. He felt a frozen lump in his heart beginning to melt. The immense barrier which had separated him and the world of Torah, the world of his past, was shrinking by the hour.

On the last night of the mourning period, David tossed and turned on his bed for a long time. Dim voices echoed within him. "Go to my sister, Odelia. Tell her that you are her destined match, that I sent you to her…"

The thunder then rolled in myriad voices between the distant mountains: "Remember your grandfather, David. Remember *Sabba!*"

R' Goldberg knocked on Odelia's door. "May I come in?"

After some small talk, he got to the point of his visit.

"The rabbi is talking about marriage with David Eliad?" she asked incredulously, addressing him in the formal third person. She couldn't believe her ears.

"It isn't my idea. It was the idea of your late brother, Shai. This was his dying wish, the last words he uttered."

Odelia's 'no' was most emphatic.

"I'm surprised at Shai. I always relied on his judgment, even when he urged me to flee from Djerba, a suggestion that seemed hopeless at the time. Even then I trusted him. But this?"

The rabbi returned to his house crestfallen, to the waiting and very agitated David.

Odelia's answer was like a violent slap in David's face.

"What's the matter?" he asked, close to tears.

The rabbi smiled sadly. He weighed his words and decided to be forthright. "You are not religious! Odelia is very observant and devout. She cannot possibly marry someone secular!"

"I used to be..."

"What?"

"I am secular now," David said evenly, "but once, actually up till several years ago, I was very religious, no less so than the rabbi himself."

"And what happened?"

David studied R' Goldberg's face, as if to see if he could trust him to understand and respect his secret.

The sun set. Night fell and David talked and talked. When R' Goldberg finally looked at his watch, he was shocked to discover that four hours had passed since David had begun his long confession.

The next day the rabbi summoned the girl to his house. "I suggest that you reconsider your reply. I think it worth your while to hear what David has to say."

And David told his story again.

"And then, on the threshold of death, Shai uttered his last words: 'Remember your grandfather!' I was dumbstruck. I had never told Shai about my grandfather, the figure by whose light I was raised and educated. How could he have known anything about him?"

"Who doesn't have a grandfather?" said Odelia, casting doubts upon his heroic tale. "Perhaps all he wanted was that you return to your roots."

"I don't think so," he replied emphatically. "I had a very eerie feeling, like some truth grasping me, forcing me to stare it in the face, to admit it and not let it slip away. I felt that Shai, a moment before death, saw everything clearly. It was not his body that spoke, but his soul. A soul sees everything. He said that he knew me and always knew who I was."

He suddenly buried his head in his hands. His shoulders shook in suppressed sobs and a thin wail escaped his throat.

"On that same day, in the very hellfire of Latrun, over Shai's fallen body, I also sought death, to lie motionless like Shai and forget this cruel world." David spoke between one burst of sobs and another.

"It would have taken no effort just to die, it was no problem... I was a sitting duck for the enemy fire. My best friends, young boys who had never experienced the taste of life, fell right and left, and in vain. Latrun remained in Jordanian hands."

"What happened there, at Latrun?"

"How do I know? Someone high up at the political level sent the cream of our youth, alongside large numbers of fresh immigrants, to the slaughter, for no reason, no purpose. The men had no idea what they were supposed to do and their fate was sealed the moment they reached the fortress courtyard. No means of defense, no armored trucks or concrete walls for coverage. Only I, who stood out like a rock and was exposed like a target for the Legionnaire sharpshooters, emerged from there without a scratch. Everyone was killed there. Leibel the Polish Jew, Shai Matzliach and dozens of new immigrants whose names no one knew. Who survived?

"I understood that if I remained alive, it was not by chance. A hidden Hand directing events saw to it that I survived. It was the same Hand that put the words in Shai's mouth to indicate to me that I return to my grandfather's way.

"Over Shai's fallen body I came to life. I decided to return to Torah and *mitzvos*, as my deceased father had raised me. One day passes and another, and the picture becomes clearer to me. Someone above is sending blunt messages to me, day after day."

"I need time to think about it," she finally replied, shocked by the revelation of his heart.

Shai had never erred in his judgment of people, neither for the good or the bad. This time, again, he had been on mark.

The wedding took place two months later. The small ceremony was held in the offices of the local rabbinate in an old grey two-story building in Hadera.

It was a sad ceremony, during a sad period. The war was not yet over. Jerusalem continued to absorb heavy losses of lives and property. The small Jewish community in Israel began to reorganize itself along normal lines, but the real rehabilitation would take many years.

R' Goldberg, the officiator at the ceremony, was shocked at the small crowd. Weddings of this kind were not so rare, and yet this particular *chassan* and *kallah* had no family whatsoever. Two friends of David from his Givati days led him to the *chupah*. Two of Odelia's loyal friends from Maayan Daniel were her chaperons.

David stood under the *chupah* frozen as a sphinx. A large *kipah* covered his head and wisps of a newly grown beard framed his immobile face. His thoughts bore him far, far away. He remembered a different *chupah*, under completely different circumstances. Other times, better times.

"*Chassan*! Be happy," he heard R' Goldberg's voice calling to him through the fog of his gloomy thoughts.

"The rabbi is speaking to me?"

"Of course, to you," the rabbi continued. "Good days lie ahead of you!"

The rabbi read the *kesubah* and honored a line of people whom he fortunately had invited at the last moment to recite the traditional seven blessings. R' Calfon, one of the prestigious members of the Tunisian community, ceremoniously trilled the words of the blessing, 'The barren one shall verily rejoice at the ingathering of her sons to her with joy'."

No one saw the *chassan*'s twisted face as he fruitlessly tried to contain his sobs.

"*Chassan*, I'd like a few words with you." R' Calfon sat by his side during the meal, looking at him thoughtfully.

Glass bottles containing an orange liquid, an ersatz orange juice with a taste as sour as lemon and a most offensive odor, stood on the table. No one dared drink this sorry concoction and the bottles had remained untouched, waiting for the next wedding.

David turned to the rabbi and absentmindedly poured a glassful of the disgusting potion. The rabbi stopped him, "Bring the *chassan* something good to drink," he called out to a waiter.

He returned with a dirty siphon bottle of seltzer.

"This is a good drink?" the rabbi said. "Don't you have anything stronger?"

"No."

The rabbi pressed a rusty copper *mil* coin into a waiting hand and the coveted bottle appeared in a flash. "Drink, *chassan*!" the rabbi winked at him mischievously. "Good days are yet ahead of you."

R' Calfon leaned towards David and asked, "Where will you be living?"

"I have a room in Chalissa, in Haifa."

"Forget about Chalissa," the rabbi said. "A neighborhood full of Arabs. A group is being organized to establish a *moshav* in the south. Rabbi Goldberg is moving there. Might you be interested?"

David sank in thought. To tell the truth, he had not planned on remaining in Chalissa forever. But the word *moshav* brought to mind Maayan Daniel, the despised kibbutz from which Odelia wanted to flee.

He weighed his answer. His head whirled from the cognac he had just downed. He stared into the silver goblet before him, a gift from R' Goldberg, a simple goblet unadorned by any embossment or etching, almost like a mirror.

And in this mirror, he suddenly saw a round face, swollen and distorted. A short man standing behind him, looking at him with satanic hatred.

Travitzky! Shalom Travitzky!

His pulse beat wildly in his temples. A cold sweat covered his forehead. Shalom Travitzky! He could still hear the man's venomous whisper, "You will hear from me. You will never get rid of me. I will pursue you wherever you go. You will remember Shalom Travitzky!"

Years had passed since then, but here he was, keeping his promise. He had come to ruin this joyous event.

Ribono shel Olam! Where can I run to?

6

David slowly turned his head around, his fists clenched.

Shalom had disappeared.

For a moment, David thought he saw a figure slipping out the door of the small hall. To the surprise of the assembled guests, the *chassan* got up and strode towards the door with rapid steps.

The darkness of night enveloped the street. By the dim yellowish glow of a streetlamp, he could see a small figure disappearing down the road.

David returned to his place, his face white. R' Calfon poured him a second tumbler full of cognac but David refused it, a dull suspicion in his heart that the entire scene had been a figment of his imagination brought on by the alcohol.

"Don't let anything spoil your *simchah*," the rabbi whispered in his ear, with an expression of one who knew everything, understood everything.

David nodded mutely and studied the rabbi suspiciously, trying to read in his eyes how much he really knew.

The rabbi ignored the questioning, frightened eyes. He continued in the vein he had begun.

"I would be most interested in having you join the group. We've received an allocation of fertile land in the northern Negev. In a month, immediately after Succos, we intend to settle it."

"Did you say 'we'?"

"Yes," he smiled his goodly smile. "I am joining the group."

～)(～

The young couple took its first steps together in life. The honeymoon had only begun and David already found himself up to his neck trying to persuade his new young bride.

Odelia did not want to hear a word about a *moshav*, no matter what. All his explanations and convincing arguments fell upon deaf ears.

"I'm fed up with the kibbutz. I want no part of communal life. I don't want cooperative anything. I want my own private life, in the holy city of Jerusalem."

David mobilized all of his powers of persuasion to explain how wrong she was and to point out the integral difference between a kibbutz and a *moshav*.

"In the *moshav* we hope to establish there will be no communal dining room. Each family will live its own private life, just like in the city. Only the buildings serving the public will be communal. The proceeds from the joint sale of our produce will go to a community chest..." David wiped away the perspiration from his brow. The long harangue was a direct quote of what R' Calfon had told him at the wedding.

"I cannot bear to hear the hated word *chaver*, comrade. It smacks of socialism," Odelia was firm in her opposition. "I've heard the word until it comes out of my ears."

Before he could rally, Odelia had jumped up on the chair, cleared her throat and brought her fist up to her lips as if she were speaking into a microphone. "*Chaver* Yugav is requested to go to the dining room to take his turn at washing the dishes," she announced dramatically. "*Chaver* Kozak is being urgently paged in the chicken coop; eight laying hens have declared a strike. *Chaver* Rachmana Litzlan is needed in the barn; Adina the cow is suffering from a stomach ache..."

David shrieked with mirth. "Enough, enough," he groaned, holding his stomach. "I'm the one with the stomach ache, not Adina the cow."

Odelia was not finished. She continued standing on the chair, shooting remarks to all sides. "I've already seen the highly touted *chaverim* and the famous fellowship at Maayan Daniel. Don't tell me tales about togetherness and other nonsense. I've seen how fake and artificial this fellowship is, and the great love everyone bears for his fellow neighbor at the kibbutz."

David was shocked. He had not imagined that she despised the kibbutz to such a degree.

"How long did you live at Maayan Daniel?"

"For half a year. But it was enough for a lifetime!" Odelia announced decisively. "To live in a *moshav*? Out of the question. Nothing but Jerusalem."

"Shai also said that he planned to take you to Jerusalem," David remembered his first conversation with his wife's deceased twin, the best friend who had only become his brother-in-law posthumously.

They went to Jerusalem before the festivals. After feverish effort, they found a one-room apartment in an ancient, gloomy building in the border neighborhood of Musrara. It was bare of all furniture, but David was resourceful. From a conversation with the *gabbai* of a nearby *beis knesses*, he learned that there were some broken benches in the courtyard which the synagogue had discarded years ago and which were lying around like so much debris.

These were quickly dragged over to the empty apartment. Together with several blankets that they had brought along to serve as mattresses, the place began to take on a semblance of human habitation. The gloom was hardly dispelled by the single candle but, weary to the bone, they collapsed upon their makeshift beds like a pair of potato sacks. They were so exhausted that they didn't even feel how hard their beds were. A deep sleep overcame them as soon as they closed their eyelids.

The wail of a siren woke Odelia about an hour later. She leaped off the hard bench in alarm and ran over to the window.

Men were rushing about in all directions to the closest shelter, which was no more than a ground-floor apartment fortified with small brown sandbags on all sides.

From a great distance they could hear a shell being fired with tremendous force. The approaching shell shrieked closer and closer, passing almost overhead. It continued its flight, only to explode with deafening noise in the next street. The siren sounded once again with a blood-curdling noise.

David was still fast asleep and didn't wake up even when the shell landed and exploded. Odelia shook the bed with all her might, calling his name over and over again.

The siren wailed a third time and then he awoke. The alarm rent the air, with a wail that rose and fell, rose and fell...

His eyes turned round with fear. He looked around, unbelieving.

"*Tatte*! Help!" he screamed in a strange voice. He leaped up from the bench and felt feverishly around in the dark for his shoes. His movements were clumsy and uncoordinated. In his frightened haste his feet wound themselves around one another and he sprawled full length on the ground.

All the while Odelia stood over him, watching in amazement. What was he, a child? Why was he so frightened? Everyone had heard the siren, but no one had reacted with such panic.

"Take it easy. You are hysterical..." she started saying, when a second shell exploded, this time in the very courtyard of their building.

The sound was deafening. Ears continued to ring even after the strange silence settled upon them. For a moment Odelia feared she had gone deaf, until she heard David groaning softly.

A small shell fragment had flown into the room through the open window and lodged in his arm. Blood dripped from the wound. David stared at it glassily.

"Look," he said, thrusting his arm towards Odelia. Blood dripped onto her palm and David whispered foolishly, "A shell fragment doesn't need any light. It found my arm even in the dark..."

≈)(≈

They left Jerusalem two days later. The experiment had failed and Odelia capitulated. She felt unable to continue in this fashion. Better to live in a detested *moshav* than to be awoken in the middle of the night by a siren and to discover that her tall soldier husband suffered from childish fears and reacted with inexplicable hysteria.

The Legionnaire soldiers who had decided to embitter the lives of Jerusalemites and crush their morale had hit the mark with regard to the Eliad family. The new residents of the capital had proven unable to withstand the pressure and accustom themselves to the nature of life in the besieged city, especially when David had had to pay the price so soon.

On that night, at the first lull in the shelling, the civil defense forces had taken him away on a stretcher for emergency treatment in the nearby Italian Hospital's clinic. The injury was only superficial, to his good fortune, and after his arm was bandaged, David was sent home. The couple packed their small bags and the first convoy that left the city the next morning returned them to the quiet southern front.

"You know what?" David asked, leaning his bandaged arm on the open window, his hair blowing in the wind. They were making their way down the coastal plain towards the south. "Now I remember that Shai spoke of two possibilities. He said that he was going to take you away from Maayan Daniel and bring you to Jerusalem. But he also spoke about a second possibility. To go to a *moshav* of observant Jews. We've already taken care of the first option. Now we're trying out the second alternative."

Odelia was quiet. A bitter expression settled on her lips. Her husband was finding great consolation for her. Apparently, Shai had been an accurate prophet, and whatever they did or planned to do had already been predicted by him…

"Did Shai say anything about the chance of your not being accepted into the *moshav*?" she said quietly. She immediately bit her lips, regretting the unfortunate remark.

She carefully glanced sideways at her new husband. He was pale as a sheet; even his lips were a bloodless white. He chewed his upper lip nervously, his eyes flitting like trapped mice. Odelia was flooded by a wave of pity. Why did he take everything so hard? One could think that life in a *moshav* had always been his life's dream.

"I didn't mean to hurt you," she whispered in regret. "That's why I pretended that my whole opposition stemmed from my deep hatred of kibbutz life. I wanted to spare you the degradation of having to stand before the admissions committee of the *moshav*."

"R' Calfon made no mention of such a committee." David was shocked, and made no effort to hide it.

"R' Calfon did not know that there would be people who would object to accepting you," Odelia said.

"Who is against me? Who doesn't want me?"

"Two people. I don't exactly know who they are, but one of the women came to tell me that there was a man by the name of Meir Tzuriel who was outspokenly against you. He says that the *moshav* should not take in members like you."

Meir Tzuriel? His forehead furrowed deep in thought. "The name means nothing to me," he said, bewildered. "Why would an unknown person oppose me?"

Odelia lowered her gaze and fixed it upon her fingernails. She felt a pang in her heart. What had Meir Tzuriel said, exactly, according to that woman? *"I know David Eliad well. He is unfit. He must not be accepted."*

"I refuse to stand before any admissions committee!" David shouted angrily. The passengers began showing interest in the arguing couple. "R' Calfon begged me to join the group and I don't intend to undergo such degradation."

"I've already explained to you that R' Calfon had no idea that there would be such strong opposition to your admission," Odelia tried to calm his rage, but the very mention of mysterious enemies incited David's anger to a greater pitch. One does not put out fires with gasoline.

"Who is this Meir Tzuriel?" David roared, ignoring the rest of the passengers. "I want to see if he can look me straight in the face!"

"It's not only Meir Tzuriel. You've got another opponent." A man with a peaked cap sitting nearby suddenly entered the stormy argument.

"Who's the second one?" David demanded wrathfully, turning towards the stranger.

"Me."

"You? Who are you, anyway? I haven't yet had the honor of meeting you."

The stranger got up from the hard seat and stood the full height allowed by the various bundles sticking out of the overhead shelf. But even with this disadvantage, David was able to see that he was dealing with a descendant of Og, king of Bashan. In full stature, the man easily surpassed the tin roof of the bus.

"I'm Yoni, coordinator of the group," his voice thundered in an obvious European accent. "I sincerely hope never to have the pleasure of your acquaintance in our *moshav.*"

David got up from his seat and faced him, his eyes shooting sparks. When standing, he was not much shorter than his opponent. The two looked like a pair of roosters about to wage a life-and-death battle. The tension in the bus was acute.

The almost inevitable clash was avoided by the clever Odelia. She slipped between the two, got up on the seat and pulled the zipper of a packed rucksack on the overhead shelf. It opened, and its assorted contents spilled all over them. David noticed it just in time and stepped neatly aside, but Yoni was buried in all sorts of clothing and foodstuffs. His cap flew off his head, revealing a bald pate. In his effort to extricate himself from the avalanche, Yoni became more and more entangled with a bundle of crumpled khaki shirts. Green socks dangling from his shining baldness and some red jam oozing down his nose and dripping into his open mouth completed the festive costume.

Peals of laughter echoed through the bus for a long time after Yoni, red faced and panting like an angry bull, succeeded in unwinding himself from the cocoon of khaki shirtsleeves and trouser legs.

7

David walked towards the green hut with mixed feelings. A small metal sign announced: Admissions Committee.

Odelia had made superhuman efforts to extract from David a half-promise that he consult R' Calfon. Ironically, it was she, the sworn enemy of kibbutz and *moshav* life, who succeeded in convincing David not to return to Haifa that very day, to the unplastered ruins in Chalissa where he had lived for the past three years.

They were shocked to discover that the distinguished rabbi was living in a small, wretched single room in an immigrant *maabarah* transit camp, together with his wife and eleven children.

"Small wonder that the rabbi wishes to move to the *moshav*," David had whispered to himself, shocked by the woeful sight. "Who can live in such subhuman conditions?"

R' Calfon himself seemed not particularly disturbed by the congestion. He sat down with his guests by a small table and conversed leisurely over a cup of steaming tea.

"Let's talk *tachlis*," he said, a mischievous glint in his eye. "What has brought you here to me?"

David carefully weighed his reply in his mind and his eyes roved about the quiet room. In spite of the aching poverty, the room sparkled with cleanliness and the simple furniture was pleasantly arranged.

Odelia left the two and went over to the little children who were playing quietly in a corner. They rejoiced to see her and offered to include her in their game. "Such nice manners," she said with a pleasant laugh and turned to their mother. "You have very well-bred children," she said. The mother beamed with pleasure.

With brief but telling words David described what had happened. From his reaction, he discovered that his tale was not news to the rabbi.

"Don't worry, Mr. Eliad," he reassured him with a pat on the shoulder. "I will be there on the committee and everything will go smoothly, please G-d."

A sour expression flitted across David's face. The perceptive rabbi understood what was on his mind and read his hidden thoughts. He took David's hand and led him to the door.

"Sometimes a man must lower himself and forget his pride. But our Sages have already promised us that honor will eventually be forthcoming. Stand before the committee with humility and you will be rewarded with the promise of Hashem to lower the proud and raise the lowly."

They did not leave the *maabarah* that night. David didn't know where the admissions office was located, and the rabbi suggested that they stay overnight on the promise that he would take David along when he traveled there the following morning for a meeting. Odelia slept at a neighbor's home and David found himself a bench in the *beis knesses*.

He stretched out on a bench well padded with cushions in the Oriental manner, but sleep evaded him. His mysterious opponents frightened him. Go fight an enemy whom you don't even know! Where did this Yoni suddenly spring from and why did he speak with such a virulent blind hatred? *May I never have the pleasure of making your acquaintance.*

In the end David succumbed to a fitful sleep and dreamed of black demons leaping all around him, thrusting their forked tongues out at him.

"We will never allow you to come to us," one ugly devil provoked him and lashed at David's face with a long whip. David screamed in fear and woke up.

"You're shouting in your sleep, young man," a hoarse voice muttered. David opened his eyes. A mustached old man reeking of tobacco leaned over him. He wagged a heavily ringed finger at him. He was busy arranging his *tallis* and its fringes struck David on the face as he enveloped himself in the prayer shawl. "In Fez, Morocco, they used to say that someone who does not steal at night will not scream during the day, and one who screams in his sleep at night will have his prayers answered during the day."

David squinted in embarrassment and got off the bench. The old man studied him with interest. "My grandmother, of blessed memory, used to say, 'If a person gets out of bed on the right foot, his enemies will surrender to him.' And you, young man, got off the bench on your right foot!"

David shrugged his shoulders. He went over to the washbasin in the entranceway and washed his hands and face. *What kind of luck will I have today?* he asked himself. *What have I come to? I sleep in a Sefardi synagogue at night and wake up in the morning to the sound of an elderly nuisance preaching his grandmother's proverbs...*

Suddenly he stopped short. The significance of the words finally filtered into his sleep-befuddled brain. What had the old man said? That his prayers would be accepted that day, that his enemies would fall before him...

He quickly dried his face and ran back to the synagogue proper.

The old man had disappeared!

"I have seen Eliyahu Hanavi," he murmured excitedly. He waited impatiently for the prayers to begin. The *beis knesses* began filling up with worshipers, most of them elderly, and the service began.

David prayed that morning with intense fervor. He already knew what to ask for; the old man had coached him.

David and R' Calfon traveled together to the admissions committee in an open van driven by one of the rabbi's admirers. David told R' Calfon in an offhand manner of the interesting episode he had had that morning, keeping his personal interpretation to himself.

"Ah, Machlof?" the rabbi chuckled. "Good. He is full of epigrams, a veritable treasurehouse of proverbs *bli ayin hara*. Double the number of Jews that left Egypt, as the saying goes..."

"But where did he disappear to so quickly?" David asked, visibly disappointed.

"Machlof is not quite all there," the rabbi said, his long beard swaying in the wind. "He prays in the chicken coop, among the roosters."

The admissions committee convened in a wooden shack in an abandoned English military camp somewhere near Ashkelon. R' Calfon let David off the van a good way from the shack. "To avoid an evil eye," he explained. David made the rest of the way on foot.

He stood in front of the closed door for a few minutes and stared at the peeling white paint. An older layer of paint yellowed with age peeked out from behind it.

With trembling fingers, he knocked on the door.

"*Yavo* (come in)," he heard a familiar voice. The tone reminded him of the German *jawohl*.

He opened the door and froze. It was Shalom Travitzky sitting there, his elbows leaning on a rectangular table, the gigantic Yoni by his side. They looked at him in silence. They were flanked by three other unfamiliar men. One chair was vacant. R' Calfon was absent.

"This is a trap," a voice cried within him. "Run for it." But his feet seemed to have a life of their own. They proceeded heavily forward like two bars of lead, and brought him to the table.

Shalom Travitzky was studying some document; he turned to Yoni. "This is Mr. Eliad."

"Pleased to meet you," said Yoni, shaking David's perspiring hand. "Mr. Eliad, I'd like you to meet the members of the committee. Yoni Avivi, that's me, the chairman; my assistant is Mr. Meir Tzuriel; Mr. Yitzchak Stefansky, Mr. Dani Morelli; Mr. Ovadya..."

David did not hear the rest.

Shalom Travitzky ... Meir Tzuriel! A flash of memory brought to mind a forgotten picture of a *tefillin* bag upon which was embroidered the words "Shalom Meir Travitzky."

"And what do you have to say, Mr. Eliad?" Travitzky-Tzuriel asked him, his voice saccharine sweet. David felt sick. *What are you scheming, you demon in sheep's clothing?*

"Gentlemen, I would like to join the new *moshav*. It is not clear to me why people are making it difficult for me to be admitted."

"Making it difficult?" Yoni's voice expressed sincere amazement. "Who has been disturbing you?"

"I was told that two members of this committee are opposed to accepting me."

Yoni turned to his colleagues. "Does anyone object to accepting Mr. Eliad?"

They all shook their heads, Travitzky included.

David stood, bewildered. How could it be? Yoni himself would have started a fistfight right there on the bus from Jerusalem, had Odelia not sidetracked him so cleverly. And Shalom Travitzky — what had happened to him?

"Gentlemen," Yoni rose to his feet and announced ceremoniously. "I ask you to confirm the admission of Mr. David Eliad, an outstanding fighter at Latrun."

A weak flurry of handclapping followed his words. The door opened and R' Calfon entered with hasty steps and sat down on the vacant seat.

"Welcome," R' Calfon shook his hand with a suppressed smile. "Whom do I have the honor of addressing?"

Aha! So you are not only an esteemed rabbi. You are also a considerable impresario… What is the meaning of this little play you've arranged for me? We will yet get to the bottom of this, some day.

The ceremony of inaugurating the new *moshav* took place a week after Succos, 5709 (1949). A government representative spoke with deep pathos, spouting hollow phrases about settling and developing the Land and of a dream that was being realized. No one paid any attention to his blathering; each one was engrossed in his own thoughts, each involved in his own private dream.

It was a small but very heterogeneous group. There were emigrants from Tunisia alongside Ashkenazim from Poland, Hungarians with a heavy accent, newly arrived Iraqis, Yemenites, Moroccans, and even two Americans who had just gotten off the boat at Haifa port.

But they had one common denominator, a very basic factor. They had all been plucked from their birthplaces in these stormy times and had found their way to *Eretz Yisrael*, their true homeland, some by choice, some by circumstances. Now they all sought a new home: a place to lay their heads down at night and firm, secure land under their feet.

After the Jewish Agency representative had finished his speech, David Eliad approached the microphone.

"I suggest that we name this new *moshav* 'Yetzivim'," his voice thundered. "Let us hope that this place will truly grant us stability. *Yetzivut*."

His suggestion was accepted to thunderous applause. David's suggestion had hit the mark and expressed a unanimous sentiment. Stability was the magic word: no more exile and wandering, no more feeling of detachment.

The wind wafted the rolling echoes to all directions. *Ye-tzi-vu-ut.*

8

And thus the years passed...

The beginning years of Yetzivim, with all their hardships, were now behind them. Families came and went. Not all of them succeeded in adapting themselves to the particular social climate and the difficult conditions that were the lot of this small *moshav* in the northern Negev in its first years.

After eleven years one could still find one hundred families hanging on to the sandy earth by their fingernails, determined to make a go of it. They stood steadfast, like a stone lighthouse amidst a sea of crashing waves.

All these years, the *fedayin* did not stop infiltrating from the Gaza Strip, stealing cows and sheep, but the horrifying murder of the Stefansky children was an unprecedented outrage.

Several weeks after the massacre, the entire *moshav* was surrounded by a dense electrified-wire fence. The lightest touch of the barbed wire was enough to set off a deafening alarm throughout the *moshav*.

To the members' surprise, the biggest opponent of this method of defending Yetzivim was none other than David Eliad. He passed from house to house collecting signatures against the plan. He mobilized all his power to persuade his friends to abandon the idea and suffice with a more modest form of defense. No one understood why. Everyone looked at him as if he were crazy. "You, of all people, David, who experienced the trauma on the night of the massacre of the Stefansky children, are the one to object?" he was asked over and again.

David could not resign himself to the fence even after the fact. Years later, he still regarded it with hostility. "How can you live like this?" he would argue angrily. "Where are we living, in Cuba or some Siberian gulag? We've come to live in a democratic country!"

"Go tell the Arab murderers from Rafiah and Gaza that you want an open democratic existence," Hillel would say. "If we had had an electric fence before, perhaps Yitzchak and his wife would not have turned into the miserable creatures they are. Look at Yitzchak; he's a veritable shadow of what he used to be. No smile, no glint of life in his eyes."

The two, Hillel and David, strode along the path surrounding the *moshav*, antiquated Sten guns swinging from their shoulders. The years of calm had had their effect. After the Sinai campaign, the *moshavniks* felt an even greater relief. The *fedayin* activities dwindled and the night watch turned into a routine duty and no more. Nerves were no longer taut.

"Yoni spoke to me today." Hillel's voice rent the stillness of the night. "Do you know that we are here already eleven years?"

"That long?" David was surprised. "I never stopped to figure it out. You're right," he agreed a moment later. "We came here in Cheshvan 5709 and now it's..."

"Elul 5719," Hillel finished.

"What did Yoni want?"

"He wanted to organize a ten-year anniversary celebration for Yetzivim..."

"Ten year?" David was surprised. "He only reminded himself now? You just said we're here eleven years."

"Very true," Hillel agreed. "I asked that very question. Do you know what he answered? He said that last year we didn't have the budget but this year it's before national elections and the government offices are just begging him to come and take the money... All he has to do is invite some cabinet ministers to the festivities."

"That is ridiculous. Does Yoni think he can make fools of people and call it a ten-year anniversary when it's already history?"

"That's it exactly!" said Hillel enthusiastically. "The notices and signs will say 'Ten-Year Anniversary'. No one is going to make a fuss. They won't even bother figuring it out."

Hillel sighed. Now came the hard part. "I want to ask you for help. Yoni is planning a gala affair spread out over an entire week. He has the budget... I think that he wants to use the event as a springboard for promoting the *moshav*. Are you listening, David?"

"What? What did you say?" David shook himself awake from his daydream. His thoughts had wandered far, far off from that time and place, as they always wandered. He had not heard a word of Hillel's last sentence.

"David, I need help."

"Hillel, for a good friend like you, anything you ask."

"Anything?"

"Anything!"

"Good, then I want Buki."

"Who?" David didn't understand.

"Your Baruch, Buki."

"How can a ten-year-old boy help Yoni?"

"Yoni is organizing a choir. He wants Buki to be the soloist."

They passed under a big lamppost. A beam of pale light focused on David's eyes.

If Hillel had been at all poetic, he would have described what he saw then in the following manner: At first the sun shone in David's eyes. They were filled with joy and glowed with happiness and *nachas*. Then clouds suddenly covered the laughing sun and a gloomy darkness blazed from the depths of his pupils with wild madness.

But Hillel was no more than a simple farmer and the language of metaphor was far beyond his experience. He had no means of expressing the revolution raging in his friend's soul and the transformation that had taken place in his gaze in the space of a split second.

"Why did you ask for Buki?" David finally asked. A freezing coldness wafted from his words and Hillel drew back. What was the matter with David? Why had he become so unrecognizable all at once?

"Don't play dumb, David," Hillel said with a fake, hollow laugh. "Everyone knows that Buki has a marvelous voice. I only wanted..."

David bent over his short friend and grabbed him by the neck. Hillel groaned in pain. David bent over until he was almost at Hillel's mouth.

"If you wish to remain my friend," he whispered hoarsely, his voice loaded with emotion, "don't you dare ever, but ever, mention such ideas to me. Is that clear?"

"Yes, yes." Hillel squirmed, trying to free himself from the vicelike grip. "What's happened to you, David? Have you gone mad?"

David opened up his iron fist and Hillel slumped to the ground limp as a rag doll, groaning and panting. He landed on the soft grass and massaged his aching neck. He looked at the retreating David with a veiled expression in his eyes.

⇐⇒

"Buki has a marvelous voice." Hillel's description fell far from doing it true justice. Buki was a child prodigy, a musical genius.

The residents of Yetzivim of 1959 were not connoisseurs of music. The *moshavniks* were involved in backbreaking manual labor from dawn to dusk. Most were farmers who tilled their lands. Even now, at the end of the *shmittah* year, they did not rest on their laurels. The large majority of the members had turned to different channels and invested their energies in the newest craze which produced considerable profits: raising geese.

Every self-respecting *moshav* member raised several geese in his yard. The *moshav* was filled with the ga-ga-ing of geese being fattened for the kill, to be sold at a hefty price to the gourmet restaurants in Tel Aviv who competed between themselves for the most delectable recipe for that royal dish, paté de foie gras.

Only the vociferous protests of several isolated *moshavniks* who claimed that they were on the verge of deafness prevented Yetzivim from turning into the major goose supplier in the country.

Thus did Yetzivim survive the Sabbatical year. On the eve of the previous year, just before Rosh Hashanah, they had all hastened to plow, sow, cultivate and do everything necessary for the land while there was still time, and now everyone was busy feeding geese.

Who in Yetzivim had the time to think about choirs?

Only Yoni.

Yoni considered himself an expert in the field of music. "In the realm of music, I am a somebody," he loved saying. He had absorbed the tradition of culture in his father's home in Budapest. He owned the only phonograph in the entire *moshav* and a rare collection of records including the classical music of Mozart, Bach, Beethoven and others. Every afternoon the sounds of the piano poured forth from his guest room to the melancholy background of sobbing violins. When Yoni had first begun playing his scratchy phonograph, he had been certain that his home would be flooded with visitors longing to revel in the lovely melodies. He was baffled to discover that most *moshavniks* would avoid the path by his home and take the long roundabout route home.

"Imbeciles, cultural philistines!" he would say dismissingly, seeing his friends shying away from the sweet sounds of the violins.

The home of Yoni Avivi adjoined that of the Eliads. He overheard Buki's singing and kept an eye on the boy.

"That dried radish, Eliad, doesn't know what a treasure he is harboring in his own home. Buki is likely to surpass even Yossele Rosenblatt. A soprano as sweet as his I have yet to hear," Yoni said to his wife, Berta, one evening, as they were sitting in their living room reading the newspapers. Berta looked up for a moment, trying to pay attention, but she dozed off immediately.

Buki's tremulous voice rang out from the Eliads' children's room. He sang a song without words, a tune that resembled an old Russian folk song. His voice penetrated deep into one's heart, evoking a yearning for sublime worlds. A tear of longing slipped from Odelia's eye. The child's singing was so pure and sweet.

David entered the house in a storm. He flew straight to the children's room and burst in with a roar.

"Enough, Buki. Stop! My head is splitting. I can't hear any more. Stop it!"

⤳⤶

"I'll be right back," Yoni said over his shoulder to the peacefully dozing Berta, her newspaper, unread, drooping in her hand. With wide purposeful strides, sharpened by anger, he went to the door.

"Where are you going?" Berta suddenly came to life.

"I can't contain myself any more," Yoni fumed. "He's mad, truly mad!"

"Who?"

"Our neighbor, what's his name. David... You're sitting here in the same room with me and you don't hear what's going on?"

Berta had not heard a thing. The drama taking place in her neighbor's house had gone over her head.

"It isn't the first time, either," Yoni explained impatiently. "You know Buki, David's son..."

"Ahhh," Berta melted at the thought. "Buki is a *wunderkindt*. I've never heard a voice like his before."

"And what would you do if our Gindush had a voice like that?" Yoni asked rhetorically.

Berta's face soured. Gindush the ruffian, Yoni and Berta's only son, had the voice of a typical raven.

"Oh, I would consider it a blessing to have a son like Buki," she blurted with outright jealousy.

"And what's one supposed to do with a child like Buki?" Yoni redirected her thoughts to the desired channel.

"I think he should be sent to a conservatory, or at least study voice development with an expert teacher."

"That's what you think. But David Eliad, our darling neighbor, is of a different mind," concluded Yoni triumphantly. "I have been keeping tabs on him for many long months and have reached the bursting point.

The Gordian Knot/ 63

Instead of developing the child's gift, he is stifling him, simply strangling the boy. Each time he sings, his father shuts him up with one excuse or another."

"I've never heard a thing like that!" Berta agreed, shaking her head in dismay. "Do you mean to say that he simply does not allow him to sing?"

"Exactly so," Yoni verified.

Berta couldn't understand it. She had heard Buki burst into song many a time. Ahhh, the pleasure of those moments. Buki would sing tunes without words, melodies unfamiliar but deeply moving.

"Have you ever noticed? Buki only sings when David is not home."

"It's crazy. I can't believe it. He must be out of his mind!"

Yoni cleared his throat. A clever retort stood poised on the tip of his tongue but he forcibly repressed it. He had solemnly given his word to R' Calfon. How many times had he almost choked upon the words he was dying to say, but he remained silent as a fish. R' Calfon had threatened him with ostracism, to put him in *cherem* if he ever breathed a word.

"So you also think it's abnormal, eh?"

"*Igen.*" In her agitated state, Berta reverted to Hungarian, her mother tongue.

"And that's why I'm going over to give him a piece of my mind," said Yoni, approaching the door again.

"No! You aren't going anywhere!"

"Didn't you just say that it's abnormal?"

"Yes, but so what? It's none of your business. Do you want to acquire a lifelong enemy?"

"But, Berta, he's ruining the life of his own child!"

"So he'll be the one to suffer from it. If David Eliad cannot stand his son's singing, it's his own problem, not yours!"

Yoni let out his breath with a slow, whistling sound. He looked like a giant balloon suddenly deflated. He sank into the armchair with a heavy sigh.

It was not in vain that the jokesters in the *moshav* would say that all of Yetzivim was afraid of a moth.

"It's a simple calculation," Moishe would explain. "All the members of the *moshav* quake from Yoni, the gigantic secretary-general. And Yoni trembles from his wife. And Berta, everyone knows, is deathly afraid of moths..."

⤳⤶

Buki ran outside, bouncing a red ball up and down. His seven-year-old brother, Yigal, ran by his side. The two played with the ball and shouted with typical childish merriment. But even as he ran after the ball, Buki pondered the perplexities of life.

Lately, his father had become exasperating. What did he want from him? Why did he keep throwing such strange looks at him and silencing him whenever he began singing spontaneously?

"Tell me, Yigal, do all kinds of tunes pop into your head all the time, too?" he suddenly asked, between one bounce of the ball and the next.

Yigal did not understand the question; even Buki himself could hardly comprehend what was happening to him. He was too young to understand that he was a born composer. Sometimes a sad melody would come to visit, other times it would be a moving one. Last year, after the memorial service for the Stefansky children, he had begun humming a melancholy tune that had been born in his mind that very moment. He had been unable to understand why his mother had stood there, dissolving into sobs.

Sometimes, when he received a high mark on a test and his father or mother complimented him, a lively, happy air would enter his head and he would burst into song. But his father would immediately send him off to do homework.

"Yigal, why doesn't Abba like me to sing? Why is he always so angry?"

The ball fell out of Yigal's hands and rolled along the yellowish sand. His childish forehead furrowed with waves of wrinkles. He was a child who thought deeply and his teachers predicted a brilliant future for him.

"I think that Abba doesn't like songs at all," he finally stated in his delicate voice.

⤳⤶

The gravel squeaked under Hillel's feet as he walked along the path leading to Yoni's house. Hillel shot fearful looks at David's window. He felt like a traitor when he knocked softly on the door. Years of friendship with David, a heart-to-heart closeness, now hung in the balance. A pity for it to vanish, if David were to learn what he was about to reveal.

The door had not opened.

"I can knock until tomorrow and he won't hear me," Hillel realized. "What should I do?"

To his good fortune, the drums announced the grand finale of the movement. Yoni got up from his armchair to switch the record to a work by the immortal Viennese Schubert. Hillel took advantage of the silence and knocked again.

"Who's there?" Yoni sang out in his Hungarian accent.

Hillel was in a quandary. All he needed now was to stand there and shout at the top of his voice, "Open up; it's me, Hillel." David was no fool. He would make the immediate connection between the incident of two nights before and his visit to Yoni. Why else would Hillel visit the *moshav* secretary? He had never made a secret of his negative opinion of Yoni, who had dominated the *moshav* for the past ten years without benefit of elections and ruled his fellow *moshavniks* with an iron fist, like the potentate of some African emirate.

He knocked on the door for the third time that evening, sending nervous glances all the while towards David's window. He offered up a silent prayer that nothing be heard, nothing be seen.

The door finally opened. Yoni broke his general rule of not opening to anyone who refused to identify himself. He was either overcome by curiosity, boredom — or a combination of both.

"Hillel?" he trumpeted. "What is the veteran opposition looking for here?"

Hillel would have liked to bury himself ten feet under. There was no doubt left now that David had heard Yoni's exuberant welcome. A *shofar* blast could not have been more explicit.

He put a finger to his lips. "Shhhh, Yoni, have pity. Not all the members of the *moshav* have to hear you," he whispered.

"What's happened?" Yoni's voice suddenly dropped several decibels. "Is this a secret visit?" he whispered, overcome with curiosity. "Come in, sit down and let's talk about it."

Yoni took a special delight in this visit for Hillel never let any opportunity pass without expressing his devastating criticism of him. The fact that he had now come to include him in a secret was a double compliment. He danced solicitously around his guest, sat him comfortably down on the living room couch and ran off to bring a cool pitcher of lemonade from the kitchen.

"Let me put on some Schubert and then we can talk without anyone hearing a word." A moment later the house was flooded with the sounds of Schubert's Fifth Symphony. The bass violas thundered dominantly to the sweet accompaniment of the flutes.

Yoni listened to the music, an expression of dreamy pleasure settling on his face. His eyes were tightly closed in reverence so that he could not see Hillel's own long-suffering expression.

"What genius!" Yoni said raptly. "Would you believe that this brilliant composer was only thirty-one when he died and had composed these wondrous masterpieces at such a young age?"

"Yoni, that's exactly what I came to talk to you about," Hillel leaped up from the couch. "I'm referring to Buki, David's gifted child."

"Ahhh, Buki. He really has great talent. But he has a problem. His father picks on him right and left."

"Are you telling me?" Hillel burst into his words. "That's exactly what I've come to discuss with you."

The discussion sank to whispered murmuring. The expressions on the faces of the two men changed several times. Amazement crept over Yoni's face and was replaced by anger. Yoni bent over and whispered something in Hillel's ear and this time, it was the latter's turn to appear astonished. Yoni added something and Hillel appeared to be on the verge of a stroke; his eyes protruded from their sockets and his fists clenched without his realizing it.

9

David went out to his fields the next morning, as he did every day. From behind the slats of the drawn shutters, two pairs of eyes watched his tall figure recede into the distance.

Several strands of silver sprinkled in his thick dark beard were the only changes which the passing years had wrought. Aside from this, David looked exactly the same as he had on the day he had come to Yetzivim eleven years before. David had always had an ageless look, an eternally youthful man whose age one could only guess at.

He was impressive looking, a handsome man. He had a broad and high forehead and dark eyebrows framing a pair of blue eyes, eyes which many people were unable to meet because of their forceful, piercing look. His cheekbones were prominent and highlighted his snub nose. A narrow split between his thin, pale lips marked the outlines of his mouth, which was generally pursed. His general appearance suggested the ascetic. After Yoni, the gigantic *moshav* coordinator, David was the second tallest person in Yetzivim.

David had always been an object of speculation in the small world of Yetzivim.

First of all, in over ten years, David had never been known to lead the prayers even once in the *beis knesses.* He made sure to be called up to the Torah on the Shabbos before the *yahrzeit* of his father and mother, but never went up before the cantor's *amud,* never on a weekday and certainly not on Shabbos. All the pleadings of the rabbis of Yetzivim fell upon deaf ears. He declined categorically and absolutely.

"David is embarrassed to show what a poor cantor he is," his friends teased. His excessive shying away from the *chazzan's* rostrum was interpreted by the *moshavniks* in only one way: David was afraid of being mocked if he revealed how far removed he was from the world of chanting.

Secondly, no one had ever heard him lift his voice in song. When all the worshipers joined in the rousing rendition of *Lecha Dodi* in greeting the Shabbos queen, David would be immersed in the *Rashi* of the weekly portion. During the joint *seudah shlishis* which was held in the main synagogue, each of the members of the *moshav,* without exception, were honored to lead the Shabbos *zemiros* by rotation. Except David, of course. In his own home, Friday night and Shabbos day, David recited the *zemiros* with a dry half-audible monotone that lacked all vitality.

But recently something had seemed to change. Hillel, David's steady neighbor in the synagogue, had caught David humming snatches of melodies to himself. His singing voice had seemed pleasing to the ear, despite its near inaudibility. Hillel began to pay attention to this earthshaking discovery until he once put his head right next to David. The latter suddenly realized that his neighbor was listening to him, and had immediately fallen silent. David's cheeks had flushed like a ripe tomato and then turned white as snow. For the next two days he was unable to exchange as much as a word with Hillel and from that time on, no one, not even Hillel, heard him humming to himself, not even the smallest fragment of a tune. And this seemed all the more strange.

Thirdly, and this surpassed the other phenomena, was David's strange attitude to his son, the child prodigy, Buki.

"We have a favor to ask, Mrs. Eliad," Yoni and Hillel repeated their request for the umpteenth time. "We understand that it must be very difficult for you, and you must be greatly disturbed by David's stubborn attitude towards your son, Baruch. But we're only trying to help."

Five people sat in the garden around an old table which had until recently stood in the living room. Yoni and Hillel, satisfied that David was safely at work in the fields, had come with their wives. "We thought it would be nice to drop in for a social visit," Tamar, Hillel's wife, explained. Berta nodded in agreement. But Odelia did not let herself be taken in for a moment. 'Royal visits' such as this did not take place on an ordinary weekday.

The conversation wound round and round. The visitors drew in lungfuls of the intoxicating fragrance of the nearby citrus orchard in bloom. The garden was a lush green; high, flowering bushes threw their shadows on the table. Berta did not stop expressing her admiration for the flourishing greenery and the multicolored abundance all around.

But despite their being surrounded by loveliness in bloom, the atmosphere around the table was far from being pleasant. In fact, it grew more melancholy by the moment.

The cold morning breeze which wafted the exciting fragrances on its wings did not particularly cool Odelia's inflamed cheeks.

"I've already explained to you several times that you are encroaching upon our private affairs," she firmly defended her husband, a hint of anger filtering into her voice. "What happens within our house need not interest anyone other than our immediate family."

Her visitors glanced at one another. At this point, according to plan, Yoni was supposed to keep silent and let Hillel, David's good friend, take over.

"Mrs. Eliad," he began with overstated formality, "no one wishes to antagonize you, G-d forbid, especially not me, your long-time friend." He stopped, as if testing her reaction. Odelia nodded in agreement.

"We've simply come to ask a favor," Hillel continued, encouraged by her response. "We are organizing a children's choir for the upcoming ten-year anniversary of Yetzivim. It will dominate the festivities. And who, if not your *wunderkindt*, your marvelous Buki, deserves to be the choir's soloist? Go ask anyone in the *moshav* and you'll hear the same opinion. Buki has a fantastic voice; it is truly fabulous."

Odelia's eyes lit up. "Thank you for the compliment," she murmured modestly.

"Hillel, forgive me for interrupting you. I'd like to say something," Yoni said. "Mrs. Eliad will not be surprised if I tell her that I am somewhat familiar with the world of music… Well then, in my mind, Yetzivim is far too small for Buki. Who can appreciate him in this remote backwater? Buki can become one of the greatest singers in the country. He has the sweetest, most lyrical soprano I have ever heard in my lifetime. If his parents only knew how to channel his talent, he could have a brilliant future ahead of him!

"I used to attend concerts before the war," Yoni lifted his head proudly. "I visited the most famous concert halls of Vienna. I've heard famous opera singers and even the king of cantors, Yossele Rosenblatt, when he was a mere youngster of *bar-mitzvah* age, giving a concert in Pressburg. And I'm telling you, your Buki can be an even greater cantor than Yossele Rosenblatt!" concluded Yoni dramatically.

Odelia remained silent. A fierce battle waged inside her heart and she felt the burden too difficult to bear. *Shai, my dear brother! Where are you now? I need your wise advice, your penetrating intuition, so badly now!*

For many years her strong yearning for her departed twin brother had lain buried and dormant. But lately, it had surfaced again to gnaw away at her heart, stronger and more demanding now than before, when the tragedy had been fresh.

David had successfully filled the painful void in her heart. He had served as her supporting and helping hand throughout difficult times, even in that gloomy period, on that black day when R' Calfon had knocked upon their door bearing the terrible news of her parents' murder in Tunis. But lately, Odelia had felt that she no longer knew her husband. Something was changing inside him. He was gradually turning into a different person, and she didn't know what was causing the change.

Yoni had cleverly touched upon her maternal pride. He didn't know — or perhaps he did — that his words were pouring salt upon open wounds.

What does Yoni think? That I don't want my Buki to be soloist in the choir? Has he come to tell me what my Buki is?

෧)෬

It was a week before this social visit that Buki had revealed to her from where he drew his tear-evoking melodies.

RIBONO SHEL OLAM! Who had ever heard anything like that! That a ten-year-old child should already be a composer!

"Do you want to tell me that you composed all those tunes from your own head?" she had asked, in open wonder.

"What does 'compose' mean, Ima?"

"It means to make up a tune. A person who makes up tunes is called a composer."

"I don't know how to make up songs," Buki explained with sweet naivete. "I suddenly hear a tune humming itself in my head and all I do is listen to it."

"And then?" Odelia interrupted with bated breath. This is what the mothers of all great composers must have felt, she thought.

"Do you remember when we were in Tel Aviv and heard that choir?" Buki asked, seeming to change the subject. Odelia nodded.

Two years before, the family had gone to Tel Aviv for Succos and stayed with the kindly sister and brother-in-law of R' Goldberg. On the evening after Simchas Torah they had attended the *hakafos shniyos* which are traditionally held in synagogues throughout *Eretz Yisrael.* These had taken place at the Great Synagogue. A large children's choir had sung festival songs to musical accompaniment and *yeshivah bachurim* had danced with fiery enthusiasm, sweeping along many of the male spectators in their circle. Odelia and the children had stood there for a long time, riveted with excitement and wondering where their father had disappeared. He had returned at the end of the festivities without as much as an explanation where he had been all the while.

"What does that choir have to do with what we're talking about?" Odelia asked, puzzled.

"Whenever a new song pops into my head, I shut my eyes tightly and I see the choir in Tel Aviv standing and singing. I imagine that I am one of the children in the choir. I listen to the soloist and suddenly, I begin singing along with him."

Odelia could no longer contain herself. She lifted Buki up, as she had when he was a year old, and hugged and kissed him for several long moments, tears of joy streaming from her eyes.

She had sent Buki off to play and cried. Even as she sobbed, she did not stop thanking Hashem for the wonderful gift He had granted her, the son with such a pure soul. She prayed that she and David would make no mistakes in raising this gifted child, that they would know how to channel him in the right direction.

But David would not leave the child alone! Whenever he heard Buki singing, something happened to him. Two nights ago, for example, Buki had sung one of the familiar tunes he liked to sing. She already knew it and its rhythm well, and had hummed along with Buki.

The notes were lyrical; they evoked an outpouring of the soul, and Yoni, who stood listening next door, could almost swear that it was an ancient Russian tune.

And then David had burst into the house, his face screwed up in a terrible grimace. He had roared at Buki, his hands and feet twitching as if in a fit of malaria. The frightened Buki had shut his mouth at once while Odelia's heart had sunk deep inside her once again.

And now Yoni and Hillel had come asking that Buki be the soloist in their choir...

A few words from Yoni's speech had lit up a red light in her head. An alarm began ringing loudly inside her with deafening force.

There are external ears affixed to the sides of one's head. These absorb most of the sounds of the outside world and channel them inward to be absorbed by the brain.

But there are ears that are more finely tuned, ears that hear better; inner ears, which absorb the sound of the soul.

She saw Yoni's lips moving, but couldn't hear a word.

She was unable to pinpoint a particular sentence that had aroused her. But her thoughts were in a whirl. She drew her breath in deeply and reviewed everything he had just said, as if the words were written in big black letters on a huge white cardboard poster. She disconnected herself from the visitors sitting by her side, staring at her with round eyes. She ignored them completely and concentrated upon what Yoni had said, but the words she was looking for refused to appear on the screen of her memory. She reviewed all of the sentences he had spoken, but one single key word, or two, rebellious and insolent, stubbornly evaded and mocked her.

"Can I help you?" Yoni asked. He looked like the epitome of good will.

Yes! Please repeat everything you said in these past two hours, word for word. Especially those annoying words which I am unable to dredge up from my subconscious mind. Repeat that key word that you uttered unintentionally...

Yoni was liable to think that she had gone mad, too.

One final, futile attempt... She shut her eyes tightly, screwing them up with painful force. What was that word he had said that had grabbed her attention? What had he said?

10

Despairing of her futile attempts to rack her memory, Odelia returned to reality: the visitors who were awaiting her reply.

"You want Buki as a soloist? Have you ever heard of a man who found a button and wove a shirt around it? A soloist without a choir? You know we don't have a choir here in the *moshav*!"

"True until now, Mrs. Eliad, but as of today..." Yoni spoke with a rolling laugh, full of happiness and permeated with self-importance, "we *do* have a choir."

"A choir here in Yetzivim?" Even Berta was surprised.

"Please make its acquaintance," Yoni announced triumphantly, withdrawing an envelope from his pocket with a grand flourish, like a magician pulling a rabbit out of a hat. "Here it is: the Children's Choir of Yetzivim!"

His fingers trembled with excitement when he tried to remove a rectangular piece of cardboard.

"What's that white postcard?" asked Hillel.

"You're looking at the wrong side; that's the back," explained Yoni, turning the 'postcard' around. There was a black-and-white photo of a group of smiling children, dressed in their Shabbos best. In the center stood a tall boy holding up a square sign which read: Children's Choir — Yetzivim.

"I am hereby unveiling the choir before your very eyes," he declared thunderously, imitating the Keren Kayemet representative removing the veil from a sign designating a new forest. He waved the picture and pushed it under Berta's nose.

"My Gindush," she cried in surprise, grabbing the picture from his hand and staring, rapt, at the tall youth holding the sign. "Yoni, what a surprise you've prepared for me! You didn't tell me a word!"

"Gindush didn't breathe a word, either, right? It's supposed to be a secret."

"But when did you manage to take a picture of the choir?" Tamar Weiss asked, overcome with emotion at the sight of her own eight-year-old Dori standing in the second row. "Hillel, did you know that our Dori was in the choir?"

"No," Hillel admitted frankly.

"We've been working on the choir in absolute secrecy for a month. (*What modesty on my part. 'We' really means 'me.'*) Everything was done quietly, I would even venture to say: underground. The children succeeded in keeping a secret just like adults. Imagine how surprised all the members and the guests will be when we open the festivity with a choir. To tell the truth, we also kept it quiet because of David. He is an unpredictable man who is liable to torpedo all our efforts.

"The choir will be the main attraction of Yetzivim's Ten-Year Celebration. We've already formed a group of twenty children and have begun practice. I brought a photographer from town one day and this is the result.

"But the center is empty!" Yoni pointed to the middle of the photo with an accusing finger. "Do you see this, Mrs. Eliad? I left a place vacant near Gindush. This is where the soloist is supposed to stand. And without Buki, the choir is not worth a cent!"

"You needn't overdo it," said Odelia. "There are other children with good voices. What's wrong with your Gindush, for example?"

"Do you want to rub it in?" Yoni sighed. "How can you compare Buki with his nightingale's voice to Gindush? I've already told you, Mrs. Eliad, that Buki can go places; he can go very far. Don't be surprised if they come and suggest that you put him in the prestigious Renanim children's choir. One of these days, when Buki becomes a world-famous singer, you'll remember Yoni Avivi, the one who rescued him from his anonymity."

"You're flattering me," smiled Odelia. "All right, I'll cooperate. Buki can be part of the choir."

"Bravo!" cried Yoni and Hillel in unison. "Thank you very much, Mrs. Eliad. At this very moment you have established the children's choir of Yetzivim."

"But only on one condition," Odelia added in a cool voice. "You've begun this as an underground affair. Continue to keep it secret. I don't want David learning anything about it."

"What am I not supposed to know about?" David asked, suddenly appearing from behind a lattice thickly covered by a leafy bougainvillaea. "And what distinguished guests have come to visit, just when I was away..."

✑✒

A successful theatrical producer would have enjoyed the scene, while an artist would surely have derived great satisfaction from the opportunity of capturing the wide range of colors that suddenly spread over the four faces. A bright white, a truly cadaverous shade of white, gave Odelia's face an other-worldly expression; Berta took on the complexion of a particularly luscious beet; two strips of pink on pasty-white cheeks gave Tamar the look — if not the sweetness — of a peppermint stick; while Hillel's usually ruddy cheeks now changed from pinkish red to grayish white and again to a greenish hue. He looked on the verge of an epileptic fit.

Yoni was the only one who didn't participate in this color kaleidoscope. "Hello, there, David," he said coolly. "It's not very polite to burst in, even in your own home. You frighten people."

"Honest people are not frightened!" declared David. "Only those who have something to hide.

"Good evening, my dear Hillel," he cried, slapping his friend across the shoulder. "So you're a partner in this celebration, as well? What are you concocting behind my back?"

An uncomfortable silence hung over the garden.

"Enough!" cried Yoni angrily after a moment. "Are you afraid of David? I'm not. I'll tell you what is bothering me.

"David, you, yourself are causing us to meet and scheme behind your back. You threaten Hillel when he makes a suggestion that any father would be proud of, to make his son the soloist in a choir!

"I don't know (*don't I?*) what you have against music in general and singers in particular. It makes no difference right now. But you can't drag another generation behind you! Why must you stifle your son Buki? He is a rising star. Let him be the soloist in our choir celebrating ten years of Yetzivim. Let him develop his G-d-given talent!"

"Over my dead body!" thundered David, his eyes shooting sparks. "I will never allow it!"

"Why not?" begged Hillel, who had succeeded in recovering his composure. "What could be so bad for Buki to sing a little?"

"You all seek the boy's good, right?" David mocked them. "And what if I tell you that you are really only concerned with your own interests? All you want is for Yetzivim to become a little famous, to bask in the limelight. To be written up in the papers. After all, we haven't had a decent *fedayin* infiltration for years, right? We have to put Yetzivim back in the news, and Buki will bestow great honor to Yetzivim, am I not right?"

Exchanging looks, the women slipped out of the garden, leaving their husbands to thrash it out themselves. David continued his harangue. "True, Buki sings fairly well and has a decent voice. Is that reason to ruin his whole future?"

"What are you talking about?" Yoni leaped out of his seat as if stung by a bee. "If a boy sings a little, it will ruin his future?"

"You were talking about a celebrated singer, right, Yoni? A world-famous singer is not one who 'sings a little.' To become that, one must mobilize all of one's emotional resources, sacrifice all of one's time. And what about studies, which are bound to suffer? To say nothing about the harm it will do to his good, sweet nature."

"Perhaps you can explain to me how a person's character is spoiled by singing and music?" Hillel demanded. "Don't you think you're exaggerating things?"

Hillel, Hillel, you've disappointed me. You, who met secretly with Yoni yesterday to scheme behind my back, now ask how one's character can be ruined?

"No, I'm not exaggerating in the least. You ask how one can ruin the soul of a child? I'll tell you how. You take a sweet innocent child and expose him to a grand performance in front of a huge audience. At first, he is embarrassed and shy. He doesn't know how to react. But, slowly, he becomes accustomed to applause and some of his rough edges are smoothed out. He becomes sophisticated and is no longer naive and bashful. The rest follows all too quickly. He becomes the idol of the public, their darling, and fame goes to his head. He soon thinks he is king. He develops absolute dependence upon the public and becomes intoxicated with fame, just like an alcoholic with his liquor. Before long, he is unable to go to sleep without the thunder of applause.

"And that's what you want to do to my Buki," concluded David. "That's why I cannot agree under any terms whatsoever. To take my gentle Buki and turn him into a world-famous singer? Emphatically and absolutely, no!"

"As a simple farmer, you show amazing expertise in a subject far removed from you," Yoni commented, his eyes veiled. "Why don't you ever visit me to hear some of my records? I have a rare collection of the greatest works in the world. Come and spend a pleasurable hour or two with me."

"I have an hour of pleasure every evening between *Minchah* and *Maariv* in the *beis knesses* when I study a page of *Gemara* together with the *rav*. I have no time for classical music from the study halls of non-Jewish composers." David's sarcasm was biting.

Yoni and Hillel left the garden without a farewell. David expelled his breath in an angry rush and collapsed on an easy chair, drained and wrung out. He lay there in the shade of a plum tree, limp, his mind empty of all thought. Why was he destined to fight this battle all his life?

≈)⌒

Vienna!

Vienna! How could I have forgotten that word? Vienna. It was the stubborn word that eluded me all that time.

Odelia sat in the kitchen sipping a cup of coffee, trying to recover from the unexpected and unpleasant encounter, hoping she would know how to smooth over this new episode. The forgotten word had made its own way through the pathways of her brain and had suddenly surfaced in her conscious mind. Who knows? Perhaps the shock she had experienced when David suddenly appeared from his hiding place and revealed that he had been listening to their secret conversation all the while had released the trapped word from the abyss of oblivion.

Actually, there were two key words: Vienna was one and 'opera' was the second.

A forgotten scene surfaced in her memory with amazing clarity, even though three years had passed. The postman had ridden up to their front gate on his motorcycle and rang the bell. She had gone out to him and he had handed her a notice.

"David, a large piece of mail has arrived for you," she said, showing him the note with its red stamp when he came home that evening from the field. "I was thinking of going to Beersheba tomorrow to do some shopping. Give me your I.D. card so that I can pick it up for you."

The next day she returned from Beersheba with a large envelope stamped with seals from a foreign country. She could feel that it contained something hard, and concluded that it must be a framed picture or certificate of some sort. But she didn't open the envelope. This is what her mother, Miriam, of blessed memory, had taught her.

The rest of the episode was surprising. David shut himself up in the living room with the envelope for a long time and when he emerged, refused to show her what it contained. "It's some stupid document that is no longer relevant," he explained. He had assumed the inscrutable expression of an ancient Chinese sage, an expression that she knew all too well, and she meekly acquiesced.

Her mother's teaching could go only so far: The following morning she searched for the "stupid document" all over the house. She went from drawer to drawer, from one closet to the next, until she found it, hidden under a pile of his winter clothes.

It was a state diploma, hung in a stylized wooden frame and protected by thick glass. To her dismay, it was in a foreign language. She tried desperately to figure out the large, curliqued, calligraphic Latin lettering. After exhausting effort she succeeded in deciphering one single word: "Opera." At the end of another few minutes of concentration, she was able to make out an additional word:

Vienna.

Suddenly she heard David's approaching footsteps. Clods of earth on the path in the yard were crushed under his boots with the familiar crunching sound. She hastened to hide the document back under his sweaters. On the following day, the diploma had disappeared from its place and to this day she had not seen it.

Could there be any connection between Yoni's story of his visit to the Viennese Opera House before the Second World War — and this?

Odelia sat quite still, her emotions in a whirl. The document! It must still be here somewhere. She had to find it!

With ironclad determination, she got up from her seat. Yes, she would find the forgotten diploma and expose the mystery behind it!

11

O delia decided to wait until David returned to his field. Then she would launch a thorough search of the entire house. She listened intently. Complete silence. Only the sound of leaves rustling in the breeze.

The ice must be broken. Since the scene in the garden not long before, she hadn't exchanged a word with her angry spouse. With hesitant steps she went out to the garden. David was sitting rigid on a chair, his eyes focused on the green aloes thriving above his head.

"I'm going to Har Lutz," he said abruptly.

Odelia stared, bewildered. What was this new complication? "What? What's Har Lutz?" she demanded.

"One of the mountains in the central Negev. Some infiltrators from Gaza murdered an army officer there. They need help."

"Who? Who needs help?"

David told her the full story. That morning the bullet-ridden body of a high-ranking army officer, Meir Fein, had been found in a deep *wadi* near Har Lutz. The prime suspects were Bedouins infiltrating from Gaza. Security forces had launched a wide search for the murderers and had asked for any aid, especially from residents of the area who were familiar with the terrain.

"How do you know all this?"

"This morning, on the way to the field, I was stopped by an army jeep and the soldiers told me the news in detail. They asked for help. That's why I came back so suddenly. I wanted to pick up some equipment I would need. I told them to pick me up in an hour."

A dreadful fear filled her heart. "You're not going anywhere!" she said forcefully.

"I'm a big boy," David answered with a small smile.

"I'm begging you. Don't go there. Bloodthirsty murderers are freely roaming about. We've had our fill of tension and fear. If you stay there long I'll be beside myself with worry."

Odelia, Odelia. How fickle you are. Just five minutes ago you wanted to send him off to the field, to work. And now you're begging him not to leave…

"It'll be all right. I won't stay away long," he promised. The next few minutes were a whirl of activity, as David prepared for a long day in the bleak desert terrain. Finally, a loud beeping sounded by the gate of the *moshav*. David ran carrying a heavy knapsack in his hand. "Don't worry," he shouted. "I'll be back by nightfall."

Odelia wiped away a tear and retreated to the secure haven that had never disappointed her, her *Tehillim*. Hers were not idle worries: The Negev swarmed with infiltrators. Murderous *fedayin* lay in ambush, waiting for innocent travelers and peaceful citizens, and striking them down mercilessly. Bedouin tribes traveled freely from place to place and were a common source of danger, both to Jewish lives and property.

As Odelia prayed for David's safekeeping, that he return home safely, she wasn't certain whether she was praying for his body or for his soul — that it, too, return to her husband in peace.

Something strange was happening to him lately. She had no doubt of that. But what that something was, she could not guess. His sleep had become more restless and agitated than usual. After several years of relative calm, David's nightmares had returned to haunt him. He would writhe and scream in the midst of a deep sleep. He would roll from side to side, drenched in a cold sweat, murmuring unintelligible words. From his flow of babbling she would barely be able to make out a few words here and there.

"David, who is Roman Spiegel?" she asked him one morning when he returned from *shul*.

He froze as if someone had lashed at his face with a whip. "Why do you ask?"

"Because you've been mentioning his name now for the third night in a row. I wanted to know who was this man who was disturbing my husband's peace."

David blushed fiercely, like a child caught redhanded. "I talk in my sleep? What else did I say?" he asked with an artificial chuckle and, she ventured to guess, a hint of fear.

"All kinds of things."

"What, for example?"

"I don't understand Yiddish or Polish, so I can't tell you," said Odelia, rising to her feet agitatedly. "Enough, David! This game is beginning to make me sick. What have you been hiding from me all this time? And who is this Roman Spiegel?"

He drew back from her in alarm, white as a sheet, his feet tottering. "Better for you not to know. No one should know of such people at all!"

≈)⌒

That had been a week ago. Now, she decided, she would unravel the mystery once and for all.

She would need a few quiet hours to herself, to turn the house upside down, to scour every square centimeter. Ironically, it was precisely this frightening trip of David's which would help her find the answer to the riddle.

They had a radio in their living room, a huge wooden cabinet with a green glass face and brown knobs protruding beneath it. Giving her *Tehillim* a kiss and placing it on a shelf, she turned the radio on full volume so as to drown out any noise she might make. The neighbors need not know what she was doing.

The diploma had to be found...

She attacked the closets first, removing every garment of clothing, every item, even searching underneath the paper shelf-liners.

Nothing!

"It's impossible!" she heard herself murmuring. "The earth did not open up its mouth and swallow it."

Perhaps that was the answer.

She took a large stick from the yard and began tapping the floor tiles, listening for a hollow sound.

Nothing.

Despairing, she moved on to the kitchen. She put up a kettle to boil and waited. A hot cup of coffee would help restore her clarity of thought.

"A cup of milk — a cup of health!" the radio blared out its advertisement at the very moment she opened the refrigerator to take out the bottle of milk. The next commercial was already on the air, and she hummed along in her mind.

Impelled by a sudden brainstorm, she slammed the door behind her and ran out.

Milk… Milk comes from the barn…

Odelia burst inside like a storm. The frightened cows pressed against one another. Over the years, the barn had grown beyond recognition. Its population now numbered thirty head of cattle, a fact that aroused no small envy among the *moshavniks*. David spent some time in the barn each day. He had two hired hands who helped him with the milking, and he had even built a small office attached to the barn where he took care of daily orders and sales to a major dairy. She first tried her luck inside the barn, but quickly gave up. She had never been able to take the smell of manure, and the odor in the barn was unbearable. She scanned the yellow-brown hay piled up along the walls in neat rectangles, up till the high asbestos roof. Go find a needle in a literal haystack…

The office was locked, but Odelia had brought its keys with her from the house.

⁓)⁓

David had put up the barn as soon as he had built their home in Yetzivim. In the beginning, she had helped with the milking. She would sit down on a low stool and milk a cow, breathing only through her mouth, her face a grotesque grimace of disgust. David would burst into laughter each time he saw her in this position, but after he expanded his activities and hired two men, she would not even set foot in the barn. Her revulsion at the smell of animals was legendary. Only a truly extraordinary reason could have brought Odelia within a hundred meters of the barn. Surely David realized Odelia would never set foot in the place. For that matter, Odelia realized with a start, David never admitted anyone into his office. The brief transaction with the dairy's representative was dealt with outside, near the milk truck.

This was the only explanation Odelia could offer in face of the shock she received upon entering the office.

On the wall opposite a small table, hung the forgotten diploma, that very one.

It did not hang there alone. Next to it was another diploma, written in calligraphy with an old-fashioned quill. The frame was simple, wooden, of a kind long since out of fashion. The language here was also foreign and unintelligible to her.

She stood there for several moments staring at the certificate, trying in vain to decipher the meaning of the words. She then shook herself out of her reverie. An eternity must have elapsed, she thought, not a mere ten minutes.

With an easy motion, she lifted both pictures off the wall. She glanced at her watch. A quarter to one. David would not be back before night. She would have plenty of time to have the certificates translated, which she was determined to do, at any cost!

She entered the house at the very moment that the radio began its afternoon newscast. "Security forces have captured the murderers of Captain Meir Fein from Kibbutz Gor Aryeh. The murderers, Bedouins who slipped in from the Sinai desert, were found not far from the site of the murder, some five kilometers from Kuseima, fifteen kilometers from Sde Boker. Joining the regular army forces were several reserve officers…"

The words descended upon her burning head like a jet of cold water. *Baruch Hashem,* David was safe. And he would be home soon. There was no time to lose.

12

"**I**'m not a professional translator, you understand, but I can try," the clerk said apologetically.

She had wasted a whole hour walking the streets of Beersheba in a fruitless search for a firm of translators. She was almost ready to lift up her hands in despair when she was suddenly struck by a brainstorm. Passing underneath a big sign, "Salzburger and Sons, Import-Export," the idea had popped into her head.

If they deal with import and export between foreign countries, why shouldn't they be familiar with foreign tongues, as well? She found herself climbing up to the second floor and explaining what she needed to the bored-looking clerk.

He tried his best. He began reading the illustrious-looking certificate. "This is in German, a language I'm familiar with."

"German?" Odelia repeated, shocked.

"Why are you surprised? Vienna is steeped with German culture. It is very likely that an important Viennese institution would use German as its official language, unless this certificate was written before the First World War, during the period of the Austro-Hungarian empire, in which case it might have been written in Hungarian."

He read the document in silence. After a moment, he took a pen and paper and began translating.

"The Opera House of Vienna." This was the title, emblazoned in full glory.

The paper danced between her trembling fingers as she read it avidly.

"The Opera House of Vienna is proud to present this certificate of honorary membership to the renowned singer, Herr Henry Horowitz, as a token of its esteem for his performances in the Opera House upon January 16th, 1935 and January 23rd, 1935.

"The appearance of the celebrated singer did us great honor."

Underneath were several lines of elaborate wishes and flowery figures of speech describing the history of the opera house. It ended with this closing sentence: "In the name of the numerous citizens of Vienna, we are proud to express our sentiments of appreciation to Herr Henry Horowitz, the giant of Polish song."

Three signatures were proudly affixed at the bottom. Two of them did not mean a thing to her but the third name... Her heart pounded wildly when she read it: "Gustav Spiegel."

While she was reading the translation of the first document, the clerk was busy working on the second one. She did not have time to recover before he handed her the paper, his brow furrowed in anger. "Who wrote this?"

"I don't know," Odelia said, drawing back in alarm at his evident fury.

"Whoever wrote this second certificate is a man lacking minimal human sensitivity. He deserves to be flogged! He tried to be clever and chose to exercise his humor on a very painful subject." The voice rose to an angry screech. "This is disgusting. The man must be mad, without an ounce of conscience. It is the height of absurdity, a forgery in the poorest taste."

"I don't understand. What are you talking about?"

"Read it for yourself and you'll see." He let the paper drop to the table with a gesture of revulsion.

"The Opera House of Maidenek," the stylized title said.

"The Opera House of the Maidenek Labor Camp is proud to issue this certificate of honorary membership to the renowned singer, the Jew, Yechiel Horowitz, for his marvelous performances during the years 1943-1944. The wonderful Jew, Horowitz, proved that with a little good will, all nations can reach a mutual understanding and find the common denominator for all nations on the face of the earth."

It was signed: "Roman Spiegel."

"It is a disgrace! A desecration!" the man shouted, his face flushed. "To joke about a death camp where hundreds of thousands of Jews met their deaths in the most cruel, sadistic manner!"

"Pinchas, why are you so upset?" the company manager, Mr. Zelzberger, had just returned from his lunch break. Hiding a yawn behind his hand, he stopped by his clerk's desk.

"Read this." Pinchas had not yet cooled off. With a rapid motion he handed the original certificate to his boss.

Mr. Zelzberger scanned it and swallowed another yawn. "Who wrote this nonsense?" he chortled, waving the paper in his hand derisively. "'The Opera House of Maidenek.' Ha, that's a good one."

She sat on the wooden seat, wrapped up in her thoughts. The bus bounced up and down along the potholed, narrow old road leading to Yetzivim. A heavy, oppressive end-of-the-summer heat filled the bus. The open windows hardly helped. A blast of steamy air hit the passengers and filled the bus with grains of yellow sticky sand and dust. The passengers mopped the constant flow of perspiration from their faces with their handkerchiefs. But Odelia was almost oblivious to the heat and dust. Thousands of thoughts swirled dizzily around in her mind. She saw herself bursting into the house, demanding an explanation, a possibility which she dismissed at once. Perhaps it would be better to ignore the episode altogether. But she rejected this idea just as quickly.

The first thing was to plan how to get David to clarify to her directly or indirectly who this Henry Horowitz was, this "King of Polish Singers." And who was Yechiel Horowitz, the "marvelous Jew" from Maidenek. Were they one and the same person? What did David know about him or them and what was his connection to them?

The bus stopped on the main road. A dirt road about two kilometers long led westward from there to Yetzivim. She plodded along by foot, fat drops of perspiration shining on her forehead. The sun was leaning to the west and its bright light shone directly into her eyes, blinding her and causing them to smart and tear. Carrying two bulky brown envelopes in her hands, holding them with all her might lest they slip and the frames break, she was unable to protect her eyes from the glaring sun.

An army vehicle approached from the main highway, its engine roaring deafeningly. She gesticulated energetically, hoping that the driver would see her waving, that the sun's rays would not blind him as well.

The driver noticed her and stopped the jeep by her side.

"Hello, Mrs. Eliad," David's head peered from the window. A mischievous glint danced in his eyes. "Have you gone out for an afternoon walk?"

From that moment on, Odelia carried on a mad race against the hands of the clock. After their happy announcement that they had returned safely, David and the driver, who had also taken part in the chase, told the suspenseful story of how they had trapped the three Bedouins who had murdered the army officer. Odelia listened with only half an ear. Her mind was feverishly calculating how much time she had until milking, and what excuse she could use to sneak into David's office. The certificates burned her palms with biting accusation. How could she get rid of this incriminating evidence?

What will you say to him? "*Listen here, David. I want to milk the cows tonight. I'm terribly drawn to the aroma of the manure...*"

Or, perhaps, forthrightly, "*What's your opinion about these two translations? The style's not bad, is it?*"

Why did I have to get myself into such a predicament? Her heart beat wildly; her breath came in rapid pants.

"Don't you feel well?" David's sharp eyes immediately discerned that something was wrong. "You look very pale."

"I'm all right." Her voice trembled. "I need to rest a bit."

The worried David forgot all about his own fatigue after a harrowing day of chase in the Negev. He fretted over her all evening, like a solicitous father watching over his only daughter. That evening she did not visit the barn.

Odelia waited impatiently for the wee hours of the night. When he was fast asleep, she would return the certificates to their place.

Someone knocked at the door. Hillel stood in the doorway.

"David," he said, his eyes fixed on the ground. "It was all your fault that I didn't work today."

"Why?"

"I've come to ask your forgiveness. I can't lose a friend like you."

"I haven't died yet. Please, don't mourn me," David thumped him on the back affectionately. The two burst into hearty tension-releasing laughter. Friendly laughter. David ran to the cabinet and took out a bottle of Baron brandy to commemorate their peace. He didn't notice Hillel approach the window and nod to someone waiting outside.

While David poured a tumblerful of brandy for Hillel and himself, there was another knock on the door. This time it was Yoni. "I heard voices and felt I had to come over. I heard that you were quite a hero today. They even mentioned you in the news."

"Big deal, big hero. I helped the security forces a little. I know that area through and through. I've been there dozens of times."

"Come, let's sit outside in the garden," suggested Hillel. "It's too hot here."

They took the bottle and the glasses and went out to the garden. David lit a powerful lamp and the celebration began: Hundreds of mosquitoes and moths collected around the light bulb. They danced and hummed around it until David was forced to turn it off. They sat in darkness, the glowing end of their cigarettes lighting up their faces with a dim, reddish light.

"I've stopped buying the old-fashioned Ascot cigarettes," Yoni said, exhaling a ring of smoke with a strong odor. "Now I'm on to Eden. It's price is outrageous. But it's worth it. The flavor is out of this world!"

"I'm a sworn fan of Dubek," said Hillel, inhaling the thick smoke into his lungs. "I'm addicted to it."

They chatted comfortably, full of good will. The quarrel that had erupted that morning in the garden seemed to be resolved and they were in high spirits. The unpleasant incident could have threatened relationships for the coming years but here, with such surprising ease, the hostilities had been smoothed over.

Don't let yourself be taken in, David. They haven't come here only to make up. Perhaps, Hillel, but not Yoni. They want something...

Their voices carried through the open window to Odelia's ears. This conversation could go on for a long time. That is, if no new argument exploded, again...

Odelia leaped agilely out of bed, bent over and took the large envelopes she had hidden underneath in the few moments David had not hovered over her with his fatherly concern.

Quiet reigned in the *moshav*. Odelia walked along the unlit paths, her heart beating wildly. She was afraid of the dark. The sound of hundreds of crickets busy with their unending labor was the only evidence of life.

If she had not been gripped by paralyzing fear, she might have stopped to inhale the refreshing fragrance of the earth and to enjoy the blessed peace, to listen to the sounds of the night — the croaking of the frogs from afar, the hooting of an owl — to study the flight of fireflies brightening up the darkness with their green phosphorescence, as she often did when walking together with David, trusting in his strength.

But now she was alone. In the dark. She trembled with every rustling leaf and fumbled her way to the barn with bated breath. Stealthily, she crept into the office, which was plunged in deathly blackness. She felt her way along the wall with trembling fingers, looking for two nails. Finally, with a sigh of relief, she replaced the certificates on the wall. Only when she had returned to the safety of her bed, quaking and shaking like a fish in a net, was she struck by a horrible idea. How easily could she have made a mistake in the darkness and put the certificates in the wrong places... But nothing in the world would be able to get her out of bed and force her to make the frightening trip once again. Not even Roman Spiegel — whoever he was.

⇀↽

The conversation flowed freely in the garden, but David felt his strength ebbing. He had undergone a grueling day and his body cried out for sleep.

"You know, David," Yoni said, lighting another cigarette, ignoring his host's obvious fatigue, "the next Knesset elections are approaching. They're scheduled to take place in Cheshvan."

"I know, I know." David was unable to control another broad yawn.

"The date of the elections is almost identical to when we settled in, the very day that we set aside for the ten-year celebration," continued Yoni. David's ears perked up automatically. Ah, it was coming. They hadn't come only to make up.

"And what of it?" All of his tiredness suddenly disappeared and he became alert and clearheaded.

"The distinguished politicians will not come to us after Succos. They will be far too busy a few days before elections. So we decided to anticipate the date and set it for Tuesday, the eleventh of Tishrei, the day after Yom Kippur, 5720. We're going to be flooded; three government ministers and six more party heads promised to attend. They jumped at the opportunity. They intend to take advantage of this gathering to do some party electioneering."

What was he driving at? "What does all this have to do with me?"

"We don't have much time left. It's already the middle of Elul. Now, at this moment of good will, I am asking you again, as a good friend: Let us have Buki."

Aha! So that's why you came to begin with. I'm glad I was not deceived into accepting the purity of your motives.

"Good evening. The meeting is adjourned," David announced coldly, and rose from his seat. "It's been very pleasant. Thank you for coming. We will meet again tomorrow at 6 a.m. in the *beis knesses.*"

13

"Paranoia. Simply paranoia."

"You're mistaken, Hillel. It isn't paranoia."

"Then what is it? Explain it to me, Yoni."

Yoni and Hillel, the two new comrades in arms, were unable to go to sleep after they had parted from David, so they took a midnight walk among the *moshav* houses. They maintained silence until they were beyond their neighbor's hearing.

Yoni, Hillel and David were neighbors. Their three single-story homes formed a triangle. A yard and garden separated one from the other. The members of the *moshav* had begun feeling cramped lately, and the small area allotted by the *moshav* no longer satisfied the needs of growing families.

The two walked along the pathways. Hillel's voice rose several decibels.

"Of course it's paranoia," he argued heatedly. "He is obsessed by a persecution complex. He thinks that something terrible will happen to Buki if he becomes a soloist. Have you noticed how tense he has become lately? On the mark and ready to shoot. Just say a word and he's on the offensive. He's coiled tight like a spring. I'm afraid he's about to explode."

"It isn't paranoia, Hillel, you've got to understand." Yoni's voice filled with self-importance. He would prove to his critical neighbor that Yoni Avivi was no mere *moshav* director; he was cultured, an intellectual. "Paranoia does not limit itself to a single area alone. If David were paranoid, he would always behave like a frightened rabbit and he would be eaten up by suspicion of everyone, under all circumstances. That's not the David you know, is it?"

"No," admitted Hillel. "David only behaves like that with regard to one subject. But when it gets to that, all of a sudden I can't recognize my good friend."

"That's the whole point, Hillel," explained Yoni. "David is normal. But his dark past has caused him to explode like that. I've learned something about this," Yoni added, with the authoritative voice of a doctor of psychology. "He is very sensitive, to an extreme, with regards to certain areas, and can't help erupting when his toes are stepped on."

"Erupting is not the word," said Hillel, rubbing the nape of his neck. "It still hurts."

"But we will have to ignore it, of course," said Yoni, as if he hadn't heard Hillel. "I intend to include Buki in the choir, as of tomorrow, even if the world goes under."

"What do you intend to do with David?" Hillel asked. "Lock him up in a closet on the day of the event? Send him up in the Russian Sputnik-2 satellite to outer space? It's scheduled for flight just around that time. 'Hello, Moscow. Can David Eliad join the crew?' 'Yes, certainly,' answers Moscow. 'The two chimpanzees on board will have to crowd together a bit, but...' No, I made a mistake. It's the Americans who are sending the monkeys into space in their Discovery, not the Russians, so there should be ample room in Sputnik-2 for Da..."

"Enough!" Yoni stopped the verbal flood with a single word. "We're talking about a serious subject, here, and you babble about a stupid race between the United States and Russia to get to the moon first. As far as I'm concerned, they can both go to blazes. As if all of the world's problems have been solved: wars, disease, poverty, hunger — and all that's left is to conquer space."

"You were talking about David," Hillel reminded him discreetly.

"Oh, yes. I don't yet know what steps I'll take, but remember Yoni's promise": and his threatening voice caused Hillel to cringe, "David will not ruin our celebration!"

The choir began practice the following day. After the first lesson of the day, the children went down to the school shelter where they held rehearsals with absolute secrecy. Buki's happiness knew no bounds. He was finally being given freedom to create his own music. All the latent talents which had been crammed deep, deep in his tender heart, out of fear of his threatening father, now burst forth in full force. He sang with all his heart and soul, with unbounded enthusiasm.

"I've never seen anything like this!" Victor, the conductor whom Yoni had brought in from Tel Aviv, said, spellbound. "I must spit blood with every boy before he learns how to sing properly, to sing in unison with the rest of the choir, not to begin too high or too low. And he — all he does is walk in and from the very first day he sings as if he had been a choir member for the past fifty years. This boy was born to sing.

"And what a voice!" Victor dissolved with pleasure. "I've never in my life heard a voice like his. He starts off in an alto minor and goes up, up, up to a high soprano. For that alone it was worth coming here. Who would have believed that a meteor would be hiding in this forsaken settlement at the end of the country. Buki is a meteor, a shining comet! A rising star! After the festivities, I intend to take him to Tel Aviv and turn him into the wonder-child of the country."

"You just try…" Yoni laughed to himself. "He's the button!" he added dreamily.

"What was that?" said the conductor. "I didn't understand you."

"Buki is the button around which the shirt was sewn," explained Yoni, his face glowing with pleasure. "The choir was formed only for him; he is the star of the choir."

"The star of the choir!" The title stuck to Buki from that day. All the children envied him his meteoric rise to glory. Some teased him, as children will, but deep in their hearts they knew the truth. Buki had entered the choir last, and had immediately risen to first place, leaving all of his friends far behind.

Ecstatic Buki paid no attention to his friends' jealousy. The backing that Yoni and Hillel gave him was strong enough to overcome any jealousy, overt or hidden, and served him as a greased shield against the poisoned arrows that some children, consumed with envy, shot his way.

Victor did a marvelous job. "Time is short and work abounds" was his constant motto. He repeated it a hundred times a day. Victor was blessed with a superior teaching ability and the children loved him. He was a tough disciplinarian but not a tyrant, and he promoted each child according to his talent. Given a group of musically ignorant children, Victor turned them into an organized choir within two weeks, through arduous daily toil and at the expense of all their school lessons. In the last week before Rosh Hashanah, rehearsal hours were doubled and the children were summoned to the shelter in the afternoon as well. The parents were told that they were preparing a play for the festivities.

The parents were not stupid. The fact of the choir had become public, a universally known secret. All the members knew about it and were sworn to keep it hidden from David Eliad.

No one knew if David was really ignorant of the existence of the clandestine choir or had built up a defensive wall of pretended ignorance around himself for the sake of appearances. The school building was not far from the *shul* where he went several times a day, and the rehearsals took place almost under his very nose. At any rate, during those two packed weeks, he left Buki strictly alone.

On Erev Rosh Hashanah, David woke Buki up before dawn. They walked together to the *beis knesses* for *Slichos*. Thousands of lights twinkling in the sky winked at the young singer from the velvety canopy spread above his head. He stopped to look at the sky and had it not been for his father's urging, he would have stood there, head flung back, until the deep blue of dawn in the east would have slowly conquered the place of the blackness.

That day passed over Buki like a dream. The prayer motions of the worshipers, wrapped in their *talleisim*, chanting the moving *Slichos* pieces in unison with the *chazzan*, wove a nebulous pattern in his mind.

"The final morning service of 5719!" R' Calfon announced; it lasted twice as long as usual.

There was a wealth of sights and experiences. His mother baked *challos* and honey cake in honor of the festival. Then came the festive evening service, the meal with the symbolic holiday foods to denote the beginning of a sweet, good new year.

The array of sights dizzied him like a kaleidoscope, like the wooden tube he had seen at a friend's house with its colored stones forming endless combinations of symmetrical designs and patterns.

That's how Buki felt now, as if the tube was whirling around rapidly, creating a mosaic of sounds and sights turning inward, deep inside his being. Something began erupting in the hidden recesses of his delicate, sensitive soul.

"Buki, I'd like to bless you," said Yigal, getting up in the middle of the meal and approaching his older brother. "*Alei vehatzlach bishnat tashach* — be successful in year 5720.*"

The rice came shooting out like bullets from David's open mouth. He almost fell off his seat laughing.

"Where did you get that rhyme?" Odelia joined the laughter.

"I don't know. It came to me all of a sudden," Yigal said. "Like Buki's tunes."

David's laughter died down at once and the smile vanished from his face. He shot a stern look at Yigal and crunched down hard upon a chicken bone. Odelia escaped into the kitchen.

Buki tossed on his bed, unable to fall asleep. He glanced at his brother, Yigal, who was sleeping peacefully, an angelic smile on his face. "He has such a cheerful nature. He's always happy and content, even in his sleep." Buki felt a pinch of envy but immediately chided himself for it. He turned over to the other side.

Something churned deep inside his soul, banishing sleep from his eyes. Weak echoes began rumbling somewhere within, bubbling up and subsiding, appearing and disappearing, as if intent on mocking him. His mind froze. The choir. The soloist. A ten-year celebration. Music… He inhaled deeply and listened. The sounds began joining one another, note after note, half a line, a musical phrase. Snatches of tunes joined hands and began dancing together.

A bright light suddenly flooded his mind. The notes finally came together into an entire song. He shut his eyes tightly and listened to the soft sound inside his soul.

And like always at a time of creativity, Buki saw the Tel Aviv soloist standing on the stage singing a new tune that Buki did not know yet, that no one had ever heard before.

A new song was born!

14

V ictor couldn't believe it. "You don't mean to tell me that *you* composed this song!" He looked at Buki to make sure he was not pulling a fast one.

It hadn't been so simple. He had fought bitterly to hold on to the tune he had created on Rosh Hashanah night. When he had arisen the next morning, he had completely forgotten it. Buki feared that it had gone the way of all the previous tunes he had composed, to sink into the abyss of oblivion. In the past he had attributed little importance to his melodies, but this time he had burst into tears. He had dedicated this tune to the Ten-Year Anniversary; he mustn't lose it!

It was the middle of *Mussaf.* The *beis knesses* was enveloped in the solemnity of sanctity and several worshipers had buried their heads in their *talleisim*, hiding tearful eyes. Wellsprings of emotion bubbled forth from the *chazzan*'s voice, plucking at heartstrings and setting them aquiver. This was the key that the *chazzan* was extending to his congregation.

Buki grasped that key and used it… He listened to the tremulous voice of the *chazzan* and suddenly felt his young heart open up. He imagined himself being swept up into enchanting palaces of music.

Suddenly the lost melody returned and struck his memory with full force, surprising him with its clarity; it was rhythmic and full, with a joy and life of its own. It cried out for a choir to sing it with the proper tempo, in harmony, with a soloist singing the high part, the chorus.

"I found it!" he shouted, jumping to his feet excitedly. "I have it."

It was like the "Eureka" cry of Archimedes, the Greek who had found the solution to a puzzling problem. Several worshipers looked at him strangely and David almost slapped him. To his good fortune, no one could scold him for his disturbance, since it was forbidden to speak until all the blasts had been sounded on the shofar, and they were still in the middle.

Buki didn't know how to hold onto the tune and prevent it from slipping away again. He sang it in his mind over and over; he hummed it incessantly, out of his father's hearing. He was ignorant of musical notes which could easily have solved his problem, and tape recorders were rare, owned only by a few people. Buki had seen one only once, when he was four, upon a visit to his German pediatrician, Dr. Ludwig Sternkucker, in the nearby settlement of Tvua.

"This is a tape recorder, my dear child," the doctor had explained congenially, opening the cover. Buki had stood mesmerized by the brown magnetic tape traveling between the two turning plastic reels. He had bent towards the little green light to discover the hiding place of the little man who was singing from the box.

"Don't touch, *mein kind*," the doctor said in alarm. "This is a very expensive device. It's a Grundig!" Dr. Sternkucker intoned the name of the prestigious manufacturer with awesome reverence.

Buki didn't know that his neighbor Yoni owned another Grundig just like it. Had he known, he wouldn't have believed that a person could preserve his voice on a length of brown tape.

But even so, without any technology or techniques, he succeeded in preserving the tune until the Fast of Gedalyah, the day when rehearsals resumed. The very moment that Victor's feet crossed the threshold, Buki ran to him so that he could teach him his song.

Victor listened with eyes shut. He understood the nature of melody; he knew them by the thousands.

This one was different, new.

It would need some adaptation, polishing, but the small flaws did not mar its beauty or dull its overall harmony and the sharpness of its notes.

"Sing it again."

Buki sang his song a second time and before he had finished, Victor found himself humming along. "And you say that you composed it yourself?" He gave Buki a veiled look. The word 'genius' was no exaggeration. The child was capable of overshadowing the greatest known composers. If Victor could have his way, the name Baruch Eliad the Israeli would rank with the greatest composers in the world.

If it was true...

"I don't believe you," he said brusquely. "Prove that it's yours, that you didn't steal it from somewhere."

Salty tears gathered in Buki's eyes. The insult was too great to bear. The word 'stole' crushed him under its weight.

"Why are you crying, Buki?"

Yoni had entered the shelter a few minutes late. He drew near and Buki rushed to him with a sigh of relief, spouting garbled sentences. Yoni grasped the importance of the situation and took Victor aside.

"It's completely true. You can believe him. The child is a born composer. I didn't know it myself, but I kept hearing new melodies, deeply moving melodies, and wondering why they were not familiar to me, since I am somewhat of a connoisseur, until his mother told me everything."

Victor became thoughtful but awakened immediately, sparks shooting from his eyes. "If so, then he's a second Mozart!" he cried, worked up. "Yoni, do you know what a treasure you have in this backwater? Buki is a gold mine! I'm going to be his manager. I'll take him for a tour all around the world. He'll bring down the rafters on Broadway. All of Europe will bow down before him. Who's his father? I must talk to him right now!"

"You can put your gears in reverse," Yoni said coolly, dashing cold water upon his heated enthusiasm. "His father is the whole problem..."

⁂

Victor transcribed the new song in musical notes and took the song-sheet to one of the major studios in Tel Aviv. He returned the next day with a finished product.

He did not come alone. The musical adapter Yitzchak Marciano accompanied him. "I must make the acquaintance of this child prodigy. I must hear him sing the song he composed."

After intensive deliberation by the triumvirate — Yoni, Victor and Yitzchak Marciano — it was decided to set the tune to the familiar words in *Tehillim*:

"*Elokim*, I shall sing to You a new song, with a ten-stringed lyre I shall make music for You.

"Rescue me and deliver me from many waters, from the hands of foreign ones."

The idea was Yoni's, to be sure, for the figure 'ten' did not leave his sight for a moment, not by day or by night.

"What could be more fitting than this verse?" he argued heatedly. "There's the phrase 'new song' and the word 'ten', to commemorate the ten years of Yetzivim."

The new song passed its maiden test and was officially launched into orbit. The choir renewed its rehearsals. The new song caught on quickly and the children did not stop singing it. It promised to be the hit of the show.

"It's going to be a real hit, don't you understand?" Yoni said, thumping his huge fist on the table.

The small secretariat of Yetzivim had met to discuss preparations for the upcoming gala affair that Yoni was planning to hold on Tuesday, the eleventh of Tishrei, 5720 (1959). But, impatient for glory, Yoni had come up with a brilliant idea: Why shouldn't the choir hold its last rehearsal in public, as a full dress preview, during the *Asseres Yemei Tshuvah*?

"A truly ingenious idea," Shaul Mazuz said mockingly. "Don't they have full rehearsals ten times a day, in the school shelter? All the singing and choir rehearsals have drowned out the sound of the geese."

"If you've already mentioned geese," a measured voice spoke — Dani Morelli always spoke quietly and deliberately — "haven't you forgotten, Yoni, that you are the *moshav* coordinator, and not an impresario? I have news for you: *Shmitta* year is over. The tractors must start working the fields but all he — " and he stabbed an accusing finger at Yoni — "has in his head is songs! Songs! And more songs! The *moshav* has turned into a kindergarten. All day long tra, la, la!"

"This is demagoguery!" Yoni thundered, and Morelli and Mazuz lowered their gaze. Yoni had always been a nonpareil expert at transforming a defense into an offense. "The tractors have already begun operating yesterday, the day after Rosh Hashanah. Thank G-d, all of our members are capable of taking care of themselves very nicely, with all due respect. But you don't understand what I'm trying to say."

"Perhaps you will be kind enough to explain," Hillel, the new member, butted into the argument. "By all means, open your mouth and let's hear what you have to say."

"Do you know who is Yetzivim's discovery of the year?" Yoni asked rhetorically, immediately answering his own question. "You have all surely heard of Buki Eliad, David's gifted son. Yes, Meir..." he stopped and looked at Meir Tzuriel, who bit his lips in an effort not to blurt out anything. "Buki is a gifted child and that's a fact. The truth is that he is far more than that; he is a natural composer of the first degree, on an international scale."

"Yoni, watch out. You're getting carried away." Tzuriel was no longer able to contain himself. "Soon you'll be calling him 'Moshe Rabbenu.' Are you sane? To call a ten-year-old 'a composer on an international scale'?"

"Yes! If you would have heard Yitzchak Marciano, the world-famous musical adaptor, rave about Buki, you would say that I am selling him short, at that!"

With that, the opposition's attack was crushed. Yoni continued to enumerate, slowly and precisely, Buki's attributes, relishing in infuriating David Eliad's sworn enemy, Meir Tzuriel. There had been a short circuit in their relations all these years; no one had ever seen them exchange as much as a single word.

"In addition to his talent as a composer, he also has a voice of rare quality. That's why he was chosen as the choir's soloist. His appearance at our Ten-Year Anniversary will be a hit! I thought," Yoni continued, in a fiery voice, "that we might make the last rehearsal a grand affair. Why hold it in the suffocating shelter when we can do it in style? Let's schedule a final public rehearsal for two days from now, on Thursday afternoon. What do you say, *chaverim*?"

Yoni was generous enough to let the other members of the *moshav* administration feel as if he was asking their opinion. In truth, the secretariat was no more than his own rubber stamp. The members didn't even have time to digest his suggestion before Yoni continued.

"We will invite the members of the nearby *moshavim*. Can you imagine the tremendous repercussions this performance will have? Next week, at the ceremony itself, you won't be able to force a pin into the crowd of people, to say nothing of the name that it will make for Yetzivim, an anonymous *moshav*."

Nods of agreement accompanied his final words and when he finished, the members of the secretariat cheered enthusiastically and thumped the smugly smiling *moshavnik* on the back. Yoni knew exactly which strings to pluck ... The patriotic sentiments for Yetzivim were shared by all and who was foolish enough to disdain the limelight and the glory? After all, Yetzivim deserved a little fame, a little *nachas*, after its eleven years of arduous toil...

Only Meir Tzuriel remained sour faced. "What's the meaning of this discrimination?" he attacked Yoni.

"What are you talking about?"

"This favoritism that you're showering upon one child. Come outside a moment," he insisted, dragging Yoni by the sleeve. "Come on, all of you."

"What do you want? What's out there?

"Come and see!"

The members of the secretariat went outside and looked all around. They saw nothing out of the ordinary. A warm sun gently caressed the lush green lawns. Kindergarten tikes played in the sandbox, birds chirped... The men exchanged glances and shrugged.

"Don't you see?" Meir Tzuriel hastened to explain. "Nature shows no preferences, no discrimination or favoritism. The sun shines equally upon everything!" He stressed every single word.

"'The sun shines equally upon everything!' A nice saying. Did you make it up?" Shaul Mazuz' eyes sparkled. He was a sworn epigram enthusiast.

"And I say the sun shines on hills and vales," Yoni produced a proverb of his own from his stock. "Listen here, Meir, there are mountains and valleys. Can't you make peace with the fact that Buki is a gifted child?"

"There are other talented children in Yetzivim. Where is your own paternal pride? Why don't you think of your own Gindush, for example? Of all the children in this *moshav* you had to go and pick Buki, David Eliad's son?"

"Your hatred towards David is blinding you. I don't have considerations like that. If Gindush had been blessed with a good voice, I'd have favored him, of course. But what to do? He's my son, but his voice... his voice is as cloying as tar."

≋)≋

Yoni's ancient jeep rapidly swallowed up the kilometers. He drove deliriously from one settlement to the next, publicizing the preview ceremony that would take place on Thursday afternoon.

"You don't have anything else to do in Yetzivim? It's the Ten Days of Repentance! *Kapparos*! *Erev Yom Kippur*! And what about post-*shmittah*? You folks kept the Sabbatical year! Aren't you swamped with work to catch up in the fields?" The secretaries of the various settlements couldn't understand Yoni. He was neglecting everything. The upcoming event had latched on to him like a dybbuk.

Yoni waved aside all of their questions impatiently. "Why waste words? Come tomorrow and you'll have a good time."

And they came. A spacious area had already been prepared. Dozens of benches were dragged over from the synagogue, the children's club and every possible place. But when the throngs filled the area, the organizers realized that it was not enough.

The crowd waited excitedly for the ceremony to begin. The appointed time passed but Yoni was nowhere in sight.

15

Yoni had turned into a bundle of jittery nerves. Standing in his office he twitched nervously, shifting his massive weight from one foot to the other. Eliad! Until now, he'd managed to ignore the threat that Buki's father represented. Would David spoil his show, his celebration, at the last minute?

A knock on the door broke his reverie. In the doorway stood Mrs. Sonia Stefansky, tenderly holding on to the hand of little Chaim Nachman, her only son, the only child she still had.

"Yitzchak asked me to tell you that he's going away with David Eliad. He made a point of my telling you, so here I am with the message."

"Where did they go?" Suddenly Yoni was the happiest of men. His question was only a gesture of courtesy; it made absolutely no difference to him where they went. For all he cared, they could go to Saudi Arabia for a secret meeting with King Faisal, to Honolulu or Swaziland, so long as they were not here…

"I don't know where. They'll be back by nighttime. Come, Chaim Nachman. We're going to the big field, to hear the choir."

Blessings upon Stefansky's head! Poor fellow was incapable of listening to music. His wound had not yet healed, so he had done the right thing at the right time and taken David Eliad away with him.

The two had gone off to some unknown destination...

⊰⊱

The dress rehearsal was perfect. The performance got off to a brilliant beginning. Everything ran smoothly: the lighting, the loudspeaker system brought in from Beersheba, and the choir, which sang in perfect tempo and rhythm, evoking thunderous applause.

As for Buki...

Buki was the star of the evening. He outdid himself. At first, he sang in a quiet voice, maintaining unswerving eye contact with Victor, who conducted with his baton. But he quickly climbed higher and higher, leaving the audience breathless and openmouthed. When he sang his song, "Hashem, I shall sing to You a new song," to the accompaniment of the choir, the audience was enchanted. Buki's pure voice plucked at heartstrings from the very first stanza and swept the huge crowd enthusiastically along with the second, faster paced and more hopeful stanza. He evoked copious tears with the third, which dripped with pathos and pain, and uplifted the crowd with the quick, rhythmic, optimistic and joyful notes of the fourth and final stanza which led again into the beginning, like a magic circle without beginning or end.

Buki split the heavens with his high soprano voice. His singing was full of pleading and longing. "Rescue me from the many waters, from the hands of gentiles." His voice climbed higher and higher and it seemed as if there was no limit to where it could soar. Yet, even when Buki soared to the limits of his capacity, his voice did not screech or lose any of its sweet, dulcet quality.

The choir sang the song twice and then a third time. By the fourth time, hundreds of people had joined along and were singing the new hit tune:

"I will sing a new song to You, a new song, a new song."

"Bravo!" thundered the crowd. "Encore!" they shouted, and would not let Buki go. He was forced to sing the song again and again, and still again, until Victor sneaked away and disconnected the loudspeaker system.

⊰⊱

Yoni beamed like a bridegroom. His round face shone like a full moon. His idea had succeeded beyond his imagination. People pushed forward to see Buki, and Odelia was beside herself with joy.

"Mrs. Eliad, your son will yet be a great singer!"

"Mrs. Eliad, Buki is a rising star!"

"Mrs. Eliad, your son will become world famous!"

"Mrs. Eliad…"

"Mrs…"

She took Buki's hand and fled away from the pushing crowd determined to shake hands with the little hero. Public attention had never been her strong point, and she was even more confused than Buki.

The admiring crowd finally dispersed. Here and there, people sought David, the soloist's father, whose son had become a star overnight, but he was nowhere to be found.

Yoni had been right. The preview performance became the talk, not only of Yetzivim, but of the entire area. The Ten-Year Anniversary Celebration itself was going to be an event that would be remembered for a long time to come. If the public preview had been so successful, how much more so would be the actual ceremony itself, which would take place with the participation of government ministers, prestigious public figures and notables, and, mainly, an overwhelming crowd the likes of which Yetzivim had never seen in all of its eleven years.

On Friday, Victor raised the members of the choir to new heights. He didn't let them rest on their laurels. "I want you to give it all you've got, your very soul," his voice thundered through the shelter. "You've got to identify with every single word in the song, to live it, breathe it, let it become part of you. That's the only way you can give it the maximum."

The nine- and ten-year-old youngsters didn't understand. "How can you breathe words?" asked Dori, Hillel's son. "Do they have air?"

But aside from a mischievous remark here and there and a prank or two, the children understood that they had to produce their best, that they must live up to the high expectations.

Yetzivim counted the hours until Tuesday, the eleventh of Tishrei, 5720 (1960).

⇒⇐

Yom Kippur was over; they had finished the evening prayer and people were rushing home to break the fast, the sooner the better: There were other *mitzvos* waiting. Immediately after some cake and coffee, the banging of hammers began. Succos was coming.

Yoni was in no rush to build his *succah*. First of all, he had to catch up on what was going on in the world. Perhaps the news broadcast would have something to say about the upcoming celebration at Yetzivim...

The radio could be heard clearly through the open windows. In his adjoining garden, David listened to the announcer while preparing his *succah*.

"With the blast of the *shofar* and cries of 'Next year in Jerusalem', the Fast of Yom Kippur came to an end.

"With the closing of the festival, the late Rav of Brisk, R' Yitzchak Zev Soloveitchik, passed away. He was seventy-three years old.

"Rabbi Soloveitchik came to Israel as a Holocaust refugee...

"His funeral will take place tomorrow in Jerusalem."

The announcer continued, but David did not listen to the rest. His hammer slipped through his fingers. The leader of the generation, the *gaon* of Brisk, had passed away! Not long after his marriage, David had gone to Rav Soloveitchik's humble home in the Geulah neighborhood to receive a blessing.

He must attend the funeral!

Yoni shared the same thought. This was the solution! He had struggled with the problem for an entire month, not knowing what to do with David, how to prevent him from ruining the whole show. The solution had fallen into his lap, straight from Heaven.

"David, I've come to ask you a favor," Yoni suddenly appeared in the doorway. "Have you heard the news? The Brisker Rav passed away."

David looked at Yoni. "Am I hearing right? Yoni mourning the loss of the Brisker Rav? Yoni, it isn't Mozart or even Albert Einstein. It's 'only' the Rav of Brisk."

"David, a mere hour ago you beat your chest with your fist and said *al cheit*. And here you are, already insulting me?"

David did not answer. *Yoni's right. It wasn't a nice thing to say.*

"I want you to go to Jerusalem tomorrow, to represent Yetzivim at the funeral."

"I was thinking of going."

"Excellent." Yoni was exuberant. He had been prepared to work very hard at convincing, brainwashing, coaxing David to agree. And here he was, ready and eager on his own. Yoni had not expected this.

"Why are you so happy? What's so excellent? It's a great loss for the Jewish people!"

"To be sure!" Yoni was suddenly alarmed. *David's no fool. My joy and relief were too obvious.* "The Rav of Brisk! What a terrible blow! All I meant was that I am glad that we will have a representative at the funeral."

"Yes," agreed David. He grasped a wooden board in one hand, a hammer in the other, and some nails between his teeth before he shot Yoni a piercing look. Yoni thought he saw a devilish glint in his eye but it immediately disappeared. "Yetzivim will have a representative at the funeral. Maybe two."

It was as if a heavy stone had rolled on to his chest, pressing on his heart. Uneasily, Yoni paced his yard for a long, long time.

"David's up to no good; he's plotting something," he whispered to himself over and over again.

The last words David had uttered had frightened him, though he didn't know why.

"Maybe two."

Who was he planning to take along? R' Goldberg, who had known the Rav of Brisk in Poland? Unlikely. He was too old, too feeble. Who then? Yitzchak Stefansky?

Yoni ran to Yitzchak's house. He had already heard about the death. He was deeply pained to hear of it. But to travel to Jerusalem? "No. I'm too weak from the fast."

Who then?

And what was the meaning of the silence that had enveloped David these past weeks? Even the tots in Yetzivim knew of the ceremony scheduled to take place the next day. People had not stopped talking about Buki since last Thursday. Today someone had even joked about them being able to retire their *chazzan* and take Buki in his place. Everyone in the synagogue had heard the joke. And David?

A heavy, oppressive feeling filtered down from Yoni's brain, shooting millions of icy splinters along his spine. The air was hot but his skin was puckered with goose pimples.

David was teasing him.

Yoni wracked his brain that evening, but all exercises in logic were fruitless. In this chess game with David, his neighbor was one move ahead.

A secret move...

Yoni went to the huge square which had been prepared for tomorrow's grand event. He examined every small detail, turned on the lighting setup, tested the loudspeaker system, scanned the seats, tables, stage. Everything was ready and in order.

Only one thing was wrong...

"Maybe two."

16

"Get up, Buki!"

A big yawn and a squinting look. His eyes were still glued together with the cobwebs of sleep and refused to open. Another yawn; Buki rolled over on the other side. *Ah, there you are, happy dreams of mine. I haven't left you. I'll be right back...*

"Buki, get up, I told you!"

Who is it? Abba?

"What time is it, Abba? I'm still so tired. I want to sleep."

"Get up."

His father shook him vigorously and threw the blanket to the floor. He wouldn't let up.

Buki got up. Shaking and shivering, he leapt out of his warm bed and washed his hands. Yigal woke from the sound of the water spilling into the metal washbasin and looked at him. The room was dark. A tiny lamp shed a bit of light. Buki looked outside. It was still night.

Just like on Erev Rosh Hashanah. But the Yamim Noraim were already over. Yom Kippur was yesterday. Did one say Slichos before Succos?

Abba was in the kitchen, preparing a cup of hot cocoa for him.

His mind suddenly cleared and his stomach did a somersault. Of course, this was the big day. Towards evening the ceremony would take place, including the performance. "Hashem, I will sing to You a new song."

How wonderful! A delightful sweetness spread through his blood, tickling his senses.

But wait a moment. It couldn't be!

Abba had not woken him up for that! Abba didn't even know about the program. It was all a secret!

In the recesses of his heart, Buki doubted it. A child's deep instinct told him that Abba was smart enough to know everything. Buki sensed what everyone already knew. It was impossible to hide something from Abba. What then? Abba had not said anything. It was his very silence that frightened Buki more than anything else.

So did the ill-boding quiet in which his father stood, pouring hot cocoa into his old blue enamel cup, the beloved cup from which Buki had drunk since he was three years old.

A terrible fear filled his heart. What did Abba want? Why had he wakened him at four in the morning?

"Abba, what's the matter?"

His father sipped his coffee leisurely. "Drink your cocoa, Buki. It's getting cold."

But his throat, his throat. A big lump was stuck somewhere in the middle of his throat. It had a strange habit, this throat of his, of getting clogged up whenever he was afraid. He was unable to get a single drop past that lump.

His father shrouded himself in secrecy and silence. His eyes enveloped Buki with a loving look. Buki thought he could detect a wetness and this frightened him all the more. Had something terrible happened, perhaps? His father got up to rinse out the cup and turned his back to him. Quick as a flash, Buki sprang like a rabbit into his mother's bed, seeking shelter.

But his mother was fast asleep.

Odelia had tossed and turned restlessly all night. David's silence filled her with an oppressive suspicion. She knew him and knew that he was preparing something unexpected. What was it?

She had wracked her brain all night long and not slept a wink. Then, just minutes before David had gotten up, she had finally fallen asleep.

Buki was a well-mannered boy. One does not wake one's mother. He went back to the kitchen. His father already had his dark jacket on and was holding a small travel bag. He held out his other hand to Buki and they left the house, very, very quietly.

Yigal's curly head watched them from the bedroom window, suppressed fear in his eyes. His child's heart predicted something terrible. Only many years later, with the hindsight of an adult, would he understand the message which his heart had transmitted.

A creaking of the garden-gate hinges one house away woke Yoni from his uneasy sleep. He flew to the window in one huge leap, like a coil suddenly sprung.

His hasty leap in the darkened room ended in a painful collision between his head and the window which opened into the room. Yoni saw stars in the middle of the night.

"Ouch!" he yelled. He felt as if his head had been split by the impact. His fingers gingerly touched the site of the blow to make sure that it was not bleeding. Thank G-d, his head was dry, but a big bump had suddenly sprung up on his forehead.

He lay on the cold floor, dazed senses registering the sound of receding footsteps.

Precious minutes had elapsed by the time he felt his way back to the window, this time with caution. He thought he could make out two figures in the distance, one tall and the other short, walking towards David Eliad's barn.

Lightning flashing in Yoni's brain.

Buki!

How did it escape me, yesterday? "*Yetzivim will have a representative at the funeral. Maybe two.*"

Buki would be the second representative.

David was going to ruin the entire show! To remove the kingpin and take Buki to Jerusalem!

They must stop him before he left the *moshav*.

Yoni galloped to the door like a young colt. His blood raced through his veins. He would show David Eliad. He wouldn't let him ruin an evening that had been constructed with such care and precision, such devotion to every detail. He had toiled for two months in planning this state ceremony that would stand the entire country on its head. He had planned it down to the smallest detail.

And David Eliad intended to ruin everything at the last minute, with one fell swoop of his hand.

Rage boiled up in his blood like a magic potion, infusing him with youthful energy. He raced to the door, turned the lock twice and shot out to the yard like a rocket.

In his headlong rush, he slipped on the dewy pebbled walk and banged his head once more, this time on the iron latch of his goose-hatch. It sprung wide open.

The blow struck precisely on the spot where he already had a big bump. The pain was unbearable. Yoni slumped to the ground in a faint. Had it not been for Berta, who slowly awoke to the ga-ga-ing of the geese strolling leisurely around the yard, he might have lain there for many hours.

⇌

A military jeep was parked behind the barn. David used it often. It belonged to one of his friends in Beersheba, but whenever he needed it, it would miraculously appear in the *moshav*.

David revved up the motor and they left through the *moshav's* front gate with a burst of speed, leaving Yetzivim behind still cuddled up in its sweet, predawn sleep.

Buki remained silent for five minutes, waiting for an explanation. When it was not forthcoming, he opened his mouth.

"Where are we going?"

"To Beersheba."

"Why?"

"To the central bus station."

"Why?"

"Why, why? Must you know everything? Wait a bit and you'll see."

The jeep slipped into a covered yard, to the back area of a lone house near the central bus station in Beersheba. Pale morning light washed the streets. Conscientious laborers hurried off to work. David and Buki slipped into a synagogue for the *vasikin* prayers.

A heightened excitement gripped the small group after prayers. Buki's ears caught puzzling sentence fragments here and there. "*Gadol hador.*" "Thousands are going to Jerusalem today." "He left a will that will be read shortly before the funeral." "He asked to be buried immediately, but because of his stature, the funeral was put off until today."

"Abba, what are they talking about?"

"The Rav of Brisk passed away."

"Who was the Rav of Brisk?"

"The *gadol hador!*"

"What's the *gadol hador*? The tallest man?"

David chuckled. He took hold of Buki's hand and they left the synagogue.

"The *gadol hador* is the greatest spiritual authority. He is like the father of everyone, a person of great spiritual stature."

Buki didn't really understand words like 'authority' and 'stature', but his sharp mind suddenly made the connection between their rapid walking along the almost deserted Beersheba streets at this early hour.

"Are we going to Jerusalem?" he suddenly asked, dreadfully frightened.

"You guessed right!" David answered evenly. "How did you know?"

"But, Abba, I-I c-can't..." Buki could hardly hold himself back.

"Why in the world can't you, my important little man?" David's eyes narrowed to two small slits. His penetrating look threw Buki into a fit of fear. "Do you have an appointment with some government ministers?"

He knew everything!

"There is nothing more important than showing our last respects to the *gadol hador*," explained David. They walked quickly. The first bus to Jerusalem was leaving in five minutes.

The last curve. The bus station seemed very close. Buki's heart raced. Soon he would be on the bus and that would be the end of the festival. What to do?

There was a long line at the Jerusalem platform. Dozens of people were waiting to get on the one bus; all wanted a seat.

"What's the matter this morning?" asked an orderly. "We hardly manage to fill half the bus on a regular morning and today we'll have to add on another one."

"Everyone's going to Jerusalem today, to the funeral of the Brisker Rav," explained a thick-bearded man.

"The who Rav?"

"Shmiel, *loz im op* (leave him alone)," his friend, a tall, thin man scolded in Yiddish. "He wouldn't understand anyway."

David and Buki approached the long line from behind. David stationed Buki at the end. "Buki, watch my bag and hold our place. I'm going to buy tickets."

David ran to the small booth on the side and forced his way among the large crowd. If he didn't get his ticket on time, he would miss the bus. He begged the people on line to let him get ahead so he could make the bus to Jerusalem. No one showed any willingness. The line inched forward.

David grumbled nervously, his glance continually flitting to the platform. The line moved with maddening slowness amidst incessant quarreling. "I was first." "You should be ashamed of yourself! To get ahead on line like that!" "Can't you move over a little?"

David calmed down somewhat. It looked like he wouldn't miss the bus, after all. But by the time his turn came, he was perspiring heavily. The tickets turned damp at his touch. He raced to the end of the long line near the platform.

"Buki. I have the tickets. Hey, Buki, where are you?"

Buki had disappeared.

The bag was still there, keeping place on line, but the boy wasn't.

"Did anyone see a ten-year-old boy here?"

In the general commotion, confusion and quarreling over places, no one bothered to listen to him. Everyone was wrapped up in the feverish attempt to find a seat on the bus for the long trip to Jerusalem.

His thoughts raced frantically. This was his last chance to grab a seat. But what about Buki?

"Mister, are you getting on or not?"

He moved aside to let the next person on. He couldn't leave a ten-year-old boy all alone in a strange city. He would go and look for him.

The boy walked quickly along a nearby street, his eyes moist. From time to time he looked back suspiciously. When he had seen his father getting into an argument with people at the ticket line, he had made a daring decision: to run away! Abba would not ruin the show! He slipped quietly out of the line, but his caution was superfluous. Even adults did not succeed in drawing any attention in the mass of humanity engaged heatedly in incessant arguing.

His tears flowed. What did his father want from him? Why was he being so cruel? Was it a sin to sing? To make up tunes? To listen to music in Yoni's house?

What kind of a strange father did he have? He had often thought about it. His father was able to laugh and be in the best of moods, but all Buki had to do was open his mouth and sing, and his father would scowl. He would turn into a different person, angry and impatient.

Today, he had outdone himself. Here he was, Buki, preparing himself for the past month to be the soloist of the choir performing today, and at the last minute, along comes his father to ruin everything.

He went over to another street near the market. From the display window of a hat store he was able to see his father's figure reflected in the distance. His heart beat faster. His father had not yet seen him, but only several meters separated them. In a few steps, his tall father would overtake him.

Like a slippery eel, Buki slipped into a fish store that had opened early.

"Hey, boy, what do you want?"

The storekeeper, a man dressed in clothing reeking heavily of fish over which he had thrown a filthy blue apron smeared with blood and fish oil, left the fish tank and drew near him with a threatening expression. He was holding a toothy metal tool for cleaning fish scales, which he now waved above Buki's head. "I know you! You're the one who stole two carp from me last week."

Buki retreated to the entrance of the store. "I-I-I n-never was here before," he stammered in fear. He ran out and fled down the street. The storekeeper chased after him, screaming, "Thief! Catch the boy! He's a thief!"

Buki ran for his life, back in the direction of the bus station. Better to fall into his father's hands than into the clutches of this dreadful creature. He stopped for a moment to catch his breath, but suddenly became afraid. A group of people was hot on his heels, led by the man in the fish store. Their shouting filled the quiet street. "Thief!" "Catch the thief!"

The distance between them was rapidly decreasing.

Buki raced like a swift horse, from street to street, alley to alley. His heart beat wildly and his breath came faster and faster. He felt his lungs burning and his strength giving out. He was about to collapse.

He ran into a narrow alley. His drumming footsteps sent some dozing cats scurrying off. He saw an open wooden door to his left. Buki slipped in, closed the door and sank to the ground. Darkness enveloped him.

17

oni swung his feet off the bed hurriedly, bent over and tied his shoes.

"Yonattan, why are you getting up?" Berta asked, rushing over. "Tell me what you want and I'll serve you in bed. Tea? Coffee?"

"Do I look so bad that you're calling me 'Yonattan'?" Yoni smiled, a pain-filled smile.

"You mustn't get up!" Berta declared authoritatively. "Look at that lump on your head! You're staying in bed today!"

"Today? What's got into you, Berta? What about the Celebration?"

"The Celebration will not begin before this afternoon. Where are you running off at five in the morning?"

Yoni was determined. "Berta, I'm going now and that's final. David ran off to Jerusalem with Buki and without him we have no Celebration."

"You're going to Jerusalem, now?" Berta could not believe her ears. "You won't be back by evening."

Yoni was already by the door, his black jacket slung over his shoulders. "I'm going to Beersheba, to the central bus station. That's where David went."

"I'm coming along." Berta was at his side in a flash, purse in hand. "I have to keep an eye on you. I also have some things to buy in the market."

The ancient jeep left Yetzivim at top speed. Its antiquated tires screeched along the dirt road, spraying sand in all directions. The roar of its motor faded slowly away in the distance.

⇌

David felt as if he were going mad. He had circled the city streets like a top spinning out of control. He had shouted Buki's name hundreds of times. He had passed through all the streets, inspected all the yards and scanned the market very carefully. After thirty rounds, he stopped counting.

The child was gone. He had disappeared.

While passing through one of the main streets, he had imagined catching sight of Buki several times from the corner of his eye. But as soon as he turned around, there was no one to be seen. It had only been a figment of wishful imagination, he decided.

The ground began shaking underfoot. A group of men rushing madly down the street like a herd of elephants gone berserk approached him rapidly. Their frightful cry echoed through the street. "Grab the thief!" He pressed himself against a wall to avoid being trampled underfoot. They must have been unemployed loafers, or madmen. What kind of a crazy thing was this, to chase after an invisible thief so early in the morning? Didn't they have anything better to do?

"Grab the boy! He's a *ganav!*" he heard another cry.

David tensed. *A boy? Perhaps...*

He joined the galloping group, his eyes scanning every corner. If it was Buki they were after, he must rescue him before they took the law into their own hands.

"There he is! He ran into that alley! Get him!"

The elephant herd galloped down the alley. To their angry frustration, their prey had vanished, as if evaporated into thin air. They had seen him running like a hunted deer, but he had disappeared without a trace.

Muttering disappointedly, the men began dispersing. "Never mind. I'll catch him yet," promised the man in the blue apron. "That thief stole two carp from me last week."

"For heaven's sake! You made us run around like fools for half an hour just for two stolen carp?" One burly man ripped the blue apron off the fishmonger and threw it aside in disgust. "I thought he stole your cashbox or at least a gold chain…"

The mob that had been ready to tear the boy limb from limb now turned its back on the fishmonger. Within a minute, he was left alone in the alley.

But there was someone else there, too. David Eliad knew his Buki. The child had not vanished into thin air. He must be somewhere in the vicinity.

He began searching yard after yard. Most of the gates were still shut. And when he examined the names on the mailboxes, his heart sank lower and lower.

The names were written in Arabic.

The jeep raced along the old road. It leaped from pothole to pothole and passed patches of unpaved highway. Yoni and Berta were flung in all directions and their bones felt it.

"With driving like this, you'll get us to Gan Eden, not to Beersheba," Berta complained. "By the way, what makes you so sure that David went via Beersheba?"

"There is no other way to get to Jerusalem," explained Yoni, his hands clutching the steering wheel. "Hold on tight, I'm going off the road."

"What are you doing?" Berta asked, alarmed. The jeep turned left and ran off onto a winding dirt road.

"It's a shortcut. It'll get us to the city before David," boasted Yoni.

"Yoni, I beg of you, get back on the road. I'm scared."

"There's nothing to be afraid of, Berta. I've taken this shortcut dozens of times. I cut through all the roads by crossing the railroad and gain at least ten kilometers."

"The railway tracks?" Berta said in a trembling voice. "That's all we need!"

They raced towards the railway tracks. "Yoni! Stop!" Berta screamed in fear, but Yoni kept on racing forward, towards the tracks.

"It's O.K. We've got plenty of time."

But he was wrong.

⇒)⇐

David climbed silently onto the high fence and peeked into the quiet yard beneath. A rain of small pebbles broke the silence. The stones fell into the yard and onto a tin surface where sunflower seeds had been spread out to dry.

"*Ruch min hohn* (scram)!" screamed a mustached man who suddenly came flying out the house.

David was not afraid. In a courteous voice he asked the angry Arab if he had seen a young boy in the yard.

"There are no children here," he said. His Hebrew had a strong Arabic accent. "You better scram before I call the police. Achmad, Yussef..."

Two teenagers ran out of the house, waving big sticks. David jumped off the stone wall and fled. It was one thing dealing with a single Arab, but a different matter to contend with three hefty louts. He went to find the Beersheba police station.

⇒)⇐

The jeep climbed onto the railroad track — and the engine stalled.

"What's this?" Berta cried.

"The engine died," sighed Yoni. "I should have changed it long ago."

He climbed out and opened up the hood. In the weak dawn light he couldn't see a thing. He took a flashlight out of his pocket.

"What about the train? Yoni, when does the train pass?" Berta was on the verge of hysterics.

"Why don't you believe me? We have another quarter of an hour, okay?"

He lit the interior of the engine with the flashlight. "I think the carburetor has had it. Everything's burnt and all the water's evaporated. Berta, bring me the water jerrycan."

Berta got out of the jeep with the jerrycan. Yoni passed the flashlight to her and emptied the contents into the engine.

"You say that your boy disappeared?" The officer at the desk was sleepy. He looked at him with watery eyes and David repeated his story over and over.

The officer behaved as if he had all the time in the world. Slowly, painstakingly, he recorded the complaint and opened a file. By the time David was about to collapse, he stretched his hand out lazily to the dial phone. "I'm notifying the patrol cars in the area to launch a search," he explained leisurely.

His finger was about to dial when the phone rang.

"Yes, who's there?" His voice reeked with self-importance. David stared at the receiver from which a muffled voice could be heard. The officer straightened up and became alert. "When? Where, exactly? How did it happen? How many? Why?" He came to life and his hand jotted some things down rapidly on a piece of paper.

"What happened?" David forgot his personal problem for a moment. The officer looked shocked and David tensed. His sixth sense whispered to him that the matter was somehow connected to him.

They stood and peered into the engine. A thin line of smoke rose from it. Berta had never before seen a car engine and she momentarily forgot her fears as she studied the complex machinery. She was particularly fascinated by the still boiling carburetor.

She marveled over the mass of metal pipes, wheels, rubber belts and things, and reveled in Yoni's knowledgeable answers as he lectured to her about the function of each part of the engine.

Yoni enjoyed showing off his expertise. Upon such occasions, he would completely forget about his surroundings.

A loud whistle split the air. The train! The chugging engine was not far off. Inside the first car the engineer saw a jeep stuck on the tracks. He gave a loud toot on his horn. As in a nightmare, he saw two figures standing on the tracks, next to the jeep, staring unbelievingly at the train bearing down on them. He pulled on the brakes, but the gap was too narrow for them to be effective.

The jeep wouldn't budge. The engineer shut his eyes tightly and waited to hear the horrible sound of iron clashing against iron, heavy steel crunching down upon a thin hunk of tin.

The frightening sounds of grinding echoed through the air. The jeep's parts were sprayed all around in a radius of dozens of meters. The engineer dared not open his eyes. The train ground to a halt only three hundred yards later. He didn't see two figures who had managed to jump away from the track at the very last minute, just steps ahead of the train speeding towards them with deafening rumble.

⤚⤙

"It was a train crash," the officer at the desk said excitedly. "They're checking what exactly happened."

"A train went off the tracks?"

"Someone else went off the tracks," explained the policeman. "A jeep got stuck on the tracks and the train smashed it to pieces."

A jeep... Why did this hidden feeling whisper to him stubbornly that it had something to do with him? And that he would yet suffer from this particular accident?

"Was anyone in the jeep?"

"They're checking it out, I told you."

The phone rang again. The officer grabbed the receiver and listened tensely. His eyes lit up.

"Only the jeep, you say? A *kapparah*. But what about the passengers? You don't know?"

"Mr. Eliad," the officer laid the receiver down in its cradle, "we have a problem with your complaint. At this moment, we have had to send a lot of men to the site of the accident, to find out exactly what happened. I'm afraid we won't be able to put more than one patrol car at your disposal to search for the boy. And that won't be free until half an hour from now."

⤚⤙

It was not one of Yetzivim's lucky days.

The Ten-Year Anniversary Celebration which Yoni had planned with such precision was canceled.

Dozens of *moshavniks* had toiled that morning to set up hundreds of chairs and benches for Buki's meteoric performance.

And then the bad news landed, like drops of poisoned rain, upon Yetzivim.

Hours passed before the picture was clarified. Rumor had it that Yoni and Berta had been killed in a horrible road accident. Yoni, the talented coordinator, the clever giant who, with all his faults, had been the one who had established Yetzivim, put it on its feet and managed it so superbly for eleven years! And the good-hearted, industrious Berta... And poor Gindush, now an orphan... What a cruel, bitter fate.

The mistake was clarified only after three hours and the moving eulogies stopped when Yoni and Berta returned, in a state of shock, towards evening, having spent a brief recovery period in the hospital. The entire *moshav* besieged them, but it was next to impossible to exchange a word with them. The two would require several days of recuperation from their narrow brush with the Angel of Death. But before he closed his door behind him, Yoni turned to the frightened *moshavniks* and uttered a single sentence that said it all, "Had we not jumped away from the jeep at the last minute, the train would have ground us to tiny pieces."

And Buki was lost!

Buki did not sing at the Ten-Year Anniversary Celebration ... He was lost in Beersheba, without a trace. The police searched the entire area, especially the alley where he had last been seen before he had evaporated into thin air, but they could not even find a hint of a clue.

And only one person was to blame for the entire commotion.

David Eliad!

18

He raced along the street, hotly pursued by the fishmonger and the mob. The fishmonger was catching up, narrowing the distance between himself and Buki. His breath was hot upon Buki's nape; he would soon nab him! One meaty hand grabbed Buki's shoulder; he wielded a stout stick with a sharp metal spike over Buki's head with the other, prepared to send it crashing down on his head...

Buki screamed with fear and awoke, drenched in a clammy sweat.

Where am I?

He lay on a hard bed in a dark room, and when he tried to get up, he understood what was hurting him. A coarse thick rope was wound about his chest, riveting him to the bed. The rope was fastened especially tight around his wrists and they burned like white-hot irons.

What am I doing here, and why am I tied up?

His head felt heavy, as if lead had been poured into it. It took a long time for him to focus his tired mind and reconstruct the chain of events that had ended with him entering the mysterious wooden door. What had happened since then? How long he had lain thus, unconscious? A fog of mystery enveloped everything. The faint beam of light filtered through a narrow slit between the iron shutters, and the window sill revealed to him that it was day and not night, as he had first thought.

Another question was added to the line of previous ones. *Who tied me to the bed?*

The answer came very quickly. The door of the room opened and a tall elderly man with a red-checkered *kaffiya* on his head entered. "Ah, the Jewish boy has woken up."

Two burly youths entered behind him, a veiled expression in their eyes. Buki felt his mouth go dry; his breath came in short pants.

The older one pressed the light switch and a small bulb spread a pale light in the room. "What do you say to this, Ahmad?" the older man laughed in satisfaction, pointing to the trussed-up boy. "And you, Yussuf? Ah? We've caught a fat fish in our net."

"A skinny little fish," answered Yussuf, "hardly a sardine."

"We can fatten him up," said Ahmad.

The three spoke an impeccable Hebrew. Only their pronounced Arab accent gave them away. Buki felt goose pimples. Who were they, slave traders? Cannibals? Why were they interested in fattening him up?

"What's your name?" the older man turned to him in a saccharine sweet voice. "My name is Samir, but no one calls me by that name. They know me as the 'electrician.' And you? What's your name?" he repeated his question.

Buki tried to answer but fear caught his tongue and it stuck to the roof of his mouth. He was unable to utter a syllable.

"Speak up!" the electrician jabbed him in the ribs.

"Bu-bu-bu-buki," he managed to blurt out with considerable effort.

"What kind of a name is that, Bu-bu-bu-buki?"

"I-i-t's a nickname. M-m-my name is B-b-baruch."

"He stutters," laughed Ahmad, revealing two rows of gleaming white teeth. "Why are you stuttering? Are you afraid? You don't have to be afraid. We're Israelis just like you. We even talk Hebrew at home... We won't do a thing to harm you."

"Why did you tie me to the bed?" asked Buki. The sudden stammering disappeared. His self-confidence returned. After all, the Arab had promised not to harm him.

The Gordian Knot/ 129

"The police were looking for you," the electrician said off-handedly. Buki's heart began racing again. If the police were looking for him, he could be sure they would find him.

"They turned the whole alley upside down in their search," he continued his description. "They entered every house, but they didn't find you!" he concluded with a exultant cry. "Do you know why? You can rely on Samir the electrician."

"The closet," Yussuf blurted out.

"Shut up!" yelled Samir, his mouth frothing. "Why do I have such a stupid son like you?"

"They went through the whole house with their bloodhounds," Ahmad said hastily. "They had a tall man with him; he had a beard and a large *kipah*. He was here first, looking for you on his own and after we chased him away, he brought the police."

"My father was here?" Buki felt hot tears running down his face. Ahmad continued his teasing description and Buki felt the sickening taste of a lost opportunity.

"The dogs barked and went wild. They police ran all around the yard, back and forth. They were here for two hours, searching every centimeter, but they didn't find a thing. In the end they took my father to the Beersheba headquarters for questioning. But what could they do? He didn't know a thing, right, Father?"

"Right," Samir agreed, his eyes glazed. "What did I do? What do I know?"

"What are you going to do to me?" asked Buki. He didn't like the sound of their voices.

"We have yet to decide. Perhaps we'll transfer you to Egypt." Samir drew close, his eyes gleaming wickedly. The ends of his waxed mustache seemed to assume a life of their own and squirmed like fat worms. "You'll have it good. The best in the world. We'll sell you to a wealthy banker in Cairo who has no children. You'll be his only son. You'll have a good life by him, with lots of money."

Buki burst into tears. "I want to go home, to my father and mother."

A resounding slap landed on his cheeks and then another and another.

"Shut up! You're not going to cry out loud and spoil all of our plans." Buki bit his tongue in fear. He ran his tongue inside around his mouth and felt the flow of a hot, thick liquid. A tooth had come out. He was afraid to spit it out lest it arouse the anger of his captors. Another tooth was shaking dangerously.

"That's only the beginning," promised the electrician. "If you make any noise, you'll be left without any teeth, or else..." he made a passing motion across his throat with a curved knife that suddenly materialized in his hand, like magic, its handle studded with tiny gems which twinkled in the pale light like thousands of colored sparks, boding only evil.

Buki felt the blood draining from his face. The memory of the Stefansky children glimmered with a red light in front of his eyes. He had no doubt that the moment they felt it necessary, these madmen would not hesitate to do whatever they liked with him.

"No one in the world knows where you are," Yussuf warned. "We can keep you here for a hundred years. If you're a good boy, we won't harm you. But if you start making trouble..." Another slap smacked across his cheeks, worse than its predecessors.

Buki's eyes turned into their sockets and his head rolled to the side. He had fainted.

When he awoke, he found himself alone in the dark room. His head was wet and he couldn't understand why. He didn't know that the three men had panicked at the sight of the unconscious boy and had tried to revive him with a dash of cold water. They were not very experienced at medical care and Buki remained unconscious for a long while.

He felt that his *kipah* had fallen off, and he tried to put it back on his head. To his surprise, he discovered that his hands obeyed him. He thus realized that the ropes that had bound him to the bed had been removed. "They probably want their merchandise in good shape. The banker won't want to buy a child that's all bruised up and wounded."

He was free!

Free? I can get off the bed, but I'm still imprisoned in this dark room, in an Arab neighborhood in some corner of Beersheba. How am I supposed to get out of here?

He was hungry and thirsty. He hadn't eaten anything since four in the morning, he suddenly remembered. Not a drop of water, to say nothing of food. From the absolute darkness by the window, he reasoned that it was already night. It had been a long day of fasting. The gap in his gums sent him reminders in the form of waves of pain intensifying every few seconds, not letting him forget the tooth that had been knocked out not long ago. A terrible weakness settled down upon him and he had the distinct feeling that a third unconscious spell was only a question of time.

Buki forced himself to get off the bed. He set his foot down on the ground and stared through the thick darkness. The chances of his escaping looked very slim. He wondered what the future held; it didn't appear very encouraging. Either his captors would really sell him to that childless Egyptian banker, or else...

A wave of self-pity flooded him and his whole body shook with strangled tears. His survival instinct whispered to him that it was better not to give in to hysteria. After he shook off a long bout of silent weeping, he felt relieved. The tears had purified him and refreshed his mind. His thoughts were clear now, as if he had just awoken from a long sleep. With a strange detachment, he reviewed the steps he must take.

And then he remembered.

"The closet." Yussef's voice echoed in his ears. "Shut up!" his father had shouted at him. What was in the closet?

With cautious steps, he walked over to the opposite wall against which stood an old wooden wardrobe with wide doors. He bumped into a chair that stood in his way and went crashing down together with it in a deafening noise.

That's it. It's all over now. One of them is going to come in, if not all three, and they're going to tie me to the bed again. His breath froze in fear and his body tensed. One moment passed. Another. No one came. Buki didn't know that it was already after midnight and the entire family was fast asleep.

When he got up from the floor, he found himself standing near the closet. He leaned against the chair with one hand and felt the wall, inch by inch, with the other.

A round box jutted out from the wall with a plastic switch in its center. He flicked it and the room was suddenly lit up with a blinding light. Buki's eyes contracted and shut in a reflex action. He couldn't decide what was better for him now: The light could help him escape, but it could also give him away...

He didn't wonder for long. He opened the closet door and peeked inside.

Dark suits hung there in a row. Is this where the Arabs had hidden him? Impossible. The bloodhounds would have traced him here and discovered the hiding place.

Then what?

Buki rubbed his forehead. There must be a secret hiding place somewhere here. During the Holocaust, he had read somewhere Jews had hidden in cellars hidden behind closets with false backs. He entered the closet and examined its back. His sharp eyes immediately noticed a runner, like those used for sliding doors.

He tried moving the plywood back of the closet. The panel slid back without a sound, exposing a flight of stairs leading downward, to a dark cellar.

Buki did not hesitate for a moment. He closed the closet door behind him, held his breath, and began climbing down.

A loud ticking hit his eardrums, like the sound of thousands of clocks in action. A heavy odor hung in the air; it was compressed and suffocating and above all, pitch black. Buki couldn't even see his own hand held up before his eyes. He had no idea how big the cellar was and certainly could not guess if it had another exit. A sense of defeat gripped him. But before succumbing to complete despair, he forced himself to think in cold logic. 'The Electrician,' Samir had called himself. Why? If this was no more than a dark cellar, why the sound of so many clocks?

The cellar could not be as innocent as it seemed. Something was hiding behind it. But if he wanted to learn anything, he must have light. He couldn't move a finger in this total blackness. There must be a light switch somewhere.

Where was it?

He began feeling his way in the thick darkness and blessed his common sense. On the left side he found not one but many switches. He played with all the buttons and the cellar was flooded with a strong light.

It took him a moment or two before he became accustomed to the glare. He studied his surroundings, stunned. For a moment, he thought he had reached the pilot's cabin in a streamlined jet. A huge panel of clocks, ticking in a uniform monotone, filled the opposite wall.

He deserves the name 'electrician', thought Buki glumly. *But how is that going to help me?* He looked around, inspecting his surroundings carefully.

Small cartons were piled high on the cement floor. An array of electrical tools and dozens of dismembered motors lay silent.

Buki had always had a love for machines. His father used to give him anything electrical that broke down and Buki would take it apart with intense satisfaction. Messing around with its innards, he would learn all about its structure. Even now, he felt a strange attraction towards the clocks and motors and all the other electric devices scattered throughout the room. Ah, yes, there were two closed doors along one wall. He didn't know if they were locked or not, but it was an opening for hope.

The door of the upstairs room was flung open suddenly. A tense silence reigned before the shout, "Ahmad, Yussuf! The Jew has escaped!"

19

*T*hat's it. Time is slipping away. Soon they'll come down into the cellar and that will be the end of me.

Buki felt like a trapped animal. He ran from one end of the room and back, looking for an escape route. Upstairs, Samir was shouting at his lazy sons, who were fast asleep. Buki couldn't understand why the Arab had not come down yet, but it was undoubtedly a question of seconds.

What could he do?

His eyes flitted from one corner to the next, looking for some way out.

From deep inside his head, a forgotten tune made itself heard, again and again:

"Save me from many waters, from the hands of gentiles…"

It was his tune, the song he had been supposed to sing that day at the big celebration. Where was the celebration and where was he?

But the message of the song — was that not the very prayer that suited this situation so perfectly? "Save me from the hands of gentiles"? From the Arabs who sought to kill him…

He heard the closet door open and then a hail of curses rained down. This was the end! Now Samir would come down with the scimitar in his hand…

Buki suddenly felt a surge of superhuman strength he never knew he possessed. He stormed upon the pile of heavy cartons and began throwing them at the stairway, one carton after another.He then fell upon the motors. With the rest of his strength he dragged a shiny new motor over to the stairs. A red button caught his attention and he pushed it without thinking. It went into action, whirring merrily as thick black smoke began rising from a thin pipe on its side.

The Arab was taking his time. Perhaps he was waiting for his sons, or feared a trap. He finally shouted from upstairs. "You just wait there, boy," he threatened. "I'll get you yet." Buki shrank with fear and pressed himself into a corner of the room.

Samir ran down the steps but tripped over the boxes and lost his balance. He reeled like a drunkard. The running motor with its smoke drew his attention and he stared at it, unbelieving. The kid had played with his gasoline-operated paint sprayer. It was a trial model that had not yet been tested.

The device whirred energetically, emitting strange gurgling noises, not at all according to plan. It had turned red hot and began shooting jets of black paint straight at Samir's face. Samir collapsed under a pile of boxes and shouted in pain. His eyes burned and his face was black as coal. The red-hot motor was still shooting jets of boiling paint at him... Samir struggled to his feet. He felt his way back up the stairs like a blind man. His shouts finally overpowered the dying grunts of the engine which had sprayed out all of its contents and gone silent.

Buki's first attempt to gain time had succeeded. A mechanical engineer like Samir had certainly planned an exit from this cellar, he concluded. Those two doors were not there as scenery.

His look focused upon a raised handle affixed in a metal square on the wall, not far from the door on the right. He hesitated for a moment. *Who knows; I might blow up the whole room if I pull it...*

I have nothing to lose, he decided. He lifted the handle and held his breath. He screwed up his eyes in fear and counted to three before opening them again.

Nothing!

Zero. No reaction. The doors remained shut. Tears of frustration and despair welled up in his eyes. "Rescue me and deliver me from many waters, from the hands of gentiles," he whispered, his eyes turned upwards.

He pulled the handle again and again. By the fifth time, he heard a slight rustling. The unbelievable had happened! Both doors swung wide open, leading to two dark hallways.

Where should he turn?

He imagined the figure of his third-grade teacher, R' Tzvi Gluskenos, waving his finger. "Children, always remember this rule," he would repeat in his nasal voice, "wherever you turn, always turn to the right, as it is written, 'Hashem's right hand does valiantly.'"

Without thinking, Buki picked up a bundle that lay at his feet and ran out the door to his right...

⸲⸱

"You wanted one funeral in Jerusalem and almost caused two funerals in Yetzivim!"

Yoni lay in bed burning with fever, muttering to himself. The shocking trauma of facing the speeding train bearing down on him haunted him and Berta and had actually made them ill. They had heard the rustling of the Angel of Death's wings above their heads and still could not understand what had pushed them aside as they had stood there, paralyzed with fear, and sent them flying away from the tracks, to lie petrified, only centimeters away from the hundreds of tons of steel hurtling forward.

His anger knew no bounds. When he was well enough to get up, he swore to himself, he would remove David Eliad from Yetzivim once and for all. That was final. How much longer could one bear the complexes of a tortured soul? It had almost brought about Yoni's death...

R' Goldberg came to visit after *Maariv* and Yoni revealed his plan.

The rabbi stroked his scraggly white beard, murmuring to himself. "So that's what you say? To banish David Eliad from the *moshav*. Well, whatever we decide, we should wait until they find Buki."

"Find who?" Yoni didn't understand.

"Buki Eliad. He's lost in Beersheba."

And that was how Yoni learned that outside of his own quiet home, all of Yetzivim was in a turmoil. The *moshavniks* were helpless. Odelia had fainted several times. David Eliad had run about with the police all day, from early morning till night, searching for a clue to Buki's whereabouts.

Yetzivim had made the headlines as Hillel had predicted. But under altogether different circumstances.

"YETZIVIM'S TEN-YEAR CELEBRATION TURNS INTO A 'TISHAH B'AV'" the headlines had blazed across the front page of an afternoon paper. Its competitor had splashed a picture of a smiling Buki across half a page, "TRAGEDY IN YETZIVIM: THE WONDER CHILD HAS DISAPPEARED." The story underneath said that "A mystery surrounds the circumstances of the disappearance of Buki Eliad, the 'wonder child' of Moshav Yetzivim. His father, Mr. David Eliad, who took him to participate in the funeral of the Brisker Rabbi in Jerusalem, was unable to explain the reasons behind his decision to take along his son, the choir soloist, to Jerusalem. The *Moshav* secretary is considering ousting the Eliad family from Yetzivim."

"Now there's an example of nonsense and gossip," said Yoni to Berta, newspaper in hand. "Such brutality! Brrrr! I feel chills running down my back when I read such things! To evict a family at such a time!"

He had apparently forgotten what he had promised himself. His wild rage had cooled off and turned to pity for the Eliads, who were experiencing such a tragedy.

"If I get back to myself by tomorrow, I want to join the search for Buki," he promised the *moshavniks* who visited him that night. And he meant every word he said, despite Berta's vehement objections.

Buki ran quickly along the corridor, which was plunged in absolute darkness. Every step was fraught with potential stumbling blocks, slips or head-on collisions.

The hallway came to a dead end. Buki thrust out a tentative foot and discovered a flight of stairs leading up. There was no railing, so he climbed up on all fours, step by step, very slowly and cautiously, until he reached a dead end. A door. A way out? He took a deep breath and prepared to burst his way through when a rustling reached his ears.

It's a trap! Someone's waiting for me on the other side.

Buki did not run. Looking desperately for something he could use as a weapon, he felt around inside the bundle he had picked up along the way and poured the contents into his hands. The objects felt like small sticks. Buki didn't know what he was doing; he let a gut reaction take over as he turned the door knob. The door was not locked and it swung wide open. He ran out, into the cold night air, straight into Yussuf's waiting arms.

In his fright, he threw the sticks in his hands directly into the Arab's face. The latter drew back in alarm. The big man knew exactly the nature of the dynamite sticks he had laid in the cellar a few days before. These were meant to explode in other people's faces, not his own!

Buki ran. Ahmad had been waiting for him at the end of the other hallway and grabbed for him. Buki heard a series of small explosions and cries of pain behind him. Now he was not being pursued by two pairs of feet, only one. Racing at a dizzying speed, he reached the gate. It was locked.

Without a second thought, Buki climbed over the wall. He grabbed onto any projection in the wall his hands could find with the agility of a cat. The adrenalin shot through his blood, infusing him with renewed energy. He reached the top of the wall and was about to jump down into the narrow alleyway, when a strong hand grabbed at his foot.

David was in despair. He was gripped by the strong impulse to bang his head against the wall a thousand times. Remorse gnawed away at his heart and sucked up the marrow of his bones. "Why did I have to take Buki to Jerusalem?"

He knew the real reason in his heart, the one which he had not been prepared to admit at the police station. But this provided no comfort either. On the contrary, on this day he had experienced the taste of *gehinnom* in this world. Odelia, always so placid and serene, roamed the house like a wounded animal, her *Tehillim* in hand and a heavy sigh escaping her heart from time to time: Buki!

David prayed that the earth would open its mouth and swallow him alive. Odelia didn't ask a thing, only looked at him with her good, wise eyes, eyes examining heart and conscience, and was silent. It was precisely this silence that oppressed David so much and rang in his ears louder than the greatest, most piercing cry...

He visited the police station again in the afternoon; perhaps they had heard something. He returned home empty handed and disheartened. Succos was on the threshold. His *succah* stood staunchly, white sheets nailed to the walls and lively colored decorations tacked on while he had been away in Beersheba. The Weiss youngsters, children of his devoted neighbor, Hillel, had toiled and labored until the *succah* stood in its full glory.

But the main thing was still missing... Buki was gone, and without him, everything seemed dark and gloomy, lifeless without his rolling laughter and beaming smile, bright eyes and good-natured features.

David felt his insides boiling and simmering within him. When he felt himself close to collapse, he went off to rest, but his black nightmares converged upon him there too.

Was Buki being held captive? Into whose hands had he fallen? Was he still alive, or had he gone the way of Avigdor, Shaul Yitzchak and Blumele?

Oy, Tatte zisser! How much more must I still suffer? How will this nightmare end?

He heard Odelia's quiet cries of despair, piercing and penetrating his very soul.

Soft knocking could be heard at the door. Was it someone who did not have the courage to knock loudly? He ran to open it with bated breath.

20

"**I** caught you!" Ahmad cried gleefully. "You're finished." He grabbed Buki's foot and tried to pull him down into the yard.

Our subconscious mind is a marvelous gift from Hashem. Sometimes we cannot act according to logic and common sense; these would only complicate matters for us. In such circumstances, our subconscious takes over and runs the show; it manipulates us like puppets and we move without any conscious thought. In many instances, it turns out that these subconscious decisions were the right ones — the product of blind instinct, but the most efficient avenue of action that could have been taken.

The conscious and subconscious minds do not work on the same planes, at the same level. The subconscious acts from the innermost strata of the soul. It is very deep and a thousand times quicker than the thinking mind.

A marvelous Divine kindness…

If Buki had weighed his chances with cold logic, he would have found it useless to resist. He had succeeded in escaping their clutches several times already, but this was it. His chances were over. His foot was in Ahmad's iron grip; Ahmad was standing two meters below him and pulling down with all his might.

But Buki did not weigh his chances on a scale of logic. He couldn't even think straight. In the split second left before he would lose his balance and fall back into the yard, he bent over, untied his shoelace and pulled his foot out of the shoe.

The shoe remained in Ahmad's grasp. Buki leaped down into the alley with lightning speed and removed his other shoe. Then he began running at a speed that could have competed with experienced marathon runners.

Ahmad was no fool, himself. He burst out of the yard and pursued the fleeing boy, leaving his father and brother, wounded and dazed, knowing that everything lay in the balance. If the boy succeeded in getting to the nearest police station...

This thought spurred him on and lent him extra energy. He ran with redoubled speed and soon closed in upon the running Buki. The distance continued to narrow. Buki could clearly hear Ahmad panting and puffing only a few steps behind. They were now running along the street parallel to the main one. A car passed near them and its driver, seeing the race, flicked the headlights on bright and honked the horn loudly as he slammed the brakes and screeched to a stop.

Ahmad had already grabbed Buki's shirt. The car door opened and a tall man leaped out. Quick as lightning, he delivered the burly mustached Arab a hefty punch in the chin which knocked him flat to the ground. At the same time, he released the boy from the Arab's clutch with his left hand and pushed him into the car. The car left the site with a screeching of tires, leaving two bright red trails as a result of the rapid friction with the asphalt.

Buki managed a look of gratitude to his rescuer before his head fell to the side and a black abyss sucked him into its bottomless depths.

The speedometer crept higher and higher: sixty kilometers per hour, seventy, eighty-five, ninety, one hundred and ten...

"Shimon, be careful, it's dangerous," remarked an older man sitting next to the driver.

"I can't wait any more, Efraim. The child has lost consciousness," replied the driver, pointing a thumb at the passenger in the back seat. Buki lay there, his eyes shut, his chest rising and falling rapidly. The driver pushed down on the accelerator, his eyes glued to the dark road before him. "A pity we didn't catch the hooligan. Did you see how brutally he pounced on the boy?"

"You did the right thing," said the older man, who answered to the name Efraim. "Time was of the essence. As soon as we bring the boy to the emergency ward, we can turn to the police. By the way, where shall we take him? It seems that he needs a hospital with expert doctors."

The driver weighed the possibilities, his foot still pumping the gas pedal. He clutched the steering wheel tightly as he snaked between the cars ahead of him, leaving them all far behind. The wind shrieked inside the car with such force that they had to shut the windows.

"Ashkelon seems to be the best bet. I know a small private hospital there."

"Small's no good. He needs a top-notch doctor."

"Let me finish. The head of this hospital is Professor Shalgi, one of the most brilliant doctors in the country. I believe that he will know what to do with the boy."

That was how the unconscious Buki arrived at the Rofeh Hospital in Ashkelon.

David reached the door, breathless. A uniformed police officer stood before him. As in a dream, David led him inside. The father's face was pale and set, almost deathlike.

It's coming… How will Odelia react?

"Mr. Eliad, we have good news for you. We've found your son!"

Buki… found?

Thank You, Hashem, for having returned my son to me, even though I don't deserve it!

"How is he? Is he all right?" David's hands were pressed to his heart. The terrible tension was beginning to tell.

The law officer hesitated. He had been told to prepare the father gradually for the meeting with his son, but dry instructions were one thing and the emotionally reality, another.

"He's all in one piece," the officer finally said. "And he'll be healthy. At the moment, he is still hazy."

≈)≈

The doctor at the hospital who greeted David and Odelia at the door of the room was more candid. "You must understand that the child has undergone a terrible trauma. He's in a coma."

"Will he come out of it?" David was laconic and cold. The doctor shivered. The man was made of steel!

"I'm no prophet," the doctor said, and pointed upward. "Only He knew how long it will take for him to come out of it. Medicine has records of people being in a coma for a duration of several minutes up to seventy years."

"Let me go in to Buki," Odelia wailed. She didn't wait for the doctor's permission but walked right in, David following behind.

Their beautiful little boy was curled up and tiny beyond recognition. His face was snow white and his eyes tightly shut. A transparent liquid dripped from a bottle suspended near his bed into a blue vein in his hand.

The steel broke. David was the first to burst into unashamed tears. Odelia held on for another minute before dissolving into a choked sobbing. They stood crying for a long while, until some doctors gently steered them out of the room.

They celebrated Succos in the hospital. Yigal stayed with the Weisses while David and Odelia spent day after day, hour after hour, next to the huge bed in which Buki looked even smaller than he was.

Odelia did not despair. She spoke to her son without end. She read chapters of *Tehillim* in his ears, prayed by his bedside three times a day, aloud, word by word.

"There is no movement yet, I am sorry to say," stated Professor Shalgi after a week. "It's really no wonder, after what he's gone through."

He pointed to the papers, which told the entire story. The security forces had been busy. They had searched for the mysterious apartment in which Buki had been held and uncovered a fat and juicy spy story.

"THE DISCOVERY OF THE WONDER CHILD LED TO THE EXPO-
SURE OF A SPY RING IN BEERSHEBA," announced the papers. The
reporters were able to disclose 'from reliable sources' all about the Israeli
Arab family, "a father and two sons, who, at first, only cooperated with
the *fedayin* across the border. Later, the family began dealing in real espionage. The father, Samir Abu Gazaala, who had been trained in the
U.S.S.R. and was known by his nickname, 'the electrician', and his sons,
Ahmad and Yussuf, built a very sophisticated underground espionage
center beneath their home, equipped with state-of-the-art radio transmit-
ters. They conveyed information to the data headquarters of Egyptian
intelligence in Sinai.

"The heads of the Israeli security system didn't believe their eyes when
they descended to the cellar. Such sophistication is only known to agents
of a world power!"

The country was in a turmoil. A flood of telegrams of good will and
wishes for speedy recovery inundated the small hospital in Ashkelon,
from the prime minister and other government ministers, down to junior
party officials. The hospital staff would step aside reverently whenever
David and Odelia passed through the corridors, and Buki received preferential treatment.

But there was no sign of improvement, no progress whatsoever. He remained unconscious until the morning of Simchas Torah.

"Buki, today is your day. It's Simchas Torah!" Odelia whispered.

Buki had always been the happiest of children on Simchas Torah. He
would sing and cavort with genuine joy and not miss a single dance.
The oldtimers of Yetzivim could not remember any child rejoicing so
exuberantly.

"Buki, wake up! I'll buy you the biggest *sefer Torah* there is. I promise
you!"

Her tears flowed ceaselessly. David was not there. He had gone to a
nearby synagogue. Odelia bent over her son's head and whispered
straight into his ear. She poured out all of her pain and emotions. She put
her very soul in her plea.

"Buki! Get up! Come, let's sing together: *Elokim, Elokim,* I will sing a new song to You; I will play for You on a ten-stringed lyre."

She sang and sobbed, sobbed and sang, his tune, the song he had composed, the familiar notes which every child in the Negev sang incessantly.

Buki opened an eye.

One eye, staring and unfocused, but open and gazing at her.

Hashem, the miracle has happened! He woke up! He woke up!

"Can you recognize me, Buki? It's me, Ima!"

He nodded. The movement could only be measured by millimeters, but the maternal seismograph registered even this infinitesimal motion.

She raced out into the hall, shouting. The doctors came running. "Call the neurologist, call Dr. Campbell!" Shalgi ordered. The latter sped to the stricken boy's room. He affirmed her discovery. The boy had emerged from the coma!

Five days passed. The happy parents did not budge from his bedside. They surrounded Buki with a protective wall of warmth and love and talked to him without stop until he fell asleep. They ignored the staff of doctors and nurses huddling together, whispering, until Professor Shalgi approached them and invited them into his office.

"The boy can't talk?" David felt as if a sledgehammer had struck his head. Odelia bit her lips hard. Her head was bowed. The world had gone black once again.

"I wish it weren't so and that I was wrong," Shalgi said, choosing his words carefully. "But the situation is not rosy. In your enthusiasm, you may not have noticed it, but Buki has not yet opened his mouth."

"Maybe..." David wanted to say something, to argue with the doctor, but his voice died down. The doctor was right. Buki had not uttered a single syllable since he had opened his eyes.

"We weren't sure of it, either," explained Shalgi. "But we've been studying the matter for several days with the help of communication experts and speech therapists. They confirmed the diagnosis. To my immense sorrow, the child is suffering from..." He expressed a long, unintelligible Latin term, but David understood its gist. "A traumatic blow to the speech center in his brain."

"The situation is severe, but not hopeless," the doctor concluded. "We've already seen cases where trauma-induced mutes recovered their faculty of speech. The lion's share of his chances depends on you, and I am encouraged. I see that you are inundating him with a sea of warmth and love."

"Buki will be able to speak fluently, just like everyone?" Odelia was impatient. She held on tightly to the back of the chair until her knuckles turned white. Her eyes were fixed upon the professor's mouth.

Shalgi took a deep breath. He looked at the worried parents with sad eyes. He knew how serious the situation was and didn't want to deceive them with false hopes. His integrity as a doctor dictated the words that followed, and each word was like a sliver of ice, a frozen stalactite from the wastelands.

"It is wishful thinking to expect Buki to speak fluently. The maximum he can expect to achieve is a heavy stammer!"

Buki stood in the quiet hallways, behind a closed door, his ear riveted to it. He listened and heard the entire conversation. Every word etched a deep groove in his tender heart. How painful it was!

A wounded heart!

The first wound in Buki Eliad's tender heart.

21

After a month's hospitalization, Buki was released into the world of speech clinics and therapists. There were varying conjectures as to his chances of recovery: David would have given his right arm to hear Buki utter a single word.

The election campaign which excited the entire country at the beginning of the winter did not interest the Eliads in the least. David and Odelia were determined to accomplish only one thing: to get Buki to talk. Most touching was Yigal's pain. At first he wept, not wanting to believe the fact. Then he made peace with the terrible reality. The third stage was the rehabilitation.

He would sit with Buki in the garden under the blooming apple tree and talk to him. On the table would be scattered their first childhood books which Odelia had not yet thrown out. Yigal would take Buki's hand and place a finger on a picture and beg him:

"Say 'ball', Buki. B-a-ll."

"A-bb-a. I-m-a. B-u-k-i."

Buki would pull his hand away and look angrily at Yigal. He refused to cooperate. David was deeply concerned about his apathy and went, again, for consultation. The doctors explained that Buki could not duplicate Yigal's swift acceptance of the situation.

"He is still in the first stage," one doctor in a major medical center in Jerusalem explained. "What his little brother was able to do in a month will take Buki about a year."

"Does that mean that each stage will take four months? The rebellion and lack of confidence, a third of a year, the acceptance another third and the rehabilitation still another four months?" Odelia's voice broke. She had hoped for a quick miracle.

"Mrs. Eliad, we are dealing with a human soul, not a machine. Every case is individual. That's why I stressed the words 'about a year.' Each one at his own pace."

Buki had his own pace, his own style. His progress was very slow, indeed. Actually, hardly any progress registered. In spite of everything, David stubbornly refused to remove him from the regular school in the *moshav* and transfer him to a special school for deaf-mutes.

"The child is not mute," he argued bitterly. "He has a temporary block which is preventing him from talking. He will yet talk fluently; just wait and see."

In the *moshav* they thought differently. "David is not being realistic. He wants to cover up his foolish, irresponsible conduct by spreading optimistic smoke."

The anger in Yetzivim was terrible. The *moshavniks* could not forgive David for having taken a flower of a child and crushed his entire future with his own hands. Their lexicon did not even have a word to describe the proper censure for a father who destroyed his own son and brought calamity upon his innocent head.

Buki — mute?

The very combination of words was unforgivable. Unbearable. Unbelievable.

The *moshav* children, the members of the choir that had fallen apart from lack of a guiding hand, came to witness the unbelievable.

Buki — the wonder child of yesterday, the star of tomorrow, the celebrated soloist whose mighty voice had shaken the rafters, rent the heavens and moved hearts — was unable to utter a single syllable.

Their childish hearts were torn asunder. Buki sat in the yard, a book in hand, unable to read a single line. Abysses of agony were mirrored in his blue eyes. Dori and Gindush, who came to visit, could not bear his pain and ran away from the yard without saying 'hello.' They hid behind Yoni's house and engaged in a stormy conversation.

"He's mute, for sure," said Gindush, weeping.

"Do you think he's deaf too?" asked Dori.

"Sure. My father says that deafness and muteness always go together," Gindush showed off his expertise.

"You mean to say that he can't hear a thing?"

"I guess so."

But Buki was not deaf. He heard every word of his friends' heated dialogue. He leaped off the bench and stamped his feet and waved his hands angrily. He wanted to run after Gindush and Dori and show them their mistake, but his feet seemed cemented to the ground as two tears rolled from his eyes onto the grassy carpet underfoot, telling the story of a great soul, filled with a wealth of warm emotions, fluttering helplessly in its captivity of chained, enforced silence.

Something in his soul shattered forever more.

This was the second wound in Buki's heart.

Odelia sat in R' Goldberg's house, seeking succor in the comforting, protective shade of the distinguished rabbi.

"I have not come to complain, G-d forbid. I know that everything comes from Hashem. But you must remember, honored rabbi, that when you were my matchmaker and suggested David for a husband, you promised me something. How did you put it? 'You won't suffer from his personal burden.' "

The rabbi nodded. She had quoted him verbatim. With the distance of eleven years, the words seemed hollow and meaningless. He knew very well what Odelia was going through, what she had been suffering since before the Ten-Year Anniversary Celebration, the concept that had become synonymous with failure and futile farce.

What could he say to this tortured woman? *Father in Heaven, put the right words into my mouth lest I stumble with my tongue. Help me say words of truth that will bring some balm and comfort to her sundered heart.* She came as a young girl from Tunisia, all alone, married a man who had been through stormy experiences in life, and was forced to see her firstborn, a true *wunderkindt* whose future was projected as a meteoric one, shrivel under her very eyes. How could he help her?

"Mrs. Eliad," he said in a shaky voice, his eyes cast downward, "I am neither a prophet nor the son of a prophet, nor do I pretend to know the future. But remember well what I am telling you: Buki will speak again!"

A mixture of colors swept across Odelia's cheeks. She wanted to cry but her eyes remained dry. Her head spun.

"When? I mean, why? How do you know? And how? Oh, I'm so excited. I'm so emotional and confused. I don't know what to say."

R' Goldberg spoke again. In her marvelous intuition, she knew she would never forget his words. They would become a source of encouragement and faith in the coming years, during her most difficult times. Each word was measured and weighed, a work of art.

"Our Sages taught us that Hashem does not bring upon a person a trial which he cannot withstand. Your pain, dear daughter, has pierced not only your heart but the hearts of everyone in Yetzivim. Many tears have been shed these past weeks in the *moshav*. It is clear as day that you will yet see much *nachas* from your dear son, Buki, from our Baruch."

He dissolved into silent weeping. Odelia felt she had never seen anyone identify so genuinely and wholeheartedly with another person's grief. She suddenly felt a sweeping sense of relief. She was not suffering alone: Her rabbi and the entire *moshav* was commiserating with her!

It was encouraging to learn that others were sharing her burden. The huge boulder that had been pressing down on her heart had suddenly become lighter by several tons.

"Will he sing again? Compose music?" This matter disturbed her no less than the faculty of speech which Buki had lost. His creative gift was an expression of the greatness of his soul. She did not ask for glory or fame. Her own soul was cut out of modesty; it was in her blood. She did not wish for a colossal composer like Mozart or Beethoven in the house, but she understood the significance of the abysmal pain reflected in Buki's eyes. She could hear the weeping of his soul, the poignant inner sobbing, the suppressed lamentation, not only for the tongue that had turned dumb. Odelia could hear in her heart the mute weeping for the violin that had been silenced, its strings broken.

The rabbi grew thoughtful again.

"Are you familiar with puzzles?"

Odelia was taken aback. What did an elderly rabbi have to do with child's play?

"Hashem's world is like a puzzle," explained the rabbi. "Yes, a puzzle of a million trillion pieces, like a gigantic mosaic which only the Creator can put together. Each and every creation, from the inanimate ones, to the vegetable kingdom, the animal kingdom and the world of human beings, is a piece in this puzzle. Every person carries out his role in life, whether willingly or not."

Odelia understood that the rabbi was leading up to something important, fatefully decisive. He did not relish figurative talk; every word he uttered was like a building block in an entire structure.

"We don't understand how, but Buki received two parts in the puzzle. He had one part which was connected to the heavenly palace of music. That role is ended. He has now received the second piece. My heart tells me that Buki's second role will overshadow the first one in its importance."

A few moments of eternity elapsed. She thought about his words and tried to fathom their deep significance.

"I am not sure," she finally said. "I am both glad and sad at the same time. You told me good news and bad. You clothed the painfully clenched fist in a silken glove and covered the bitter pill with chocolate."

"No!" the rabbi was adamant. "You will yet see that it is not a thin layer of silk or of crunchy chocolate. This is a reality that will reveal itself at the proper day and time."

The Eliad family suffered a difficult winter. Buki finally began uttering single syllables, but his progress stopped at this point.

The winter of 5720 was an interesting one. Many changes took place in the world at large. Khrushchev, the premier of the U.S.S.R., visited the United States at the beginning of the year and a short-lived air of appeasement blew between the two great world powers after years of bitter quarreling. In Israel, the Labor party won the elections, as usual, and Ben Gurion established a broad coalition according to the years-old tradition: "Without Herut and the Communists." Several new representatives entered the fourth Knesset: Moshe Dayan, Shimon Peres and R' Menachem Porush.

The winter was cold and the radio broadcast an advertising war between the different kerosene-heater companies. 'Fireside' offered the public their product, the stove with the nonfolding wick and the tap on the side. 'Fireperfect,' on the other hand, fervently claimed that "happiness went hand in hand with warmth, and warmth went hand in hand with Fireperfect, the kerosene heater by..." The local cigarette companies and the importers also waged an advertising war, as the popularity shifted from one brand to another: Eden; Montblanc with the cool menthol flavor; Arbel, with its superb Oriental blend; the flat Atlas cigarettes; the simple Silon ones and the prestigious Nelson brand. Margarine manufacturers advised Israeli mothers to fatten up their children on their vitamin A and D enriched product.

New one-, five- and ten-lira denomination bills were introduced into the Israeli currency. The single lira was blue and pictured a bearded fisherman bearing an anchor on his shoulder, with the Kinneret in the background. The five-lira bill depicted a scientist staring in wonder at a test tube and the ten-lira bill starred the Dead Sea scrolls.

≈)⌒

Purim arrived. The *moshavniks* gathered in the home of the Sefardi rabbi of the *moshav*, R' Calfon, to celebrate around laden tables, as they did each year.

The absence of one particular celebrant was pronounced: David Eliad preferred to remain home.

"I'm going to bring him," announced Yoni, already by the door. "Mr. Avivi, come right back here," insisted R' Calfon with a note of pleading. "Leave him be. It is better for him to stay away."

Yoni did not listen. The rabbi sent his two sons, Saadya and Rami, to fetch him back. They ran after Yoni but couldn't catch up with him. He strode towards David's house with his long gait and returned five minutes later together with David, Buki and Yigal. Their expression said everything. The boys were overjoyed at joining the rest of the *moshav* folk. David came as if he were being dragged by a demon.

"Come, sit with us," the rabbi invited, pouring him a large glassful of vintage whiskey. "Drink, my son. It is a *mitzvah* to get drunk on Purim."

David had always shied away from strong liquor for reasons of his own. This time, something must have given way. Perhaps he sought to drown his bitter lot in the hard liquor. In one motion he emptied the contents of the glass straight down his gullet.

Someone filled it again and David absentmindedly downed that too. R' Calfon watched and whispered something in Saadya's ear. His son got up silently and began transferring all the bottles to the other table.

The assembled crowd burst into lively singing. Hillel sang a medley of satiric Purim songs and everyone held on to their stomachs from laughter. No one noticed David guzzling glassful after glassful. His long arm reached all the bottles which the frustrated Saadya kept on taking away: shnaps, arak, vodka, beer, sweet red wine…

And then, suddenly, a voice was heard. A mighty, powerful voice. Everyone stared at David Eliad as if they saw the sun rising in the west. The eighth Wonder of the World: David Eliad singing?

He was drunk. They could tell he was no longer connected with his surroundings. He had gradually lost all association with reality and had returned to bygone days, days which he had sought to hide and obscure, to bury as if they had never existed.

His eyes were transfixed and he sang in the sweetest voice anyone had ever heard.

"David! You know how to sing?" asked Mazuz in shock. "I thought that you and music were two opposite poles."

"Do I know how to sing? You make me laugh. Do you know who I am?" David's voice thundered. He climbed up onto the table. "What would you like to hear, *chevrah? Hamalach Hagoel?* Fine, let it be that. The first song my father composed, at the age of ten."

Before anyone could open his mouth, he began. His voice crept up to the highest notes anyone had ever heard, and kept on rising. He was a perfect tenor, strong and powerful. There seemed no limit to his capability. Buki had been a pale copy of his father, the legendary source.

Buki and Yigal stared at their father wide eyed. Yigal got up and drew near to see if this was truly his father. Buki sat paralyzed on the bench, his mouth opening and closing but not producing a single sound.

No one had dreamed of such a discovery. David sang and sang. He sang unfamiliar excerpts, joyful songs, sweeping, poignant songs. "All these are my father's songs, his most famous pieces," he boasted in the typical drunkard's voice that left no room for doubt.

"The surprise of the century," whispered the *moshavniks*. "An endless repertoire..."

22

He was drunk and lost all control over himself. The audience demanded an encore; David was not stingy with his response.

He sang in a lyric tenor, a high voice that was also soft and tender, velvety and caressing. At Yoni's request, he sang some Yossele Rosenblatt favorites. In one song he ran through the entire range of octaves, from a thick, low bass to a baritone, ending up with a tenor so powerful that the *moshavniks* had to cover their ears. Then his voice suddenly sank to a thin, delicate falsetto of a little boy, and the resemblance to Buki's lost voice was incredible.

"We used to call this a *kop shtimme*," Yoni said, shivering with pleasure. "Only Yossele Rosenblatt was able to combine a full coloratura range and climb again from the powerful tenor up to the lofty *kop shtimme*. You need a very large larynx to accomplish such a feat, and David does not fall short of Yossele Rosenblatt, believe me."

"David, show them what you really know," Meir Tzuriel suddenly jumped up, having sat quietly until now, frozen in a corner of the room. "Sing a passage from Verdi."

"Who spoke? Ah, it is you, my good friend, Shalom Travitzky." David called out mockingly. "You want Verdi? Like in the good old days? Fine... I'll sing Rosenblatt's *Uvimnuchoh Yomar*. This is a song composed by the famous Italian opera composer, Verdi..."

He sang a perfect and powerful imitation of Rosenblatt's *Uvimnuchoh Yomar* that left all of those present spellbound. Whoever shut his eyes could have sworn that the late Yossele Rosenblatt had risen up from the grave for the performance.

"No, it even surpasses the original..." said Yoni, his eyes shut, a dreamy expression on his face.

They sat riveted to their seats, oblivious of the passing of time. David's unexpected performance transported them to a different world, to a divine palace of music and notes.

"Does anyone have a violin?" he suddenly asked. "I have one at home," offered the redheaded Moishe. The instrument was quickly brought and David stood on the table, singing to his own accompaniment, like a famous concert-hall artist. A general feeling of astonishment gripped the audience and held them spellbound.

It was a volcanic eruption: A volcano named David Eliad suddenly exploded, shooting hot lava on all sides. As mighty as his repression had been until now, so powerful was its eruption.

"Enter wine — exit secret," cried out Shmuel Kastel in his American accent. "David a singer! Very nice! I thought he couldn't even carry a tune."

All of them had thought so. It was clear that the bottles of liquor which David had guzzled down had removed the cork that had plugged up the active volcano. David had successfully concealed his power of song for eleven years. Who would have believed that behind the facade of a simple *moshavnik* hid a virtuoso violinist, a colossal singer and *chazzan*?

"Why were you silent all these years?" demanded Dani Morelli. "You could put all the great singers in the world in your back pocket! Not only our *chazzan* in Yetzivim!"

"Go know something like that," grumbled Chaim Segal, the elderly *gabbai* of the central synagogue in the moshav. "How many times did I beg you to stand before the *amud* and lead the prayers, and you refused? Not on festivals, not on Shabbos, not even for a simple weekday *Minchah* service. You always refused. Why?"

Yes, that was the question which everyone asked. Why had David systematically concealed his awesome talent?

But there was no longer anyone to ask. By now, David was wallowing on the floor in his own vomit. He gesticulated drunkenly with his hands and feet and murmured broken phrases. The violin had slipped out of his hands and lay shamed on the floor by his side. R' Calfon's sons picked David up gently and laid him on a folding bed in a corner of the room.

"I know the answer!" a voice cried out. Meir Tzuriel sprang to the center of the room.

R' Calfon rose from his seat and waved his hand frantically. "Meir, I beg of you, sit down and be quiet."

But Meir showed no desire to obey. On the contrary. His eyes shot sparks. "You've been silencing me for eleven years. There's a limit to everything. I will be quiet no longer!" He turned to his comrades.

People crowded around him. A thick cloud hung suspended in the large room. Something terrible was about to be revealed.

"Friends," cried Meir, "have you noticed that some people in this room were not as surprised as the rest of you? Myself, Yoni Avivi, R' Calfon: Did anyone hear us express a word of surprise like you all did?

"Do you know why? It's no news to us. We knew David's big secret all these years. Everyone masquerades on Purim, but some folk masquerade all year round. David Eliad is one big act.

"What you discovered only this evening and was hinted to you not long ago through the lost talents of poor Buki are historical episodes for us."

"If so, why were you silent all these years?" people demanded to know. "Why did you make a mutual pact of secrecy?"

"It was not a pact of secrecy," Meir screamed, holding his throat as if he were choking. "It was a forced silence, not of our own design. R' Calfon made us swear not to talk. He threatened us with bans and curses if we dared open our mouths."

"True, it's true," Yoni interjected.

"Meir, I beg of you, stop right now!" cried the rabbi. "Have mercy on yourself, at least, if not on David Eliad."

"You can't frighten me any longer, Rabbi. I was afraid for eleven years, but no more! I'm not afraid of bans and ostracism. I think that the time has come for the public to know who David Eliad is!"

Silence reigned in the room. No one moved. Only the faint buzzing of the fluorescent bulbs could be heard.

"Do you all see David Eliad?" Meir pointed a finger at the bed. "A decent farmer, G-d-fearing, earning his living respectably, ha, ha, ha.

"My friends," shouted Meir in a strange voice, "it's a gross lie! A deception! A cowardly farce!

"Do you know who David Eliad is? I know! He doesn't deserve to be called a human being! He is the most despicable rogue I ever saw in my life! Give cheers to the Jewish kapo, the Nazi collaborator, David Eliad!"

"Meir, stop it! Take back your words!" shouted R' Calfon. "Don't accuse a person who can't answer back."

"I will not take back what I said!" Meir shouted back. "Were you with him in Maidenek? Did you see how he put his good services at the disposal of the camp commanders? I was there! I heard all the beautiful songs he just sang now. I heard him singing enthusiastically and playing his violin while they killed my father, my mother and all my brothers and sisters. He stood at Roman Spiegel's side and sang from music sheets, as if he were in a concert hall. The Nazis slaughtered, the Nazis massacred tens of thousands of Jews, and he sang. They were asphyxiated in the gas chambers and burned in the crematoriums, but he was saved. The accursed Roman Spiegel watched over him; Roman was his protector and Eliad was his protege. Look at his arm: he doesn't even have a blue tattooed number. He was privileged, the famous Polish singer, the music idol, the primo don, the object of adulation. That's him — David Eliad. It is he and none other!"

Tears choked his throat. He sipped some water and continued:

"After that, when only the two of us survived, he asked me, he begged me to hold my tongue, not to reveal it to anyone. He intended to cover up his past, to deny the musical side of his personality and pretend to be totally ignorant of the world of music.

"Why didn't you suspect him? Did you ever see a bigger enemy of music? It's abnormal! Even the worst tone-deaf, off-key singer, with a croaking voice of a raven, does not despise music like David. Didn't it ever occur to you how strange this is? Didn't you understand that David fled from music like from fire, because it constituted an incriminating testimony against him?

"Then, after Maidenek was captured by the Soviet forces, David asked me to keep quiet, but I promised him the opposite. I swore to publicize throughout the world how David Eliad had turned traitor against his Jewish brethren and collaborated with the Nazis. After that he disappeared, and I discovered that he had come to *Eretz Yisrael* and was living in Haifa. I traveled to Haifa and monitored his movements for a month to make sure it was he. And it was. But without a *kipah* on his head. David the secularist. You should have seen him in his prime... An orthodox Jew par excellence, replete with long, curly sidelocks, a *tzaddik* and *chassid*...

"When I wanted to publicize his identity in Haifa, he suddenly disappeared. I learned that he had been drafted into the army. He served in Latrun in the War of Independence. After the war I continued keeping tabs on him and even came to his wedding. That's when I learned that R' Calfon had asked him to join the pioneer founding group of Yetzivim.

"Then I met Yoni Avivi, formerly Fisher, and I volunteered to join the group. It seemed that Yoni already knew about David. He had heard him in Vienna, in the opera house and concert halls. But he had never met him personally. I revealed who and what he was and both of us agreed to sabotage David's attempts to be accepted to the *moshav*. We decided to confront him at the interview before the acceptance committee.

"But at this point, R' Calfon intervened. He claimed that he knew from an indisputable source that it was not the whole truth, and that David was an honest, innocent person. It was *he,* apparently, who had been at Maidenek, and not I... He made a scene that I will never forget. If we dared open our mouths, he warned, we would suffer bitter consequences. But he can't intimidate me any more. I've been agonizing over these memories for many long years but have been afraid to open my mouth. I was afraid of the bitter fate that might await me, afraid of R' Calfon's censure. But I have reached the breaking point. How long can a person keep quiet? The choice is now in your hands. Judge David as you see fit."

R' Calfon rose to his feet. He cleared his throat, looked at his spellbound audience, and began:

"My dear friends, the choice is, indeed, in your hands, whether for good or bad, whether for *Gan Eden* or *Gehinnom*, but the Torah commands us to 'choose life.'

"I don't presume to have been in Maidenek. David and Meir were, and they were among the few survivors from a multitude of people. But one thing I can tell you: I know one thing clearly, and when the time comes, I will reveal my sources. There are reliable witnesses who will testify that whatever Meir Tzuriel said is pure fabrication, lacking all credibility."

"Who are your witnesses?" Meir jumped up as if bitten by a snake. "Produce one man who can refute what I claim! And furthermore, if this is all a figment of my imagination, who sang before you tonight? Was it me, or, perhaps, the honorable rabbi? Why did David Eliad conceal his true identity all these years?"

"He has his own reasons, and they are perfectly justified," said the rabbi, holding his own. "My friends, there is a rule that says that any secret known to three people is no longer secret. Therefore, I cannot ask the seventy-odd people present here to keep this in confidence, as I asked Meir and Yoni. But you should know, my friends, a rabbi has the power to issue a decree, and I am avowing you all, unreservedly with all my rabbinic authority: Whoever persecutes David in any way or causes him distress on the basis of Meir Tzuriel's words shall live to regret it!"

The *moshavniks* recited the *Bircas Hamazon* and rose to leave. Many found it difficult to digest what they had heard. Some were quick to express their opinion and honored the sleeping David with kicks and saliva as they exited. Others sufficed with expressions of disgust aimed at David, who was oblivious to the fact that his secret had been revealed and his identity exposed.

Buki and Yigal had seen everything, heard everything... for in the heat of the discussion, no one had thought to remove them from the arena.

This was the third blow to Buki's heart.

The deepest, most painful one.

"Wait a moment," someone grabbed Meir Tzuriel before he left. "What did you mean that he concealed his identity? Wasn't he called David Eliad then?"

"David Eliad?" snorted Meir. "I forgot to tell you the main thing; we've become so accustomed to the name he assumed after the war."

"What was his real name?" one impatient *moshavnik* demanded, pulling at Meir's sleeve. "Tell us his previous name."

"They called him..." Meir tapped his forehead as if trying to remember. He spoke slowly and deliberately, self-importantly, realizing the drama of the occasion. "Ah, yes. His name was Yechiel Horowitz. Yechiel David Halevi Horowitz."

PART TWO
CHILIK AND SHALOM
Lublin
5675-5704 1915-1944

23

The thousands of people in the immense opera hall stood on their feet, cheering long and lustily. The performance of the beloved popular singer, Henry Horowitz, had just come to an end.

A tall figure stood on the wide stage. He was in his early twenties, thin and imposing, dressed in tuxedo and bowtie, his dark hair immaculately groomed. He bowed slightly to all sides, acknowledging the cheering, waving crowd. People tried to rush up to the stage but were repelled by teams of determined ushers.

"Patience," begged Henry. "I'll be down to you in a few minutes to hand out autographs."

The crowd increased its fervor. "Hen-ry! Hen-ry! Hen-ry!" they shouted in rhythm. "Encore, give us an encore!"

Henry acquiesced. He understood his fans; he knew when to give in for another encore and when to disappear behind the curtains.

"What should I sing?" Henry asked simply. The crowd roared unanimously, "The Princess." Henry pretended not to understand, and repeated his question several times until the crowd shouted in unison, "Prin-cess!" with a power that almost shattered the specially built acoustic ceiling of the Lublinska Sahl where the public idol had just made his dazzling performance.

Henry sang the well-known song based on a Polish folk tale. It told of Princess Ludmilla, daughter of the Polish king Jason Sovyeski, who had been kidnaped by forest outlaws. They planned to kill her, but the clever princess succeeded in outwitting her captors and escaping by leading them on a dangerous chase straight into the arms of the king's soldiers and palace guards.

The audience sat enthralled. Henry's powerful voice soared to incredible heights as he described the princess pleading for her life in fluent Polish. The audience completely identified with the words of the song, despite the fact that they had heard this favorite tale dozens, if not hundreds, of times. But Henry imbued a new life into the familiar saga as he described the weeping Ludmilla. The women sobbed along with her and soaked snowy-white handkerchiefs with their tears. And when Henry described in his dramatic tenor, to the accompaniment of the percussion drums, how she escaped into the forest among the hungry beasts of prey, the male members of the audience leaped stormily to their feet, their hands clenched in suspense, until the happy resolution of the fairy tale. In the nick of time, the princess succeeds in slipping out of the clutches of the vulgar ruffians and fleeing to her father's palace, while her pursuers fall victim to the waiting swords of the palace guards! The huge audience cheered long and loud, waving their fists in victorious exultation.

The epic story seemed to be taking place right then and there, due to Henry Horowitz's powerful talent. When he described the events, people felt a part of them. There was a mesmerizing, suggestive power in his singing that made one identify strongly and tangibly with the story.

This was just one facet of Henry Horowitz's talent. One of a dozen.

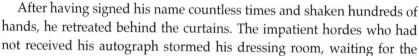

After having signed his name countless times and shaken hundreds of hands, he retreated behind the curtains. The impatient hordes who had not received his autograph stormed his dressing room, waiting for the star to emerge, but the experienced ushers did their job well and pushed back all of his enthusiastic admirers.

"Your performance today was a tremendous hit!" Karol, the impresario, said flatteringly. "The people are wild about you. The opera house manager, Dr. Zbignew Blyzhynsky, wants to know when you plan to return."

Henry shrugged his shoulders and sank into thought. It was not so simple. Each appearance of his in this hall was a painful knife thrust in his father's back. His father knew everything but contained himself; he bit his lips and kept silent. But the deep gnawing pain in his heart found release in the form of quiet moans, at night when he was supposedly asleep.

And the Rebbe, what of him? He also knew what was happening to Henry lately. The Rebbe chose to ignore the fact, as if he didn't see the change that was taking place in him, but his tender look smote Henry's conscience even more than a sharp rebuke.

"Henry, I'm waiting for your answer. We can't continue in such a disorganized manner. We must plan a series of appearances before the beginning of the winter season."

Karol's voice roused Henry from his reveries. He shook his head and shrugged his shoulders once again. "I don't know yet," he finally said, troubled and confused. "I'll give you an answer tomorrow."

"Are you afraid of your Jews?" Karol's sarcasm was stinging. Henry winced, disclosing the storm of emotions taking place inside him. "A pity, Henry. A pity for your talents. Do you want to bury your golden talents in the court of your *rabbin* for the rest of your days? You are destined for greatness, not to sing in a Sabbath choir with your Jewish frogs..."

Enough! He had overstepped the mark. Henry left the dressing room with an angry slam of the door. Karol realized he had gone too far and ran after Henry to appease him. "Henry, I was only joking. Don't take it to heart. You know I didn't mean it seriously."

Henry walked the dark streets of Lublin with long, rapid strides, not bothering to look behind him. Karol was panting heavily by the time he succeeded in catching up.

"You can't leave just like that, with a slam of the door," he complained angrily. "Henry, don't be a fool. Come, let's shake hands and forget our words," he pleaded. *That's all I need, that the Jew leave me. He is a rising star, a public idol, and he doesn't even know his own worth...* Each performance inflated Karol's bank account with astronomical sums. How many times had he awoken from a nightmare in which Henry Horowitz demanded to look over his account books and see how much money each of his appearances really raked in. But, thankfully, the Jew was not yet confident in his new role. He was still filled with doubts and qualms, so that meanwhile he was happy to receive the substantial sums which Karol threw his way — and still thank him.

Henry stopped. He reveled in the pleading voice of the impresario who had catapulted so many Polish singers and stage stars into fame and was bowing and scraping obsequiously in the streets of Lublin... Ah, what a scene! Go and tell your Chassidic friends how worthwhile it is to go out into the big, wide world, to breathe in some of the air beyond the stifling ghetto walls, to occasionally break away from the embracing bear hug of the Jewish audience of enthusiasts which did not give him a moment's peace.

"Alright. Listen, Karol," he finally agreed. "I can't come next week; we have a holiday, Shavuos. In another two weeks."

"You agree to a performance in another two weeks?" Karol thumped him on the shoulder. Joy spread all over the impresario's face. "Henry, I want to suggest something bigger for you. Come to Warsaw. The public is eager for you there."

"Warsaw?" Henry frowned thoughtfully. An anonymous threatening letter from a Warsaw zealot still lay in his drawer. "It doesn't come into the question."

"You're afraid of fanatics? Henry, you're bigger than all of them. Come to Warsaw and we'll see who will dare harm the fingernail on your pinkie!"

"We'll discuss it next week," Henry said lightly, and turned to go. "Good night, Karol."

"What do you mean, next week?" Karol shouted. "If you're going to appear in Warsaw, I must go there tomorrow and prepare the hall for you. I have to talk to the orchestra manager and print up music sheets for the accompaniment."

Henry capitulated, "Fine, all right." He found it pleasant to think about a crowd of admirers overflowing the tremendous auditorium in the capital. Ah! That would be a performance to be talked about for a long time to come. As for the fanatic *chassidim*? Let them threaten! *I'm a chassid just like they... or am I?*

Karol left him with a hearty handshake. He raced off to his office to begin the organizational work necessary for Henry's performance in Warsaw.

⇒)(⇐

It was a warm and pleasant summer evening. A pale moon hung lightly in the sky and throngs of stars winked at him with friendliness. The streets were quiet and not a living soul could be seen.

Henry was already planning his Warsaw performance and the pieces he would sing. What technique should he use this time?

He didn't notice an anonymous figure that had latched onto him a short distance behind from the moment he had left the Lublinska Sahl. The unknown stalker knew his work well and followed soundlessly behind him.

And there was a third person, more clever than either. This third figure followed both Henry and his tracker. "Interesting," he thought to himself. "Someone else is also following Henry Horowitz." The second stalker made note of the fact and proceeded to be even more cautious.

⇒)(⇐

A large suitcase in his hand, Henry walked the length of Bramova Street, taking the usual route around the marketplace and city square. He dared not expose himself in these areas, despite the late hour. You never knew where Jews might show up, even late at night, and all he needed was for one of his acquaintances to meet him. He could see the windows of the Tribunal, the royal Polish courthouse, from the distance. This had once been a monumental landmark, a magnificent edifice. But in the beginning of the 19th century the Russians had come and 'renovated' the building so thoroughly that all of its architectural beauty and historic value had been stripped. Legend had it that this had been the site of notorious blood libel trials in the past.

He went down Grodzka-Zamkova Street, crossed the large square and the municipal park, and five minutes later was at the gate of the Jewish quarter, better known as the Cracow Gate. He stopped a moment before entering the ghetto and slipped into the narrow alcove of a nearby store.

These alcoves had the interesting feature of a recessed window above a wall from which it was possible to transact business with the shopkeeper. This was originally a Jewish device designed to protect shopkeepers during difficult times when it was too dangerous to expose oneself to the street. Here one could risk doing business from the window, or shut it completely if need be.

Henry removed his clothes from the suitcase and quickly changed into a dark suit and velvet wide brimmed hat. The two sidelocks which had been tied to one another on top of his head were let down to dangle freely, after having been duly curled to a corkscrew spiral down the sides of his face.

When he entered the Cracow Gate of the ghetto, he was again Yechiel Horowitz, the well-known *chazzan*, adored by all of Lublin, idolized for his legendary voice; Yechiel Horowitz, the composer and musical arranger, the colossal singer of the Jewish street who had climbed with dizzying speed to the heights of fame in the Jewish world of song and threatened to overshadow all of the well-known *chazzanim*. Reverently they called him the "second Yossele Rosenblatt" in Jewish Poland. Many claimed that Yechiel Horowitz surpassed him, if not as a *chazzan*, then surely as a singer.

Yechiel took out his gold watch from his vest pocket and peered at it. Already one a.m. The streets were deserted. From Kovlaska St. he turned right to Siroka St. and headed for No. 6, where he lived.

His two trackers stopped at a sensible distance from the house. The first did not dream that he, too, was being followed at that very hour, and allowed himself to relax his vigil. He lit up a cigarette and blew smoke rings into the empty sky.

The second figure did not budge from the street corner.

≋)⋐

Henry entered the house on tiptoe. A thick, luxurious Persian carpet soundlessly swallowed up his soft footsteps into its close-knit texture. He lit a candle and entered his large living room. He looked into the thick *siddur* and *davened Maariv* by the dancing yellow-orange light. To be sure, in the Lublinska Sahl, among the throngs of Polish gentiles, he had not even been able to think about his evening prayers... An aching lethargy crept over him and he almost fell asleep with the open *siddur* before him, on his feet, while reciting the *Shemoneh Esrei*. He finished with difficulty, murmured the blessing over the counting of the *omer* with his eyes closed and his mind asleep. "Today is forty-three days which are..." He suppressed an immense yawn with his hand. "...which are?" *Don't you know your arithmetic, you utter goy! You opera singer!*

"Which are six weeks and one day," he yawned again, "*la'omer.*"

"*Harachaman*... may the All-Merciful One restore to us the *Beis Hamikdash*..." He could barely drag his weary feet up the flight of stairs to his lavish bedroom on the second floor. He sank down onto the comfortable bed, stretching out in pleasure. "Rest has come to the weary," he hummed the popular Zionist pioneer song. In consonance with his profession as a singer, Yechiel had an all-encompassing repertoire which also included the songs of the atheistic pioneers from Beit Alfa and Nahalal.

His weary but self-satisfied and happy gaze wandered around the spacious room. One did not even see such bedrooms in the homes of gentiles of the upper class and certainly not in the poor homes of Lublin's Jewish quarter.

But Yechiel Horowitz was different. He was rich. In one month he earned as much as a Polish Jew earned in years of toil, if not more, now that the government had intensified its commerce tax on small businesses, a decree which directly and primarily affected Polish Jewry. Yechiel Horowitz was able to allow himself to reside in one of the most resplendent mansions in Lublin, a two-story house, with several servants living below in quarters in the basement.

Ita awoke and opened a sleepy eye. "You're back already, Yechiel? Thank G-d. I was beginning to get worried."

"What's there to worry about?" Yechiel said lightly. "The audience demanded encore after encore and the performance just wouldn't end."

"As usual," murmured Ita with satisfaction. All of Lublin was intoxicated with admiration for Yechiel Horowitz. And she was his wife! The decision to burst upon the gentile world was purely hers. True, Mirushka had pushed in this direction, but Yechiel would not have taken such a decisive step without her wholehearted backing.

"How are the children?" Yechiel murmured, half asleep.

"Avigdor is as usual, with all his clever sayings. Shaul Yitzchak cried all night. His stomach hurt; he screamed just like you…"

But Yechiel was already in the thralls of a deep sleep and did not catch her snide but affectionate remark.

The figure at the street corner finally left its post and slipped silently out of the ghetto. The smoker also decided to leave. How long could one stand and stare at a dark house? He walked slowly along Lubertovska Street. The person who had sent him would be most interested in the information he had to report that evening, after an extended vigil of seven hours…

24

Yechiel Horowitz was a *chazzan* and the son of a *chazzan*.
More accurately, he had been born into a long line of *chazzanim*, a family that was steeped in song and music through and through, to their very marrow, a family which revolved around an axis of music, notes and scales throughout most of the year.

His father, Baruch Horowitz, was the 'court singer' of R' Avremele, the Rebbe of Lublin.

R' Avremele did not boast a very large court of adherents. His *chassidim* did not number in the thousands. He did not compete with the major Chassidic courts whose members filled every town throughout Poland, such as Ger and Alexander. His following did not even approach the size of an average Chassidic court.

But he had a priceless prize. He had his own private court singer, a court singer of such repute that his small court was known in every corner of Jewish Poland.

Baruch Horowitz was blessed with a legendary talent, a gift from Heaven. He was a composer par excellence. His melodies were masterpieces. His tunes were sung throughout the courts of the major *admorim* in Poland and Galicia. His original repertoire included difficult, complex tunes, intricate and detailed compositions which less than a handful of people were able to master. But he also created many simple, light tunes, lyrical folk melodies full of joy and a lively tempo. Many of his rhythmic songs even found their way to gentile choirs, and there were Jews who could swear they had overheard local church choirs singing them.

Baruch Horowitz himself was a descendant of a many-branched family of *chazzanim*, but his father, Avigdor Horowitz, had excelled in a different area altogether, of tomes rather than tunes. He was a kabbalist who spent his days and nights delving in the mystic secrets of Torah. Rumor had it in Lublin that he had mastered the esoteric branches of "practical Kabbalah" and stories circulated that he had performed several miracles. But R' Avigdor was a reticent, humble person who secluded himself in his cellar in the company of his ancient books, spending the majority of his days by the dim light of an oil lamp. His family could tell many things about him, secrets they could barely contain in their own hearts, to reveal the hidden greatness of this unassuming Jew. From their early childhood, each of his children stood firm against the strong urge to go and tell their friends who and what their father was, though the desire burned in them to let the world know the extent of his holiness and righteousness.

But R' Avigdor remained a hidden saint. Not a single one of his sons or daughters dared disobey him and go against his express will not to reveal what went on within the walls of their home.

≈≈

R' Avigdor departed this world in 5655 (1895), leaving behind two wills for his sons. The first was opened on the day of his death and included the usual family requests which every father exacts of his offspring. But when the bereaved children reached the last paragraph, they were stunned.

Their father had informed them that this was only the revealed part of the will. The second part, called 'The Hidden Scroll', must not be opened under any circumstances. The sons' role was limited to keeping scrupulous vigil over this scroll and transmitting it to the coming generations. This will, said R' Avigdor, must only be opened one hundred years after his death!

The sons sought the advice of the rabbis of the city and the members of Lublin's *beis din* regarding the will and if they were required to obey the unusual request. What was to guarantee that a member of the family would survive in a hundred years' time? To whom, specifically, was the will charged by their father? Perhaps their descendants would be alienated from the world of Judaism and mock this strange request? Perhaps the world might come to an end... Go know what would be a hundred years from now! A double jubilee. Who could foresee such a distant future?

Many questions gnawed at their hearts, but to tell the truth, the uppermost one revolved around their natural curiosity to peek into the mysterious will and be partner to its great secret, to see with their own eyes what a person was capable of writing to such children as would be born some five generations in the future... For even if they themselves enjoyed a long life to the full extent of the proverbial one hundred and twenty years, they would not know their great-great-great-grandsons.

The rabbis whom they consulted had been well acquainted with R' Avigdor; they had known him intimately and they believed in his mystic powers. They unanimously ruled: Obey the will blindly.

The mysterious will, a long blue wooden tube sealed with red sealing wax at both ends, was placed for safekeeping in the home of R' Avigdor's oldest son, Moshe. But by the time Moshe passed away, childless, the middle son, Tzvi, was no longer in Poland, having emigrated to America several years before. The wooden scroll, therefore, passed into the possession of R' Avigdor's youngest son, Baruch Horowitz, who had been born to him at a very advanced age.

Baruch Horowitz was called 'the singer', not only because of his skill as a prolific composer who produced hundreds, if not thousands, of tunes, but also because of his dulcet voice. True, he was not a tenor; his voice was limited to within the range of an average baritone.

But he was a veritable living violin.

He had a voice sweeter than honey; it touched even the coldest and hardest of hearts. Baruch Horowitz knew how to reach the depths of emotion. He, himself, was all feeling and soul, and he performed wonders in his limitless capacity to utilize the delicate vocal chords which the Creator had placed within him. They were like clay in the potter's hand, and he knew how to produce the sweetest, most heavenly sound from that golden throat.

"When our Baruch sings, he takes you by the hand and strolls with you through *Gan Eden*," his fellow *chassidim* from R' Avrumele's court would explain.

When he sang on Friday nights at the *tish* with the *kappele*, the choir, in his lilting, outpouring voice, it made no difference whether it was *Menuchah Vesimchah* or *Kah Ribon Olam*, or any other of the Shabbos *zemiros*; the entire *beis midrash* would rapidly fill up with hundreds of people. Lublin Jews enjoyed a weekly concert free of charge.

The permanent place of the singer was on '*the kappele's paranche,*' a wide wooden platform of steps stationed behind the Rebbe's seat. His choir numbered ten adults and six children, with the adults standing on the bottom step, and the children on the raised level behind them so as to be visible.

Baruch always stood among the children. The audience would joke that this was because of his small stature. "He feels at home, there, with his peers." The truth was different. Baruch loved children with all his heart; they sensed it and returned his affection many times over.

In the second and third stanzas his rendition of *Kah Echsof*, whose words forcefully exuded emotion, Baruch would become enrapt and his baritone would gradually turn into a baritone-tenor. But this would not last long and would soon fade away to his more natural range. He would wave his hands in conductor's style, leading the choir, and all sixteen voices would swell through the *beis midrash* in magnificent harmony and perfect accord. At this stage, the face of the Rebbe, R' Avrumele, would blaze a beet-red from intense spiritual effort, and tears would gather in the corners of his tightly shut eyes.

The *beis midrash* rested in partial darkness. The dim light of the oil lamps emphasized the darkness more than they illuminated. The vast audience would look at the gigantic shadows outlined on the walls as in an eerie, bewitched scene, trying to reveal which figure was Baruch

Horowitz's, and which belonged to his son, Chilik, his wonder child, who was rapidly soaring upward, both in height and in musical talent.

Yechiel Horowitz's birth was cloaked in miracles. Baruch and Mirushka Horowitz produced three sons, all of whom died of crib death before their first birthday. When the fourth was born, on Shavuos of 5675 (1915), Baruch came before the Rebbe and wept copious tears. "Hashem gave me three sons, and took all three away. Will the fourth have a similar fate?"

"Call him Yechiel," said the Rebbe. "May the Almighty sustain him in life."

Baruch sufficed with this terse blessing and turned to go. R' Avrumele beckoned with his finger. "He was born on Shavuos, the anniversary of King David's death."

Baruch listened to the Rebbe's words, not understanding what the Rebbe meant. The Rebbe clarified the mystery. "Call him David, as well, after King David, of blessed memory. Let us hope that your son will also be a sweet singer of Israel."

Thus did the infant receive the double name Yechiel David at his *bris*. Thirteen years later, he walked regally and proudly through the streets of Lublin with a *tefillin* bag upon which his full name was emblazoned in embroidery: Yechiel David Halevi Horowitz.

But Mirushka, the mother, did not like the name David and the infant was dubbed Chilik. The name David sank in the abyss of oblivion, forgotten…

Chilik demonstrated his capabilities at a tender age. Baruch Horowitz decided to include him in his choir at the age of five, since the youngster was blessed with a sweet voice that captured the hearts of his listeners from the very first note.

He brought him to R' Avrumele's *beis midrash* on Krakovska Street and the child stretched himself out on the hard bench and fell asleep even before the Rebbe made *kiddush*.

"Baruch, what do you want from the child?" his friends wondered. "Leave him be. He still needs to sleep at home."

"You'll soon understand," said Baruch inscrutably, letting Chilik sleep on the bench for the next two hours. When the Rebbe asked for a rendition of *Kah Echsof*, Baruch woke little Chilik up and placed him by his side on the topmost step. The child yawned and rubbed his sleep-webbed eyes as if he had no inkling what was wanted of him.

"Baruch, what are you doing?" thundered Mendele-the-second-voice, that is, Mendel Schwartz, the unchallenged second to the soloist, Baruch Horowitz. "Why isn't your child at home?"

"Wait until you hear my 'child'," answered Baruch tersely.

Mendele discovered to his astonishment that on that Friday evening, he served as the 'second-voice' to a child of five.

Chilik 'delivered' the solo parts reserved for his father. And whoever heard him upon that occasion understood that a new star was rising on the horizon of Jewish music in Poland. Chilik's singing made the term *wunderkind* seem trite, empty. Whoever heard those few passages understood that talent such as his descended to earth only once in a generation. The five-year-old tot had been blessed with a voice whose likes no one had ever yet heard. But that was not all; he had a complete and perfect grasp of the most convoluted complexities in his father's intricate compositions, an unprecedented phenomenon.

On the coming *Shabbosim*, the Rebbe directed Baruch to keep the child at home, lest an evil eye harm him. Only after two years did the Rebbe give in to Baruch's pleas and agree to remove his ban upon the child's appearances. Yechiel Horowitz was seven years old when he actually joined the choir. And masses of people began streaming to R' Avrumele's *beis midrash* from that time on to hear the singing of the "Lublin Nightingale," Yechiel Horowitz.

25

Yechiel became a living legend before he turned ten. R' Avrumele begged Baruch not to expose the tender child to a voracious public. "He will suffer much from it," he explained to the proud father. Baruch Horowitz, a loyal *chassid*, was prepared to swallow his pride and degrade Chilik's public profile, but at this point Mirushka entered the picture.

Miriam Kaplinsky came from a wealthy family. She had seven brothers and sisters, each of whom achieved their particular measure of fame and success. Two brothers managed a flourishing textile firm, Kaplinsky Textiles, in the industrial city of Lodz. Her twin brother, Yehoshua, succeeded in the diamond business, and his frequent trips to the diamond centers in Antwerp left his acquaintances openmouthed and more than a little jealous. The younger brother, Moshe Chaim, ventured into real estate, and the brokerage percentages which he accrued soon turned him into a wealthy man. Mirushka's sisters also did well for themselves, or at least their husbands did.

Only Mirushka, blessed with talents, who in her youth had been considered the genius of the Kaplinsky house, did not follow the family's pattern of success. Her husband, Baruch Horowitz, was a nonpareil composer, but he lacked the drive and expertise to translate his rare talent into financial success. The concept of copyright held no meaning for him. He did not have a begrudging bone in his body, and the knowledge that every chassidic court in Poland sang his songs only gladdened him and caused him pleasure and *nachas*.

Mirushka gnashed her teeth at his lackadaisical good-heartedness. She imagined that had he been born to non-Jewish parents in western Europe, he would surely have become one of the wealthiest individuals in the world.

But these were mere fantasies. Mirushka grew up in a chassidic home and had absorbed a solid knowledge and understanding of Judaism. She knew that while her siblings were accumulating wealth and property, her husband was gathering assets of an altogether different nature. Baruch Horowitz's list of assets included many acts of kindness performed in private, far from seeing eyes; hundreds of pages of *Gemara* studied by candlelight in the wee hours of the night; and dozens of tunes 'lent out' indefinitely to his colleagues, the court composers of famous chassidic dynasties who found themselves before a festival without a suitable melody for *Mechalkel Chaim*, a moving waltz tune for *U'Nesaneh Tokef*, or a lively march to *Ein Kitzvah Lishnosecha*.

"Baruch, you just pick the tunes out of your hat," was the usual refrain of his professional colleagues as they slipped in clandestinely to pick his brain, while glancing suspiciously on all sides to make sure they were not detected in their moment of weakness.

But his comrades did not know that even Baruch Horowitz, whose well known title in Lublin was 'the factory for melodies,' the *niggun fabrikant*, did not pull melodies out of a hat.

True, as with every great composer, the tunes and compositions flowed from somewhere deep in his soul, germinated and ripened in his subconscious mind as a result of personal events and experiences he underwent and the different emotions that struck him. Sometimes the tunes would erupt with violence from the depths of his soul, like phenomena of nature, over which he had absolutely no control. He was liable to awaken in the middle of the night with a new tune and feverishly search for a piece of paper upon which to jot down its notes.

This is how many of his soul-songs were born. These were songs which plucked at heartstrings, evoking fervent yearning in his listeners to purify themselves, to become nobler, more refined, more genuinely spiritual.

But Baruch slaved over many of his melodies, investing arduous effort. At times of spiritual infertility, during dry spells, he would go forth into the nearby forest to receive inspiration from the silence, the chirping of the birds. Or he would stroll along the banks of the river, and gaze for hours, transfixed and turned inward, at the flowing water. Then he would let his thoughts range freely and widely. And as he turned, dreamy and disconnected, he would be blessed with fruitful inspiration.

This way or that, his most beautiful works came into being.

Mirushka made peace, for lack of an alternative, with her husband's good and soft nature, but when Chilik began showing signs of prodigious musical talents, she decided that she would bring an end to this profitless inefficiency.

"This child is going to become a second Yossele Rosenblatt. He will surpass the greatest *chazzanim*. You will yet see him outshine them all!" she argued heatedly in Baruch's ears, even though he, too, was already certain of it. In her exuberant energy, Mirushka tried to persuade those already convinced. Baruch had a sharp eye and an absolute grasp in the field of music, and he predicted that his little son would reach the epitome of his musical career in the world of Jewish music within about twenty years, if he received the proper guidance and training.

Mirushka knew that from now on she would be able to look her brothers in the eye; she would not have to lower her gaze in embarrassment at family gatherings, for she had a 'goose with golden eggs.' It might be still small, but its future worth was unimaginable. She was determined to hoist her Chilik up the ladder of success as quickly as possible. The Creator had granted him one of His most beautiful gifts and blessed her only son with the voice of a nightingale. She would prove to her husband and all of her family that in her world of mathematics, there existed a simple equation: Talent was equal to glory and money, lots of glory and lots of money.

"But you must understand, Mirushka, your outlook is not exactly a pure, wholesome Jewish attitude. I also want the boy to grow and blossom, but my purpose is one and only: Honor Hashem with your innate gifts. If Hashem blessed our son with the voice of a nightingale, he must utilize this gift to draw Jews closer to their G-dly service and to rouse them to repent. But to exploit his talents only for honor and the pursuit of money?"

"Baruch, don't be such a self-righteous fool. Chilik will yet bring back many Jews to the fold, but first show me anywhere in the Torah where it is written that it is forbidden to utilize one's talents for the sake of earning a livelihood!"

"Mirushka," Baruch pleaded aloud, "do you really have Chilik's good in mind, or are you looking for peacock feathers to glory in before your sisters and sisters-in-law?"

At this point, the ongoing argument between the couple would grow heated. Mirushka knew that Baruch had struck at her weak point. But she would not let him have the last word. In times of distress, she had her own ace to expose, a card which he could not top, an argument which Baruch could not rebut: "Perhaps you can tell me in which chassidic book it is written that one must hand out one's best melodies to friends who deck themselves in feathers that are not their own and pretend to have composed the songs themselves? Hundreds of your tunes, worth a cumulative fortune, have gone down the drain, because you gave them away free.

"Is it a *mitzvah* to be a fool? To sell oneself short for pennies?" Mirushka would conclude in a hoarse, infuriated rasp.

Baruch would lower his eyes. There was no point in arguing with facts. The clever Mirushka knew exactly where his own weak point lay.

Chilik sat by the sidelines, taking in every word of the heated argument. He didn't understand everything, but his alert senses conveyed to him that his mother wanted to promote his talent, to push him upward, and this fact pleased him more than anything...

At the Rebbe's command, Baruch stopped bringing Chilik for performances at the regular *tish*, and except for rare occasions such as festivals, his voice was not heard. This was despite Mirushka's disappointment and Chilik's own desire to surrender his voice to song. The Rebbe's command was stringent and binding.

A turning point was reached on the threshold of his tenth year. R' Avrumele hinted to Baruch that if he wished to bring Chilik every *Shabbos Mevarchim*, when the coming month was heralded and blessed, he — R' Avrumele — would not object.

Shabbos Mevarchim became a regular monthly festival for the worshipers of the *beis midrash*. Word spread rapidly and R' Avrumele's *beis midrash* soon became too small to contain the vast crowds that flocked there each month. But the matter did not stop here. The wonder child did not remain the sole property of the ghetto. The news of the marvelous discovery crossed the lines of the Jewish quarter of Lublin and spread throughout the city. In honor of the upcoming *Shabbos Mevarchim* of Sivan, whispered someone in the ears of Beilka the butcher's wife, the ghetto would be in for a surprise.

This was big news. Beilka could not contain it, and her butcher shop on Yatzena Street turned into the top news agency for the Jews of the area. Between serving one customer a cut of meat and weighing some bones and *shmaltz* for another, she casually let slip an innocent remark: "You must have heard the news already, no? We are going to have guests next Friday night. The gentiles are coming to hear Chilik."

The news spread like wildfire. There was a massive convergence upon Rebbe Avrumele's *beis midrash* that Friday night. A huge crowd of curious people stood waiting impatiently to see 'them' coming. And indeed, Beilka had been right. At about 10 p.m., a group of seven men made its way from the market square to the Jewish quarter. From the moment the group crossed the Cracow Gate, they were accompanied by an entourage of dozens of excited Jewish children who volunteered to show them the way to the *beis midrash*.

These were not common folk; you could tell by the elegant way they dressed. The group of curious people lapsed into excited silence and waited to see what the non-Jews would do. A tall, thin man with a monocle left the group and drew near. "Is this where the young Caruso is scheduled to sing?"

"Who?"

"Caruso."

"Caruso?"

"You never heard of Caruso?" he snorted derisively. "Caruso, from Naples. The biggest singer of all."

This is how the *chassidim* learned about the famous Italian singer, Enrico Caruso, who had earned a worldwide reputation due to his powerful voice. And their little Chilik was competing with him!

"Yes," one person chuckled. "You'll soon hear our Caruso."

When Chilik trilled one of the difficult passages together with his father, his clear soprano voice cutting through the air with its piercing sweetness and reverberating like a delicate bell to great distances, the group of gentiles standing under the window held their breaths; they were flabbergasted.

"Ah, this is unique. Nothing of his like has ever been heard," said the tall one. "Call his father out, please."

Before *Bircas Hamazon*, Baruch went out. He was curious to know who the gentile was who wished to meet him on Friday night.

"*Pan* Horowitz, are you the father of the *solovei* (singer)?"

"Yes," Baruch answered in Polish.

"I have an offer for you," said the tall one. "I am Dr. Blyzhynsky, manager of the Lublin opera."

Baruch was stunned. Dr. Zbignew Blyzhynsky's name was famous throughout Poland. He was considered the greatest music authority in the country. What had brought him here?

Deeply moved, Baruch shook the expert's hand.

"Listen carefully," said Dr. Blyzhynsky. "I want to tell you that I have heard dozens of child prodigies in my life and they don't impress me. But a voice like your son's I have yet to hear in all my days! He began in a low alto and within seconds, had climbed all the way up to a mezzo-soprano and from there to a high soprano, sharp and clear, without an ounce of effort. And what is even more astonishing is that the higher his voice, the sweeter it is to the ear."

Baruch smiled with satisfaction. That was the whole point, the very essence of the matter. Most wonder children became painful to the ear when they began climbing octaves. Their nightingale voices turned to raucous screeching.

"This phenomenon is almost miraculous; it is beyond my comprehension!" continued the expert. "If we suggested the legendary Caruso before, let me tell you, your son makes him stand in the shade!"

"*Zinkouya*," Baruch, much moved, thanked him, again shaking the hand of his eminent visitor.

"I would like to suggest that if you have the child's good in mind," Dr. Blyzhnysky enunciated ceremoniously, "that you send him to me, to my school of opera. Many young talents have passed through my hands. The famous singer Thadeus Mazoveitzky, for example, is one of our products, and he is considered one of the greatest Polish singers today. But he does not even approach your son's ankles. Your child can go far under my tutelage."

Baruch was shaken.

"Dr. Blyzhynsky, I am far too insignificant for all the honor you are showering upon me tonight," he replied tensely. Only a perceptive eye could detect that his lips were almost white. "But my Chilik is still a tender child, not even ten years old. He still needs his mother's apron."

A wide circle of curious bystanders congregated around them. "*Vos reden zei?*" some youngsters asked in Yiddish, hungry for news.

"*Pan* Horowitz, you look to me like an intelligent person. Don't brush off such a generous offer so lightly."

Baruch weighed each word before speaking. The last thing he wished was to offend the opera manager of Lublin, who had connections and adherents throughout the world. His revenge might be very painful.

The crowd around them continued to swell. The young boys sensed that Baruch was in a quandary, but couldn't fathom what was going on. Only a few of these chassidic youths knew Polish. After a moment of consternation, one youth drew up to Baruch and whispered something in his ear.

"Dr. Blyzhynsky, they tell me that my *rabbin* is waiting for me in the synagogue. We will continue this conversation upon a different occasion."

Zbignew Blyzhynsky was as cold as ice. He withdrew a calling card from his pocket and handed it to Baruch with a rigid, frigid expression. "If you change your mind, you will find my address here and my reception hours."

Baruch took the card and took leave of his unusual visitors. He went up to the *beis midrash* and threw the card away in disgust. He hoped that the opera house manager would not find his way to Chilik's mother…

A round squat figure bent over from behind and quickly snatched up the rejected card. "Baruch Horowitz, what a fool you are!" Shevach Travitzky hissed quietly between his teeth. "What isn't good enough for your Chilik is very good for my own Shalom!"

26

Shalom Travitzky was Chilik Horowitz's best friend.

Shalom was two weeks older, and they were in the same class since they began attending *cheder*. They began learning their *alef-beis* together under Yankel Erlichman at the age of three, and from that time on they were inseparable. They were always seen together, romping, playing, quarreling…

Shevach Travitzky was a simple man of the lower class. He worked very hard to make a living but earned no more than pennies. His dilapidated house on 4 Ruska Street, or Reisha Street, as the Jews called it, was one of the poorest houses in the Lublin ghetto. He was the assistant to the fishmonger in the market, not far from Cracow Gate, and the smell of smoked lox, pickled herring and decayed fish innards among which he toiled from morning to evening clung to him like a leech. Wherever he went, he was accompanied by the reek of putrid fish, and people shied away from him. He was consumed by feelings of inferiority and sought comfort in his only son among eight daughters — Shalom.

Shalom displayed talents from the early grades. He understood at the age of six what his eight sisters had not learned by their teens: His father was not respected. As a matter of fact, Shevach was one of the most shunned figures in society. In the *beis knesses,* during the daily *shiur* between *Minchah* and *Maariv*, no one would dream of sitting near him because of the offensive odor that enveloped him. The same applied on Shabbos. Thus, when R' Avrumele held his *tish*, people gave Shevach a wide berth.

Shalom was a good student and when he was tested on Shabbos afternoon by local yeshivah students, they would report to his father that Shalom'ke had known his lessons well. And then a spark of *nachas* and pleasure would light up the father's dulled eyes for a brief moment. Shalom was prepared to exert himself all week long and be an exemplary student just to see the gleam of pleasure in his father's eyes on Shabbos afternoon.

Shevach Travitzky had given up on himself long ago. He cast all of his hopes upon his young Shalom'ke. Chilik Horowitz, his son's best friend, did not find favor in his eyes. He was a spoiled, pampered child, product of a well-born family, and his father, Baruch Horowitz, was very high up the Jewish social ladder in Lublin, on the topmost levels, while he, *Shevach der fisher*, just about scraped the bottom rung.

The stronger the bond between the unlikely pair, Chilik and Shalom, the more Shevach despised the boy. He was no fool and understood that in the course of time, Chilik would climb high up the social ladder, pushing his Shalom aside. He tried many times to separate the two, but failed repeatedly.

Shevach was a regular worshiper in R' Avrumele's *beis midrash*. And when Chilik got up on the wooden platform on *Shabbos Mevarchim* for the first time and trilled with his voice, he felt a lump choking his throat. He devoured the wonder child with his envious, embittered eyes and resolved at that moment to turn his own Shalom into a prodigy.

Shalom was indeed blessed with a pleasant voice. Shevach tested him privately on Shabbos afternoon, and in his opinion, the child was on par with Chilik Horowitz. He decided to take him to a private music teacher. He would take the bread from his own mouth to see that his child become a singer, no less than Chilik Horowitz.

≈)⊂

His legs shook and his knees knocked incessantly. He held on tightly to the calling card which he had salvaged on Friday night. Shalom stood near him. The two had washed up and put on their best clothing; the smell of fish was hardly noticeable.

"According to this card, it should be somewhere around here," whispered Shevach. "Here, it says: 7 Okopova Street."

They had come to Dr. Blyzhynsky's house. The bottom line of his card read: Musical Consultation and Reception between 6 - 8 p.m. The municipal theater was not far. People were flocking to the show from all sides. They walked along the street and flung surprised looks at the pair. Shevach felt embarrassed and for a moment considered turning around and going back to the Jewish quarter, but he felt embarrassed to do so because of his son, Shalom.

A beautifully tended and aromatic rose garden surrounded the home of the famous opera director. Shevach knocked on the iron garden gate. An elderly, heavy-set maid tottered forward on her short legs and opened the gate.

"We've come to see Dr. Blyzhynysky," Shevach said, waving the cardboard rectangle.

The short woman respectfully turned aside and showed them the way up a dirt path. If these *zhids* had the *doktor's* calling card, they couldn't be as common as they looked.

They entered the house. The woman told them to wait in the hallway. Their eyes grew round with surprise at the opulence they beheld, which surpassed their wildest imagination.

Dr. Blyzhynysky sat ensconced in his library on the top floor, engrossed in a thick, leather-bound tome. When the elderly maid entered and told him of a Jewish father and child awaiting him below, he smiled broadly.

"Aha, so they've come," he exclaimed gleefully, whipping the monocle off his eye. "I knew it! From the very first moment, I knew they'd come. *Pan* Horowitz is no fool." He shut the book and snapped the gold clasp. In Dr. Blyzhynysky's house, every book was tenderly and scrupulously cared for.

Maria Ruskanina turned away, a satisfied smile on her wrinkled face. No, she never misjudged people. Hadn't she understood at once that the people with the calling card were acquainted with the distinguished director?

Dr. Blyzhynysky descended the winding staircase to the first floor with light steps, then stopped short.

"*Donner und blitzen!*" he spat out, adjusting his monocle, his eyes shooting sparks as he studied the father and son sitting comfortably in his fine leather armchairs. "This man is not *Pan* Horowitz!"

Shevach Travitzky arose at the sight of the master of the house, his hand extended in greeting with exaggerated obsequiousness.

"Who are you?" Zbignew snorted, his hands thrust arrogantly in his jacket pocket. Shevach's outstretched hand remained suspended in the air like a scarecrow's.

"My son wishes to study singing under your honored patronage," Shevach managed to say with considerable effort. "He has a voice just like Chilik Horowitz." Before the *doktor* could rally, he turned to his son, "Shalom, please sing for the honorable *Pan* Blyzyhnsky the song Chilik sang on Friday night."

Shalom was terrified by the sight of the distinguished gentile whose goatee stood on end. The boy opened his mouth to sing, but only a croak emerged. Zbignew drew near, not believing his ears, when the stench of rotten fish suddenly hit him...

This had gone too far. Was this farce really taking place right here? In his very house?

"Out!" he screamed at the top of his voice. He held his nose with his fingers and opened the door wide with his other hand. "Out, but fast!" He pushed Shevach out, his high forehead red with rage. "My house is not a shelter for beggars."

Shevach and Shalom found themselves on the other side of the door. The agitated Shevach pressed his face against the glass door panel. "*Pan* Horowitz threw your card away in contempt and I picked it up from the ground," he shouted at the barred window. Dr. Zbignew was already at the top of the stairs, racing for the bathroom to wash his hands with carbolic soap, but Shevach's loud cry reached his ears and penetrated deep into his consciousness.

The elderly Maria Roskina ran off to her room, shaking and weeping. What had come over the *doktor*? He had been so happy to hear that the Jews had come. Why had he chased them away with such anger?

From that unfortunate morning onward, Shevach's hatred towards Chilik grew violently. He dripped his venom into Shalom's ears upon every occasion, and slowly Shalom was influenced by his words. Nevertheless, he did not relinquish his close bond with Chilik despite his father's express wish. Shevach had designed a totally new creative direction for this relationship.

Chilik began, as expected, his meteoric rise upward. He had just turned twelve, and his singing was causing reverberations throughout Jewish Poland. From all sides, people streamed to hear him. He appeared in R' Avrumele's *beis midrash* every other Shabbos. Aside from this, Mirushka organized performances in the Jewish theater house on the narrow, winding Yazuitzka Street.

The Pantheon Theater did not belong to a Jew. Its owner was a Pole by the name of Makovski, but certain less scrupulous Jews attended the Jewish folk evenings and the low grade entertainment offered there. It was situated somewhat inside the Jewish quarter, and this fact seemed to lend it some cover and respectability. Audiences of hundreds would roar with laughter at the humorous presentations such as "Simcha Plachti" or "Chanchi in America," and would duly weep along with the touching story of "Gluckel von Hameln." Her Chilik would appear there, Mirushka decided.

Baruch tried to prevent this disgrace with all his might, but after a long, exhausting argument, he gave in. Mirushka won and Chilik appeared before an audience of a thousand people, his first performance before such an immense crowd.

The conditions in the theaters of poverty-stricken Poland were far from ideal. There were no spotlights to highlight Chilik while he made his maiden appearance, though the large theater was well lit, as usual, with kerosene lamps. Only in the center of the stage, above the head of the wonder child, was a single large electric bulb of sixty watts, a considerable achievement. Though there was no loudspeaker system to carry the sound of the 'nightingale' to the far corners of the hall, two factors combined decisively to contribute to the overwhelming success of the evening. One was an excellent acoustical ceiling that had been especially designed and built to reverberate each and every note. The second factor was Chilik's resonant voice itself. He had been born with especially strong vocal chords, and his uplifting song was so powerful that it reached the very last row in the balcony. No one could complain that he had not heard him. His clear voice cut the air with an inexpressible sweetness and reached every ear in the concert hall.

Most of the audience was not from Orthodox circles. The center of gravity of the public life in Jewish Poland had begun shifting left. Lublin was then filled with cells of Bundist youth, *hachsharah* (emigration) devotees, *Tarbut* culture organizations and so on. These groups kept a healthy distance from the *beis midrash* of the extremist R' Avrumele, and had never heard of the chassidic child prodigy called Chilik Horowitz. The evening was an overwhelming revelation for them.

Chilik stood in the center of the stage dressed in shining satin. He was at the height of his bloom, young and handsome, and his curly blond *payos* added the element of charm and innocence to his gentle face. The atmosphere in the large hall was charged with electricity; the huge crowd listened to his melodious singing, bewitched.

His voice had an other-worldly character. Chilik sang choice excerpts from his repertoire. His marvelous voice rose and dipped alternately, beginning from a low alto, through a mezzo-soprano, which parallels the adult male baritone, and finally soaring all the way to the highest soprano. The overflowing sweetness of his alto in the emotional passages moved the audience to unabashed tears, causing them to lower their damp faces in embarrassment. But when Chilik passed on to his happy, sweeping songs, the audience went wild. The narrow area before the stage was filled with men and boys who could not contain their excitement and who had burst into spontaneous dancing. Groups of curious people in the audience tried to climb up to the stage to see the star from close up, and the entire evening almost turned into bedlam before the ushers succeeded in restoring a semblance of decorum.

The Pantheon was witness to the loudest and longest applause it had ever heard. The thunderous handclapping threatened to literally bring down the rafters.

And that was only the beginning. At the end of the evening, the crowd stormed up to Chilik and his mother, begging to become acquainted with the new star. Mirushka did not object. She had never pushed away any honor due her, and the crowd warmly pressed Chilik's hand as Mirushka stood by and beamed with pride.

The Jewish newspaper of Lublin, the *Lubliner Tagblatt*, came out the next day with banner headlines: "The Child Who Is Bigger Than All." Mirushka could envision the eyes of her brothers and sisters grow wide when they heard the news. Until now, they heard very little about Chilik and his talents, and had taken no interest in it. But now, when he appeared in the skies of Poland like a rising comet, they would be unable to ignore her little *nachas'l*. All of Poland was talking about him. Yechiel Horowitz was the most talked-about child in the entire country, by Jews and non-Jews alike. Would his very own uncles ignore him?

She erred in singling out the enemy. Chilik's uncles and aunts were prestigious business people, but they did not begrudge their nephew's dizzying success. On the contrary, they even took pride in it.

The danger threatened Chilik in his immediate environment. In his neighborhood, many pairs of eyes gazed upon him with open jealousy, but no one envied him more than his best friend, Shalom Travitzky...

27

Chilik felt the first blow land on him during his third musical lesson with his Dutch teacher of voice development, Henrik von Florsheim.

The teacher had instructed him in proper breathing exercises. "You must expel the air from your lungs and use it in the process. You cannot rely only upon your vocal chords — they will collapse from the effort and leave you hoarse. You must utilize the air you breathe. Like this..." He taught Chilik an old technique he had acquired during his years of study in the College of Music in Amsterdam. Chilik felt the process foreign and disturbing. He reviewed the exercises with pronounced dissatisfaction.

The elderly teacher looked at him in a strange manner all the while. At the end of the lesson, he requested that Chilik empty his pockets.

"What? But why?" Chilik exclaimed, stunned.

The teacher looked at him, weighing in his mind whether to reveal the secret. Finally he went to the adjoining room and brought a letter he had received the previous day. Chilik read the paper and almost fainted. The anonymous letter warned von Florsheim not to be taken in by his student's innocent facade but to take note that he was an experienced pickpocket, and had already sat in jail for his crimes more than once!

"It's a lie!" wept Chilik. "What a terrible accusation to make!" Pale and struck with shame, he dragged his feet through the streets of Lublin. He would never to return to that gentile teacher again, he vowed.

At home, he announced ceremoniously that from now on, he would only go to a Jewish voice-development teacher, the famous R' Shlomo Eckstein. "All the famous *chazzanim* studied under him. Isn't he good enough for me too?"

≈⊂

Baruch Horowitz had made an uneasy peace with his wife's unbridled ambitions. Her grandiose plans to turn Yechiel into a singing idol had never appealed to him, but in these days Mirushka resembled a steamroller, and he moved aside to avoid being crushed, knowing full well that his objection was worth less than an onion peel. She was determined, with an iron will, to push Chilik to the heady heights of the world of music, at all costs.

Yechiel Horowitz was a clever, astute child. His studies at the *cheder* would have suffered drastically, had it not been for his blessed talents. Between daydreaming about the past week's performance and looking forward to the afternoon lesson with his piano teacher, he forced himself to pay attention to the *Gemara* lesson for at least ten minutes. This was sufficient for him to grasp the material as well as had Shalom Travitzky, who did not let his eye wander from the rebbe's mouth from the beginning of the lesson to the end.

Over the years his teachers had had no grounds for complaint. Yechiel was a good student and had a full command over the material. But they were far from being satisfied with him.

"True, Chilik is a good student," they would sigh in his father's ear, "but if these are his achievements at only thirty percent of his capacity, what could he accomplish if he studied with zest, with all his heart and soul? The Torah world of Poland is losing a potential giant in Torah. Why, he could become another R' Meir Shapiro of Lublin!"

Yes, R' Meir Shapiro, the famous rabbi of Pietrokov, had laid the cornerstone of the great Torah center, Yeshivas Chachmei Lublin, several years before, on Lag B'Omer, 1924 (5684), on the huge plot on

Lubertovska Street. It was donated by the philanthropist Shmuel Eichenbaum. The grand yeshivah was being built at a rapid rate before the eyes of Chilik and his friends. On their way home from *cheder*, they would stop to watch the construction workers pouring cement and arranging the bricks, row upon row. Their eyes devoured the sight of the long building rising up, story by story. And the boys would take bets on which one of them would eventually merit to become a student. In Lublin it was rumored that only the very best would be accepted, learned students who could prove expertise in hundreds of *Gemara blatt* by heart.

"Yechiel, you could get in easily," his seatmate in class, Chezki Lustig, commented to him one day. "But your head is buried in music. Do you know that the human body is composed of a mind, and not only vocal chords?"

This was a nasty remark and Chilik felt his throat choke with suppressed tears. He hurried off to tell his mother but she dismissed the matter in her way, with a wave of her hand.

"I've already told you a thousand times, Chilik, that your friends are eaten up with jealousy at your success. Your friend, Chezki Lustig, would not even be accepted as a *chazzan* at the cemetery."

But Chilik felt she was whitewashing the issue. Chezki's remark hid an incisive truth. He thought about it and felt his soul being torn between the will to devote at least part of his talents to the study of *Gemara* and *Mishnah* and his unbridled compulsion to reach the peak of the music world.

He was the product of mixed drives. His character was a combination of the contrasting traits of Baruch and Mirushka, his parents, and his tender soul was continually catapulting from one extreme to the other. He felt torn between two poles: his refined and modest chassidic father, who could, with a heartwarming, wholesome smile, give away a tune in which he had invested days and nights of effort. And his mother, with her megalomaniac aspirations, who was subverting his talents and channeling them to directions of her own design. His young heart threatened to burst from the effort of dealing with the force of the conflict.

≈)(≈

"You want to turn me into a baby?"

"Yes, *yingele*, don't look at me with those big eyes. Why are you surprised? I want to turn you into a baby."

Chilik had come to his first lesson with the "Mr. Day and Night," R' Shlomo Eckstein, at his home on Grodsaka Street, and the famous teacher had not concealed his joy. "What a surprise! The famous Chilik has come to me to learn voice development. I was sure that you would go to bigger experts, like Henrik von Florsheim, for example."

Chilik blushed as he recalled how his Dutch teacher had made a thorough search of his pockets, and was silent. Eckstein interpreted this as a sign of modesty on the part of the charming boy.

But when they began to the actual lesson, Chilik was dismayed. Was his teacher mentally deficient? What did he mean, turning him into a baby?

"I will teach you to sing like a baby," Eckstein explained. "Did you ever see how a baby cries? His whole body moves: his hands, feet, stomach. Do you know why?

"A baby is the ultimate reflection of the natural person. He has not yet been spoiled or ruined. He looks exactly as the Creator made him."

Chilik didn't understand a word.

Eckstein rose to his feet to demonstrate to his new student. He was a middle-aged man, and his beard was one of the most fascinating natural phenomena of Lublin. This famous beard had earned for him the name Mr. Day and Night; half of it was coal black and half, snow white. Looking at him from his right profile, a person might assume that he was thirty years old, while one standing at his left would be certain that the man was seventy.

But Chilik did not stand from the side. He sat exactly opposite him and studied the evenly divided beard with astonishment.

R' Shlomo flung his head back and stretched his throat. He opened his mouth and belted out in a deep bass voice. Chilik, a fun-loving, zestful child, watched the performance, trying desperately to suppress the laughter beginning to bubble up inside him. The teacher did not notice a thing and continued with his demonstration. He suddenly produced a sound as mighty as a *shofar* blast.

Chilik gave up his internal struggle and burst into laughter. His shoulders shook and his face was buried between his hands.

"Are you weeping, *yingele*?" asked Eckstein. "What a sensitive child! True, I was going to give a rendition of the piece *Hineni He'ani Mimaash* by cantor Zvulun Kwartin, a most moving selection, but to cry already?"

The laughter swelled and swelled until Chilik thought his stomach would burst. He rose quickly to his feet and escaped out the door to catch a breath of fresh air.

To his good fortune, Eckstein was an easy-going person, quick to be appeased. He was prepared to overlook the unfortunate episode and begin teaching him the fundamentals of his unique approach to voice development.

"I want to demonstrate to you how one can sing a difficult passage without any exertion whatsoever," explained the teacher. He asked Chilik to sing a well-known cantorial piece. Chilik turned red with the effort.

"Now you can understand what I am driving at," R' Shlomo said enthusiastically. "Have you ever thought why a baby is able to scream for hours on end at the top of his lungs without getting hoarse?"

Now he was talking sense. Chilik felt the question applying directly to him. "Not really. Why?"

"Every average teacher of voice development will tell you that it's because he cries from his stomach. A baby's belly is as round as a bottle and he doesn't have to strain his vocal chords to produce a loud sound."

"Is that correct?" Chilik wished to understand.

"No!" Eckstein's voice thundered like that of a prophet of yore, and the thin-stemmed crystal shnaps glasses on the shelf near the liquor cabinet tinkled against one another.

"To be more precise, yes and no. A baby does cry from his stomach," the teacher lectured heatedly. "But not only from there. He cries with his whole body, and that's why his whole body vibrates. The sound is not only produced from his vocal chords but also from every single limb and organ in his body.

"I am going to turn you into a baby. I only pray that you truly learn to sing like a baby!" R' Shlomo said, full of enthusiasm, his eyes sparkling and his thick beard jutting forward like a two-colored horn. Chilik felt his inner struggle beginning anew. He bit his lips and studied his fingernails, a tried and tested method to stem unwanted laughter.

"The various teachers of voice development teach different techniques. One will tell you to thrust your stomach out when you sing quietly in a bass voice, and to hold it in as you go up the musical scale. Another will tell you the opposite. Which one is correct?

"The answer is," Eckstein intoned with a *Gemara* sing-song, "that both are right. Sometimes you must pull in your stomach, and sometimes, release it. But that's only half the story. A third teacher will tell you that you must concentrate your vocal effort upon the sinuses and nasal cavities, while his counterpart will dismiss this practice with scorn and say that this is not a voice, only a nasal sound. A certain instructor in Galicia teaches how to sing from the chambers of the stomach, from the walls covering the liver.

"And I ask you? Are they all crazy?"

Chilik was fascinated. Mr. Day and Night was suddenly revealed in a new light. He made sense and Chilik felt that he was going to teach him a technique that would serve him for the rest of his life.

"They're all right and all mistaken at the same time," began Eckstein. "Let me explain how this is possible.

"A person must sing as King David described in *Tehillim*.. 'My soul, bless Hashem, and all my innards, His holy Name.' And furthermore: 'All my bones shall declare…' Do you think this is a mere figure of speech? Not at all, my friend. It is the pure, simple truth!

"He must sing like an infant, with all of his 248 organs and 365 sinews. Every cell in his body must sing. He must breathe like a baby, inhale and exhale just like they do, and produce a sound from his throat in the proper manner. I will teach you to sing without effort. You will sing in the easiest manner possible and everyone will hear you!"

"With all due respect, sir, but everyone can hear me well, now, too," said Chilik modestly.

"True," agreed the teacher, "but what effort must you invest to achieve that!"

Chilik's silence was his tacit admission.

"After you acquire my techniques, you will sing with your full voice, and the entire world will fall before you on their knees," boasted Eckstein. "You will sing in a thin voice that will trill like a bird, and a sharp voice that will cut the air like a honed knife, a sound that will be heard at a distance of hundreds of meters and will still be sweet and pleasant to the ear.

"You will sing with your sinuses and your forehead; with your stomach and your ribs. You will sing from the very marrow of your bones and from the soles of your feet, until you and your song will turn into one inseparable entity. Do you know the meaning of King David's words, 'And I am prayer'? This is not only a goal for *tzaddikim*. You and your prayer will coalesce into one totality!"

Chilik did not hear his last sentences. He was already floating in the biggest concert halls of Europe, America, Palestine. The entire world would bow down before him and pay him homage! The future was spread before him like a red carpet. All that was left for him was to bend down and gather up success into his arms. He rose suddenly from his seat and ran over to the surprised Eckstein, and before the latter could recover, hugged him warmly. "Thank you, Rabbi Eckstein! Thank you!"

"What's come over you?" R' Shlomo extricated himself from the boy's excited embrace. "'Let the one who girds his weapons not boast like the hero who removes them after battle,' he quoted the Biblical warning. "You will have to practice for months and years until you reach half of what I described. Just don't get tired and run away in the middle."

But Chilik knew that he would not run away in the middle. He would study under Eckstein until he reached musical perfection. He was a perfectionist by nature and loved flawlessness. He would prove to the entire world what could be achieved if one utilized one's talent to the fullest!

The first lesson was over. He rose to leave, but Eckstein held him back for a moment. "Before you go," he said to him thoughtfully, "I'd first like to show you something."

He went over to a drawer and took out a piece of paper. "Are you familiar with this handwriting?"

Chilik felt the blood rushing to his head. Those poisonous letters were pursuing him again!

"Someone thought it necessary to bring to my attention the fact that you are not planning to put on *tefillin* after your *bar-mitzvah*, and that your mother is thinking of taking you to America. Is that true?" Eckstein looked at him incisively to see how he would react.

His vision became blurred. Tears blinded his eyes. A despicable creature was trying to ruin his life and was persecuting him every step of the way.

Who could it be?

A wild idea suddenly hit him. "Give me the letter," he demanded, and he grabbed it away from his teacher with trembling fingers. He drew it close to his nose.

It reeked of rotten fish.

28

"**Y**our friend is a spy. You must break off all relations with him," Mirushka ordered Chilik. "Such disgusting behavior! To write such scandalous letters against you! Whoever heard of such a thing!"

"But Mother, it isn't him," Chilik defended his best friend heatedly.

"Who else could it be? You yourself said you smelled fish on the letter. If you would have smelled the letter he sent to von Florsheim you would have detected the same odor!"

"Shalom doesn't smell of fish!" Chilik stubbornly insisted.

"Oh, sure. He is as innocent as an angel; he doesn't do a thing. He only spies on you. But his father spreads evil rumors about you all over the city. Wait, wait. We don't even know the extent of harm that Shevach the fishmonger has caused you, and you go and stand up for him?"

Though Chilik broke off his ties with Shalom, his nature could not resist Shalom's pleading eyes. After two or three months, he began a restrained, reserved friendship with the very person who had struck at him behind his back.

Chilik had made a fateful mistake. Mirushka had been right. Chilik should have stayed away from Shalom as an animal flees from fire. In the end, he would pay dearly for his mistake.

For the rest of his life.

≈)⌒

Chilik's parents celebrated his *bar-mitzvah* in a modest celebration held in the *kloiz*, the ancient *beis midrash* of the Chozeh of Lublin, on Siroka Street. Interestingly, it was Mirushka's own uncharacteristic suggestion that they forego a grandiose affair. She understood that one could not hold a formal and lavish initiation into *mitzvos* with the participation of gentiles from the society of the musical elite of Poland.

In anticipation of the great day, Chilik went with his father to the Rebbe, R' Avrumele, to receive a blessing. R' Avrumele asked about the boy's studies and wanted to know if he had good friends. Chilik, embarrassed and flustered, told the Rebbe in a muddled style foreign to him that he had many good friends.

"Who, for example?" inquired R' Avrumele. Chilik mentioned Srulik Tannenbaum, Chezki Lustig and Shalom Travitzky. The Rebbe listened and murmured under his breath in a manner that made it impossible to guess whether he was pleased or not. Then he raised his eyes, which were normally lowered to the ground, and studied Chilik intensely.

"Do you study *Gemara* with the fear of Heaven?" The surprising words shot through the room like bullets. This time it was Baruch's turn to blush. Chilik's studies had taken a drastic turn for the worst in the past few months. His afternoons were filled with music studies which included learning the notes, voice development, piano lessons, and becoming familiar with the violin and flute. He showed a phenomenal mastery in every aspect of the world of notes and scales and Mirushka had decided that the boy might as well acquire expertise in musical instruments. The inevitable regression took place in his *cheder* studies. While his friends were beginning to study the commentaries, *Rishonim* and *Acharonim*, Chilik practiced his violin.

"He is excelling in music," Baruch admitted painfully. "His head is filled only with music and he has fallen very far behind in his *Gemara* studies."

R' Avrumele looked at him for a long time. Chilik's face burned fire-red. He had never felt such terrible disgrace. What had happened to his father? Why had he decided to reveal his shame before the Rebbe?

R' Avrumele tapped the sheet of glass that covered the table and hummed to himself. His long white beard lent him a venerable, patriarchal look. His eyes studied Chilik again, this time with a pleasant expression, and the child relaxed. He felt that his worth had not fallen short in the Rebbe's eyes because of what he had heard about him. Chilik didn't know, however, that the Rebbe had been monitoring his progress closely for years. Baruch's 'tattling' was no earthshaking revelation to the rebbe.

"Music is not a negative thing," he said slowly, as if counting his words like coins. Chilik's ears perked up. The Rebbe was on his side! Hurrah!

"Music is not a negative thing," the Rebbe repeated. "It all depends on what one does with it." He looked at Chilik again. "Tomorrow you will be called up to the Torah. Which *aliyah* will you get?"

What a question. "*Levi.*"

"Fine. You are a *Levi*, the son of a *Levi* who is the son of a *Levi* and so on down until *Levi*, the son of Yaakov. You are the grandchild of *Leviim* who served in the *Beis Hamikdash*. Do you know if your ancestors were among the gatekeepers or the musicians?"

"Of course." The answer came without hesitation. Chilik had imbibed the details of his lineage together with his mother's milk. "We are from the musicians."

"How long did the neophyte *Leviim* study the art of music playing?" the Rebbe tested him.

Chilik was flustered. No one had taught him this.

"Five years," the Rebbe whispered. "A *Levi* studied five full years before he was qualified to be a musician and stand together with the members of the choir, his fellow musicians, along the length of the fifteen steps in the *Beis Hamikdash*. So Chilik is also studying, just like his ancestors, the *Leviim*, did in their time. You're studying music, right, Yechiel?"

Chilik burst into happy laughter. The Rebbe was on his side, praised be Hashem. He would soon run off to tell his mother.

"When did the *Leviim* sing in the *Beis Hamikdash*?" the Rebbe queried again. Baruch stood, perplexed. He had known R' Avrumele for many years. The Rebbe was a taciturn person, his words were measured like precious coins. Yet here he was, conversing leisurely and pleasantly. He must be driving at something. At what?

"The *Leviim* sang the Daily Psalm!" Chilik answered easily. If only they asked such simple questions in *cheder*!

"When else?"

Silence. The exam was suddenly becoming more difficult.

"When offerings were sacrificed," he finally recalled.

"He knows," the Rebbe exclaimed with genuine joy. "And what happened when the *Leviim* sang?" Chilik began to tremble. He suddenly understood that the wise Rebbe was steering the conversation to unexpected channels, and the uncertainty frightened him.

"Let me tell you a true story," the Rebbe said quietly. "A Jew, let us call him Nechunya from Kfar Chittin, committed a terrible sin. He knew that his sin could not be atoned before he brought a sacrifice to the *Beis Hamikdash*. Before long, he went up to Jerusalem to bring his sacrifice. Upon arrival, Nechunya was deeply impressed by the glory and grandeur, by the *Kohanim* dressed all in white, and by the aura of holiness which surrounded everything. But his heart was still sealed shut. He led the sheep to the *Kohen*, the sacrifice was slaughtered and its blood was sprinkled.

"The *Leviim* stood upon the fifteen steps. The *Kohen* knew through his Divine intuition how the man had sinned. He signaled the choir of *Leviim* and they burst into song.

"The *Leviim* were thoroughly versed in all areas of music. They knew how to adapt every tune to the roots of a particular sin. Their pure, clear voices rose up in the air, an exhilarating sound. The tune seemed to emerge directly from *Gan Eden*. The delicate, ethereal strains were other-worldly. The *Leviim* sang in first, second, third voices and so on, creating a magnificent harmony. This was pure heavenly mystical music that reduces a person to his basic components and crumbles his soul to tiny fragments. The notes plucked at his heartstrings, each note and its significance, each movement and its distinct meaning and connotation. It would soar to great heights one moment and then pull the person down to the depths of such pain, sorrow and remorse that he felt he would die.

"Do you know," the Rebbe's voice grew deep, as if it were emanating from a cavern, "according to the holy books, the palace of music in Heaven is next to the palace of repentance. Now you surely understand why. Nechunya from Kfar Chittin was transformed into a new person after the singing of the *Leviim*. His heart was bathed with pure waters; his soul was purged and purified. He became a *baal teshuvah* in the absolute meaning of the term. A real penitent.

"Nechunya from Kfar Chittin is no more than a allegory, an example. He is me and you and everyone else. Indeed, who not?" The Rebbe pointed to imaginary figures in the room and fell silent.

Baruch and Chilik were bewitched. A similar thought passed through both their heads. They had thought, up to this moment, that they had known something about music. And yet R' Avrumele, who could be expected to know as much as the average person, had, today, revealed to them secrets that a person heard only once in a lifetime, if he merits it.

"All the music in the world emanates from the ancient singing of the *Leviim*," concluded R' Avrumele. "But from the day that the *Beis Hamikdash* was destroyed, the glow and glory of music was dimmed. The *Leviim* were familiar with many more notes and scales than are known to us today. Ancient music was a thousand times richer than modern music. If you were to hear today a song the way the *Leviim* sang it, you would swoon and die from its sheer sweetness. Really and truly." R' Avrumele nodded emphatically. "Today's music is only a pale reflection of the song of the *Leviim* in the *Beis Hamikdash*.

"Do you know why? It's very simple. Melodies are created in order to purify a person and bring him back to his roots. When the *Beis Hamikdash* was destroyed and the sacrifices abolished, the true melodies were forgotten and only a faint memory lingered on — and only by Jews! Gentile music is only a counterfeit, a poor imitation of the real thing.

"The *Leviim* were familiar with all kinds of tunes and all possible rhythms. Music was like clay in their hands. But they did not use it for their personal benefit; their tunes were holy unto Hashem. Do you understand, Yechiel?" The Rebbe lifted his head and looked at him with two fiery eyes. "If you use music as your ancestors did, you will be fulfilling your purpose on this world. For this you were created. But if you take the gift of the Creator, your magnificent voice and blessed musical talents, and lower them to the dregs, if you glory in them before gentiles in opera houses and concert halls foreign to the spirit of *Yisrael Sabba*, Jewish tradition through the ages, you will eventually sing — coerced and subjugated — before the enemies of Israel. You will sing until you vomit from disgust and rue the day you were born with your musical talents, and wish you had never possessed them, like your friend, Shalom Travitzky, for example."

He knows everything, thought Chilik fearfully. *Nothing is hidden from his sight.*

The audience was over. The Rebbe shook their hands. He blessed Chilik and asked him to welcome his newcomer, his *yetzer tov* — the good inclination which would become his new partner when he came of age, upon his *bar-mitzvah* — with gracious hospitality. "Think about what I said to you today. Guard the words in your heart forever," the Rebbe called out to him as he stood on the threshold. "They are your key to a happy future."

≈≈

R' Avrumele's words had such a strong influence that Chilik stopped all of his music lessons. He sang on Friday nights in his father's choir in the *beis midrash* and began leading the prayers on festivals and special Shabbosim in the huge central *beis midrash* of the Maharshal. Chilik knew that he possessed an instrument that should be used to repair and mend souls, but that could be misused too. And he tried to utilize his G-d-given tool only for the good. Mirushka begged him not to burn all of his bridges behind him, but her words fell upon deaf ears. The youth began immersing himself heart and soul in his studies. He entered R' Pesach Shuldiner's *mesivta* immediately after his *bar-mitzvah* and began excelling in his *Gemara* studies in measure with his talents. He acquired expertise in hundreds of *Gemara* pages and seriously intended to apply and be accepted into R' Meir Shapira's yeshivah, *Yeshivas Chachmei Lublin*.

≈≈

Two years passed.

The enormous dedication ceremony of *Yeshivas Chachmei Lublin* lifted the entire city from its general routine. The event itself was confined to a single day, but the preparation and commotion surrounding it spread over many long weeks.

Tuesday morning, the 28th of Sivan, 5690 (June 24, 1930), dawned as a normal summer morning, but the festive atmosphere could be felt immediately. The city filled up with tens of thousands of guests: Chassidic leaders, famous Torah figures, rabbinical personalities, and hundreds of reporters from all over Poland and beyond who had come to participate in this rare event.

Chilik was fifteen and hoped with all his heart that the hundreds of pages of Talmud he had studied in depth and scope would serve as his good ambassadors. But he was quickly disappointed. Several days after the celebrations passed and the dazzlingly beautiful yeshivah opened its gates, Chilik learned, to his dismay, that a very long line of young boys seeking admission, like himself, had formed before the *rosh yeshivah*'s office. His chances to enter the room were slim indeed. The long waiting line included youths who knew a thousand pages of *Gemara* with *Tosfos*! Chilik felt like a baby next to them. He was certain that when his turn came to stand before the *rosh yeshivah*, R' Meir Shapira, who would hereafter also serve as the chief rabbi of Lublin, he would put him in his place. The *rosh yeshivah* would explain that he would be better off remaining in the *mesivta*.

Pursued by his foolish imagination and unjustified feelings of inferiority, Chilik left his place in the long line and slowly returned home.

⁀)⁀

Mirushka renewed her attack.

"Hundreds of people stood outside the *beis knesses* last Shabbos to hear you lead the service," she complimented Chilik. He bowed his head modestly. She had been stingy with her compliments of late, and had seemed peeved and dissatisfied with him.

"But you surely know what they all say. Yechiel Horowitz is slipping. He's not what he used to be."

"That's not true," Chilik cried out, tears gathering in his eyes.

"You're not arguing with your mother. It's easy to argue with her... You're arguing with facts!" she said bitterly. "You're already fifteen and your voice is soon going to change. You know that, don't you?"

Chilik nodded. He dreaded this in his heart. Up till now, his voice had not changed at all. He still sang with a child's alto and soprano, but he knew that he was not immune to the ravages of time.

"If you don't renew the lessons which you've neglected these past two years, you will lose your legendary voice," his mother warned. "Yechiel Horowitz, the child prodigy of all Poland, will sing in a hoarse voice. The nightingale will turn into a raven!"

29

He didn't sleep a wink that night. He tossed in bed and turned restlessly from side to side. The clever Mirushka had shot her honed arrow straight to the heart of the target.

Chilik was afraid.

He had received a gift from his Creator, gratis. And he was about to lose it through foolishness.

"Yechiel Horowitz, the child prodigy of all Poland, will sing in a hoarse voice. The nightingale will turn into a raven!" His mother's words rang in his ears like alarm bells. He loved his mother with all his heart, and felt that this time she was not thinking of herself. She was genuinely concerned for him. She had sent him a painful message and he had received and absorbed it. Towards morning, after hours of sleeplessness, he got out of bed with a resolute decision. He shuffled to the kitchen in his slippers and made himself a cup of coffee. The blackness of night had begun dispersing in the east, making way for a deep dark blue. A new dawn was about to break upon the world.

Mirushka awoke and surprised Chilik in the kitchen.

"I made my decision, Mother," he informed her ceremoniously, his voice shaking. "I am renewing my lessons with R' Eckstein."

Glints of joy sparkled in Mirushka's eyes, but she carefully controlled her emotions. "I am very happy about your wise decision, but you must first receive permission from your father."

Something has come over her, thought Chilik. *She's changed for the better. She was always the decision-maker.*

Baruch entered the kitchen, full of vigor and energy. "What's going on? Is this some secret council?"

They told him everything and he replied at once, "I have no objections, only one condition — that your studies in yeshivah are not disturbed. R' Eckstein can teach you in the evenings."

≈)⊂

Sixteen-year-old Chilik waited in fear. His voice had not changed yet. What kind of a voice would he get as an adult?

"You have nothing to be afraid of, my child," Eckstein would reassure him. "It isn't in your hands, anyway. If Hashem desires it, you will receive such a mighty voice that it will demolish all the buildings in your vicinity."

Chilik began walking around with a scarf around his throat. His good friends had warned him that if he did not take care of himself during the transitional period, he would surely lose his voice. He was even afraid to talk.

Then Moshe Koussovitzky came to Lublin.

All of Lublin flocked to hear the concert given by the 'King of Cantors,' Moshe Koussovitzky. Yossele Rosenblatt was the 'Sweet Cantor' of the Jewish people, and his outpouring heart won him a place in the 'eastern wall' of the world of Jewish music. But Moshe Koussovitzky was king.

Chilik stood near him and followed each movement of the world-famous *chazzan* with spellbound attention. He knew in his heart that here was perfection incarnate, and he was determined to reach the very same pinnacle himself.

On the following day, he went with his father to visit the *chazzan* in his luxurious lodgings. Koussovitzky was staying in a friend's home in the most beautiful apartment house in all of Lublin, the Spoldum on Provostva

Street. Here, in contrast to the stifling atmosphere in the congested Jewish quarter, a cool, pleasant breeze blew. The Spoldum overlooked luxuriant gardens and blooming fields. The waters of the Bistshitza River flowed leisurely along the horizon.

Koussovitzky shook his hand vigorously. "Ah, so you're the nightingale. I've heard great things about you."

They were very moved. The 'king' only complimented rare individuals.

Baruch told the famous *chazzan* about Chilik's fears and the latter shook his head.

"No, don't be frightened. What's a scarf doing around your neck on such a warm day? Are you crazy? Why do you need it?"

He whipped the length of silk from the embarrassed youth's throat and taught him several rules.

"Please G-d, you will have a good voice, even if you act normal and don't lift a finger to watch your health. If He wishes otherwise, nothing will help, not seven scarfs wound around your neck, nor refraining from speaking."

"What, then, should I do?" asked Chilik fearfully.

"You must resolve to sanctify Hashem's Name in all of your performances," the famous *chazzan* shot at him. "If you ask Hashem to give you a good voice so that you can draw Jews closer to their Father in Heaven, and to bring back wayward sons, the gates of Heavenly assistance will be opened for you at their very widest."

He's talking like R' Avrumele! Chilik could not believe his ears.

"You can go back to singing like before," Koussovitzky said, thumping him on the shoulder. "Just don't sing at the top of your lungs and don't shout like a voice in the desert. I would like to pray along with you on Shabbos morning at the *beis midrash* of the Maharshal. Please organize the choir."

It was a Shabbos unlike any Lublin had ever experienced before. From dawn onwards, hundreds upon hundreds of Jews began streaming towards the large synagogue of R' Shlomo Luria, the revered Talmud commentator. Not a single notice had heralded the concert, but the news spread like wildfire in a cornfield.

The early risers were stunned to find that they were not the first ones. Those who were even more eager and enterprising had remained in the *beis midrash* all night to be assured of a place. Better to be safe than sorry.

Half an hour before the designated time for prayers, it was impossible to push a pin into the place, and people continued to come. Thousands remained outside, their ears perked with tense anticipation so as not to lose a single note of the rare event.

"How grateful we must be that the voice of our child prodigy, Chilik Horowitz, has not yet changed," wrote Mottel Morgenstern, top reporter for the newspaper *Moment*, who was present at this unique concert. "I have never heard such symphonic perfection before in my life, and doubt that I ever will again. Cantor Koussovitzky with his powerful tenor, accompanied by the second voice of Yechiel Horowitz, the ultimate soprano, is no less than a fantastic dream! Koussovitzky sang *Mimkomcha Malkeinu* and Chilik accompanied him. Baruch Horowitz provided the baritone and Mendele, the second voice, was the bass. Moshe Minsky was the unidentified *kop shtimme* and in the background were two choirs, the adult choir of R' Avrumele, and the children's choir of the Maharshal synagogue which was especially arranged for Chilik.

"The choirs sang in harmony of two, three, four, six, eight and even ten different voices! Actually, in a medley of innumerable voices. The voices surrounded us and came from all sides, above and below, from the front and the back, from the right and the left... In all the octaves, with infinite variations and nuances, with the proper modulation, a full, perfect harmonious ensemble.

"I know that on Shabbos it is forbidden to weep," concluded the deeply stirred Mottel Morgenstern, "but I shamelessly admit that I cried like a baby. And weeping together with me were hundreds upon hundreds of men, overcome by this heavenly musical experience. This must be what the singing was like when the *Leviim* sang in the *Beis Hamikdash*."

"So Mottel Morgenstern also knows about the song of the *Leviim*?" said Chilik as he laid the newspaper down on the table and looked at R' Eckstein expectantly.

"Why are you surprised, *yingele*? It's no secret," laughed R' Shlomo comfortably.

A year ago Baruch had told him about the talk R' Avrumele had had with Yechiel before his *bar-mitzvah*. This would be a good time to elaborate a bit on the subject, he thought, not realizing where his words would lead...

To Chilik's catastrophe, to his personal holocaust.

"What do you know about the *Leviim*'s musical instruments?"

"I've heard about the tambourine and the harp," Chilik said, leaning all the way back to study the ceiling while he racked his brain to remember. "But what difference does it make?"

"I know what the *Leviim* sang in the *Beis Hamikdash*," R' Eckstein suddenly burst out, as if he had discovered the hidden secret just now. "Only the words, of course, not the melody," he added, looking at Chilik, who was shrugging his shoulders.

"Almost every baby knows that. They sang the Psalm of the Day," said Chilik disdainfully.

"Correct. But they also sang the other psalms of *Tehillim*, the Book written by the Divine songster, King David." R' Eckstein's eyes grew cloudy and an air of mystery spread over his face.

Many psalms in *Tehillim* begin with the introductory word of *mizmor, shir, michtam, lamnatzeiach* and similar words, which indicate that they were sung by the choir of the *Beis Hamikdash*.

"The conductors stood on the top step with the choir below them. Do you know how many instruments they used?"

The question was rhetorical. R' Eckstein was clearly in his element now. "There were violins, harps, cymbals, horns, trumpets, flutes, organs, drums... They sang the psalms to the accompaniment of all these instruments.

"Just try to imagine," said R' Eckstein, his gaze bright as fiery coals, "the double mouthed flute they had which produced a humming sound like that of a swarm of bees. It was called the *nechilos*. They had many other instruments that are lost, instruments which produced natural sounds, not the discordant, false notes of modern-day instruments."

"Which instruments were lost?" asked Chilik with interest.

"Oh, a great many. They had a special one called *yedusun*. I have no idea what it was like. And the *gittis, alamos, shoshanim, machol* and many more."

Chilik tried to digest this information. R' Shlomo apparently knew more about musical technique than merely how to expel one's breath while singing.

"How many voices were you on Shabbos, altogether?"

"Fifty!" said Chilik proudly. He had never sung with such a large choir. R' Avrumele's had twenty members, and that was considered the maximum.

"Aha!" R' Shlomo suppressed a smile. "What an enormous choir. But do you know that Shlomo Hamelech established a choir of *Leviim* in the First Temple that numbered four thousand men?"

"Four thousand?" Chilik jumped up from his seat. "That's impossible!"

"Take a *Tanach* and check it out. Open up to *Divrei Hayamim* I, Chapter 23," said R' Eckstein with absolute confidence. "And all of them played an instrument. Every member of the choir was also a musician in the orchestra. Try to imagine how it sounded. I don't know if they all sang simultaneously, but it must have been the biggest philharmonic orchestra in the world!"

"If so, the *Beis Hamikdash* must have been all music!" Chilik said, stunned.

"Yes, there was music, but not only that. The *Beis Hamikdash* was first and foremost a House of Hashem. It was the heart and soul of the Jewish people, a sanctuary of holiness on earth. A gateway to Heaven. Sacrifices were offered up in the *Beis Hamikdash* to atone for the Jewish people. They prayed there; the Sanhedrin sat in judgment and determined the laws. And there was also singing.

"It was a different type of singing." R' Eckstein's voice grew thick. His eyes looked off into the distant past, through an imaginary time tunnel. He was now transported to Jerusalem, to the *Beis Hamikdash* of yore.

"The singing of the *Leviim* could be heard for a distance of dozens of kilometers. This was its physical, actual dimension. As for the spiritual dimension, it reverberated throughout the entire world!

"The whole world was pure and pristine because of their singing. It was a perfected world, a world aspiring to fulfill its created purpose."

"This is why we mourn the destruction of the *Beis Hamikdash*," Chilik burst out. For the first time in his life he was able to feel genuine sorrow for the Temple in Jerusalem that had been consumed by fire.

"Did you ever notice that there are certain tunes that are highly captivating, while other tunes do not move you at all?" R' Eckstein seemed to have gone off on a tangent.

"Yes, that's true."

"Do you know why? It's very simple. The closer a tune is to the original pure singing of the *Leviim*, the more it touches your soul. The further away it gets from their pure source, the more contaminated it becomes. The soul, which can recognize truth, abhors the fraud.

"We are searching for the lost music of the *Leviim*," moaned Eckstein. "We are looking for the tunes that were lost during the conflagration. When a pure-minded composer like your father concentrates and searches within himself, he becomes inspired by the ancient music which visits him, and he unites with the roots of that tune. This develops into a lovely musical movement, the offshoot of a passage that was sung and played in the *Beis Hamikdash*. This is true music.

"Everything else, all music that floats around rootlessly in the air, is no more than cacophony, a meaningless combination of sounds."

The conversation was a fateful mistake.

Chilik told his mother about his talk with R' Eckstein and she became enthusiastic. "Do you hear that, Chilik? The *Leviim* reached their peak of perfection only because they mastered musical instruments!"

"What are you driving at?"

"You know exactly. Not what I am hinting, but what I am saying explicitly, Chilik. Why don't you go back to your music instruction, to your piano and violin lessons, your flute lessons? What was permissible for the *Leviim* in ancient times is surely permissible for you."

Chilik argued. He said that the *Leviim* had not needed special sanction or permission to study music. It had been their G-dly service in the Temple.

Mirushka was not impressed by his sophistries. "I am taking you to the piano teacher tomorrow."

This time, Chilik noted, she said nothing about seeking his father's permission.

~)(~

He went back to practicing on various musical instruments until he had a perfect mastery over them. The year completed its cycle and when Chilik was seventeen, his voice changed.

"The legend called Yechiel Horowitz the Wonder Child is now a legend forever more," exulted the newspapers, which had awaited his changing voice with trepidation. "Yechiel Horowitz, the adult, is the best tenor in Poland, after the 'King,' Moshe Koussovitzky."

He was granted narrow vocal chords which turned him into a tenor. Had he possessed broad chords, he would have only reached the range of a baritone. But when he wished, Yechiel could be an excellent baritone as well as a bass.

Under R' Eckstein's tutelage, Yechiel, whose childhood nickname became eternally buried under the remains of his alto and soprano voices, learned how to use his voice and talents to their maximum.

He sang bass and bass profundo; he sang baritone when he liked, and sang tenor. He could also sing the entire range of notes of a tenor: first tenor, second tenor, lyric tenor, spinto tenor and dramatic tenor.

R' Shlomo also taught him to use the thin falsetto head voice.

"The word falsetto is like *false*. You fake your real voice and sing high and thin, different from your real voice. But see how Yossele Rosenblatt is able to turn his falsetto voice into an art in itself, how he embellishes every cantorial piece of his with it."

Rumor had it that Rosenblatt did this because of a weak heart, and his doctors' warnings not to overexert himself in singing. But Eckstein thought otherwise.

Yechiel Horowitz's star zoomed up higher and higher. The press and public opinion worshiped him blindly, but he was careful not to transgress R' Avrumele's directives, and never appeared before audiences in concert halls, only in the *beis knesses*.

The matchmakers ran after him. Really, who didn't...

At the age of eighteen, Yechiel married Ita, the highly accomplished daughter of Nachman Schneider, the wealthy industrialist of Lodz, in a resplendent wedding held in one of the grandest halls in Warsaw. All of Poland's Who's Who attended the wedding, people from all circles and streams, and, of course, the creme of both the Jewish and non-Jewish music world. It was the most talked-about wedding in Poland in 1933 (5693).

Their first son, Avigdor, born a year later, was named after his grandfather, the mystical *tzaddik*. The months rolled on leisurely, and Yechiel felt as if he had never had it so good.

And then the earth began quaking. An invitation from the Viennese Opera House arrived at Yechiel's house.

30

Yechiel Horowitz almost reached the peak of his career before turning twenty. Aside from a full command of his vocal faculties, of the resonance that he could produce from that mighty vibration box in his larynx, he also displayed a facility in everything connected to music. He mastered the violin and piano, the flute and clarinet, the trumpet and drums. He read musical notes quicker than the average person reads a newspaper, and his musical ear was so acute that he was able to identify the composer of a tune from the first opening notes. Nor could he bear any degree of discordance. "Yechiel is the calmest person I have ever met," his wife, Ita, was fond of saying, "but woe to anyone who sings off key within his hearing."

He had lately begun studying musical arrangement. A tune that underwent his treatment emerged as highly polished as a diamond. His father, Baruch, was astonished to hear the very songs he had composed in the past, his well-liked and familiar melodies, emerge from under his son Yechiel's hand many times more beautiful and perfect.

His home teemed with young and old musicians who sought to gain expertise under his tutelage or who had brought a new song to undergo his arrangement.

It was a form of compensation for Yechiel, who competed with his father and surpassed him in everything except for composition. Yechiel had also tried composing and had created several lovely melodies, but his talent in this area was a far cry from his father's legendary capacity.

"There is no comparison," concluded the Lublin public. "Baruch is a giant of a composer and a mediocre *chazzan*; Yechiel is the Number One *chazzan* in Europe but a less-than-average composer."

≈)⊂

Yechiel returned home from R' Avrumele's *beis knesses* surrounded by a crowd of admirers. It was a cold *motzaei Shabbos* evening and snow fell with stinging sharpness; it was also the first night of Chanukah. R' Avrumele had just finished lighting the first candle. Yechiel had outdone himself in honor of the occasion and the results were commensurate. The choir had sung long and well and Yechiel now felt drained and exhausted. He sought to shake off the flock of young admirers which had encircled him relentlessly from the moment he had emerged to the street. But admirers, as they always will, had no consideration for their idol's personal feelings. They regarded him as an object of their youthful enthusiasm, and they gave their feelings the appropriate release, not sensing that their bear hug had become too stifling.

"Fellows," Yechiel said, raising his arms upward, "*a gutte vach* to you and a happy Chanukah. See you tomorrow morning."

They didn't have a chance to recover before Yechiel leaped over his locked gate like an agile cat, to the laughter of the group. He wished to enter his house without a royal escort. Ita had lately complained that her young husband was bringing home guests without a limit, and that she could not run a house in such a manner.

"*A gutte vach*," Ita greeted him. "I can see that you outdid yourself tonight."

"And how!" Yechiel answered. "I'm going to sleep now."

"Before you go to sleep, you had better see what the postman brought."

"The postman? Tonight?"

"Yes. There's a telegram for you from Vienna."

"A telegram? From Vienna?"

"Yechiel, stop being a parrot. Go over to the sideboard and see what it is yourself."

He went over to the dark-red mahogany sideboard, with its clusters of ornately carved grapes on every corner. The crystal mirrors lining the cabinet lent the rest of the lavish furniture in the living room an added touch of elegance and splendor. Nachman Schneider knew which gifts to give his son-in-law.

He read the Latin letters but didn't understand much. "It's written in German, I think."

Ita leaned forward. As a young girl, her wealthy father had hired a private tutor to teach her French and German.

"Let me translate it for you."

She read the telegram with a festive air:

"The director of the Royal Opera of Vienna is honored to address the singer, the esteemed Herr Horowitz:

"Dear Mr. Horowitz,

"Allow us to send our sincere greetings. Your fame precedes you. We have heard much about you and in the estimation of the newspaper *Der Zeitung* you are considered the Number One Jewish singer in the world. It would do us great honor if you would deem to come and sing before the culture-loving Viennese public. We are most interested in inviting you to participate in a series of performances of guest artists in honor of Xmas and the end-of-the-year celebrations which are scheduled a month hence.

"As you surely know, an appearance in the Viennese Opera House is a calling card for a successful career throughout the world. This is not the place to specify the high remuneration which the opera house awards its guest performers.

"I extend my best wishes to you and hope that you will reply to our invitation affirmatively.

"Professor Gustav Spiegel, Manager, Viennese Opera House."

"That isn't a telegram," exclaimed Yechiel, somewhat shaken. "It's a letter. A cable like this costs a fortune!"

"The opera house in Vienna is willing to spend a lot of money on you." Ita was drunk with pride. "Yechiel, do you know the significance of this? The most prestigious institution in all of Europe is inviting you to appear on its stage!"

"Calm down," said Yechiel, cooling off her ardor. "You don't seriously think that I would go there, do you?"

"Well, why not?" Ita retorted with a sour expression.

"What's come over you? They're telling me to come and sing on their Xmas and New Year! Me, Yechiel Horowitz, a Lubliner *chassid*, should sing at a *goyish* festival?"

Ita lowered her head in silence. She had not been prepared for such an attack. She had been certain that Yechiel would ignore the inconvenient dates. Since when had he become such a *frummack*? Such self-righteousness and piety was not in character.

Yechiel was alarmed by her bowed head. He thought that she was insulted by the tone of rebuke in his voice. "Look here, Ita," he spoke appeasingly. "It surely is a great honor to receive such an invitation..."

"All the newspapers in the world will write it up," Ita interrupted. She could already imagine Yechiel's pictures splashed all over the front pages.

"I've had my fill of publicity and the press," he answered indifferently, but in his heart of hearts, he had his doubts if he really was sated with fame or if his appetite had only become whetted. "As a believing Jew, I am forbidden to participate in *goyishe* ceremonies. What would Tatte say; what would my mother say..."

His voice suddenly faded out. He quickly put his hand to his mouth, but it was already too late. A mischievous glint sparkled in Ita's eye. *Thanks for the idea,* she laughed to herself. *I will go tomorrow and hear what Mirushka has to say about the idea. It should be interesting...*

≈)⊆

Ita was stunned. She knew that her mother-in-law was blessed with many talents and with a sharp, quick mind. But such speed?

She had only showed her the telegram and already Mirushka had anticipated all the problems and seen all the possibilities.

"Yechiel doesn't want to go, right?"

"Very true. How did you know? Do you also read German?" Ita could not get over her rapid power of absorption.

"Since I was ten," said Mirushka proudly. "German is like my mother tongue."

"Well, what are we supposed to do?" asked Ita.

Mirushka thought for a few seconds. Ita could almost hear the cogs whirring inside her mind.

"Tell Yechiel three things," she replied quickly. "First of all, that he is right. He must not sing on a Christian holiday. But who's to stop him from singing afterwards?

"Secondly, he can grab the bull by the horns. By all means, let him appear in Vienna and sanctify Hashem's Name in public. It will be a marvelous *kiddush Hashem*; he will be able to draw so many Jews closer to their source. It's been seven years since R' Avrumule brainwashed him on the eve of his *bar-mitzvah*. He doesn't stop talking about *kiddush Hashem*.

"And thirdly, tell him to come to me as soon as possible."

Yechiel understood at once that Mirushka's long arm had already succeeded in stirring up the pot. Ita tried at first to pretend that the two reasons were the products of her own thinking, but Yechiel detected his clever mother's fingerprints in the matter. "True," she finally conceded goodnaturedly, "and she also urgently asked that you go to her."

Thus did Yechiel find himself standing, head bowed, absorbing a rich dressing-down from his mother for his foolish refusal to accept the royal invitation of the prestigious Viennese institution.

"Kings and counts bow before you and pay you homage, and you run off to your chassidic *shtiebel*," she scolded. "Yechiel, what happened to your brains? Can't you identify the signs of international success looming on the horizon? Instead of progressing, you are regressing one hundred years back!"

"What will Tatte say?" Yechiel tried to play an emotional note.

Baruch had been gone from the house for a fortnight. He had been invited to Galicia to help a well-known chassidic court assemble a large choir.

Mirushka hesitated for a moment. Now was the time to tread between the raindrops. On the one hand, she was very careful with her husband's honor, especially in the eyes of her only son. On the other hand, in her eyes, her husband lived two generations back. Many things had happened to her since she had been a pure Orthodox girl in her parents' home. The winds of Enlightenment which blew in Poland had swept up many people bigger and better than she.

"Yechiel," she finally replied, "do you want to be the heir of Yontil Klezmer, or do you want to be a world-famous singer?"

Yechiel grimaced at the suggestion. Yontil, a popular chassidic violinist and a well-known figure in the folk history of Lublin and Warsaw, was a highly talented artist who had given up great honor in order to remain a devout Jew.

"You've got to understand," Mirushka explained. "Your father is still riding along in an old-fashioned horse-and-buggy while you're already speeding on an express train."

He lifted tear-filled eyes and looked at his mother. She expected a positive answer. She had nurtured and cultivated him for twenty years in anticipation of this very moment. Here he was, on the verge of reaching the pinnacle of her hopes. Would he let go of the rope at the last minute?

He felt asphyxiated. His heart beat wildly. He would not sing in Vienna in the month of the Christian festival. But afterwards? What was so wrong about that?

R' Avrumele's warning rang in his ears, erasing the gap of seven years. "If you seek glory in your voice before gentiles in their opera houses and concert halls, you will yet sing, coerced and degraded, before Jewish enemies. You will regret it."

What had he meant?

Jewish enemies? Wait a moment… That was the solution. "Mother, you certainly know that Vienna is terribly anti-Semitic. It is full of Germans who idolize Hitler, the mad chancellor of Germany. Perhaps they will try to harm me."

"Do you see any signs of anti-Semitism in the telegram from the opera house?" Mirushka asked, shrugging her shoulders. "I don't. Don't be afraid, Yechiel. Two hundred thousand Jews live in Vienna in peace and comfort. Who would wish to harm you?"

Yechiel, cried a voice from deep inside, *don't hesitate. Grab the lifeline being thrown to you.*

Yechiel, cried out a second voice, *Tatte travels in an old-fashioned horse-and-buggy. Travel along with him. Don't ride in an express train. Speeding trains can send one hurtling into oblivion.*

This was the last cry of his conscience. But Yechiel ignored it. He felt that he could not disappoint his mother. Slowly, he agreed. Shouts of glee exploded in the house. Ita had been standing behind the door listening to the conversation between mother and son. Now she could no longer contain herself and rushed into the room with unbounded enthusiasm and exuberance.

"Yechiel, you are going to be the greatest singer in the world."

"By the way," Mirushka suddenly remembered, "you can't appear in Vienna with a name like Yechiel! It's a name the *goyim* would be unable to pronounce. From today on you're going to be Henry."

"I refuse!" shouted Yechiel in anger. "I have a nice Jewish name. Why should I be ashamed of it?"

"True, it is a Jewish name, but it is not a commercial name." Mirushka was teaching him an important business principle. "At home you will always remain Yechiel. But outside you must choose a different name for your performances, a more catchy name that's easy to pronounce, a name that expresses power. Henry is a nice name. You will be the first singer named Henry."

"Henry Horowitz?" Yechiel grimaced in disgust. "What kind of a revolting hybrid creature is that?"

"Yechiel, don't you hear me?" Mirushka lowered her voice to a whisper, as she always did when she was angry. "You are not Henry Horowitz, do you understand? You are Henry the Singer, that's all!"

≈)⌒

Baruch Horowitz remained in the Galician town for two months, and therefore knew nothing about the Viennese connection being formed by Yechiel with the encouragement of his mother and wife. Yechiel sent a reply telegram to Professor Spiegel the following day, informing him of his acceptance of the honored request. He explained that due to certain constraints, he was unable to appear on the date specified on, but he was available a month later.

"Well, what do you know," Professor Spiegel asked, showing the cable to his son, Roman. "The mouse has entered the trap… The Jew agrees. Ah! What a performance that will be!"

"Why are you so enthused, Pappa?" asked Roman, a tall, blond Aryan with sharp handsome features, that now bore a dissatisfied look. "Our Adolf says that they are a sick people, and a rotten limb must be amputated from a healthy body!" His clenched fist moved swiftly from right to left, leaving no doubt as to his intentions as how to treat a Jew who had the ill luck of falling into his clutches.

Gustav was not impressed by his zealous son's words. "Roman, you are still young. You still see the world in black and white. But there are many shades in between that allow for enjoying the performance of a Jew."

"Pappa, *ich bin den Juden feind*, I hate the Jews," declared Roman vehemently, his icy blue eyes gleaming with fire for an instant.

"Roman," said Gustav, "you are getting worked up. Anger can harm you. If you really want to know, I'll tell you the truth."

He opened up a top drawer of his massive wooden secretary and, after rummaging around briefly, found the paper he was looking for.

"Do you see this?" he waved the typed sheet. "This was written by Minister Goebbels himself. He asks me to help him prove to the entire world that Germany and Austria maintain a pleasant, congenial environment for Jews. *You must invite famous Jewish artists to appear in the opera house and theater,* he writes. *The world must be convinced that Jews are not being persecuted, neither in Germany nor in Austria,* end quote. Now you understand? I must assist Goebbels' propaganda machine. He is involved in an international campaign and I have been chosen to prove to American and British statesmen, and to the world public opinion at large, that Jews enjoy equal rights."

Roman's blue icebergs sparkled with a strange light. "I will prepare a welcome reception which he will never forget, the pretty *Jude*."

"No!" thundered Gustav. "You must reserve your Nazi zeal for a different occasion. On the contrary, you must serve as Horowitz's host when he comes; you must be his best friend."

31

Yechiel left Lublin clandestinely. To avoid being noticed, he took the midnight express to Katowitz. But his fears were unnecessary. Even his clever mother, Mirushka, who had labored for hours with his makeup, could hardly recognize him in the end.

"Yechiel," she succumbed to a fit of laughter, "excuse me, Henry, you are simply perfect!"

'Henry' studied himself in the mirror and was taken aback by the rascal who faced him. He was dressed in a short checkered suit jacket and a sports cap. He had tied his two long *payos* together on the top of his head. His beard had been chemically bleached while a pair of round rimless glasses perfected the masquerade. He did not even look like a relation of the singer, the *chassid*, Yechiel Horowitz.

For reasons of secrecy, Ita waived her strong desire to accompany him. It was clear that her presence at his side would expose his identity.

Though everything went perfectly Yechiel felt a heaviness in his heart, and despite his comfortable seat in the first-class compartment, he could not relax for even a moment.

You have a long journey ahead of you, Yechiel. No — Henry. You've got to rest before you get to Vienna, he tried to convince himself. He adjusted the small cushion under his head and leaned on the wide window sill, eyes shut.

A futile gesture. He was restless and kept changing position. He felt ill at ease and he knew exactly why.

Nonsense. R' Avrumele doesn't know a thing about this trip to Vienna. He doesn't know and will never find out.

He was afraid. This trip would serve as a springboard to exceptional world fame. But instead of feeling the pleasure of anticipation, he was full of fears. He was afraid of the elderly Jew in Lublin who had given him a warning seven years before and had sealed off the soaring of his spirit and imprisoned his soul forever inside his *shtiebel*.

Forever?

Here he was, leaving the spiritual prison. He was going forth to embrace the entire world and its fullness, to become acquainted with new people, different approaches, varied experiences.

But deeper, under all of these thoughts, lay the thought that did not succeed in penetrating through the many strata that covered it. It was an ephemeral thought that dared not express itself in so many words:

He's right, R' Avrumele. He's right and you will yet pay the price!

This tiny glimmer of a thought which had not succeeded in blazing a trail upward into his consciousness did, nevertheless, disturb his peace of mind. He constantly shifted his position from right to left and left to right, to the annoyance of his seatmates in the compartment. Finally, one burst into vociferous complaint: "Please be still. I paid a lot of money for peace and quiet, and you are constantly making noise!"

Yechiel froze in his place, overcome by guilt. From that moment on, he hardly budged. But he did not succeed in shutting his eyes and resigned himself hopelessly to the bitter knowledge that he would reach Vienna worn out by the twenty-four-hour journey.

Somewhere, in the back compartments of the train, a young man took a seat. He intently studied a small picture he held in his hand, trying to imprint the features of its subject upon his mind. When he was certain he knew them by heart, he ripped up the photo and threw the pieces under his seat.

‿◠

The train hurtled rapidly along its long, winding route which crossed Dembitz, Cracow, and towards morning, reached the last stop. 'Katowicze,' announced the signs. Jews called the place Katowitz. Most of the passengers had reached their final destination, but many had to continue on and rushed forward with their luggage to the train on the parallel track.

"Is this the train to Vienna?" Yechiel asked one of the men sitting in the first-class compartment. When the latter replied in the affirmative, he spread out on the upholstered seat and shut his eyes. After six exhausting hours of restless travel, Yechiel finally sank into a deep sleep. The tumult about him was great. The door opened and closed, passengers entered and left, but he slept on. He did not notice one particular man open the door and study the passengers one by one, dismissing each with a negative expression, until finally letting his gaze rest upon Yechiel. He stopped for a moment, and then shook his head once again.

The loud whistle announced the resumption of the journey. The engine pulled sixteen additional cars after it on its route from Katowitz to Susnowitz, and from there to Tichi. An hour later, the train crossed the bridge spanning the Visla River. Another hour's travel brought them to the border town of Ostrova.

"Halt! Border ahead!" screamed the signs in red and black.

Yechiel awoke with a start. "We're entering Czechoslovakia," one of the passengers noted. "Prepare your passport."

He held his breath and felt icy metal fingers gripping his heart. How had he not thought of it?

The picture on the passport was that of Yechiel Horowitz, a typical young chassidic Jew with long sidelocks, and without eyeglasses. The latter was no problem to explain away. He could also show his *payos* to the officer. But what would he say about the change of colors? The passport stated: 'Hair color — brown', but his beard was light blond.

The border control would throw him directly into prison.

"Excuse me," he jostled his seatmate roughly. "My stomach." He held his stomach with a genuine gesture of pain and rushed off to the bathroom.

He burst out of the bathroom ten minutes later. None of the passengers looked at the door, which was to his good fortune. He had partially returned to his original appearance. His beard looked catastrophic. The blond bleaching powder stuck to it like a plague, and even though he had washed it several times with soap and water, many strands still remained blondish.

"So what?" he thought encouragingly. "There are lots of people who have mixed hair color."

He strode cautiously to the last car and mingled in the crowd. Two unbelieving eyes stared at him from the opposite seat. *That's the very man I'm looking for! Where did he suddenly pop up from?* thought the young stranger.

Yechiel remained sitting in the last compartment until after passport control. To his good fortune, the Czech soldier was half asleep and barely glanced at his passport.

After the inspection, he did not dare return to the first-class car. What he saw in the cracked and distorted mirror in the bathroom was enough. He looked strange, neither here nor there. He could not possibly appear thus among first-class passengers.

The train climbed up the Sudeten mountains and crossed through Zilina, Tranchin, Pishtini, and by afternoon, came to a stop in Bratislava, or Pressburg, as it was called by the Jewish inhabitants. This was the city of the Chasam Sofer.

A group of loud and merry youths got on the train. They looked like *yeshivah bachurim,* and from their conversation, Yechiel learned that they were studying in the Pressburg yeshivah.

"Where are you going?" he asked them cautiously.

"What a question? To Vienna, of course."

"What is a group of yeshivah students looking for in Vienna?"

"A funny question, Yonoson," Yechiel's seatmate said to his friend, a burly youth who had to stand for lack of space. He was so tall he almost reached the ceiling. "What do you know! Here's a Jewish young man who must have fallen off the moon; he's asking what we're looking for in Vienna."

Yonoson laughed. This man with the oddly colored beard must surely be ignorant. "Haven't you ever heard of Yechiel Horowitz?" he said con-descendingly.

"Yechiel Horowitz," parroted Yechiel's seatmate in a strong American accent. "It was worth coming all the way from America for this alone! Just to hear Yechiel Horowitz sing. He's the Number One Jewish singer in the whole world and this yokel asks his stupid questions..."

This was the first time that Yechiel heard of his worldwide reputation. He felt overcome by an intoxicating sweetness and a strong desire to re-veal himself before his unidentified admirers, but, on second thought, chose to remain incognito.

The border inspection on the Austrian side was said to be very strict. The soldiers studied every passport slowly and thoroughly, and Yechiel was certain that this time he would be caught.

The sun set and the evening shadows spread over the wooded hills. The dim electric light in the ceiling of the car did not help the soldier's weary eyes. He had already checked hundreds of passports and wanted to finish the job quickly. He briefly scanned Yechiel's passport picture. "*Gut,*" he murmured, and let the passport fall into his hands. Yechiel breathed free. The train crossed the border after a two-hour stop. He was now in Austria.

His American neighbor turned out to be an inveterate gossip. He in-troduced himself as Yosef — Joe — Berniker, and pointed out his friends by name. Yechiel was interested in the gigantic one. "That's Yonoson Fisher, a budding *maskil*, a cultured fellow, the only one in yeshivah who has any interest in classical music." Joe was very gener-ous with his information.

"How did you learn about the performance?"

"From the posters."

The streets of Pressburg were full of notices advertising this perfor-mance, he offered. Not plastered by the Opera House, of course. That elite institution had never sought Jewish patronage. The Jewish *Gemeinde* (community) of Vienna had taken the trouble to inform its neighboring city of the upcoming event.

"A week of performances, man! Do you understand what that means?

A pity we can only attend the first one, two days from now," said Joe, looking downcast.

As an afterthought, he added, "I just don't understand one thing. Why is he calling himself Henry, all of a sudden? What's the connection between Yechiel and Henry?"

≈≈

Yechiel had difficulty slipping away from the lively group once they left the train at the busy Viennese terminal. He went to a public convenience and emerged, camouflaged by his original masquerade. Thus attired, he set off to Professor Spiegel's house.

The unknown figure that followed all of his steps so carefully crossed the broad avenues and the snow-covered gardens.

Yechiel reached Franz Josef Strasse and looked for No. 25. He felt himself choking back a cry of wonder. "And I thought that I lived in luxury!" he murmured.

This was not a house; it was a castle! A three-story mansion, protected from the eyes of passersby by rows of ancient oak trees in a gigantic garden with luxuriant growth of many different kinds of flora. It boasted several marble fountains which now stood beneath a layer of snow, the water frozen in their basins.

He pulled the door bell and a moment later, a tall, imposing figure appeared to open the gate.

Roman Spiegel stretched out a hand in greeting. "You must be Henry Horowitz," he said in impeccable Hebrew. "*Baruch haba.*"

≈≈

The succeeding hours taught Professor Gustav Spiegel that Henry Horowitz had not earned his reputation as the Number One Jewish singer in vain.

They sat in leather-upholstered armchairs in the resplendent living room, sipping hot tea in front of the glowing fireplace. Yechiel agreed to the tea out of courtesy, but declined anything else for reasons of *kashrus*. The German professor understood.

They spoke in German, and Yechiel now understood why Mirushka had insisted that he learn German in private lessons.

Spiegel cautiously asked Henry which pieces he had planned to sing, and almost fainted when he heard that Yechiel had not prepared anything.

"I am unfamiliar with opera. I only know Jewish songs. But I can learn," he replied lightly.

"You can sing Jewish music on the opening night," Spiegel agreed. "We posted advertisements in the Jewish quarter and all the tickets have been sold out. There is a great demand for more, and we are considering arranging another evening for the Jewish public. But what about the cultured Viennese public?"

"The Jewish public is not cultured?" Yechiel asked innocently.

"Don't pick on my words," said Gustav coldly. "The Jewish public is not very interested in opera. It likes cantorial pieces and light music."

"And the general Viennese public?" Yechiel felt his way carefully.

"Ah, there is a big demand for classical concerts, operas, good theater. Our public loves culture."

Yechiel was well aware that under the surface the professor held the Jewish Viennese public in great disdain, and relegated them in his mind to the Middle Ages. This came as a surprise, as Yechiel knew that Viennese Jews had a strong affinity to the world of gentile culture, much to the strong disapproval of its rabbis. A quick thought passed through his mind: Could this be an exercise in discrimination between Jews and gentiles, trying to show Jews up as a backward, primitive and uncultured people? Was he not being an accessory to this attempt?

"Why did you come?" Gustav hurled the words at him. "If you are not prepared, what will you sing?"

"Bring me a music book," replied Yechiel complacently.

Gustav Spiegel almost fainted for the second time that evening. Yechiel absorbed within half an hour what took regular musicians an entire month to learn. The young Jew flipped through the booklet, asked a few questions, and then sang some selections.

Gustav and Roman stared at him in awe mingled with disbelief. This

Jew was good. Too good. He would overshadow all the talent they had to offer. After him, who would want to hear anyone else?

Before leaving, Yechiel borrowed a few dozen music booklets and a huge sheaf of classical opera songs. He promised Spiegel he would know them fluently by the following day, and the latter believed him, after the private performance they had already witnessed. Roman accompanied him to the Jewish hotel, Blaue Donau, which was not far from the Jewish quarter.

"What do you do during the day?" asked Yechiel.

"Oh, lots of things," replied Roman in perfect Hebrew.

Yechiel had been curious about this blond man since his surprising welcome some hours before. "Why... where did you learn Hebrew? he asked, hoping he sounded curious but not rude.

"Why are you so surprised? Here you are, a Polish Jew, speaking a fluent German."

"Yes, but..." Yechiel was baffled.

"I studied the Bible in the original," boasted Roman. "At the age of sixteen I was tested at the *gymnasium* on the entire Bible by heart."

"And what do you do now?"

"I am studying in the Academy of Music. I am learning to conduct. I read a lot, give private lessons in mathematics and manage the opera house together with my father." Roman insisted on speaking Hebrew. Yechiel only knew *lashon kodesh*, ancient Hebrew with a different pronunciation, and following along took great effort.

"Do you sing?" Yechiel fired his spontaneous question, but immediately regretted it. He could tell that he had accidentally stepped upon a sensitive issue. Roman looked at him with burning eyes but didn't say a word.

32

H enry's first performance was a historic event that would long be remembered in the annals of Jewish Vienna. Masses of people began streaming towards the opera house before evening; surprisingly, there were many non-Jews among them.

The huge auditorium was packed long before the performance was scheduled to begin and hundreds gathered outside, trying in vain to obtain a ticket. Speculators had already sold their last tickets hours before at astronomical prices, and there were none to be had at any cost.

Yechiel climbed up to the stage from the steps behind the curtain, his heart pounding. He had held numerous rehearsals with the orchestra and choir for two days but he was still as excited as a child. He had never seen such size and splendor. Heavy velvet purple curtains hung in gathered folds along all the walls of the auditorium and crystal chandeliers sparkled brilliantly, lending the place a royal atmosphere. The Polish halls which Yechiel had seen were stables compared to this.

The orchestra sat on the left side of the huge stage. It was composed of seventy-five musicians, their music sheets ready on stands before them. The instruments ran the full range, from pianos and saxophones to harmonicas and flutes. But the dominant feature were the string instruments, which were fully represented, beginning with the violins, all twenty of them; five violas, two cellos, and six contrabass, producing the lowest sound of all the stringed instruments.

The choir spread behind them, a huge body of one hundred and fifty voices, seventy men and eighty children.

The children's choir had been forced upon the opera house's managers. Yechiel had stubbornly refused to sing with women in the choir, and these were replaced for the children's choir of the Academy of Music to fill in the necessary alto and soprano voices.

It was a major production, of the kind that only Vienna excelled in. And 'Henry' was the star, the highlight of the evening. All eyes were riveted upon him alone.

Among the crowd of thousands was one who had little or no interest in music of this sort. A lusty beer-hall tune, accompanied by a foaming glass, was all the culture he needed. Still, his Lubliner employer had promised him a lot of money to keep tabs on Yechiel Horowitz — too much to turn down.

≈)⌒

'Henry' outdid himself that evening, and the audience was electrified. He appeared in full evening dress, as befit the cultural event, and wore the high cantorial hat that was the accepted style. Thousands of people turned their opera glasses upon the tall, imposing figure highlighted by a pale beam of stage light. From time to time, the glasses would be removed after having become suspiciously damp. Henry and his choir, together with the Viennese Philharmonic Opera Orchestra, were an overwhelming combination which left everyone opened mouthed with amazement and wonder. People felt that this was a one-time event, close to the celestial singing of angels.

Professor Gustav Spiegel and his son, Roman, sat in a private box off the balcony, viewing the performance from large field glasses.

"I have never heard the likes of this in my life," Gustav admitted honestly, hand upon his heart. "That Jew puts all of our artists into his back pocket. None of them can achieve half of the quality of his voice. What a beautiful voice, a dream."

Roman didn't know what to say, and sat in angry silence. He wondered how the Jew would react to his particular hobby. Would he admit that it surpassed his own skill?

The second evening was even more successful than its predecessor. This time Henry sang for the greater Viennese public, but, again, many hundreds of Jews came to enjoy the excellent opera, a production of William Tell.

Henry took the part of William's father, who was forced by command of the robber chief to shoot an arrow into the apple sitting on his son's head. He also starred in additional roles. Henry changed his costume five times during the course of the evening and was surprised, himself, at his amazing command of all areas of opera performance. During a momentary lull, he discovered that the conductor was none other than Roman Spiegel. In the front row of the balcony reserved for the aristocracy, Henry spied Gustav Spiegel, who winked at him in a friendly manner. Next to him sat none other than the Chancellor of Austria, Dr. Kurt von Schoshnig, in grand splendor. The Defense and Police Minister, Dr. Arthur Seis Inquart, sat at his left. The entire top government echelon was represented.

Henry stopped for a moment, thunderstruck, but immediately resumed his composure and continued to sing in a mighty voice that shook the ancient walls of the opera house. The audience reacted with stormy applause that was not at all in character with the cold, proper and reserved Viennese mien.

The next two evening performances took place after Shabbos. Henry let the Viennese public wait patiently for three days and spent Shabbos in the midst of the Jewish community, which welcomed him with warmth and affection. He was honored with leading the services in the Schiff Shul, and moved the huge crowd of worshipers to tears with his ardent prayers that rose up from the depths of his heart. "When a Jew like you sanctifies the Shabbos upon such an occasion, he is sanctifying Hashem's Name among gentiles!" said the rabbi of the congregation, R' Shimon Furst, with deep feeling.

He broke the box office for the next four concerts which he granted to the Viennese public. Henry's success was sweeping; the Jewish virtuoso's performance was electrifying and became the talk of the entire city.

The press went wild, and Henry's pictures, alongside full-page articles, appeared on the front pages of all the papers. Henry's modest room at the Blaue Donau Hotel was filled with reporters demanding interviews, since no newspaper dared appear without some scoop connected with Vienna's newest rage.

The New York Times outdid them all. In a prominently placed article, Bob Zealand, their reporter stationed in Vienna, crowned Henry with an unforgettable title: "Mister Music."

❦

Henry was about to leave Vienna. After an encore evening for the Jewish community, his week of performances came to an end. He had come to Spiegel's mansion to complete the financial arrangements. His eyes almost popped out of their sockets. The check made out to him was so huge that it boggled his imagination. He knew that if he told his friends in Lublin, they wouldn't believe him. On the spot, he decided to donate half of it to the poor of Lublin.

"The time has come to part," Gustav said, shaking his hand warmly. Yechiel was somewhat repulsed by the contact, as if a cold, slimy creature had just touched him. "Before you go, Roman would like to invite you to his room."

He went down with the professor to the ground floor. There his host showed him a white carved wooden door. Gustav bowed and gestured to Henry to enter.

Yechiel was attacked by a sudden fear. A dull sense of danger gripped his guts, as if a murderer with drawn knife awaited him inside. *Nonsense,* he thought to himself, dismissing the disturbing thought from his mind. *Roman has been very pleasant. What's come over you? Have you turned paranoid?*

He entered the room with assumed nonchalance.

Roman was waiting for him, a smile on his face. "I wanted to show you my hobby," he said, opening a small door in a side cabinet and removing a large glass bowl.

Yechiel stared into the bowl at three eggs. They were decorated with tiny black marks. When he looked closer, he saw that they were miniature letters, the like of which he had never seen in his entire life.

"Micrography," explained Roman. "This is my hobby. I write mainly on eggs, but also on wheat kernels. Here, look at this." He rotated an egg carefully on his fingertips. "Look what's written here."

Yechiel drew near. Roman gave him a magnifying glass and he was able to read:

"Bereishis bara Elokim..."

"It's in Hebrew," he said, amazed.

"The entire Book of Genesis on one egg," Roman boasted.

"How can you do that?" wondered Yechiel.

"The same way you sing," said Roman challengingly. He was balancing the scorecard with the arrogant Jew from Lublin. "This is my talent, a talent I developed and perfected."

"Is the egg hollow?"

"Yes. I empty out the contents."

"How come it doesn't break?"

"It's a complicated technique that you wouldn't understand. Perhaps some day I'll tell you more about it. But why waste time? Here, I wanted to give this to you as a goodbye gift."

He removed one of the eggs with a loving motion and laid it in Yechiel's palm. Yechiel was shaken to discover his own likeness in miniature, composed of tiny letters which spelled out the verses of the Book of *Tehillim*.

"I made note of the fact that in your performance before the Jewish public all the songs you sang were from the Psalms, so I decided to dedicate this Book to you in your own likeness."

Yechiel was overcome with amazement and shook Roman's hand heartily. "I've acquired a true friend!" he said ceremoniously. "I have a true friend in Vienna."

Roman wrapped the egg carefully in a skein of flax and laid it on a soft velvet lining in a round metal box. "Watch over this egg. It is a souvenir from me."

⁓⁓

The ceremonies were not yet over. In the evening, shortly before he left the city, Yechiel was picked up by a limousine and taken to the opera house. This mode of transportation was a luxury only the very wealthy allowed themselves, or a privilege provided only to special guests of honor, such as Henry Horowitz, for example.

Present and waiting in the office were the Minister of Defense and Police and the three managers of the establishment. In an impressive ceremony, they presented Yechiel with a certificate of honor, duly embellished and framed. It read:

> The Opera House of Vienna is proud to bestow this certificate of honorary membership to the famous singer, Mr. Henry Horowitz, as a token of its esteem.
>
> In the name of the numerous citizens of Vienna, we are proud to express our sentiments of thanks to Mr. Henry Horowitz, the giant of Polish song.

The certificate was already signed and framed, and Yechiel accepted it with care. The cameras flashed and commemorated the occasion for future generations.

≈⌒

"I have a true friend in Vienna." Gustav and Roman held their stomachs in laughter after the limousine bearing the music idol had drawn away. "If he only knew what kind of 'true friends' we were."

Dr. Seim Inquart silenced them. "The main thing is that you discharged your mission. You did a wonderful service for our beloved Fuehrer."

His arm shot out in the Nazi salute. All those present rose to their feet at the sound of the chancellor's revered name, Adolf Hitler.

"I'm curious to know if Henry will bother to read the entire text I wrote on the egg," chortled Roman from a corner of the room.

"What did you write?"

"Half the Book of Psalms in Hebrew."

"And what else?" asked Gustav. His Roman had surely planted some trap. He always had such ingenious ideas.

Roman told them. They all laughed in satisfaction.

≈)(≈

The train set out on its long journey back to Poland via Czechoslovakia. Yechiel had learned his lesson from the first trip and before embarking removed all signs of camouflage. He even released his two long *payos* from the top of his head and let them dangle down the sides of his face.

He sat in one of the last cars, a fact that greatly eased the surveillance of one particular person who studied his moves from behind a newspaper. No, he was not mistaken. With the long sidelocks, this singer looked just like the picture he had been given. He would have a lot to report in Lublin. Many things to tell...

33

An anonymous stranger knocked upon R' Avrumele's door after midnight. The elderly rabbi was ensconced in a rickety armchair and half sat, half leaned on the table. His eyes, red from a chronic lack of sleep, were fixed with intense concentration upon the yellowed pages of an old, worn *Gemara*. One of the boys who took turns sleeping in his house and attending the revered rabbi awoke at the sound and leaped towards the door in long strides so that the Rebbe's rest not be disturbed. He did not know that every night, while he himself was fast asleep, the Rebbe studied page after page, occasionally checking if his young attendant was sleeping deeply and if he was well covered.

"Let me in to see the Rebbe," demanded a stout figure wrapped in a black silk scarf around the lower part of his face.

The youth was taken aback. He slammed the door in the person's face and ran to ask his master what to do.

"Let him come in," said R' Avrumele casually.

Only when he was standing right by the table did the stranger remove the scarf from his face. The Rebbe's surprised eyes could now identify Shalom Travitzky.

"What has brought you here in the middle of the night?" he asked in astonishment.

"Rebbe, I have some important information for you." Shalom rolled his eyes upward until only the whites could be seen. "Someone in our community is breaking all barriers of decency."

"And this can't wait until the morning?" asked the astute Rebbe, suspicious of Shalom's sudden religious zeal.

Shalom did not want to reveal his real reasons. "I only substantiated it a short while ago."

"What is it all about?"

Shalom told the Rebbe the news. He launched into a fully detailed account of Yechiel Horowitz's visit to Vienna and the concerts he had held before thousands of non-Jews, men and women, which breached all the accepted norms of modesty and decency in the Jewish community. "Can you imagine, holy Rebbe, that Yechiel is ashamed of his Jewish name, and in all of the notices publicizing his performance throughout the streets of Vienna he appeared as Henry. Just 'Henry', nothing more."

"And what is the source of all this information?" asked the Rebbe in a singsong voice.

Shalom thought he heard a note of enthusiasm in the Rebbe's voice, and he was swept up with emotion. "I sent a person to watch him. He followed him from the moment he left Lublin until he returned."

"Really!" The Rebbe was shocked. "Who was this spy?"

"Oh, some professional non-Jewish detective whom I hired and paid well. He used to work for the police."

"How did the man know whom to follow?" The Rebbe would not let up. Full of self-importance, Shalom told how he had given him a portrait of Yechiel.

The rabbi sank into thought. His eyes closed and Shalom thought that he had fallen asleep. Half an hour later, R' Avrumele opened his eyes and looked straight at Shalom. Shalom shuddered beneath his severe, reproving gaze. "Shalom'ke, come here," he said, wagging a finger.

Shalom drew closer. His face was bathed with perspiration; he felt that the Rebbe was dissatisfied with him.

"You're a Torah scholar, aren't you?" the rebbe said in a weary voice. "You are thoroughly versed in entire tractates."

"I know how to learn a little," said Shalom with assumed modesty.

"Your rosh yeshivah, R' Zalman Schreiber, told me that he has set his eye on you to become his son-in-law."

Shalom blushed with pleasure. The happy rumor had reached his ears as well, and now that R' Avrumele verified it, there was no doubt that it was true.

"Why aren't you happy with what you have?" the Rebbe changed the direction of the conversation with surprising sharpness. "Under your father's prompting, you have dedicated yourself to a single purpose in life: to ruin Yechiel Horowitz. This jealousy is driving you mad," the Rebbe whispered. "You are prepared to pay a fortune for detectives to watch all of Yechiel's movements, at the very same time that all the papers in the world are stepping all over themselves to report in elaborate detail all of Horowitz's public appearances. Did you think that I needed your detectives? Fool that you are!"

Shalom wanted to flee from the room. The words hit him like a cold shower. He suddenly understood that the elderly rabbi was wide awake and fully informed, far more than he had imagined. He had his own sources of information.

Shalom did not imagine the real reason for R' Avrumele's surveillance of the singer. Yechiel was the apple of the Rebbe's eye. He watched over him like a mother hen.

"No one has appointed you a guardian over Lublin Jewry," the Rebbe continued to lash at him with his sharp remarks. "'A rotting of bones', that's what jealousy is. You are destroying yourself, you are wasting your time and forfeiting all pleasure in life just because of the success of your former friend, Yechiel Horowitz. You are ruining your life through aggravation. Envy will never turn you into a singer like Yechiel. But it will cause you to lose all the good that you do possess!"

"I wanted so much to be a singer like Yechiel!" Shalom said, suddenly bursting into tears. "I've envied him ever since he was a little boy standing on the *paranche* on Friday night."

"Now you're speaking the truth, at least," said the Rebbe with delicate irony. "You're not pretending to be religiously zealous for Hashem's sake. This is your entire error. You are not zealous — you're jealous! And this is a clear sign that your faith is shaky and its foundations unstable."

"Why does the Rebbe accuse me of such things?" he whispered weakly.

"If you truly believed with all your heart that everything that happens in this world is through the direct providence and guidance of Hashem, you would know that He provides you with what you deserve, and provides your friend with what he deserves. Then you would not be envious of Yechiel's singing talent just as he does not envy you your success in Torah study!"

The Rebbe was thoughtful. He considered adding that Shalom should really be happy for Yechiel. He should be happy that Yechiel was blessed with the power of song in the same measure that he should be happy with his own lot. But he knew that he could not ask that of this creature consumed by jealousy standing before him. It was beyond him to rise that high. Instead, the rebbe dismissed him with a wave of his hand.

Shalom had heard things he had never known. He had never considered matters in this perspective. He thought them over on his way home, but in the end remained fixed in his own opinion. He did not absorb the Rebbe's lesson and made no attempt to carry out his advice. A few days later, he remembered the nocturnal visit to the Rebbe as an unfortunate episode, no more. He continued to weave dreams of getting Yechiel off the track of success, thus unknowingly preparing Yechiel's escape from the clutches of imminent death, and his own survival a few years later.

The next day after prayers, R' Avrumele asked Yechiel to come to him in the afternoon. When they were alone, the Rebbe inquired where he had been the previous Friday night.

"I was in Vienna," he said, blushing suddenly.

"*Shalom aleichem,*" said the Rebbe, extending his delicate hand. "And what brought a Jew to Vienna?"

"I went there to sing before the public," said Yechiel simply.

"All the way to Vienna, just to sing?"

Yechiel had understood from the start that the Rebbe already knew everything and was only leading him on, stage by stage. He played along according to R' Avrumele's own rules.

"I was invited."

"By whom?"

Enough! Yechiel had decided to skip several steps in this annoying dialogue. "I made a tremendous *kiddush Hashem* in Vienna. I went to draw assimilated Jews closer to a life of Torah. I kept Shabbos openly with the knowledge of many non-Jews."

"How does one draw assimilated Jews closer?" the Rebbe asked innocently.

"By singing songs of faith before them, songs of adherence, of the soul. Rebbe, you should have seen how thousands of Jews, alienated from religion, sang these songs with feeling, with tears in their eyes, songs like 'I will not die, for I will live to sing the works of Hashem', 'From out of the straits, I called to Hashem' and 'For it is our life'."

"And where are they?"

"Who?"

"Those assimilated Jews whom you were *mekarev*. Where are they now?"

Yechiel grasped the sting fully. "Rebbe, I sowed the seeds. They must be left to germinate."

The Rebbe took Yechiel's hand in both of his and pressed them warmly to his heart. "Yechiel, *mein kindt.* You dug yourself a deep pit there in Vienna. You went there, not intending to influence Jews but to further your own career. You can still draw back. Come back!"

Yechiel was shocked by the strong words. "Rebbe," he protested heatedly, "I caused a tremendous sanctification of Hashem's Name. A *goy* named Roman Spiegel wrote the Book of *Tehillim* upon an egg, in my honor, so deeply moved was he!"

"What?" It was the Rebbe's turn to be shocked. "A non-Jew wrote the *Tehillim* for your sake?"

"Yes, and that's not all. It was in my own likeness, upon a hen's egg," answered Yechiel proudly.

"Destroy it immediately!" shouted R' Avrumele, agitated. Yechiel had never seen him so upset.

"Why?"

"Don't ask questions," the Rebbe shouted again hoarsely. "*Destroy it immediately!*"

Yechiel returned home. He opened the box, his hands shaking. His look caressed the egg covered with its painstakingly small marks. He studied the verses which formed his likeness and tried to decipher the tiny words.

"Be gracious to me, Hashem, in Your kindness; in Your great mercy, erase my sins," he succeeded in making out an entire verse. His eyes hurt from the concentrated effort.

It was incredible. That a gentile, in a Christian city like Vienna, should write verses in such miniature letters, in Hebrew, upon eggs!

He stood there for a long time, deep in thought. He tried to understand the Rebbe's words, especially his warning that it was not too late to turn back. To turn back from what?

A sheet of grey clouds hovering over the Lublin skies suddenly parted, and through the rift shone the reddish beams of sunset. He stood there, bathed in this light, the egg held in his hand, staring at the pedestrians below. He finally shook his head and laid the egg carefully back upon its soft lining.

❧

The invitation from Dr. Blyzhynsky was not long in coming. "Your performance in Vienna has caused tremendous waves throughout Europe," wrote the manager of the Lublin opera house. "And I ask, would you refuse to grant the residents of your own native city the pleasure you granted to the Viennese public?"

As usual, when faced with such dilemmas Yechiel found his way to his mother. He simply could not make any critical decisions on his own. He needed his mother to tell to him what to do.

"What a question!" Mirushka exclaimed enthusiastically. She did not know that Dr. Blyzhynsky had tried to draw her son to him ten years before. "Yechiel, Vienna opened the gates of the world to you. Keep up your good work. I expect great things from you. But not here."

"Then where?"

"In America, of course, my simple child," Mirushka laughed good-naturedly. "Did you think for a moment that you could remain here in backwater Poland? The great and wonderful continent of America was created for giants like you!"

≈⊃⊂

Yechiel accepted the invitation of the Lublin opera's manager. He began giving concerts here and there before huge audiences, though he often refused grand opportunities. He was afraid of R' Avrumele, and finally understood what he had meant when he had said that it was not too late to turn back. For two years he straddled the two worlds, but he was finally swept up by his tremendous success. The Polish audiences idolized him. He performed a repertoire of popular songs and opera, accompanying himself with most of the known musical instruments, and outdid himself every time anew.

In the end, he committed himself to a contract with Karol, the impresario who had catapulted most Polish singers and actors to fame. Shortly afterwards, he acquired his new two-story home on Siroka Street.

His second son, Shaul Yitzchak, was born, and Yechiel Horowitz imagined that there was no happier person than he.

He was unaware of the constant surveillance that Shalom Travitzky had posted on him. Shalom had married the daughter of R' Zalman Schreiber the year before, and had been appointed as a *maggid shiur* in his father-in-law's prestigious yeshivah. He could have been the happiest of people. But his obsessive jealousy of Yechiel warped his mind. He spent huge sums of money in keeping tabs on Yechiel's movements and his detective, a former police officer, verified the facts: Dressed in gentile fashion, Yechiel Horowitz was appearing before mixed crowds of non-Jews in theaters and opera houses far from the Jewish quarter.

Shalom immersed himself in his next project, hiring a photographer to immortalize the star in his performances before his new audiences, and circulating the pictures in public. He would blacken Yechiel's face throughout Jewish circles until he would be forced to flee or to stop singing altogether.

⋙⋘

There was another detective assigned to follow Yechiel on the night when he returned from the Lublinska Sahl.

Thadeus Mazoveitzky, the foremost Polish singer, had felt himself threatened of late. He was about to lose his crown to the unknown Jew who had suddenly catapulted from the ghetto and launched himself with meteoric speed upon the Polish public.

"You are very good, Thadeus," one of his close friends had said, slapping him on the back in a moment of candor as they sat drinking their mugs of foaming beer in a pub on Lipova Street. "But what can you do if the Jew sings far better than you?"

Thadeus almost choked. He coughed violently and the beer ran out of his nostrils in a foamy stream. He looked ridiculous.

"He sings better than me?" he asked, still gurgling helplessly, trying to rid himself of the liquid that still remained in his windpipe, threatening to choke him.

"Of course. Go and hear him for yourself," suggested the friend.

Thadeus already despised Yechiel, but after he heard him in the Lublin opera house performing classical pieces together with a choir, and witnessed the audience screaming and stamping its feet with wild enthusiasm, his hatred reached the boiling point and he resolved to take action. This accursed Jew must be eliminated before he pushed him aside.

He went to Warsaw and hired 'The Professional,' a nonpareil expert gangster, for five thousand zloty. He latched on to Yechiel like a powerful magnet. He followed him that night back from the Lublinska Sahl all the way to his house on 6 Siroka Street. in the Jewish quarter.

"This is where the Jew lives," he murmured in satisfaction and jotted something down in a small notebook.

The Professional's real name was Alex Petrof. Every policeman in Warsaw and Lublin had heard of him and held his picture in his wallet for identification. At the same time, they were so scared of him that no one wished to have the honor of confronting him in a dark alley.

Alex Petrof was a hired assassin.

The most deadly murderer in Poland.

34

Yechiel left for Warsaw two days after Shavuos. Karol, his impresario, had arranged a prestigious concert for him. Yechiel sat in the first-class compartment. Compared to the long trip to Vienna which he had taken two years before, this was child's play. In the second car, some twenty yards behind, sat Alex Petrof, engrossed in his daily newspaper. He was keeping an eye on things through two tiny pinholes that he had pierced in the paper.

His surveillance was professional and excellent, and thus Petrof immediately noticed the former policeman whom Shalom Travitzky had put on Yechiel's tail, and who sat in a parallel seat three rows in front of him but to the left.

"Don't forget," Shalom had warned his man as he had handed over a handsome retaining fee. "You must hire a professional photographer in Warsaw. If you return from Warsaw without two or three clear pictures of Henry during his performance before the non-Jewish audience, you needn't bother coming back."

Alex Petrof had no interest whatsoever in Henry Horowitz's public appearance in Warsaw. According to his original plan, Henry would have arrived in Warsaw as a corpse. But the presence of the small-time detective forced him to rethink his plans somewhat.

Petrof studied the train route on a map of Poland. The train was scheduled to make two stops, in Polvei and Otvotzk, from where it would continue non-stop to Warsaw.

He had planned to utilize the tumult at the stations for his purpose, and had set his mind on Otvotzk, a well-known resort town. He would approach his quarry with a knife hidden beneath his suit jacket; a quick thrust and he could easily disappear into the milling crowds.

But this second tail might spoil things, he decided. After some reflection, he came up with an even more brilliant solution. A hundred miles after Polvei, the train crossed the Vistula through an underground tunnel. Two minutes of pitch blackness were more than enough for him to complete his mission speedily and efficiently.

Alex put down the newspaper and waited impatiently for the Polvei station.

Yechiel took out an egg and mustard sandwich from his traveling bag and looked around for a sink to wash his hands.

The train stopped. "Polvei," announced the ticket collector. A few passengers got on and even fewer got off.

The deafening whistle sounded, the wheels began to move as the train left Polvei.

A short while later, the Vistula River winked at them in the distance. The greenish-silvery water was as smooth as a mirror and reflected the sun with a blinding brilliance. Alex Petrof tensed his muscles.

The train sped along on the tracks and began its descent towards the underground tunnel.

A thick darkness reigned in the train. Alex Petrof leaped forward, agile and speedy as a jaguar, and crossed over from one car to the next. He collided with an unknown figure that came towards him. A particularly heavy passenger who had become frightened by the sudden darkness had run out of the bathroom. Petrof was flung to the ground and banged his head violently. Two or three precious minutes passed before he succeeded in getting to his feet, cursing under his breath.

The train began climbing out of the tunnel and light bathed everyone in the car. The moment of surprise was lost.

⁀⁀

Not in vain did Petrof earn the title 'The Professional.' With the failure of one plan, he proceeded to hatch an alternate one.

The alternative was called Otvotzk.

Four hours later, the train stopped in the health resort. As expected, there was an unending stream of passengers boarding and leaving the train. The vacation season had already begun and hundreds of vacationers were coming and going in busy commotion.

Travitzky's detective looked as if he were deliberating what to do next. Finally he descended the iron stairs to the platform.

This is it! This is your opportunity, Alex. Now you can carry out your plan without any complications.

He leaped up from his seat and went quickly towards the first-class car. Through the glass window, between the gaps in the white silk curtain, he could make out Yechiel's form as he sat hunched over a book.

He felt for the weapon in his pocket and opened the door, prepared for action.

A tumult suddenly made itself heard from the stairs of the second car. Alex stopped for a moment and looked behind him. His blood froze.

The detective was getting into the car, accompanied by four burly policemen.

"That's him!" he shouted, pointing to the stunned Petrof. "There he is! The number one murderer in the country. Grab him!"

Petrof's eyes roved wildly, like mice caught in a trap. He tensed his muscles and gauged the distance to the nearby window, ready to spring and jump. But the police were quicker and stronger and within seconds Alex was sprawled on the floor, beaten, his hands cuffed and several of his teeth on the floor. A body search revealed two needle-sharp steel knives.

"Whom did you want to eliminate?" the policemen demanded as they pummeled him roughly with their fists. "Confess or we'll beat you to a pulp."

Stubbornly Alex refused to talk, though the blows rained down mercilessly on every inch of his body.

A circle of people surrounded the police. Suddenly Yechiel appeared, having left his compartment to find out what the commotion was all about.

When Alex saw Yechiel, something burst inside him. "Him," he groaned from a mouth oozing blood, and he pointed to the singer.

≈)⌒

Yechiel canceled his Warsaw performance. He was unable to free himself from the horror he had felt when the assassin had pointed to him. The police had dragged the criminal to the police station and there, under a hail of more blows, extracted the rest of the details from him. Poland became embroiled in a shameful scandal; Thadeus Mazoveitzky was censured and became an object of scorn and ostracism. Public opinion was thoroughly disgusted with him.

Had he tried to eliminate a different Jew he might have turned into a national hero, but to attempt to kill Henry Horowitz? The apple of Poland's eye?

It could have been Henry Horowitz's greatest hour. All of Poland sought to idolize and worship him, to raise him on high. A blink of his eye could send a troop of reporters running, and the slightest gesture of his finger caused hundreds of admirers to flock to his side.

This was an ironic situation, since anti-Semitism was running rampant in Poland at this time. The heads of the Nazi regime were considered Polish guests of honor in Warsaw and the broader public opinion was consistently hostile towards Jews.

But even the most anti-Semitic Poles were not prepared to pass up Henry Horowitz's heavenly singing.

And here, at the very height of his career, he decided to withdraw completely from the arena.

"Henry Horowitz Refuses to Sing" screamed the headlines. The papers noted the trip to Warsaw as the beginning of the crisis and commentators filled lengthy columns with their involved explanations and conjectures about the emotional breakdown he was undergoing because of the attempt on his life.

"Will He Sing or Not?" The newspapers took bets on the fateful question. Delegations came to the artist to beg him to return to the stage, but left emptyhanded.

Yechiel categorically refused to be interviewed. Not a single one of the many reporters who hounded him knew of the nocturnal visit he had paid to R' Avrumele together with his father, Baruch, immediately upon his return from Warsaw, and of the hand he had given to R' Avrumele to seal his promise never again to sing in concert halls before non-Jews, for the rest of his life!

"Henry Horowitz Has Returned to the Ghetto!" announced the disappointed newspapers when they learned that Yechiel Horowitz had repented and would no longer sing in public, except before his fellow *chassidim*, on Friday nights at R' Avrumele's *tish*, and on Shabbos morning, as the chief *chazzan* in the Maharshal's *beis knesses*.

"Yechiel," said Mirushka, her eyes dull, their light extinguished, "you've become a little boy again. A baby hiding under your elderly rabbi's *tallis*. You're afraid to deal with the big wide world."

"They wanted to murder me, Mama! I'd prefer to be a small Jewish *chazzan* and alive than a world-famous singer six feet under the ground."

"Go to America," said Mirushka sharply. "I told you that a long time ago. Poland is too small for you. In America, no one will try to kill you because of competition."

"You're right, Mama," Yechiel ended the discussion. "I will take out my immigration papers." He did intend to do so, but somehow postponed the trip to the district office of the Ministry of Interior from one day to the next. His self-confidence had been shaken by the event in the train. America frightened him. He would be lost on that gigantic continent. Who would bother to look at him there?

Another year passed. Germany began sharpening its claws in preparation for the second World War. The plan of Austria's annexation, the *Anschluss*, had already been taken out of its drawer.

"Why don't we invite that Jew, Horowitz, once more?" Professor Gustav Spiegel asked his dearly beloved son, Roman. "A visit of his now would take the minds of the American and British government off our political doings. It would throw them off and confuse the entire world."

"He doesn't sing any more, Pappa," Roman reminded him.

"He doesn't sing in backward Poland, but if we invite him, he'll sing. Oh, how he'll sing!"

"It depends. If he's read the writing on the egg, he won't come," said Roman doubtfully.

"Let's send him an invitation," said Gustav, determined, "and see what he does."

The invitation was sent with a large check enclosed, as a retainer.

Yechiel read the letter and looked at the huge sum on the check with round eyes. In the coming nights he was unable to sleep, gnawed as he was by doubts and questions, but he did not utter a word. To his fortune, his wife Ita was not home when the postman delivered the letter, so that he was spared extra pressure.

After three sleepless nights, he had arrived at a decision. He ripped up the invitation and check to tiny pieces and burned them.

A month later Germany invaded Austria, an act previously coordinated with that government, which had become a mere satellite, and captured it without firing a single shot. They called this annexation the *Anschluss*. The S.S. soldiers were greeted by the Austrian citizens with flowers. On that infamous day Austrian Jews, who had not suffered any discrimination until then, were stripped of all their rights. In one full swoop, they plummeted from the apex of franchisement and security to the depths of fear and insecurity. A wave of deportations was immediately launched, and most of the Jews were herded into congested ghettos. Large numbers of people chose to put an end to their lives out of despair and depression.

That was on *Rosh Chodesh Adar Sheini*, 5698 (1938). Yechiel remembered that date as the very one designated on the invitation, and his flesh tingled with horror. He had been invited to Vienna during the very week of the *Anschluss*!

A handshake and a promise had saved his life.

35

The flood which wiped out European Jewry did not descend all at once. It was presaged by thousands of preliminary signs, though no one could imagine the catastrophic dimensions of coming events.

In the beginning of that year before the war, Yechiel became happier than ever with the birth of his daughter, Bluma. His father, Baruch, the legendary composer, had begun suffering from several illnesses that left him greatly depressed, but the birth of his granddaughter raised his spirits. That very week Baruch composed one of his happiest songs, a lively, rhythmic tune that set all of European Jews dancing and was put to the words "*Ba'erev yalin bechi* — At night, he retires in tears, to awaken with joy."

The collective Jewish mood did not generally lean towards joy. Ominous black clouds covered the horizon and an evil foreboding filled the air. People were afraid to predict what the future might hold for Poland, though the optimistic Jewish nature sought to push aside the premonitions that sat heavy on people's hearts. Thus Baruch's new hit became an overnight success that lifted up the general Jewish morale.

But the dancing did not last long.

In the winter of 5699 (1939), shortly before Purim, R' Avrumele suddenly suffered a stroke. It took place at a Friday night *tish*, in the presence of a large crowd. He had finished a brief *dvar Torah,* as was his practice, and then added a few sentences whose meaning became clear only later: it had been a farewell message.

> *Dear Jews. If you maintain unity, you will be able to survive the diffi-cult times ahead. The Torah states, 'My enemies speak evil of me — when will he die and his name be effaced?' Our enemies are uniting in order to uproot us from the world, but if they talk of us in the singular, 'when will he die' and not 'they', then we will merit the realization of the continuation, 'But, Hashem, do be gracious unto me and raise me up so that I may repay them!'*

Six months later the Jews of Lublin understood his words. But it was too late.

R' Avrumele had lifted his eyes and looked at the people sadly. "Yechiel, please sing for us *'Chasdei Hashem ki lo samnu.'"*

Yechiel burst into one of his father's favorite tunes and hundreds of *chassidim* joined him. R' Avrumele's head suddenly fell to the table and his eyes closed. The panic-stricken men shouted and pushed each other in an attempt to revive the unconscious Rebbe.

The doctor who was summoned ordered the Rebbe transferred immedi-ately to a hospital. He was taken to the Jewish hospital on Lubertovska Street. After a comprehensive examination the head of the department, Dr. Hirsh Mandelbaum, went out to the throngs of *chassidim* waiting expectantly.

"His condition is not good. The Rebbe has suffered a stroke and he is unconscious."

Prayers were held in every synagogue in Lublin for the recovery of the beloved and revered leader. But the weak body could not fight for long. At midnight, *motzaei Shabbos,* the Rebbe passed away, surrounded by his family and closest followers, including Baruch and Yechiel Horowitz. Yechiel did not shut an eye that entire night. He wept until his eyes were red and swollen. He felt orphaned, despite the fact that his fa-ther stood right next to him. They embraced and wept upon one another's shoulders, but these were two kinds of weepings, very differ-ent in nature. Baruch's stormy weeping told of a broken heart, of love and a close relationship spanning fifty years, which had come to such an abrupt end. Yechiel's sobbing voice communicated a helpless despair. His mentor had departed. Who would encourage him and help him withstand all of his internal pressures? He was afraid of lures which he would be unable to combat. How would Mirushka and Ita take advantage of the new situation that had materialized? Surely they would join forces to try to topple the protective wall he had constructed around him in these recent years.

On the following day, Sunday, R' Avrumele was laid to his eternal rest in the ancient cemetery of Lublin, in a massive funeral attended by tens of thousands of weeping people.

Baruch and Yechiel felt as if their world had collapsed on them. It was a personal calamity. But aside from their personal misfortune, a terrible feeling of foreboding gripped the hearts of the Lublin community. The tree which had sheltered them for so many years had suddenly been uprooted and they were now exposed to danger, left without any protective shade.

≈)≈

The wail of sirens rent the tense air on that Friday, the seventeenth of Elul, 5699 (September 1, 1939). A few days later, Poland was overrun by countless of arrogant German soldiers in their impeccable uniforms.

The Germans began bombing Lublin towards evening of the second day of Rosh Hashanah. The people fled from collapsing houses to the open fields and squares. German planes circled so low that people could see the satanic expressions on the faces of the pilots, as they chuckled with glee at the sight of people scurrying helplessly to and fro, and then dipped their planes to cut them down with their machine guns. After three days of bombing, the German army invaded Lublin, on the fifth of Tishrei, 5700 (1939). The spine chilling cries of *'Heil Hitler'* and *'Heil seig'* could be heard on all sides.

After several days of doubt and uncertainty, the brutal victor ripped the mask off his face and began ruthlessly and systematically persecuting the Jews.

≈)≈

There were three quiet knocks on Yechiel's door. The anonymous visitor had leaped over the thorny hedge that surrounded his garden and reached the front door.

Yechiel jumped out of bed in alarm. The hands on the big grandfather clock pointed to 3 o'clock in the morning. He had intended getting up early, anyway, to do *kapparos* and hurry afterwards to the *Erev Yom Kippur Selichos*.

Dressed in a light robe, he ran breathlessly to the door.

"Who's there?"

"A good friend," answered an unidentifiable voice. "I risked coming here to deliver an important message. The president of the congregation received a letter today from the German army headquarters in the city. It contains a list of twenty distinguished Jews of the community, all of them wanted by the authorities. They include rabbis, Chassidic rebbes, *roshei yeshivah* and... you..."

"I don't understand," said Yechiel. "Come in and speak clearly."

"I cannot. If word gets out that I was here, my life is not worth anything," said the voice. "Yechiel, watch out! You are being targeted by the Nazis. They want you!"

Terrified, Yechiel froze. The echoes of footsteps faded. The unknown visitor had leaped over the hedge and disappeared. Yechiel recovered enough after several moments to open the door. The street lamps had been extinguished since the beginning of the war, but by the light of the distant half-moon and the thousands of stars he could make out a form leaping over the hedge.

⁂

It was an hour before the beginning of the fast. Yechiel, wearing felt slippers, was making his way towards the Maharshal Shul. His right hand held six-year-old Avigdor, his eldest son; his left hand held three-year-old Shaul Yitzchak. He knew that people would be crying that evening. Oh, how they would weep! The Germans had already killed dozens of people within a few days. Little room was left for the imagination. It was clear to any sensible person that they wouldn't allow the Jews to sit quietly in their homes.

When they were not far from the synagogue, Yechiel suddenly flattened himself on the ground, and his intelligent son, Avigdor, who imitated everything his father did, followed suit. Only Shaul Yitzchak remained standing and surprised. Yechiel quickly pulled him down beside him.

"*Tatte, vos is geshein?*" he asked, wondering what was happening. Yechiel's broad palm quickly covered up his mouth, suppressing any further speech.

He raised himself a bit and looked around. Across the street, about one hundred meters away from them, stood a tall helmeted soldier holding a rifle. He was shouting in Hebrew, of all languages, to the frightened landlady.

"Where does he live? Tell me quick."

The woman was hysterical and screamed in Yiddish, "I don't understand what you're saying!"

"I am a German and I'm talking Hebrew, and you're a Jew, and you don't understand?" the soldier screamed, this time in German. "Tell me where he lives, your singer, Henry Horowitz."

Yechiel did not lead the prayers that Yom Kippur. He fled from the place as quickly as his legs could carry him, and went underground that very day.

Roman Spiegel, the proud officer of the S.S., had come directly from Vienna. He carried out a house-to-house search for Yechiel. Yechiel did not wait to hear if the woman actually revealed his address or not. He was two steps ahead in this forced chess match. He raced home as fast as he could and immediately removed Ita and the three children. They went to live in the cellar of Chezki Lustig's house until the danger passed.

The Jewish community gallantly shielded Yechiel. Suddenly no one knew who the singer, Henry Horowitz, was, and certainly not where he lived. Several Jews had to pay for their silence with their lives, but Roman Spiegel did not come any closer to his prey in his stubborn search.

≈⌒

The door burst open with a swift motion. A tall officer stood in the door.

"Where does your singer, Henry Horowitz, live?"

Shevach Travitzky had aged considerably in the last few years and his mind had become unhinged. Of all his eight daughters, he had managed to marry off only two, besides his son, Shalom, his pride and joy. Six daughters still lived with him in their spinster misery, the spark of youth dying down, leaving grey hairs and a future that was turning into the past. The many bitter years which Shevach suffered had affected his body and soul, and left him a wreck of a man, half senile and partially blind. His hearing, however, had not been affected.

"We have no singer called Henry. He's named Yech…"

A dreadful shout came from the other room. "Tatte, no! No!"

Shalom Travitzky had come to visit his elderly father. He stood petrified. To betray a Jew to the Nazis? Even he was incapable of descending to such depths.

"Who shouted there?" barked the officer.

"I have a crazy son," explained Shevach. "Pay no attention to him. If you are looking for Henry Horowitz, you'll never find him."

"Who should I be looking for?"

"Yechiel Horowitz."

This he remembered! The burning hatred for Chilik.

Roman Spiegel breathed in relief. He had finally found a Jew willing to cooperate.

"Where does he live?"

"Don't remember," said Shevach helplessly. His Jewish conscience was aroused, but too late. He suddenly realized the terrible thing he had done.

Roman Spiegel had no patience for his slow speech. He grabbed the old man by the nape of his neck and jammed the butt of his rifle into his side. He led him thus through the streets of Lublin.

"Tell me where he lives, at once, or you're a dead man," he bent over the stocky figure and hissed his words into his ear.

The old man whimpered with fear. The street had suddenly emptied. Everyone had fled to their homes and were watching the scene from between the slats of drawn shutters.

Roman punched Shevach in the stomach. The old man doubled over and fell to the dusty sidewalk.

"*Sag schoen!*" Roman spat. "If you tell me now, I'll spare your life."

The old man believed him. "He lives on 6 Siroka Street, in a two-story house," he groaned, panting with fear. The fist had punched all the air out of his lungs.

A single shot rang out and Shevach's body rolled lifelessly to the gutter.

≈)⌒

The house was deserted. Yechiel had not managed to take much along with him before making his hasty getaway. Roman concluded from the state of things that his quarry had not been in the house for over a week.

He turned the cupboards upside down in search of documents and photo albums. He would need a picture of the Jew in person to circulate and publicize everywhere, among soldiers and civilians. He had taken along several pictures of Henry from Vienna, some of which he had cut out of newspapers and some which he had taken from the opera house archives, but the bundle had disappeared during the first days of the war in the storm of battle.

Yechiel was clever. Among the few things he had salvaged from his house had been all the family documents and albums. He knew that Roman would want to lay his hands upon his pictures, and refused to perform this service for him.

Roman went wild. He emptied drawers and entire closets onto the huge Persian rug.

"*Kroitz, dunner...*" he cursed madly. "*Vo ist ihn gekommen die alle dokumenten und alle bilder* (Where have all the documents and pictures disappeared to)?"

A small metal box rolled onto the rug.

He leaped forward and picked it up. He opened the round lid slowly.

Inside, resting upon its padded lining, lay the decorated egg, whole and gleaming white.

Yechiel's handsome face, the work of Roman's own hands, painstakingly constructed from miniature verses of *Tehillim*, smiled up at him, sharp and clear.

"*Fahter in himmel!*" murmured Roman in wonder. "I forgot exactly how he looked, but this picture will be my perfect model. I'll have no difficulty reproducing this."

⁂

"Yechiel, did you know that your likeness is plastered all over Lublin?"

Yechiel turned white as a sheet. Chezki Lustig, the good friend in whose cellar he was hiding out, was trying to hint at something. It was as if he were saying, in so many words, that Yechiel's presence was endangering him.

"A drawing or a photograph?"

"A drawing as exact as any photograph. The man who produced it is a first-class artist."

Yechiel knew who had drawn his face. Only the devil's specter from Vienna, the talented Roman Spiegel, could have produced such an exact likeness. But where had he obtained an original to copy? Had he done it from memory?

"I have a true friend in Vienna," the words echoed from the recesses of his memory, words he had uttered five years before. They returned now to mock him.

A friend, indeed! Idiot that you are, Yechiel, how could you have been so blind not to see that the young Nazi was only drawing you into a trap?

Wait a minute! When did I say those words? Wasn't it then, when I held the egg in my hand?

The egg!

The egg bore his likeness. That was the incriminating evidence! The dead giveaway! Roman Spiegel had surely found the egg and copied his face from it.

"*Destroy the egg!*" R' Avrumele's words of warning clanged like thousands of alarm bells in Yechiel's memory. Alas, the Rebbe was now in *Gan Eden*, but he had known.

Alas, saintly Rebbe! Yechiel's face was bathed with hot, salty tears. *Be my good advocate, Rebbe. Intercede for Yechiel David ben Miriam, for my wife and two sons, for my infant daughter, for my father and mother, for the entire Jewish people in Poland...*

He almost choked upon his wracking sobs. *Beloved, saintly Rebbe, you were right in everything you told me. Had I destroyed the egg, Roman might not have found any identification to help him find me.* The Jewish population had gone out of its way to protect Yechiel, the apple of their eye. Roman would never have found a picture of him without searching at length among old archives and among dusty library shelves. Such searching belonged to peaceful, leisurely periods, not to hectic wartime.

What else had the Rebbe said? *"If you sing before non-Jews in their concert halls and opera houses, you will eventually be compelled and coerced to sing before the enemies of Israel!"*

That's why Roman Spiegel was searching for him.

He held on tightly to a long, round wooden tube, painted blue and sealed at both ends with red sealing wax, containing his grandfather Avigdor's will. He had watched over it for the past two years, ever since his father had suffered his first heart attack and had transmitted it to him for safekeeping.

Yechiel was prepared for the worst. He knew that his fate was sealed.

36

Roman Spiegel had detested Yechiel Horowitz even before he had laid eyes on him. After he heard him sing, his aversion had developed into a deep-seated hatred, and for four years he built up his great dream of destroying the Jewish artist.

Professor Gustav Spiegel had emigrated from Germany towards the end of the 1920s. He never forgot the beloved Fatherland and regarded his residence in Vienna as a state mission.

Gustav Spiegel was riddled with unbridled ambition. He willed his son, Roman, to fame and had given him a grandiose name to suit his destiny: Roman Wilhelm Karl Spiegel.

His prime ambition, to turn Roman into a top opera star, failed.

"A lack of coordination," he would explain to his friends who wondered why he did not keep his promise of turning Roman into the world's greatest opera singer. And it truly was a problem of coordinating talent with destiny, for Roman possessed a weak voice, very weak, in fact.

He did enjoy superior musical talents, an ear highly attuned to the lowest sounds audible to humans. But Gustav would not be consoled with this: He poured all of his frustration upon his son's head and made his childhood and youth miserable.

Roman tried to satisfy his despotic father's will with the varied range of his other talents. It helped. Until Gustav heard a singer with a lovely voice. Then his expression would sour and he would express himself with open bitterness. *Everyone knows how to sing. Only my son is an absolute zero.*

Roman was certain from the start that Yechiel Horowitz's invitation to Vienna was only a tactic designed to degrade him. *Just look, Roman. Even the detested Jews are capable of producing a great singer. And you? What are you worth?*

When Roman heard Yechiel, his hatred increased sevenfold. The Jew sang in the voice of Roman's dreams. It was more than he could take.

When Yechiel had asked him if he could sing, his bitterness almost reached the bursting point. The Jew was deliberately prodding a painful wound.

When 'Henry' sang, Roman cringed with envy. The Jew had taken the loveliest voice in the world all for himself. Unforgivable!

Roman believed in the Fuehrer's mission. The day would come when he would be a soldier in his army, a soldier who would invade Eastern Europe and help decimate the Jewish people.

For four years he waited. Day and night he weaved his plan of revenge upon the Jew who had stolen his voice, and dared to be more talented and successful than he. A year before the outbreak of the Second World War he returned to Germany and enlisted in the army. As a sturdily built and conscientious soldier, he found his way to the storm troops, the S.S. He rose quickly up the ladder of military success and reached the degree of *haupt-sturmfuehrer* with relative ease. He was soon promoted to *uber-sturmfuehrer*. At Roman's behest, his father utilized all of his connections and influence in getting his son placed in the troops assigned to invade Lublin.

❦

"Where are you going, Yechiel?" Ita asked in alarm.

"I can't stand this any longer," he replied angrily. "I'm suffocating here. Just a bit of fresh air won't harm me."

"What's wrong with you? You're a wanted man!"

"Enough! I'm sick of it. How long can one breathe this stifling air? I haven't seen the sky for four months now."

Ita begged him not to go. Yechiel stubbornly ignored her. It was late at night and he pulled up his coat collar and put on his "Viennese" eyeglasses.

Chezki Lustig lived at the edge of the ghetto in a large apartment house. One side faced the Jewish quarter and the other, the Christian one. The cellar had an opening to the Christian side of Lublin. Yechiel hesitated for a moment and then decided to go out from the latter exit. He was not as well known there: The chances of identification were smaller.

He wandered around the empty streets, breathing the cold night air deeply into his lungs for about half an hour. His head moved ceaselessly from side to side. He shivered at the sound of approaching footsteps and buried his head deep inside his coat. An unfamiliar Lublin gentile studied him carefully from head to foot and Yechiel hoped that his face was adequately concealed.

After half an hour, he felt the ground burning under his feet and he hurried back to the stifling cellar. This was the curse of the ghetto: You couldn't even walk about like a free man near your own home.

Roman Spiegel paced Gestapo headquarters. The odor of cigarettes filled the small room. He did not smoke as a general rule, but he was now chain-smoking compulsively. He lit another cigarette from the butt he was about to discard. He inhaled and coughed, coughed and inhaled.

His nerves were taut. He had invested four years in his plan to destroy the singer and now, precisely in Lublin itself, where he was so close to the realization of his dreams, his goal seemed so distant and elusive. The Jew had evaporated into thin air. Suddenly, no one knew him; no one knew where he was. Spiegel was no fool, and he understood that the Jews had united in protecting their beloved and revered singer. He had killed dozens of them, but the frustrating searches had not brought him any closer to his target.

Until he had found the elderly Jew who had spilled vital information before Roman had shot him down. He had finally found where Henry lived.

But to his frustration, he had again been confronted by a blank wall. Henry's portrait had been splashed all over Lublin, but there was still no sign of the man.

A new doubt began gnawing away at him. Perhaps the Jew really was not in Lublin! *Do you have any proof that he's hiding out here, Roman?* he found himself musing aloud. *Perhaps he read everything you wrote to him on the egg and ran away in time?*

You're wasting your time, Roman. Henry Horowitz has fled to America!

Someone knocked softly on the door.

His military attache stood there, duly submissive. Sigmund Schmidt was a shallow person of low intelligence. Roman would have liked to rid himself of this lackey but Sigmund's father, Professor Felix Schmidt, was a top man in the political hierarchy, and he mustn't initiate a confrontation with his beloved son.

Sigmund handed him a paper with hieroglyphic symbols scratched on it. "Someone pushed this under the door."

"Who?"

"I didn't see."

"You should have opened the door and caught him, you helpless ninny!" yelled Roman in frustration. He studied the paper and his eyes lit up.

"Your *zhid* is in Lublin," wrote the unknown person in broken German. "I saw him last night taking a stroll. He was walking rapidly towards the ghetto."

It wasn't signed, but, like a drowning man clutching at a straw, Roman took the chance that it was true.

The next question was: how to force the mouse out of its hole.

And then he was struck by a devilish idea.

≈)⊂

Five units of S.S. soldiers in long dark coats and metal helmets arrived at the offices of the Judenraat, the puppet council that the invading army had appointed in most major cities.

The soldiers descended systematically from two trucks and immediately dispersed like trained hunting dogs and surrounded the building. Ten soldiers entered the building. When they emerged, they were accompanied by the chairman of the council, Dr. Adam Altman. He held an attache case with dozens of documents and seemed frightened. He was taken into the truck, the soldiers jumped on, and they drove into the ghetto.

They returned two hours later, together with a group of forty Jews, bound and handcuffed like sheep being led to slaughter. These were the leaders and distinguished figures of the Jewish community, the *créme de la créme* of Jewish Lublin society, who now stood, terrified, their faces devoid of all color.

This group, which had been arrested at Roman Spiegel's orders, included *admorim, roshei yeshivah*, rabbis, public figures, renowned doctors and Baruch Horowitz, the famous Jewish composer.

The forty men were lined up facing a brick wall. Tens of soldiers, their rifles aimed and cocked, were stationed to guard them.

Several military cars left the square, equipped with megaphones, motors revved up loudly. They headed in all directions inside the ghetto.

"Yechiel Henry Horowitz, leave your hiding place," shouted the loudspeakers, "or else we will kill all the distinguished men in Lublin at the rate of one per hour. The first will be your father, Baruch Horowitz."

It was Roman who had hit upon the connection between Baruch Horowitz, one of the people on the Who's Who list of the Judenraat, and the name of the wanted singer. "Who is he?" he had barked at Altman, as his men had rounded up everyone on the list in a house-to-house search and arrest.

Altman cringed in fear. "It's Horowitz, the famous composer."

"Is he related to Henry?" Roman asked impatiently.

"He's his father."

Roman exulted. He could have released the other thirty-nine notables at that very point. All he needed was the singer's father. But he had staged such a good show. Why ruin it?

Yechiel heard the loudspeaker from his hiding place in his childhood friend's cellar where he had been staying for the past months. His face turned ashen at the sound of the booming announcement. It had finally come. The hangman's noose was being waved before his nose.

"I'm going out," he said to Ita, who sat with him in the cellar, protecting her three little ones.

Ita wept. She accepted the verdict with submission and resignation. Yechiel revered his father and would not allow him to die in his stead, to say nothing of all the other respected figures who were on the lineup.

Yechiel kissed his children goodbye. His tears mingled with those of Avigdor and Shaul Yitzchak. Bluma, his ten-month-old daughter, lay asleep in her crib and Yechiel stood silently by her side, listening to her quiet measured breathing. His finger gently stroked her pale cheek, trying to draw part of her soul into his innermost being. He sought to freeze this moment, to stop the flow of time.

The finger continued moving across the warm baby's cheek. Yechiel was storing away chips of time, fragments of eternity.

"*Tatte, ich vil kummen mit dir* (Pappa, I want to come along with you)," wailed Avigdor. Ita rushed to pull him back. She still imagined that she and the children could remain safe within their shelter…

⁓⊃⊂

Yechiel climbed up the stairs of the cellar with heavy steps. He blinked in the light of day. He was immediately surrounded by ten rifles and led to a closed black armored car with two swastikas painted on the front. Part of his mind seemed to dissociate itself and think clearly and objectively. If the soldiers shot him, would he be able to hear the shot before he… What was quicker, the speed of sound or that of a flying bullet?

The soldiers did not harm him. Their orders were unequivocal: Bring Yechiel Horowitz back alive and well.

Roman awaited him in the city square, near the municipal council house, beaming with pleasure. He was celebrating his victory.

"*Shalom aleichem!*" he greeted him in Hebrew, and slapped his hand into Yechiel's in a fervent handshake. "How nice it is to meet again, my friend."

Yechiel quickly pulled his hand away.

"I am not your friend," he said in German. "Why do you waste your time? Take your gun and get it over with."

"What are you talking about?" Roman looked at him in surprise, being careful to reply in Hebrew. "Since when does one shoot good friends? Have you already forgotten our merry Viennese days?"

Several heads along the long line in front of the wall turned involuntarily, to watch with rising astonishment the absurd comedy taking place. The soldiers on guard chose to ignore their curious stares. Roman had staged a little scene and was not prepared to lose even a precious nuance in the drama. On the contrary, he wanted certain things to filter into the public awareness and resonate fully among the Jewish population of the city.

"My dear Henry," he said, laying his hand upon Yechiel's shoulder in an affectionate gesture, "the songs you sang in Vienna are engraved upon my very bones."

Yechiel was bewildered. What was this fiend scheming? What was the meaning of this outspoken friendliness, here, in the city square, in front of all the distinguished figures of Lublin Jewry?

Roman continued, turning to Baruch Horowitz, "Did you know that you had such a talented son? He raised a big commotion in Vienna, back in '35."

Baruch had been in Galicia at the time and the Viennese chapter of Yechiel's life had remained a hidden secret from him. He was hearing about it now for the first time, and didn't know how to react to it.

Roman noticed the exchange of glances between the people standing in front of the wall. He understood that he had succeeded in disconcerting Yechiel. The naive artist had displayed innocent trust and had revealed to him, in a moment of closeness, back in Vienna, that he had come secretly for reasons of religion. Roman had taken all this in account when he had planned his long and painful revenge.

"Why are you so surprised?" Roman turned theatrically to his audience of forty, still talking in Hebrew, throwing them all off and confusing them. His reasoning was cold and simple. Jews understood Hebrew, even if they only spoke Yiddish all their lives. It was the language of their prayers, of their Bible.

"Didn't you know that your Yechiel performed in Vienna? Did you imagine that one of you was friendly with a Nazi? Yechiel and I have been good friends for the past five years!"

They didn't believe the young boastful Nazi officer.

The heads of Lublin's Jewish community were not fooled by Roman Spiegel's words. They believed in the innocence of the man they dearly loved and revered. And yet something seemed strange in this exchange, in which the officer spoke only in the language of the *Tanach*, with a pronounced and jarring German accent.

With a magician's flourish, Roman whipped out a small metal box from his pocket, and with deft, dramatic movements, withdrew an egg with writing on it.

"And what would you say about this?" he asked, waving the egg in front of his audience's eyes. Here was concrete proof of the nature of his relationship with the Jewish performer. "I drew this in Vienna during Henry, excuse me, your Yechiel's visit to Vienna. We became fast friends there, didn't we?"

Two soldiers took the open box with the egg and passed along the line of notables, displaying it before their eyes.

"And now you are coming with me," Roman said to Yechiel. "The Jews here can return to their stuffy cubbyholes in the ghetto. But a distinguished person like you does not deserve to live in a moldy hole. You will come to live with me, in my house in the Christian quarter of Lublin."

Yechiel was taken from the city square, his face deathly white. The show was over. The hostages had played their roles and were returned to the ghetto. The Jewish population in Lublin did not know how to digest the strange tale. Most of them tended to reject the version presented by the young murderer. In any case, most Lublin Jews had worries of their own. The Nazis had begun their *aktions*, the infamous deportations. The Gestapo murderers circulated among the ghetto streets day and night, wantonly humiliating, kidnaping, beating and killing to their hearts' content. Young men were mobilized for hard labor; life in Lublin turned to a living hell. Who had time to think about what Yechiel Horowitz had done or not done?

But the seed of the horrors to come had already been sown. The protective barrier that had surrounded Yechiel was breached.

37

Yechiel was imprisoned in one of the rooms of a spacious apartment confiscated by the occupying German forces. While the Jews of Lublin suffered want and hunger, he received plenty of food and his room was light, airy and comfortably furnished.

In his generosity, Roman had allowed him to return to his cellar and pack a small suitcase containing his personal articles. Yechiel put in his *tallis* and *tefillin*, a small *siddur*, and a long blue wooden tube, hoping that his nemesis would not search among his personal effects.

Roman allowed him one day to sit in peace. Then the nightmare began.

Yechiel awoke to the sound of children crying. Alarmed, he sat up in bed and looked all around. It took him a few moments for his thoughts to clear. And then he remembered: He was being held in captivity in a golden cage. But what did *he* want from him?

The crying sounded familiar; it was Avigdor.

"Avigdor!" he shouted. "What are they doing to you?"

The key turned in the lock and the door opened. Roman stood framed in the doorway, smart in a crisp uniform, exuding authority and superiority.

"Why are you yelling?" he laughed. "Your children have been waiting for the past hour, waiting for their father to wake up."

What was he talking about?

"Get up!" Roman ordered. "Go and wish your wife and children a 'good morning'."

Ita was seated in the next room, Blumele in her arms and her two sons clinging to her in fear. When they saw their father, they burst out crying.

"Yechiel," Ita looked up at him bleary eyed. "The Gestapo soldiers surrounded the house two minutes after you left. There was nothing we could do."

Her apologetic tone surprised Yechiel. Was she to blame that she was no longer free? All of Polish Jewry had forfeited its freedom.

Roman let them converse for a long time without disturbing them. His plan was proceeding as scheduled.

The moment of parting arrived, accompanied by tears and words. Why was the Nazi doing this? To what was this leading?

Yechiel felt like a mouse being hunted by a sadistic cat. The cat was allowing him to run away, but not too far, before he caught him again. A measure of release and then, again, the trap. When would he put an end to this cruel game?

Ita and the children were taken from the house to an unknown prison apartment. Roman let Yechiel cry for half an hour, then entered his room.

"How do you feel, my dear friend?" he asked with a pleasant smile. He took a chair and sat down near Yechiel.

Yechiel sat, his head buried in his hands. He felt the moment of truth approaching. The Nazi was about to reveal his cards.

"Your wife and children are in our hands," Roman began without further introduction. "So are your father and mother. They are enjoying excellent living conditions. Any *Jude* would be happy for a tenth of what they are getting."

"What do you want from me?" Yechiel asked dully. He would not allow the Nazi to tease him.

"Why are you in such a hurry? That's one of your nasty habits, always in a rush. Come, let's talk leisurely. Let's understand one another so that we can work together."

Work together? Aha! So that's what he's driving at.

"You can kill me this very minute, if you expect me to cooperate with you against my fellow Jews." Yechiel shot up from his seat, eyes flashing. "I will not harm a Jew or hurt a hair on anyone's head."

A thick cudgel suddenly appeared in Roman's hand. "Sit!" he barked in a cold, commanding voice. "This is not an opera house; you can forget the dramatics.

"You are not expected to harm any Jews," continued Roman. "All you must do is sing."

Yechiel looked at him, shocked. "Sing?"

"Just so. You and several other artists will prove to the whole world that Jews in captivity do not suffer that much. In fact, they are in such fine spirits that they sing and appear in concert halls before audiences."

The cat was out of the bag. The satanic Nazi was now baring his claws.

"I will never do such a thing!" shouted Yechiel in a terrible voice. "Kill me right now!"

Roman's ice-blue eyes narrowed. He lost his patience.

"Swine! Accursed Jew! You will not raise your voice to me unless I ask you to." He took a deep breath. When he continued, his voice was controlled. Yechiel imagined he heard the hissing of a viper. "You will sing whenever I ask you to, because if you don't, I will kill your wife, your oldest son, your second son and your baby daughter, before I put an end to the life of the legendary composer, Baruch Horowitz, and his wife."

"Why are you picking on me?" Yechiel wanted to know.

"Because you're a thief!" the Nazi said. "You stole my voice."

Yechiel laughed aloud. The circumstances were too strange. Though the Nazi could kill him without any warning, he couldn't control his mirth.

"You are crazy!" he said. "How can one steal a voice? A voice is something a person is born with."

"That's precisely it," said Roman excitedly. "You were exchanged with me at birth."

Yechiel was no longer laughing. "I suspected that you were a little insane. Now I know that you are completely mad."

Roman rummaged around in an inner pocket and took out a document.

"Are you familiar with this?"

Yechiel nodded. It was a page from his passport. "You must have stolen it from my house."

"Not at all. I have had this for five years, ever since your first visit to my father's house."

He was bewildered. "But my passport was not missing any of its pages?"

Roman laughed with satisfaction. "You are standing next to one of the most talented people in the generation. The forger of the century. I forged this page. I planted the forgery in your passport and kept the original for myself. Even the top officer in the Ministry of Interior would not notice the difference."

"But..why?"

"For my own amusement. I wondered if they would catch you on the train at the border control."

Yechiel remembered that examination and shuddered.

"You and I were born on the same day, on May 20, 1915." Roman went over to the window and stared out. "At what time were you born?"

"At 4 a.m.," answered Yechiel. Mirushka had told him about it dozens of times. The birth hour of her only living son was etched upon her memory.

"See? I was also born at 4 in the morning," said the Nazi. "Do you understand what happened? Our constellations got themselves mixed up. You received the voice I was supposed to receive. I never understood why I was drawn to the *Tanach* or why I was attracted to Hebrew, of all languages. Have you ever seen a German speaking fluent Hebrew?

"When I opened your passport and saw the date of your birth, it all became clear to me. From where did I get this great love for letters, in general, and for Hebrew letters in particular? Thief! Robber! I decided on the spot to ruin you, to empty you of all content and leave you empty."

Yechiel was petrified. The man was mad! For a moment he toyed with the idea of leaping forward and throwing Roman out the window. They were on the third floor and the scoundrel's head would be smashed upon the sidewalk below. But two guards were stationed in opposite corners of the room with fingers poised on their triggers, precisely to discourage such foolish notions.

"I studied Torah, do you know?" Roman turned away from the window. His eyes were covered over with a film of reflection. "Did you ever hear the teaching, 'One does not punish before giving warning'?

"Well, I'm warning you," he said in a monotone. "I am warning you explicitly: Watch out for me. I told you in detail what I intend to do with you."

"It's a lie!" shouted Yechiel.

Roman continued to maintain his stony, maddening smile. He took out the box with the egg. "*Komme, Jude*," he said enticingly. "Let us see if it is a lie."

He took out a powerful magnifying glass from a nearby drawer. The egg revolved upon his fingertips and he studied it intently.

"Here it is," he pointed to a certain spot. "Come and see for yourself. Here is where I planted the trap," he chuckled satanically. "I knew you wouldn't think of reading everything on the egg."

Yechiel peered at his likeness. The beard was constructed from tiny, closely written letters. He studied the writing.

"*Keili, Keili,...* Hashem, why have You abandoned me...

"It is true, Henry Horowitz. One day you will scream to heaven: Why have You abandoned me?

"One day we will invade Poland. The beloved Fuehrer is preparing us for this fateful moment. I will be there among the invaders. I will search for you and I will find you. When you are in my power, I will turn you into a miserable creature. You will curse the moment you were born. You will rue your marvelous voice.

"Wait for me, Henry Horowitz. Even if it takes years, I will come.

"Roman Wilhelm Karl Spiegel."

꿈

"Destroy the egg!" R' Avrumele had shouted. And he had disobeyed. If only he had listened, or at least taken the trouble to read the horrible text... But he had done neither. He had simply watched over the viper's egg like an idiot. The fiend had given him a warning five years in advance. *I could have run away to America in time, at the first signs of war. Dear Mother, I would have been saved if I had listened to you. You told me that my natural place was in America.* These were his last bitter thoughts before he fainted.

When he awoke there was no one in the room. The door was locked and the window barred. Roman had taken every possibility into consideration and had removed every means of suicide. The Nazi had prepared a key role for Yechiel in his drama: the worst act of treason.

Jews would die and he would protect their murderers. He would be the smoke screen of the Nazis. He would be photographed, filmed, and would provide the entire world with the illusion that life for Jews in the ghetto was not so terrible. The Nazi extermination machine was built with characteristic German efficiency, well greased down to the smallest screw. Josef Goebbels, Ministry of Propaganda in the Nazi government, had taken care of all the details.

≈)⌒

"Artist's Performance" screamed all the posters in gigantic letters. Lublin's Jewish population was thinning out at an alarming pace. The conqueror massacred them without mercy. One after the other, deadly decrees landed on the community's head like hailstones.

And then suddenly, in the midst of the storm — a concert!

It wasn't even a bad joke; it was abuse for its own sake, a death-concert.

The district Gestapo command did not wait for the Jews to be kind enough to come and attend a concert between one *aktion* and the next, between one mass killing of thousands in the open fields and the next. Trucks were stationed by the ghetto gates into which thousands were forcibly herded. Those who attempted to protest were shot down on the spot without the blinking of an eyelid. The trucks sped towards the Lublinska Sahl and disgorged its human freight at the doorstep.

Photo teams of the S.S. were awaiting their arrival but the filming was delayed. Roman Spiegel wrinkled his nose at the sight of the shuffling crowd being prodded at gunpoint.

"What's this?" he screamed. "Is this how you want to film them? Is this how cultured people rush to attend a concert?"

He changed his mind about filming the line outside the hall.

Before the performance Yechiel was imprisoned in a cramped cubicle at the side of the hall. He hoped to make contact with one of the thousands who had been forced to hear him and to clarify the misconception, to explain that he was being coerced just as they were. At first he had refused to listen to anything about the concert, but his entire family had been brought to the apartment and he had heard Ita's heartbreaking cries at the sight of a soldier wielding his rifle butt over Blumele's head.

Roman had weapons of the highest degree of effectiveness. "Yechiel is no hero. His heart is made of butter. Just touch the fingernail of a member of his family and he will immediately cooperate. He will do whatever you say," he explained to one of his officers as he rubbed his hands together in gleeful anticipation.

These were secret weapons since none of the Jewish public knew that Yechiel's family was under threat. Roman had coldly calculated his satanic scheme. The Jews would despise Yechiel the traitor, who sang at concerts while they were being butchered!

Yechiel was determined to reveal this secret, to explode the myth. He waited for the slightest chance to exchange a word with a fellow Jew.

The hall filled up, the curtain rose and Yechiel went out of the wings, dressed in tuxedo and bowtie.

The audience of thousands stared at him unbelievingly. *Is this our Yechiel?* Horrified whispers filled the hall. No one could see the rifles aimed at him from behind the curtains, prepared for the event that he would try to convey any message to someone in the audience.

The cameras hummed and filmed the wide-eyed audience. *Die Jude haben liebe musik,* the narrator would be heard commenting when the film was developed and shown. Yechiel began singing *"Lemaan Achay Vereiay."* He had purposely chosen this particular song, certain that the audience would interpret it correctly.

He was mistaken.

Yechiel rose to the limits of his tenor voice and at that moment a riot broke out. Shouts of "boo" and "shame" thundered throughout the auditorium, drowning out his voice.

The machine guns stuttered into action and the place turned into a slaughterhouse.

Thirty corpses were removed from the hall. The wounded were taken out and shot to death. Yechiel pretended to faint but the doctor who had been waiting in advance on the sidelines reassured Roman Spiegel. "It's nothing, only a minor excitement."

Quiet and decorum were restored and the audience sat in their seats in tense silence. No one wished to leave on a death wagon.

Yechiel resumed his concert. He tried a different hint. "*Zeidim Helitzuni* (Enemies coerced me)," he sang in a mournful tune. Baruch Horowitz sat in the front row. He burst into tears and fainted, his hand clutching his chest.

Baruch's heart disease had quickly reached its terminal stage. His heart broke within him at this sight. With the sensitive intuition of a loving father, he understood that Yechiel was under duress, that he was being held captive in corrupt hands and was singing against his will. A thin wail escaped from his throat. His face turned purple and he fell to the ground.

"Tatte!" screamed Yechiel helplessly. He tried to jump down to the audience, but was restrained by a pair of hefty soldiers.

Baruch Horowitz convulsed on the ground and a few moments later was removed from the hall, dead.

The show went on. Yechiel almost choked. He tried to fake his voice and sing in a different voice.

The note reached him within seconds.

"Remember Blumele."

He remembered Blumele. He wanted to spare her. How he wanted her safe. For her sake and for the sake of Avigdor and Shaul Yitzchak and Ita and Mirushka, he sang as he had in the past, in the good days.

The audience — less thirty-one spectators — returned to the ghetto. Yechiel had suddenly turned into the most despised person in the city, even more hated than Hillel Buber, the figure of Lublin's underground who had become the symbol of treason and collaboration with the Nazi enemy.

"All right, Hillel. He never did have a conscience. But Yechiel Horowitz?"

There were more performances. Yechiel's name became a thing of loathing and repulsion.

And that was before Maidenek.

38

"**D**o you know, Yechiel, your singing lacks conviction."

"And what did you imagine, Roman, that I would be bursting with happiness?"

"No, it's not that!" Roman retorted angrily. Two years had elapsed since the German occupation. The first films he had produced had been sent to Berlin and were hailed with joy. The propaganda department spliced excerpts of the concert into dozens of films depicting similar cultural events throughout the areas under German occupational rule. Jews appeared carrying on with their lives, their daily affairs, as usual: working, shopping, enjoying their leisure and… attending concerts. The enlightened free world could see with its own eyes that Jews were not suffering. Their consciences could continue to slumber peacefully. The Nazis were not such terrible conquerors as they were made out to be. The facts spoke for themselves.

But the last film which Roman produced had evoked Goebbels' destructive criticism. "Your *Jude* sings like a corpse. The duress is evident in every motion. A film like this cannot serve our purposes."

The bottom line of the letter which came from Berlin hinted that the military headquarters in Lublin should consider removing the one responsible for the propaganda films. Roman didn't like that, not one bit.

"Listen here!" his voice rose to a hysterical shout. Yechiel's stomach turned over with fear. Roman had never shouted like this before.

"This cannot continue!" he screamed. "You gave four performances, each one worse than the next. Someone will have to pay for this. How old is your mother?"

Yechiel leaped up from the bed on which he had been sitting. "You wouldn't dare touch my mother," he said, approaching Roman, his eyes bulging with virulent anger. Losing all self-control, his fists pummeled the Nazi. He kneaded his enemy's flesh with all his might, venting all of his bitterness and frustration, his pain and fear. Two years of suppressed rage burst forth from within him like a burst of pent-up steam.

The surprised Roman lay sprawled on the wooden floor. He had not expected such a violent reaction. To his bad luck there was no one in the room besides themselves. The Jew was liable to finish him off with his blows.

But two years of prison conditions had done their bit. Yechiel had been fed well before each performance, but between one concert and the next he had been undernourished. Even in his prison in the Lublin apartment he had felt the biting pangs of hunger, the mortifying pain of going without a drop of water for three days. In times like those he had wondered about the fate of Ita and the children, and how his mother was faring.

Roman was a methodical sadist. From time to time he would slacken the rope. Yechiel enjoyed a visit from his family once every two or three months. The children were growing and had become very thin. He understood that they suffered from hunger and threatened not to sing if they did not receive adequate nourishment.

It worked. At the next visit, two months later, Yechiel could see the difference. For the first time since the German capture, his children's cheeks were rosy. Blumele was now three years old.

Yechiel saw Mirushka only once, the previous year. He couldn't recognize her. She had turned prematurely old and looked like an eighty-year-old when she was barely sixty. Her world had collapsed on her. Her revered husband had been wise enough to flee to a world that was wholly good at the very beginning of the destruction and she remained alone, all alone... Roman stubbornly insisted in keeping her completely isolated in a solitary cellar, and she became nearly deranged from the gravelike silence that enveloped her twenty-four hours a day.

Outside, in Lublin itself, only ten percent of the Jews remained. The great majority were deported at first to the death camp in Lozitz, and those imprisoned in the small ghetto in the city dwindled at a precisely calculated rate until they were also deported to the enclosed ghetto in the suburb of Maiden-Tatarsky.

The Gestapo intended to transfer the remaining twenty-three thousand of Lublin's Jews, together with another several hundred thousand Jews from near and far, to a death camp which had just been completed: Maidenek.

꙳꙳

The nutritional difference had its effect. The balance of power weighed heavily in favor of the strong, well-stuffed officer, as opposed to the emaciated and weakened Yechiel. Yechiel had the first advantage: The shocked Nazi could not believe that the Jew was striking back at him!

Yechiel was hitting with all his might. He was determined to finish Roman off here and now, despite the fact that he would have to pay for it with his life. It would not be long before one of the officers in the high command who stayed in the apartment would come in and see the bleeding corpse. He didn't care; there was no point left to living, anyway.

Slowly but surely, Roman succeeded in slipping out from under the pummeling fists that struck with maddened wrath. His right hand withdrew a club from his belt and, quick as lightning, sent it crashing down on Yechiel's head.

Yechiel's eyes turned in their sockets and he sank to the ground unconscious.

Roman got up and wavered on his feet like a drunkard. His eyes were bloodshot and glazed with a murder lust. He drew his gun and planted it at the forehead pulsing rapidly but weakly.

He stood there for several moments, toying with thoughts of murder. Finally he replaced the gun in its holster.

"No, *Jude*, I will not give you the pleasure of dying in one moment. I want you to die slowly, gradually, through terrible suffering," he whispered with venom. "I will kill you ten times over, and will revive you ten times to kill you again, until you remain the last Jew on earth. Then you will sing your swan song, the swan song of the Jewish people, which the Fuehrer will wipe off from the face of the earth."

~)(~

The *auszidlung* was a transfer program, a deportation plan for the remainder of Lublin Jewry to the Maidenek death camp. It took place in the months of Cheshvan and Kislev, 5703 (1943).

Maidenek was originally a Polish village four miles from Lublin; the death camp built nearby received its name. At first it was called a prison camp and held Soviet prisoners-of-war. Later it was expanded, and transports of hundreds of thousands of Jews were brought there from Czechoslovakia, Greece and France.

Yechiel was transferred to Maidenek in Roman Spiegel's private car. In those days Roman was in a creative mood and his mind feverishly schemed with plans for 'music evenings' and concerts within the camp. He would prove to Goebbels that he still had it in him. The new propaganda movies which would be filmed in the camp, next to the gas chambers and crematoria, would surpass those he had produced in Lublin!

Yechiel was kept separate for two months before his preferential treatment ended. He now wore a blue-striped suit and received a bunk in the big barracks together with several hundred other prisoners.

He sat on his bunk, ostracized like a leper. No one would exchange a word with him. "You're a traitor to your people, Yechiel," someone called out from the other side. Yechiel had no trouble identifying Shalom Travitzky's familiar voice. His long-time enemy's face looked thin and wizened. Shalom hurled caustic accusations at him until he had worked up the entire barracks against Yechiel. All of the latter's attempts to defend himself failed. A babble of shouts and curses drowned out his voice. No one wanted to hear him out. Some hands were raised and blows landed on all parts of his body.

The barracks door was flung open and a tall form stood in the doorway, hiding the floodlights outside with its broad shoulders.

Roman Spiegel stood surveying the scene, his uniform looking even smarter and neater than usual. His expression was that of deep satisfaction and arrogance. Excellent! Matters were developing as he wanted. This was his plan, to incite the entire camp against Yechiel. When someone would attempt to kill him, he would rescue him at the very last moment. The Jew would feel gratitude towards him and would develop a total dependence upon him. He, Roman Spiegel, would become his protector.

He beckoned to Yechiel, who came instantly, his body trembling.

"They wanted to kill you?" he asked gently. Yechiel shook his head.

"Don't protect anyone. Tell the truth."

"You've turned them all into animals," Yechiel accused him, to everyone's surprise. "You accursed Nazis have caused us to lose our Divine image. You are inciting us against one another."

Roman reacted differently than usual. He whispered something into Yechiel's ear and then left the barracks. Yechiel followed.

Ita and the children awaited him by the barbed-wire fence. It had been a year since he'd seen them. His heart was torn to shreds at the sight. They looked like walking skeletons. Avigdor, a child who had been full of life and joy, looked pale and listless. Shaul Yitzchak leaned weakly against the concrete wall of the nearby barracks. He tried to smile, baring gums without teeth. Blumele was dressed in rags and her face was yellow as parchment.

"We are still being held in relatively good conditions," said Ita, her eyes dull. "All to your credit, of course. Roman told us that so long as you cooperate and sing, he will keep us alive. We are his hostages and you are our insurance policy."

She burst into quiet tears and wept for a long time. Yechiel imagined he saw the destruction of the entire Jewish people reflected in her.

"Where is Mama?"

"I don't think she is alive," she replied weakly.

"You don't think so?"

"Roman came to us one day and shouted that a mother who raised a son who lifted a hand against a German officer did not deserve to remain alive. A year has passed since then."

So he would have to bear the burden of his mother's death upon his conscience as well!

Roman had promised to ruin his life and he was keeping his promise. He was draining his lifeblood slowly, with calculated, icelike slowness, drop by drop.

The children talked among themselves. Shaul Yitzchak pointed to the smoking chimney. "Is it true that that is Jewish smoke?"

"No, it isn't!" replied Avigdor. "That isn't smoke. It's angels. Inside the incinerators, Jews turn into angels and they go up to Heaven through the chimney."

Shaul Yitzchak tugged at Yechiel's hand. His round eyes glowed with childlike simplicity. "Abba, does it hurt to turn into an angel?"

"The festive encounter is over," announced Roman, suddenly materializing before them from nowhere. "The next meeting will take place right here, at the same time, next month, if you behave well and sing with your full voice, through joy and happiness, at your maiden appearance in the Maidenek Opera House."

Dozens of eyes followed the strange meeting. Many of the workers who had not filled their daily quota peered at the group huddling by the fence with stealthy glances.

"Yechiel has it made," whispers passed from ear to ear. "Who else has the privilege of having his entire family kept alive? What's the wonder? He made a pact with the devil. Yechiel is organizing concerts for the skeletons in the gas chambers and the incinerators, and Roman Spiegel is keeping him and his entire family alive!"

The rumors about the upcoming concert spread several days in advance. Even before Roman bothered to tell Yechiel of his new role, all the prisoners knew about the Opera House, the huge barracks being erected in a corner of the camp.

They knew and they fumed.

They had already heard about traitors who had sold their souls to the devil, but in such a fashion? To stand and sing right in front of the smoking incinerators?

"I've known him for a long time!" Shalom Travitzky claimed heatedly. "In his good days in Lublin I already saw that he was corrupt, but no one believed me. You were all blinded by him, you idolized him. Now see to what depths he has fallen, to the lowest of the low!"

Roman began pampering Yechiel once again. Yechiel received rich foods in the room in which he was now being kept separately. He refused to eat the meat because of *kashrus* reasons, but even the fruits and vegetables stuck in his throat like a bone.

How could he eat so much bread while his fellow prisoners fought for every crumb in their barracks? To bite into a juicy apple? His companions pining away in the camp would have been happy just to look at this forgotten fruit, to see an apple or pear…

He did not bear a grudge towards his fellow prisoners who had beaten him. He would not have acted otherwise. And yet when he thought of Shalom Travitzky inciting the entire camp against him, he felt a stab of fury. He kept the fruits and vegetable for the upcoming visit of Ita and the children but the fruits turned into a fermenting mush long before.

Roman worked hard at organizing the concert. His orderlies passed from one barracks to the next and made their own private selection. Whoever knew how to hold a musical instrument of any sort gained himself an insurance policy for the near future. "Henry himself can play several instruments," Roman remembered with relief, and reduced the number of musicians. The orchestra included ten instruments: two violins, two drums, a trumpet, trombone, three flutes and one mouth organ. A poor showing under normal circumstances, but very rich considering these extraordinary conditions. Roman had a most macabre sense of humor: to play the "Blue Danube Waltz" to the odor of Jews being burned in the crematoria was not a thing to be passed over lightly. The Fuehrer himself would congratulate him for this brilliant idea!

The festive evening arrived. Several professional cameramen stood prepared with their cameras. Feverish activity could be felt in the camp;

in honor of the event, the prisoners were assigned new prison uniforms.

The lights went on in the big barracks. A huge sign hung above the entrance announced "The Opera House of Maidenek" in German. The hundreds of seats in the 'auditorium' were filled with *musselmen*, walking skeletons devoid of any human expression, virtual robots who barely comprehended what was happening all around them.

Roman stood on the makeshift stage and scanned the audience disappointedly. "No good. No one will buy this. The staging is too transparent."

"Search the general barracks," he instructed his soldiers. A few minutes later a few dozen non-Jewish prisoners were rounded up and placed in the front rows. Some of them were given black *kipahs* to put on their shaven heads.

"Ah, that's much better," he smiled with satisfaction. These prisoners looked far more convincing. Their bones did not jut out as much.

The door of his cell opened. Yechiel felt like a circus lion being led from his cage to the ring.

You are really no more than a trained animal. Who says that your blood is redder than your brothers' who are being asphyxiated by the hundreds daily in the gas chambers, whose burnt bodies give off the sickening stench that fills the atmosphere?

This question had been revolving in his head for several days. Consumed by pangs of conscience he left the room, accompanied by a heavy guard, to be led to the illuminated barracks.

They walked near the camp's barbed wire. Exposed electric wires encircled the mass of barbed wire; the fence was electrified. A high voltage ran through the bare wires.

He felt an irresistible urge. His feet leaped of their own accord, bearing his body.

He ran towards the electrified fence. His stunned guards did not have time to react before Yechiel found himself leaning on the fence, embracing the metal wires.

39

The general silence that reigned in Maidenek suddenly turned into chaos. The large siren began wailing and the projectors flooded the corner where Yechiel stood hugging the electrified fence with a wide beam of white light.

Two soldiers from security broke away from their companions and ran to tell Roman what had happened.

He stood on the stage and stamped his feet impatiently on the wooden floor.

"What's all this commotion? Why did you turn on the alarm?"

"Horowitz committed suicide!" the two replied simultaneously.

"How?" asked Roman coolly, a thin, almost imperceptible smile hovering at the corners of his lips.

"He electrocuted himself on the fence."

Roman burst into a mighty peal of laughter. The soldiers thought he had gone mad. His hands clutched his stomach as if he had heard a terrific joke.

"He threw himself on the wire? Ha, ha, ha. *Yechiel, mein zisser*, you are so predictable and unoriginal.

"Go, you fools," said Roman, finally recovering from his lengthy bout of laughter. "Go and bring him here. I disconnected the electricity an hour ago."

⋘⋙

Yechiel had been emotionally prepared to die. The encounter with the Angel of Death no longer frightened him. He had rushed to the gate, expecting a mighty electric shock which would burn up his flesh and bones.

He had flung himself upon the fence with outspread arms and lost consciousness.

When he was aroused by the streams of cold water which doused his head, he could not understand what was happening. "Do they wash sinners in cold water in the World to Come? I thought they worked with fire..."

When he finally realized what had actually happened to him, he became filled with a seething anger. A few scratches on his hands and feet were all he had to show for his close encounter with electrocution. Dozens of people had already put an end to their lives this way; only he was prevented from doing so. "Roman, you wretch," he swore in his heart. "The day will come when you will pay dearly for this ."

After a brief period of recuperation, he was forced to put on his tuxedo. Roman had thought of all the minute details. A colorful silk bowtie was snapped nattily on the collar of his snowy white shirt. His hair was combed and his face made up by a cosmetician. Yechiel let them do whatever they wanted.

His will had been broken in the two years that had passed. He had turned into a marionette, a rag doll controlled by strings.

Roman greeted him when he was brought, weak and shaky, to the 'Opera House.' He awaited him in a side corner, a mocking smile on his face.

"My dear Yechiel, have you forgotten that we have the same horoscope?" he whispered in his ear. Many heads turned to see him whispering with the Jew. That was exactly what he wanted.

"Don't you think I know what goes on in your Jewish head? I know you even better than you know yourself! You are a poor chess player. I can anticipate you two or three moves ahead. You are as open and transparent as if you were made of glass. I can also guess what you will think tomorrow, when you are told that Ita and Avigdor have gone for a stroll in the gas chambers."

Yechiel's fists clenched. Here, then, was a reason to live. He would remain alive in order to take revenge against Roman Spiegel. Even if it took ten years, it would come.

"Ita and Avigdor in the gas chambers? Why?" he murmured weakly.

"It all depends on you. If you sing like in the good days, when you and your singing were one, they will remain alive."

He came back to himself at that performance. The vocal chords which had fallen into disuse for so long did not betray him. His voice soared to great heights, just as in former times. He sang Jewish songs for his Jewish audience, and classic songs for the general prisoners, those who occupied the front rows and who enjoyed his performance tremendously. They applauded him enthusiastically.

He identified the shriveled face and burning eyes of Shalom Travitzky in the fifth row, but it made no difference. He recognized some other Jewish faces among the crowd, grayish-green death masks stretched across sunken cheeks. These people, he knew, did not have much longer to live. Tomorrow or the next day they would be asphyxiated with Zyklon-B gas and their bodies would be gathered and piled up on the crematoria wheelbarrows. And when the small gas chambers would not be able to stand up to the huge numbers, thousands would be taken to the nearby Krampitz Forest where they would be murdered en masse.

He knew this all. Roman Spiegel came to visit him every two days to update him on everything with obvious glee. He reveled in seeing Yechiel cringe in pain at the painful news of the death of thousands and tens of thousands. The pain of this particular Jew filled his life with a sweet pleasure.

The last thing he wanted to do was sing. To sing? 'How can we sing the song of Hashem?'

But that evening Roman had injected an elixir into his veins. He now had cause to live, a reason, a goal. Revenge!

He adapted one of his father's most famous tunes, one with which all of Poland was familiar, and fitted it to the words, "*Kel Nekamos Hashem* — Hashem, G-d of Revenge, G-d of Revenge, Appear." And before anyone caught on, he also sang the words, "To take revenge upon the gentiles."

He was certain that the audience would finally understand him.

A faint humming could be heard in the audience. It swelled until it turned into a rousing, sweeping song. Hope suddenly appeared in dimmed eyes. Yechiel singing about revenge upon the *goyim*? It must mean something. Perhaps the knife he had jabbed into the back of his people was not struck by his own will but through coercion?

The humming grew stronger. The cameras immortalized the Jewish audience singing along with Yechiel. Roman, who had gone out for a few moments, did not hear the Jews singing of revenge.

"He's lying!" a loud voice suddenly rang out. The singing was abruptly cut off and all eyes turned towards the shouter.

It was Shalom Travitzky. He screeched at the top of his voice and his pale face turned red.

"He is deceiving us, Yechiel the traitor. They'll be leading us to the incinerators tomorrow. No one is going to get out of here alive. Only Yechiel Horowitz and his family are going to remain alive. Roman Spiegel promised him. He has a pact written and sealed by the devil!"

The door of the barracks was flung open. Roman burst in like a wild beast, his eyes shooting sparks, a short bludgeon gripped in his left hand and a gun in his right.

"Who shouted?"

Silence. No one breathed a word.

"I am counting until ten. If the one who shouted does not get up on his feet, all of you will leave here, and I mean all of you," his hand indicated the non-Jews seated in the first four rows, "immediately to the gas chambers!"

The threat worked. "It's that one, that *zhid* over there." Someone from the fourth row got up and pointed to Shalom Travitzky. Shalom cringed with fear.

Roman leaped forward like a leopard, lunging at Shalom, waving his gun. He drew the trigger and was almost upon him.

Everyone watched the developing scene in paralyzed fear. No one dared draw a breath.

Yechiel did not lose his wits. He ran towards the Nazi standing ready to shoot. "Leave him be. If you want me to continue singing, leave him alone."

His hand wrenched Roman's gun from him and he aimed the barrel at his own head.

Roman opened a pair of wide eyes. This Jew had depths he had not anticipated, after all.

"Do you know him?"

"Yes."

"Do you know that his father informed on you?"

"Yes."

"And you're protecting him?" Roman's voice was filled with astonishment. "You Jews are a strange people, a strange people, indeed!"

Yechiel had studied in yeshivah in his youth. The famous words of the Rambam in *Hilchos Daios* passed before his eyes. How does one distance oneself from an undesirable trait? By leaning all the way to the other extreme and doing the opposite of what one would have naturally done.

You'd like to take revenge on Shalom for all he did to you, wouldn't you?

Thou shalt not take revenge.

Then save him from death!

He whispered in Roman's ear. "Do you want me to perform here like then, in Vienna? Then add Shalom onto my family."

Roman looked at him in wonder. He nodded and left Shalom whimpering in fear. The evening continued as scheduled.

The concert was the turning point in Yechiel Horowitz's status. He sang beautifully that evening and Roman understood that the despised Jew could help promote him further in his climb to the top. The rolls of film were sent to the government film office and developed in the propaganda department labs in Berlin. Three weeks later he received a telegram from Goebbels' office:

EXCELLENT STOP CONTINUE STOP GIVE THE JUDE WHAT-EVER HE WANTS STOP JOSEF GOEBBELS END

Goebbels himself had addressed him! Roman was beside himself with joy. That very day he freed Yechiel from his isolated cell, gave him back his bag with his personal effects, and transferred him to the officers' quarters. He also gave the artist a personal gift...

"What is this?" Yechiel asked, looking at the framed certificate.

"A diploma," Roman exulted, proud at his devilish invention. "A certificate of esteem to the greatest singer of all."

He handed the framed certificate to Yechiel, whose fingers shook with rage.

> *The Opera House of the Maidenek Labor Camp is proud to issue this certificate of honorary membership to the famous singer, the Jew, Yechiel Horowitz, for his marvelous performances during the years 1943-1944. The wonderful Jew, Horowitz, proved that with a little good will, all nations can reach a mutual understanding and find the common denominator for all nations on the face of the earth.*
>
> *(Signed) Roman Spiegel*

He threw the certificate from his hand as if it were a repulsive thing. "Aren't you ashamed of yourself?" he shouted angrily. "What do you want from me? Why are you tormenting me so?"

Roman pretended to be insulted. He picked the certificate up from the ground and cleaned it off. "I already have one certificate of yours, if you recall. The one from the Viennese Opera House. How happy you were to receive it at the time. Well, I have it, and now, I will have another one, too," he said lightly.

Yechiel was now under Roman's supervision for many hours of the day. Still he was permitted to roam freely throughout the camp and was even given a key to the officers' apartment.

He came and went among the officers' barracks as in his own quarters. His bravado grew and increased. He hid his *tefillin* bag inside the administration quarters and every morning, while the officers were out for breakfast, he would steal in silently to the danger zone and put on his *tefillin* for a moment, murmur a few hurried verses of the *Shema* and then slip out with beating heart.

He was never caught. The Nazi officers loved eating. They starved millions of people to death without a moment's twinge of guilt, but could not bear a delay of a few minutes in their meals being served. Every morning Yechiel would steal into the administrative quarters. Sometimes he would take the secret will out of its hiding place and lovingly caress the blue wooden tube.

Life would carry on, he knew. His saintly grandfather had left his will for the future generations. All the members of his family had already been killed. Only Yechiel and his sons remained.

Life would continue; it was a prophetic promise.

It was a lone moment of comfort, a single straw floating on the surface of a sea filled with destruction and death.

Until that morning…

On that morning he had a premonition of disaster. A deep inexplicable feeling paralyzed him with fear when he wound the black leather straps around his arm. He knew it was illogical. The strict order of the camp did not allow officers to be in that part of the camp at this particular time. It was only due to this inflexible rule had he been fortunate enough never to be caught for an entire year.

He promised himself that today he would remove all of his things, the *tefillin* and the will, and hide them elsewhere. Yechiel did not know if he would find a safer place than the administration quarters, but his heart told him that he could not return here again.

He adjusted the straps on his hand and head, murmured several blessings and phrases and laid his hand over his eyes.

Suddenly his heart stopped. There was a jangling of keys outside and the door opened.

"What?!" The roar shook the very walls. It was Klaus Reiter, one of the most brutal officers in Maidenek. Among themselves, the prisoners called him 'Klaus Schneider,' because of his thrill in cutting live flesh.

"Here? In my very room?" Klaus screamed. A hail of murderous blows fell upon his head, back and every portion of his tortured body.

Klaus saw the ring of keys and understood that the Jew had used his room as a hiding place.

"What else are you hiding here?" Yechiel pointed helplessly to the hiding place and Reiter removed the blue wooden tube from a hidden niche in the wooden wall panel. He tried to remove the red seal but couldn't. "I'll open it tonight," he murmured to himself.

That was only the beginning. The cruel Reiter whipped every inch of his body and had Yechiel put in solitary confinement. Death seemed very near.

40

Yechiel lay on the concrete floor of the isolation cell, wishing he could die. His life had lost all meaning years ago and now he no longer possessed his grandfather's sacred will — nor the will to live. His wish might have been granted, but Roman looked for him in his room and thus learned from Klaus Reiter what had happened.

"Fool!" he screamed at the stunned Reiter. "Don't you know that this *Jude* is Goebbels' property?"

Yechiel's *tefillin* were returned when he was released to his room, but the will remained in Roman's hands.

The death industry continued to flourish. Roman kept Shalom Travitzky alive. "My word is a word," he promised ceremoniously, hand held dramatically on his heart. At the very time that hundreds of thousands of Jews were being sent to their deaths, Shalom Travitzky was added to the list of privileged persons.

Roman had another purpose, an evil one, which Yechiel learned of only later.

Roman organized three concerts in Maidenek. Yechiel's final performance was on the most important night of all, the night of the gigantic slaughter in which all the Jews of Lublin and Maidenek were liquidated in the Krampitz Forest and other areas in the vicinity.

It was shortly before the end of the war. The scales were tilting against Hitler. The German army was being routed on all fronts. It was clear that the Nazi dream of a Thousand-Year Reich was going up in the smoke of Allied bombers.

The Nazis hastened to complete their genocide. They were determined to wipe out the Jewish race from the face of the earth, but their dream had failed. However, in all of their death camps they hastened to murder the remaining survivors.

Yechiel knew nothing of this. In all innocence, he thought that this was another concert just like its predecessors. But when he got up on the stage in the 'Opera House,' he discovered that aside from him and Shalom Travitzky, there was not a single Jew in the audience. All the rows were occupied by the regular non-Jewish prisoners.

"Where is everyone?" he whispered.

"They took them to the Krampitz Forest. All of them," replied Shalom. He also whispered. "They also took my mother there tonight. Do you intend to sing?"

"Have I got a choice?"

A glint of malicious joy was ignited in Shalom's dispirited gaze. "Sing well tonight. I have something to tell you afterwards."

"What?" Yechiel was very wary of the strange glitter in Shalom's eyes. He knew something; that was dangerous!

Shalom kept silent. Yechiel despaired of gleaning any information from him and five minutes later, when Roman entered, his last performance began.

It was the Jew's swan song, just as Roman had wished. Yechiel wrung out the best he could from himself and soared to the forgotten peaks of years ago. Later on, he learned that the echoes of his singing had reached all the way to the Krampitz Forest.

Roman stood, smiling broadly to himself with great satisfaction all evening long. Occasionally, when Yechiel sang an especially lovely rendition of an opera piece, he was unable to contain himself, and laughed, his face buried in the sleeve of his army uniform.

A premonition of evil suddenly gripped Yechiel. Iron tongs as cold as ice suddenly clamped his heart so tightly that he felt like shouting in pain.

He suddenly understood everything.

Ita and the children! They had been taken to the forest, together with the rest of the Jews!

So that was the explanation of the laughter. The laughter of the Angel of Death. The fiend!

He jumped off the stage to the astonishment of his audience of hundreds of prisoners and ran to Roman. "Where are my wife and children?"

Roman measured him with an even expression, somewhat amused. "In a safe place."

Yechiel gave up on him. "Shalom!" he roared in a mighty voice. "What do you know?"

Shalom exulted in his victory. "Whoever sows wind will reap a storm."

"Cut out your nonsense!" he shouted, and slapped Shalom across the face . "Tell me what happened."

Shalom stepped back. "Your family was taken to the Krampitz Forest tonight."

Yechiel lost consciousness.

≈⌒

The Soviet forces captured Maidenek in Av, 5704 (1944). The camp itself was liquidated shortly before. Yechiel was a broken man. He walked around like a shadow, his heart a shell. Roman made sure to remove all sharp instruments or heavy, blunt things lest he do something foolish. His revenge was complete. The Jew would remain alive and all the other Jews who survived the war would despise and shun him.

He made sure to leave an eyewitness, Yechiel Horowitz's sworn enemy, who would tell all the Jews in the world how the revered singer had turned traitor to his people.

Shalom Travitzky!

≈⌒

The war ended. The armed forces of the Soviet Union captured Lublin and its environs. Yechiel was free, free to go wherever he wished.

He had nowhere to go. Nor did he have any reason to live.

He was a wreck of a man, neither alive nor dead. Not in Heaven, not in Hell. He was in an inexorable catapult, eternally slung and flung into the depths of the nether regions.

The first place he went to was the Krampitz Forest, to the wide trenches which had been dug on the night of the mass slaughter when the Nazis had killed eighteen thousand Jews, on *motzaei Shabbos, parshas Vayeira,* the eve of the sixteenth of Cheshvan, 5704.

He searched in vain for the burial spot of Ita and the children. Special units of the infamous Sunderkommand 1005 had burned all the bodies and ground the bones to dust to obliterate all incriminating evidence of the mass murder.

Yechiel stood between the trees, his eyes reflecting abysses of bereavement and agony. At that moment he made a vow between himself and his Creator:

This mouth which sang while my brothers and sisters, my mother and father, my wife and children, were being slaughtered; this mouth which was punished because it refused to listen to R' Avrumele's warning and drank the goblet of bitterness down to its dregs...

This mouth shall sing no more. Ever!

Not on Rosh Chodesh nor on Shabbos, not on a festival nor on any other occasion, not a melody nor a tune. This mouth shall be dammed up forevermore.

This mouth shall never sing again!

The vow was superfluous. Yechiel had no need to force himself not to sing. The wellsprings of song had withered and died inside him. The channel of song that connected the heavenly Palace of Music to Yechiel's soul had been broken somewhere along its length and its ends had been plugged up forevermore.

≈)⁓

"Hello, there, Yechiel." Shalom surprised him as he suddenly appeared from between the tree trunks, a knapsack slung over his shoulders. The thin short figure had been partially concealed by the thick green foliage. "I'm going away. Don't worry; I'll make sure to publicize everywhere, wherever I go, who and what Yechiel Horowitz is."

Yechiel closed his eyes in contempt.

"Remember your rescuer, Shalom. If not for me, you would have turned into a heap of ashes."

Shalom was not moved. He didn't even blink. "I'm no fool. You staged the whole show there, that night. Roman did not dream of killing me for a moment."

"Roman didn't dream of ki..." Yechiel's voice fell silent. He was stunned by this gross lie. "Who ever told you that?"

"Roman himself! He told me that it was all a show."

Yechiel was silent, in shock. Shalom continued, *"You will yet hear from me,"* he whispered softly. *"You will never be able to rid yourself of me. I will pursue you everywhere. You will remember Shalom Travitzky."*

Yechiel returned to Maidenek to get his bag. The will had disappeared, but the coming generations had also been destroyed. The righteous Saba Avigdor had erred in his prediction of the future. There was no one left for whom to preserve the long blue cylinder with its two red wax seals at both ends.

He recalled the last conversation he had with Roman Spiegel, an hour before the arrogant officer had fled in stolen civilian clothing from the approaching Soviet forces.

"'This is my solace'," said Roman, pointing at him, quoting the verse from *Tehillim*. "I will leap gladly into my grave knowing clearly that I fulfilled the will of the Fuehrer. I did my part in destroying the Jewish people, and left you hollowed out, a ruined relic. Your life will never have any significance. When you arise each morning, you will ask yourself why, and at night you will pray for the release of eternal sleep. Jews like you I like."

Yechiel had needed to enlist all his mental faculties so that his heart would not fail at the sound of such abuse. He dredged up that strength and found it. From where? He knew not.

"The day will come when I will avenge myself on you, Roman. We will both survive. I, in order to repay you in kind, and you, in order to witness with your very eyes, the coming generations of the Jewish people. My own sons and daughters."

Roman burst into laughter. He was in good spirits. He held the blue cylinder containing the will and waved it in mock warning before Yechiel's eyes.

"When I reach safety, I will open this cylinder. I see that it is very dear to you; it is apparently very valuable. I have your diploma, as well. Do you want it?"

"The day will come when my sons will catch up with you and exact my revenge," Yechiel said, eyes flashing.

Roman stared mockingly at the shaking skeleton standing before him and laughed again. "You will die childless, Yechiel-Henry. No Jewish woman will want to marry someone who stuck a knife into the back of the Jewish people when it was down."

"Time will tell." Yechiel had the last word. Roman fled. The curtain had fallen on the most horrific drama in the world.

Yechiel dragged his weary feet through Europe en route to *Eretz Yisrael*, amidst thousands of Jewish refugees. He buried his incriminating name and turned himself into David Eliad.

Eli-ad, my G-d is eternal. Eli-aid, my G-d is my witness.

He thought about the promise he had made to Roman and wondered about his solid conviction. It had been a promise without any substantial backing.

"Time will tell."

What would it tell?

PART THREE
MEITAR AND AVI
Moshav Yetzivim
5755-1995

41

"**D**o you understand, dear Avi and Meitar? Do you understand your grandfather?"

They nodded hesitantly even though, in truth, they didn't understand at all. They would require many long hours to digest his words before they began to comprehend a fraction of the shocking human drama that had taken place.

Avi and Meitar, both grandsons of Saba David Eliad, but so different from one another, so distant in their respective worlds. A bridge of tens of miles long could not span the vast abyss separating the two.

Anyone seeing Avi need not think twice before fitting him into the niche of a typical yeshivah student, even without his suit and hat. He was a *ben yeshivah* in his very essence and radiated a rare quality which only others of his kind, other students who toiled arduously in Torah, emitted.

Meitar was the complete opposite, an Israeli teenager rebelling against every convention. Elliptical glasses rested loosely upon his snub nose; his long hair blew out in the wind. He was a star product of the secular Israeli society of the '90s.

The bond between Avi and Meitar, cousins, had dwindled over the years to rare meetings on festivals and *shabbasim* at the home of their grandfather and grandmother in the *moshav*. Aside from a hasty greeting, they hardly exchanged a word between them.

But something had happened today. Saba had summoned Avi urgently from his yeshivah in the south where his father, R' Yigal Eliad, served as *rosh yeshivah*, and Meitar from one of the prestigious high schools in Rehovot. Meitar sped to Yetzivim on his motorcycle, his pride and joy, and in his breakneck haste had almost forgotten to tell his father, the eminent scientist Baruch Eliad, about the sudden summons.

They were now seated around a picnic table in Saba David's large back yard. Saba David, as they had been accustomed to calling him, sat on a chaise lounge, slightly removed. A mild end-of-winter breeze was blowing, sending the green leaves on the broad trees atremble. Saba shivered and covered his shoulders with a light woolen blanket.

"I'm afraid that you don't understand a thing." He was wise; you couldn't fool him. His penetrating eyes saw everything.

"Rome wasn't built in one day," quoted Meitar. "You can't throw an atom bomb of a story at me and expect me to understand it immediately. Give me a month or two to digest everything, to think about what I just heard."

"And what do you say, Avi?" The blue-gray eyes rested upon him. David Eliad's piercing steel eyes were still strong and firm; they had not dwindled with his eighty years.

Avi was plunged deep in thought. His fingers combed the fringes of his *tzitzis*, as they did when he was concentrating. Yes, this was a new *sugya*, a far more difficult topic than the one he had been dealing with lately in yeshivah. A living story, moving, still taking place at this very moment, its epilogue deeply affecting their lives, changing everything he had always taken for granted. He would have to work hard to crack the difficult core of this terrible story.

"So what do you say, Avi?" Saba would not desist.

Avi thought each word over before he spoke. "The story is true, that's for certain. If I understand it or not is a secondary question. The main question is: Why did you summon us now, at this particular time? Why did you tell us your story today, after so many years of silence?"

"Excellent! That's the very point!" David exulted like a child. "Do you hear that, Meitar? That's how a yeshivah student talks. He does not evade the issue but meets it head-on. He doesn't ask for two months to think it over. His brain is at work, and that's the main thing!"

Avi blushed in embarrassment. He was sure now that Meitar would get up and leave. Saba had insulted him. Saba had dared insult the famous singer, Meitar Eliad, the revered soloist of a well-known rock group, the idol of Israeli youth, unchallenged hero of Israeli teenagers.

But for a change, Meitar showed no signs of embarrassment or insult. He was thinking about what his grandfather had just said. This was new to both Saba and Avi. Meitar thinking?

"Good, listen to me," David broke the tense silence. "Avi, you've addressed the issue. Why did I summon you here and why did I decide to break my silence after so many years?"

Avi and Meitar both rose, as if they had planned it beforehand, and moved their plastic lawn chairs very close to their grandfather. He was going to transmit an important message, one well worth listening to.

"You are right, Avi," said David, suddenly rising impatiently from his upholstered chaise lounge. "I don't need two psychiatrists to listen to what presses upon my heart, not even if the two sweet psychiatrists are my own beloved grandsons.

"The truth is," and David's voice suddenly fell several octaves, "that if I didn't have this one vital major reason for which I summoned you here, you wouldn't have heard a word from me to the day of my death. I've learned to live with abuse and degradation. I have been the most despised person in Yetzivim for the past thirty-five years, as you surely know, and have made peace with the idea that they will even spit on my grave."

"Saba, you are getting carried away. Don't be so extreme." This was Meitar, of course; Meitar, who had no reservations but said what he liked, interrupted David's flow of words. "Aside from two harmless old men, Meir Tzuriel and Yoni Avivi, the *moshav's* former secretary, no one abuses you. Everyone respects you for what you are."

"Are you calling Shalom Travitzky harmless?" David spoke in a cracked voice. "That man who had been ruining my life since I was a child? The father began the work of destruction and even betrayed me to the accursed Nazi, and the son continued his work. He slandered me falsely as having sung for my own pleasure while his father was being murdered by the Nazis in Maidenek. In reality Shevach Travitzky was killed by the Nazi a moment after he delivered me into his hands.

"And you call him, Shalom Travitzky, 'harmless'?" David laughed bitterly, a laugh that had nothing to do with mirth or joy. But a moment later he came back to himself. He was again fresh and energetic, as if he had received a shot of adrenalin. It was incredible how after decades of suffering and bitterness, the man remained young in spirit. He had a surprising emotional fortitude that amazed everyone.

"Who is this Shalom Travitzky?" Meitar asked, baffled for a moment. "Ah, I remember, that's Meir Tzuriel's *galut* name."

"It's not a *galuti* or native *sabra* name," David interrupted wearily. "His full name is Shalom Meir Travitzky, but here, he suddenly changed it to Meir Tzuriel."

"Just like you changed your name from Yechiel David Horowitz to David Eliad," the well-mannered Avi spoke up. "Savta Odelia says that she was married to someone called David Eliad before she suddenly discovered that her husband had a different name altogether."

David was silent for a moment. He recalled the difficult days. The old wounds had not yet healed; they were not even so old. This picking at the scabs evoked all the nightmares of the past.

He fell back into his chair and huddled into his cozy blanket. The wise Odelia had understood that he would need a lot of warmth this afternoon in the garden, and not because of the lingering winter breeze.

His look focused upon the top of a tall cypress tree, the one he had planted as a tender sapling in his first year at Yetzivim. It had climbed up very high, while he had fallen very low...

"Do you know, life is full of surprises." His voice was low, directed at his grandsons who were drawing closer, centimeter by centimeter. "Here is an interesting paradox. Your great-grandfather, R' Baruch Horowitz the composer, gave me the name Yechiel David, but my mother, Mirushka, didn't like the name David and called me Chilik. The interesting thing is that when I still sang, I was called Yechiel by everyone. But from the day that my vocal chords broke and I stopped singing forever, I began being called David, after King David, the divine songster, the Sweet Psalmster of Israel."

Avi drew a little closer and took hold of his grandfather's sunburned hand.

"Saba, your vocal chords did not break. The accursed Nazis forced you to sing while they led the people to the slaughter. Roman Spiegel cruelly made you sing."

"Don't mention his name!" David suddenly shouted with visible fear. "Don't defile your mouth with his name!"

He trembled all over. For the first time in their lives, Avi and Meitar saw several tears rolling down his cheeks, slipping into his silvery beard.

They had never seen him weep. Not a single tear, even in those days when tears could have helped him, when he would have wanted to cry. And now? Tears?

"Saba!" Meitar cried in alarm. "Don't you feel well? Perhaps you'd like to go inside the house?"

"No, I'm not a small child," David grumbled. "I still haven't gotten to the point. How do they say at an executive meeting: Let us now get to the issue for which we have convened today." A mischievous glint flickered in his eyes once again.

Avi and Meitar breathed in relief. Saba Eliad was truly a rare phenomenon. A mighty emotional strength flowed in his veins, as if some secret cause had kept him going all these long, difficult years.

Meitar, in his youthful optimism, was wrong; David was right. David Eliad had been pushed out and shunned from the society of Yetzivim ever since that bitter Purim of 5720 (1960).

When David had awoken, sober in R' Calfon's house and returned home, feeling the dizzying aftereffects of the wine, he had not understood why some of the *moshavniks* had spat upon him. But when everyone kept their distance from him the next morning in the synagogue as if he were a leper, he understood that something had happened.

"What's going on?" he asked, grabbing hold of Shaul Mazuz's sleeve after prayers. "What did I do? I got a little drunk, that's all. It happens."

Shaul withdrew his hand hastily and stepped away from David, murmuring, "Yechiel Horowitz, the singer of Maidenek, asks what he did?"

David felt as if a mighty fist had slammed into his head. An invisible pipeline seemed to suck up all of his vitality. His face was drained of all expression; his chin sharpened and the skin on his cheeks stretched until they hurt. His head looked like an ancient skull dug out of its grave.

He felt as if he were living through a nightmare. He saw all the worshipers looking at him with somber expressions and then leaving the synagogue one by one. He heard voices outside. "The lowly traitor. Impostor! Pretender!"

And much more...

The secret was out, then. Wine enters, secrets leave.

But how could it be? David knew himself. He kept away from the bitter drop as if from fire, and aside from a small tumbler here and there over the years, he had not drunk at all. He was afraid of what might leak out from him while under alcohol's influence. In addition, David knew his own emotional powers and knew that even a professional hypnotist would not have been able to extract his terrible secret from him.

Who had leaked the story?

A friendly hand was laid warmly on his shoulder.

"David, there's nothing to be done." It was R' Calfon who had stayed behind. "Your secret became known yesterday, in the presence of almost all the members of the *moshav*. They were all surprised at your singing, and someone talked."

"It was Meir Tzuriel." David didn't ask; he stated a fact. The rabbi nodded heavily. David grasped his head as if to prevent it from splitting apart. "My sons, Buki and Yigal. They were in your house at the time?"

He didn't wait for an answer but raced home wildly, sobbing like a child. He suddenly understood what he had done to Buki all these years. Pursued by his own nightmares, he had imposed upon this gifted child an additional holocaust, a private holocaust of his own making.

"Buki!" David burst stormily into the house. "Buki, where are you?"

Buki was not at home. "Where's Buki?" David rushed through the rooms like a hurricane until it dawned on him to look in the garden.

Buki was sitting on a chair in the garden, among the gardenias, his chin leaning on his fist. He sat silent.

David approached him with hesitant steps, his heart pounding loudly.

"Buki?"

No reaction.

"Buki?" His hand gently stroked the boy's shoulder. Buki got up and moved away. He did not speak; he didn't even utter a single syllable, but David would never forget the terrible look on the boy's face. He was never able to properly define that expression.

It was a deadly mixture of anger, shame, repulsion and indifference, a terrible pain and suffering that had no parallel, rebellion and defiance. David had been prepared for all this. But to his deep pain, the suffering face also reflected a terrible message, something like:

"I will never forgive you, Abba, for what you did to me. Not for the muteness which you imposed upon me, nor for the shame you caused the entire family last night."

This was not the face of an eleven-year-old. This was an adult face, of a child who had matured before his time.

David saw all this in a flash, a split second. He felt his heart being crushed under the burden of his elder son's pain and understood that he had lost Buki forever. The thread of love and friendship, trust and purity which had attached the two hearts had been rent asunder for all eternity.

Paradoxically, in the long run, Meir Tzuriel had done David a service. From that day, David came out of the closet, so to speak, and ceased living in constant fear lest his secret be discovered. The worst had already happened; nothing could be ruined beyond that. An indifferent expression rested permanently on his face and the searing pain was no longer reflected in his eyes.

David peered at the slowly setting sun painting the Negev skies a bright violet that turned an orange-purple as it sank westward.

"I called you for another purpose and not to pour out my heart," he repeated, like a girl declaiming a graduation speech from a written page. "Did you understand the main message from my story? The point I was driving at?"

"No," said Meitar; "Yes," said Avi, simultaneously.

"What did you understand, Avi?"

"You were talking about your grandfather's will."

"What a quick grasp!" marveled David. "Do you see, Meitar? See what the yeshivah does to your cousin, how it sharpens his mind."

Long evening shadows darkened the garden, hiding the angry look that appeared on Meitar's face.

"I absorbed the message, Saba. You called me in order to pick on me. Thanks a lot and good evening."

He got up from his white plastic chair but Avi was quicker. He grabbed him by the hand and pleaded, "Don't get insulted, Meitar. Saba is in a very emotional state; he really didn't mean to hurt you."

"Exactly," said David quietly. "My dear Meitar, would I want to hurt you?" He tousled the long reddish locks tenderly. (*If only there were a kipah on his head*, he thought, but did not say.)

"We have no time for games of prestige." David rose quickly from his seat, vigorous and decisive, like a man of forty. "Gentlemen, it is a burning issue. Time is running out and something must be done."

"What are you talking about, Saba?" It was Avi, now. "What's burning?"

"Time is burning. Do you know when the will was written?" David's eyes flashed feverishly. "Zeide Avigdor, after whom you are named, wrote it in Teves 5655 (1895), six months before his death. He wrote that if the will was not opened one hundred years after his death, a grave danger would face the Jewish people living in *Eretz Yisrael*, if not the entire people. He stated it explicitly. Now do you understand?"

"Take it easy, Saba," said Meitar in English. "We're in danger all the time," he chuckled. "Why are you making such a big to-do about some antique will?"

"Do you have time to joke around, my wise man? Do you know when Zeide Avigdor passed away?"

"No." Meitar shrugged his shoulders.

"He died on the twentieth of Sivan, 5655 (1895)!" shouted David.

"And we're now at the end of Adar Beit, 5755 (1995)," cried Avi excitedly. "That means that w…"

"It means that we have less than three months," David interrupted. "Just about ninety days. You must search for the will. You must find it!"

42

"**L**ook for the will; find it!" echoed Meitar, a hint of mockery in his melodious voice. "There's nothing easier, Saba. Tomorrow morning we will go to the government archives in Jerusalem and ask to see Zeide Avigdor's will. They have a special department there for historically fateful wills."

"Meitar!" Avi's voice was loaded. He stared at Meitar disapprovingly. They say that eyes are the windows of the soul, and Meitar read the hinted message that remained unspoken: "How can you ridicule Saba this way?"

Meitar was embarrassed. He combed his thick hair with his fingers. He suddenly had enough of this meeting in the garden with Saba and Avi, both with their *kipot*. He felt uncomfortable and wanted out, to go off to his room with his electric guitar and synthesizer and compose a new song. 'Serenade,' the musical group with which he was chief soloist, was reaping spectacular successes and was vastly popular with Israeli youth, thanks to his wildly rhythmic songs.

"Saba, could you give us any idea how we could locate the will?" asked Avi gently.

"To tell the truth, no!" said David surprisingly. "I haven't the slightest idea. Not even the faintest."

"So how do you expect us to know?" asked Meitar directly.

"I don't know," sighed David. "I am old. Perhaps I am turning somewhat senile. Why did I think that you would be able to find the missing will? What a foolish notion..."

⤚⤙

"He's right," said Baruch to Meitar. "How does he expect you to find the will?"

"Abba, what is this story? Is there really a will or is the old man dreaming?"

Baruch raced on his exercise bicycle. The speedometer read thirty m.p.h. His heart-lung monitor showed that he was not overexerting himself, which was a good sign. His cardiologist, Professor Zimmerman, would be happy to hear about the improvement.

"Look here," Baruch panted, his feet whirling on the pedals at high speed, "I don't think he made up the story with the will."

"Why?"

"Because a person does not repeat the same story for thirty years if he really just imagined it."

"He's been talking about it for thirty years? How come you never told me anything about it?"

Baruch got off the exercise bicycle and wiped his perspiring face with a towel. He sat down to rest on an easy chair in a corner of the modern exercise room. Ever since he had suffered two consecutive heart attacks, Baruch had turned into an exercise buff. The doctors had warned him that his sedentary lifestyle, the hours spent bent over his test tubes and electron microscope in his underground laboratories, were liable to be fatal. He was an obedient patient but running around the neighborhood towards evening dressed in a jogging outfit did not especially appeal to him. What would the neighbors say? In these times, you could do everything at home. All you needed to do was open your purse. And so Baruch purchased the best and most expensive equipment and began exercising. He lifted weights and pulled coils; he ran several kilometers each evening on his sophisticated electronic treadmill and raced nowhere on his digital exercise bicycle.

"Meitar, I want you to understand. I'm not exactly interested in this subject. But Savta Odelia once told me that almost every night he talked about the will that was stolen from him. He talked about Roman Spiegel and the will alternately, one night this and the next, the other."

"Whew!" whistled Meitar in wonder. "He's been talking about the will in his sleep for thirty years? I must write a song about it. What a hit of a song it could be. It will be on Serenade's newest release."

"M-m-meitar, t-t-take it easy," said Baruch. His heavy stammer had long since disappeared but it returned to haunt him whenever he became angry or excited. He took a deep breath before continuing. "The intimate emotions of your grandfather and his personal secrets are not a subject for a musical group, is that clear?"

"Oh, Abba, don't be so serious. I was only joking."

"I'm not so sure." Baruch was angry. "You compose songs indiscriminately. Anything you experience turns into a song, like that stupid song of yours, 'A Hundred Grams of Yellow Cheese.' You call that a song? It's nonsense!"

"That's not so," Meitar protested vehemently. "It's one of our nicest hits. They're singing it throughout the country."

"It only goes to show the level of our youth," Baruch defended his position. "Our youth is truly driven by a sense of destiny and mission concerning the hunk of cheese weighing one hundred grams! Where are the songs of yore? The beautiful songs of idealism? Everything is dead."

"Abba, what about the will?" Meitar returned to the forgotten subject.

Baruch sipped some cold water and sank into thought for a moment or two, then rallied.

"I don't know what to say. I think I'll call up Yigal."

⁂

R' Yigal Eliad was leaning over his worn *shtender* in his house in the southern settlement of Mesilot. He stroked the hairs of his long black beard and squinted pensively at the difficult text before him. The *shiur* he was scheduled to deliver in yeshivah the following day had been elaborately constructed, but his study partner, Shimon Elyassian, a young and brilliant youth who heard him give the lecture in the evening before he delivered it to the entire yeshivah, had suddenly asked an incisive question that had toppled the entire lovely structure.

The telephone rang in the background. At first R' Eliad didn't hear it. His concentration was absolute. The ringing was stubbornly persistent. He shook his head and remembered that his wife had gone out to a student's wedding. The children were fast asleep and the disturbing ringing might waken them.

He rushed to the old telephone in the hall, the only one in the house, an old black rotary model. His students always joked that Graham Bell must have spoken his first transmitted sentence into this receiver. But in the home of R' Eliad, sufficiency and frugality were a life credo.

His older brother, Baruch Eliad, the famous scientist, was on the other end of the line.

"Hello, Baruch," said Yigal, excited. "We haven't spoken for months. What's up?"

The bond between the brothers seemed rather lukewarm to the outsider, but deep in their hearts they loved one another dearly, as in their childhood. The bond had weakened in the next generation. Yigal did not encourage his children to associate with the children of his secular brother. Geographically only seventy kilometers separated the brothers, but in actuality, a high, impassible barrier kept them apart.

"Avi didn't tell you anything?"

"What happened?" cried Yigal in alarm.

"Calm down. Nothing happened. Abba summoned our sons and told them everything about himself. Meitar talked to me for several hours about it. I think Abba told them things we, ourselves, never even knew."

"True, Abba is not a talkative person," agreed Yigal. "So that's the news?"

"No," the antiquated receiver rendered his voice with a metallic overtone. "Do you remember Zeide Avigdor's will?"

Yigal screwed his eyes up. Yes, he did recall. Abba had never spoken of it. His mother Odelia was the one who had told him about its theft and that Abba had continual nightmares about the fate of the ancient will which had been forcibly removed from his possession.

"Listen, Yigal. We must sit down and talk it over. Could you hop over to Rehovot tomorrow? Come visit me. You haven't been here since I was recuperating from my heart attack."

"I can't, Baruch. I have to give three *shiurim* in yeshivah tomorrow, aside from a monthly exam and several other urgent matters on the agenda."

"Do you think that I play around in my laboratories in the Weizmann Institute?" Baruch teased him goodnaturedly. "I don't have any extra time, either."

"Come visit me." It was only a cold plastic telephone receiver, but Baruch was able to feel the powerful love that was poured into that plastic tube, from the depths of his younger brother's heart straight to his own heart yearning for love. He melted like beeswax. "All right. I'll come tomorrow evening."

The silver Pontiac stopped by the gate with a screech, attracting many pairs of eyes. A fancy car like this was a rare sight in the Torah community of the southern town of Mesilot.

Baruch got out of the car, barely noticing the little children gathering around it because he was involved in a telephone conversation. He was arguing with a lab technician who stubbornly insisted on putting all the test tubes remaining on his table into the refrigerator.

"Don't put the yellow one in," Baruch commanded authoritatively. "I left it outside on purpose. It must remain at room temperature all night. It's the X tube, do you understand? Don't dare touch it."

An entire group of children escorted the bareheaded scientist speaking so authoritatively into his cellular phone. He stopped for a moment and opened his eyes. "Where am I? Can you tell me where Yigal lives?"

"Yigal?"

"Sorry." He quickly corrected himself. "Rabbi Eliad."

"Oh, the *rosh yeshivah*?" A buzz of surprise swept through the group of kids. "He's talking about the *rosh yeshivah*. This *chiloni* has come to see the *rosh yeshivah*…"

The whispers reached his ears and singed his heart with a searing pain. "I was once like you too," he wanted to shout, but he bit his lips in pain. No one had forced him to become different.

Forgotten pictures floated to the surface of his memory.

≋)≋

"My dear Baruch, Baruch *mein kindt,*" R' Goldberg stroked the boy's head. "You will speak again just like everyone else. You'll see."

Buki was then fifteen and a source of frustration and bitterness to his parents. He had been expelled from several yeshivos. The teachers and students had shown a high sensitivity to his almost complete muteness. No one ridiculed him; on the contrary, everyone befriended him and tried to help him acclimatize.

But Buki was filled with bitterness. He stammered very badly and he preferred absolute silence to helpless, pitiful attempts at speaking. Not every place was like the yeshivah. There were places with people lacking the minimal sensitivity and they found an easy prey: a stammerer! And how he stammered! Buki heard all the abuse being said behind his back and sometimes to his face. He was very sensitive and absorbed everything with his sharp senses, all the jokes that cropped up like mushrooms and followed him like a smelly trail wherever he went.

In his misery, he would run off to seek refuge in the home of the elderly rabbi of Yetzivim. R' Shraga Feivel Goldberg had always understood the boy. He was blessed with a perennially young spirit and wise, seeing eyes which danced with youthful mischief. Two round flames, small as pinpoints, burned behind the thick lenses of his eyeglasses. A thread of marvelous camaraderie was woven between the elderly rabbi and the embittered youth. R' Goldberg was the suffering boy's Wailing Wall.

"R-r-rebbe," Buki wept, burying his head on the rabbi's shoulders. "W-w-why d- d-do I have it s-s-so bad?"

"Baruch, my dear," the rabbi whispered gently, his tender heart enveloping the words, "if only *Mashiach* would come as quickly as you are going to be able to speak again."

Buki didn't know that each visit of his cost R' Goldberg a considerable part of his health. Rebbetzin Batya never revealed that after each visit the elderly rabbi would open up his *Tehillim* and pray with heartbreaking tears for the recovery of the young boy. Dozens of pages in his *Tehillim* had crumbled because of the rivers of tears he had shed.

"*Oy, Ribono shel Olam,*" he wept, dissolving in tears, " '*Lamnatzeiach al yonas ileim...*' Oy Tatte zisser, yonas ileim... Won't You redeem our mute dove? Restore his power of speech!"

His shoulders shook with sobs. His soul pined to see Buki speaking again like a normal person. He did not believe that the power of music would return to him. That was lost forever. His soul whispered to him that Buki had been banished from the heavenly palace of music due to some special decree.

But let him speak again!

Let him speak again, fluently, without his embarrassing, exhausting stammering. The youth was being destroyed by the shame. He saw everything and felt everything. How could people be so ruthless to ridicule a handicapped person? Who could guarantee their own future, for that matter?

Buki knew nothing of the weeping and prayers which undoubtedly hastened R' Goldberg's demise before he saw his prayers answered and the great miracle taking place.

≈)≈

Two small children volunteered to show him the way to Yigal's house and another ten trailed behind. He had not been here for many years and felt a repugnance at the sight of this poor, neglected neighborhood. "Slums," he murmured. "Why is the brilliant Yigal living in such slums?"

"This is where the *rosh yeshivah* lives," one tot pointed to the wooden door whose white paint had peeled off in wide strips.

The door opened wide even before he had time to knock. "Baruch!" Yigal embraced him warmly and lovingly. "Come inside."

"How did you know I had arrived?"

Yigal pointed to his heart. "I felt it here. Besides," he chuckled, "I heard the commotion of the children outside."

Baruch studied the decrepit house. The chairs were rickety; the paint was coming off the walls; the beds stood on shaky legs. The bookcase was the most impressive piece of furniture in the entire house. Thousands of books took up most of the wall space in the living room, children's rooms, and hallway. What surprised Baruch each time was the interesting fact that no book seemed dusty, though all the gold lettering on the covers had long since faded through use.

He compared Yigal's humble home with his own comfortable three-level cottage in Rehovot. But where was there room for comparison? His luxurious home was surrounded by a beautiful garden in front and a large blue-tiled swimming pool in the back. Two expensive cars were parked in his garage. The contrast inside reflected by his carpets and chandeliers, lithographs and paintings by famous artists, his state-of-the-art American kitchen was something he didn't even want to think about, it being so vast. He felt a slight dizziness at the shocking difference.

One thought gnawed away somewhere in his mind and would not let him rest. *Yigal looks happier than I do. His face radiates an inner quality of vitality that I cannot pinpoint and a certain unshaken confidence in the truth of his way of life.*

It was this thought that made him feel uneasy about coming.

"How are you, Baruch?" Yigal asked, sitting him down by the living room table. "You've been out of the country recently, haven't you?"

"Correct. After I recovered from my second heart attack, I went abroad for a lecture series in various universities." He didn't want to tell Yigal how much money he received for a single lecture. Yigal probably did not get that much from three years' salary. But he was mistaken if he thought that Yigal would have envied him. Yigal worked hard at uprooting the trait of jealousy. "I was even in Washington where I appeared before the Senate Subcommittee on Bac..." He caught himself in time, before spilling the crucial word. In the home of his brother, who radiated amity and love, he always forgot to guard his tongue.

"Come, let's get to the point," Yigal said, rescuing him from his embarrassment. "Avi was here already today, during the yeshivah lunch break, and told me everything."

"What's your opinion about this strange story, Yigal?"

"I think it is very serious. We, the great-grandsons of Zeide R' Avigdor, must find a way to locate the lost will before the one hundred years are up," he replied emphatically.

"So you buy the story?" Baruch inquired.

"Without reservation."

"So what's to be done? How does one go about finding something that doesn't exist?"

"The accursed Roman Spiegel took it with him when he fled at the end of the war," Yigal thought aloud. "How can we find out if Roman Spiegel is alive and where he is? He must be hiding somewhere in Argentina or Brazil where all the Nazi war criminals hide."

"Yigal, you're the family genius," sighed Baruch. "Tell us what to do. Find us a clue."

"Come with me to R' Aharonowitz," said Yigal, rising lightly to his feet.

"To whom?"

"R' Aharonowitz, the *mashgiach* in our yeshivah. He is a very distinguished Jew, a kabbalist and saint. I don't do a thing without consulting him. Come, let's go to him. He will organize our thoughts and put this mess into a semblance of order."

43

David Eliad walked in his garden, angry and disturbed. He wanted to think about the present, to find some solution to the riddle of the vanished will, for if it would not be opened in three months, some terrible calamity would take place. But his thoughts kept wandering backwards. Roman Spiegel had succeeded in ruining his life, as he had promised back in Maidenek. He had put a watchdog on him, Meir Tzuriel, the former Shalom Travitzky, who had clung to him like a tick all these years, and upon the right opportunity, had revealed David's terrible secret. Eleven years of relative peace had passed in Yetzivim, only to be shattered from that fateful Purim onward. Since then, his life had turned into *gehinnom*. Almost all the people of Yetzivim turned their backs on him. " 'Is this Naomi?' " they seemed to say, in Biblical paraphrase, by their turned backs. "This so-called righteous Jew — who devotes study time to Torah and who raises his children according to the best Jewish tradition — was a traitor to his people?"

He recalled those gloomy days, towards the end of 5720 (1960), when a spontaneous meeting was organized against him in the synagogue courtyard.

"It's like coming and saying that Yossele Rosenblatt, to make a thousand distinctions, went and converted to Christianity," said Yoni heatedly in the courtyard. His thunderous voice rolled into the synagogue, where David could hear it.

"Do you know what a disappointment it was to me when I heard about it from Meir Tzuriel?" continued Yoni volubly. "I, myself, traveled to Vienna to hear him as a yeshivah student in Pressburg. How we revered him! How we laughed upon discovering that the naive-looking young man who had traveled with us in the same train and who pretended to know nothing about Yechiel Horowitz was none other than the famous singer himself! He was not a bad actor, believe me. I saw him perform in the opera 'William Tell,' a day after his appearance before the Jewish audience. He was a master of the art, let me tell you."

"You're talking about David in the past tense. 'He was, he knew.' But he's still living in our midst," said Hillel Weiss. He reserved a warm place in his heart for David and continued to visit him secretly.

"No!" thundered Yoni. "For me, David no longer exists. I despised him from the moment I heard from Meir what he did at Maidenek. But over the years, the memories became dulled and I ignored them. I wasn't looking for revenge. I even agreed to make his son, Buki, the rising musical star, the chief soloist in the choir, without paying attention to what the father had done. Then along came that fool and destroyed his son on the grounds of pious excuses. Did you ever hear anything like that? To kidnap a soloist and take him to Jerusalem to the Brisker Rav's funeral? What had Buki done that he deserved to be made so miserable? And fool that I was, I even gave him the idea of going to Jerusalem…"

"Are you a paid lecturer?" asked Moishe the redhead, suddenly popping up from the gathered crowd. "If so, we can all expect to go bankrupt very soon."

Everyone laughed, except for Yoni, who continued to speak. "Everything that I forgot exploded in your faces on that Purim gathering in R' Calfon's house. You should know that treachery like that is unforgivable. David must be expelled from Yetzivim, the sooner the better."

"Perhaps he was under coercion? Perhaps the Nazis forced him to sing? We've already heard of things like that," Dani Morelli attempted to defend him.

"If you would have seen with what pleasure he sang at Maidenek, you wouldn't say that," Meir Tzuriel said heatedly, foaming at the mouth. "Even if you say that the Nazis threatened him from behind the curtain with cocked guns, he should have jumped into the audience and chosen to die rather than live a life of treachery."

"That's right," Yoni joined in. "An honorable death is preferable. He surely had hundreds of opportunities to be so good as to put an end to his life and to rid the Jewish people from the disgraceful stain of such treachery. And when? During our people's most difficult times in history! He did not utilize them. He is a traitor."

"Look at the righteous zealot, a reincarnation of Pinchas ben Elazar ben Aharon the *Kohen*." No one had seen R' Calfon approaching and all took a step back in reverence. "You are jealous for the sake of Hashem, right, Yoni? The savior of the Jewish people... Have you ever heard the expression: 'Don't judge someone until you're standing in his shoes'?

"Tell me, my friend, would you be prepared to forfeit the lives of your children who were serving as hostages?"

Yoni turned white as a sheet. This was very surprising. The big bully before whom all of Yetzivim trembled bowed his head before the rabbi and sought to leave but his feet were rooted to the ground. He didn't budge; he hardly breathed.

The crowd shifted uneasily. People suddenly heard how one must look at the other side of a controversy, even if the antagonist is a despised person, and make an honest appraisal from the true viewpoint of Judaism. But then, as ever, it was Meir Tzuriel, David's eternal enemy, who stirred up the winds and incited the people, nipping the feeling in the bud.

"To be sure, Rabbi Calfon." His voice was razor sharp with sarcasm. "Surely you were in Maidenek so that you are able to so favorably judge that lowest of human creatures, David Eliad, a man devoid of all Jewish feeling. Hostages! Grandma's tales! How do I know? Simply enough. Perhaps I was in Djerba during the war, reclining upon the soft cushions of the *beis midrash*."

When they say that one jibe can refute a hundred reproofs, they are talking about such a moment. Peals of laughter rang out between the crowded rows. Still, R' Calfon was not one to let a sliver of eternity, a moment of true arousal, slip between his fingers.

It was the evening of a hot day. An Indian summer's sun had beaten down all day and warmed the air of this northern Negev settlement. Only towards evening had a cool, refreshing wind begun to blow, and between *Minchah* and *Maariv*, many had gone out to breathe in some fresh air in the shade of the towering cypresses. The synagogue square was filled with people. R' Calfon was standing in the center of a circle. He was short and his thin pale face framed by its grey beard showed that he was no hedonist. He possessed a charismatic personality that shed a special magic quality mixed with old-fashioned good humor. An extremely erudite Torah scholar, he could easily have vied for the rabbinate of a major city, but he preferred the peaceful life in this small, quiet *moshav*. Now, everyone hung on his words.

"My friends, Rosh Hashanah is three weeks away. It is a day of judgment for all creations. The *shofar* is blown on Rosh Hashanah. We will all blow the *shofar*, won't we? Everyone will buy himself a *shofar* and blow it, right?"

"What? What's he talking about?" Shmuel Kastel jumped up, confused. He did not realize that the clever rabbi was leading them on with a rhetorical question. "Only one *baal tokeia*, only Kalman Schlesinger, of course," Shmuel said in English, in a pronounced American accent. People could not help smiling.

R' Calfon turned around and pointed a finger at him. "Very true, my friend, Mr. Kastel. You're right. There is only one *shofar* blower. Tell me, can one person alone discharge everyone of his obligation?"

Everyone was quiet. It was clear that R' Calfon wanted to say something. Kastel jumped up again.

"Of course," he said in English, with his characteristic American enthusiasm. "For sure."

"If so, I ask you," the rabbi continued, his voice shooting sparks, "why in the instance of such a major *mitzvah* as blowing the *shofar*, you are all prepared to be dissolved of your obligation by sending one representative to blow for all of you, but when it comes to the '*mitzvah*' of dissension, which is not in the Torah and not from our Sages, you do not suffice with one representative but feel impelled to be involved in it yourself, personally, and to go forth with swords and spears against an innocent man?

Enough that there is one Jew here who has dedicated his life to hatred of David Eliad. He is discharging the duty of all of you here!"

All heads spontaneously turned towards Meir Tzuriel, who stood in the center of the circle, his cheeks aflame. He inched himself out and slipped away.

The spontaneous gathering dispersed. R' Calfon's short sermon had made a mighty impression upon the people. For weeks and months afterwards, the people of Yetzivim did not stop repeating his apt comparison between *shofar* blowing and controversy, until the clever insight wandered forth and reached the big cities, where many rabbis used it in time of need.

And in Yetzivim itself... Yoni became silent as a fish from that day on and even Meir Tzuriel did not dare utter a word in R' Calfon's hearing.

But Tzuriel was not one to surrender so easily. He continued to quietly fan the fire of hatred towards David and to await another opportunity to serve his purpose. He and Yoni were determined, and had almost sworn, to oust David from Yetzivim at the first opportunity. But that did not present itself...

⮑⮐

R' Calfon succeeded in breaking up the lynch mob. Yet it became clear that while blows and expulsion would not fall upon him, friends could not be acquired by force. David remained isolated, almost completed ostracized. Only a hidden stubbornness burning in his bones succeeded in preserving him all those years. He believed that the day would come when his innocence would come to light. The mills of justice ground exceedingly slow, but they revolved all the time. He hoped that Zeide Avigdor's mysterious will would provide a solution to his personal distress. Zeide Avigdor had been no simple person; perhaps he had also foreseen his grandson's dark future, his unhappiness?

But Roman Spiegel had cruelly denied him this dream. Had the marvelous will been in his hands, he would have been able to study it, to learn what his saintly grandfather had wished to bequeath to the coming generations. Now, in three months' time, it would be one hundred years from the time of his grandfather's death, but an unyielding fate had played a trick on him. *You're still alive; you've produced two successive generations, but the revenge you promised to exact against Roman Spiegel was not carried out, not even after fifty years. That evil fiend is still alive mocking you and sticking his long tongue out at you...*

Was he alive? Was Roman Spiegel still alive?

Yes, of course. Who, if not he, saw to it to send David those occasional painful reminders? In the beginning, he sent the forgotten certificates, the diploma from the Viennese Opera House and the one from the Maidenek 'Opera House.' David had hung them up in his office by the barn, his private *yizkor* corner. And even after Odelia had discovered them and accidentally exchanged them on the wall, he did not remove them. From time to time he would sit in this place and allow his thoughts to wander to his murdered children, calling them by name: Avigdor, Shaul Yitzchak, Blumele. Here he also occasionally felt deep pangs of sorrow over the loss of Ita, wife of his youth, penetrating anew to his very marrow. He did not weep; the fountain of his tears had emptied out on that dreadful night in the Krampitz Forest.

He found no explanation for it, but whenever he saw the framed certificates, he did not think of those evening performances in Vienna and Maidenek. Instead, the figures of his family, murdered so brutally in the Krampitz Forest, arose before his eyes.

After the Six Day War, Blumele's embroidered blouse came to him by registered mail. A small note in Hebrew accompanied it: "To commemorate the victory of the Jewish people over its enemies, I have decided to return all of your property to you. Roman Spiegel." David had fainted when he opened the small package. Only as a result of Odelia's vast intuitive wisdom and tact did he succeed in recovering from the shock.

Roman chose original occasions. Before holidays, after wars. But he always, always remembered David's Hebrew birthday, just as he always made sure to send his mementos by registered mail to make sure that they were duly received by the addressee.

On the eve of David's sixtieth birthday, close to Shavuos 5735 (1975), a package arrived containing Avigdor's shoes. A year later, Shaul Yitzchak's Shabbos shirt and *tallis kattan* arrived, and in the midst of the Galilee campaign, Roman sent him Ita's head kerchief with a note: "This is not a victory like the Six Day War was, but it is also not a war of shame, like the Yom Kippur War. With my compliments."

David's heart burned like fire each time, and a small cabinet in his bedroom turned into his own miniature Holocaust museum.

Before the Knesset elections in the summer of 5752 (1992), Roman sent him his forgotten Polish identification card with the mocking message: "You need an identification card in order to vote."

The worst package of all arrived in 5754 (1994), directly from the depths of hell. It aroused an unbearable emotion in David and evoked afresh all of the past atrocities. It contained a round metal box with an attached label '*Giftgaz* (poison gas),' under which glared the skull and crossbones with another label 'Zyklon B' and 'Manufactured by the Farben Co.'

A homemade sticker was attached on the reverse side. "Dear Yechiel. Your wife was not shot in the Krampitz Forest. She was poisoned in Maidenek with gas from this container. You really should open it."

Had it not been for the previous dispatches which had dulled his sensitivity somewhat and prepared him for this, David would have gone out of his mind. Such depravity, such fiendishness the human mind cannot even imagine! He dug a small hole in his yard in the middle of the night at the foot of a peach tree, and hid the poison container in it. Who knew? Perhaps it contained one of Ita's bones, salvaged on purpose from the incinerator, which would require proper burial.

He did not have the strength, nor the will, to open the box. There was a limit to every joke. *I refuse to play the game according to his rules. Roman, I refuse to open the box!*

He tried to find a clue to Roman's whereabouts from the postmarks on the wrappings, but Roman had foreseen this and had mocked him in this too. The list of countries from which the different packages had been sent was long: England, France, Spain, Belgium...

David was sure that Roman was circulating somewhere in Europe, but then packages began arriving from Buenos Aires, Argentina; Rio de Janeiro, Brazil; Capetown, South Africa; Jamaica and India.

How could it be? David's head ached as he tried to crack the riddle. Was Roman Spiegel a modern-day Marco Polo, a traveler circling the globe?

Another enigma had painfully puzzled him all these years, a conundrum for which he had no answer:

How had Roman Spiegel learned his address in Moshav Yetzivim?

And the second question, even more difficult: How, in G-d's Name, had Roman found out that Yechiel Horowitz was David Eliad?

And if David had forgotten Zeide Avigdor's strict command concerning opening the missing will 100 years after his passing, after Purim of 5755 (1995) the most difficult memento of all arrived, a reminder that shocked all of his senses and shook up his nerves, causing him to urgently summon Meitar and Avi to Yetzivim.

The last package in the series arrived. A long wooden blue cylinder.

"He sent Zeide's will," David cried, when he'd opened the package. He scanned the tube with longing eyes. The red wax seals had disappeared.

"He opened it," he cried in a strange voice. With shaking hands he removed the protective plastic casing and peered inside. His body trembled at the sight of the desecration. The tube was empty. A gold-bordered sheet of white paper fell out.

"The will was most interesting, despite the fact that I opened it fifty years prematurely. I first read it in 1945 and since then, fifty years of amusement and pleasure have passed for me. Your grandfather was a genius, but mad and visionary. Yours, in eternal friendship, Roman Spiegel."

The package had been sent from Vienna. The letter had been written on the gold-bordered stationery of the Royal Opera House of Vienna.

Yigal and Baruch stood by the bed of R' Gershon Aharonowitz, spiritual leader of the famous yeshivah *Amal HaTorah* in the southern town of Mesilot. A malignant illness was gnawing away at the elderly rabbi's body like a hungry worm. He was too weak to get out of bed, and even a visitor without medical knowledge could readily see that his days were numbered. Baruch was astonished by his eyes. They were consumed by suffering, yet they radiated an extraordinarily pure sweetness. He was suddenly beset by a strong urge to draw up some of the cancerous cells from the rabbi's body into a hypodermic needle, crack the genetic code in his laboratory and turn them into healthy cells. Oh, couldn't he find some cure for this terrible disease?

The rabbi looked at his visitors and his face lit up. "My dear R' Yigal. You brought me an important visitor? Who is he?"

Baruch had put on a clean, ironed black *kipah* before entering. As he bent submissively and pressed the rabbi's extended hand, it slipped from his head directly into the oxygen mask that covered the sick man's face.

Yigal quickly replaced the *kipah* on Baruch's head. "This is my older brother. He is a top scientist in the Weizmann Institute in Rehovot and does much good for the Jewish people."

"You work in secret matters?" asked the rabbi. Baruch was taken aback by his quick intuitive grasp.

Yes, very true. I work in a special department of whose existence no one even is aware except for the prime minister and a select group of workers, he would have liked to boast. Instead he quoted, "'Silence suits the sage.'"

"Certainly," smiled the rabbi in understanding. "I realize that you are in charge of certain security secrets of the top degree. You must surely have been checked over many times before you were accepted into the institute to see if you could keep a secret."

The patient's face turned serious. He became thoughtful, holding on to Baruch's hand all the while. Finally he asked, "Are they all like you there?"

"Every employee passes a strict screening before he is accepted there," replied Baruch. "This is one of the most highly classified institutes in the country."

"It were well to check it out thoroughly. Perhaps in your very vicinity there may be dangerous elements," the rabbi said cryptically, leaving Baruch openmouthed.

"How did you get there? Why didn't you turn to Torah study, like your brother?"

If anyone else had asked this, Baruch would have exploded like a nuclear bomb. But the eyes before him were gentle and tender. R'

Aharonowitz did not invade the privacy of another. He was a man of truth and only asked in order to learn the truth. You can never reach another person's heart unless there is absolute honesty between you.

Baruch spoke. The personal story which had pressed upon his heart for many years but which he had never divulged to a soul now burst forth in a gushing flow. He spoke about the difficult stammer which had barred his way wherever he had turned, of the gnawing bitterness which had caused him to rebel against the establishment, and the friction he had generated with the rabbinical staff until he had been expelled from every yeshivah. He told how he had returned home and wept for days and nights and slowly had arrived at the decision to learn what had actually happened to him, to understand how such a trauma and fear could have caused such irreversible damage in his brain. He was filled with a strong urge to investigate everything from the foundation, to descend to the very depths of the matter and understand why things happened one way and not another.

"I enlisted in the army and became nonobservant, under the influence of my friends," he revealed with an ease that surprised himself. "After my release I was accepted to university and I began studying the natural sciences. I learned about the structure of the molecule and from research into the human cell I discovered the wonderful world of our genetic code."

"I understand. I understand," the rabbi whispered gently. "Better stop here, lest you let slip some professional secrets. Just tell me, did you never consult with rabbis? You experienced very difficult times, I agree with you. But why did you never search for a person of a higher spiritual caliber, removed from mundane cares, from whom to draw hope and encouragement in your hard times? 'Appoint yourself a rabbi,' our Sages advise us."

"I did have a rabbi." Unabashed tears fell from Baruch's eyes. The memory of R' Goldberg always aroused in him painful longing. He still felt orphaned from his spiritual father. "If he were still alive, I would not have left religion. He died on the eve of my army mobilization."

He recalled the huge funeral which had taken place in Yetzivim for R' Shraga Feivel Goldberg. The elderly rabbi had passed away at a very advanced age and all of Yetzivim had been astounded at the streams of people who flocked to the *moshav* to pay him their last respects. But no one had mourned him more than Buki Eliad. He had wept all night after the funeral, until David and Odelia had feared for his health. Buki felt that his support, his refuge and solace had been uprooted and removed forever more.

"He spoke with me often," Baruch reminisced. "I drew so much encouragement from him. And then, suddenly, he died. Interestingly, it was only a short time afterwards that the big miracle occurred. One day I suddenly found myself able to talk normally, like everyone else, without stuttering or stammering. But in his absence, there was no one to support me further. I was already too far gone even before, and from then on, galloped full speed downhill."

"Greater are the righteous in their death than in their lives," said R' Aharonowitz. "R' Goldberg must have prayed for your recovery in his lifetime, but in the Other World, he succeeded in doing for you what had been denied him while he was still chained to earth."

"What?" Baruch was shocked. "Are you saying that I regained my power of speech because R' Goldberg's soul interceded for me in Heaven?"

"Exactly so," smiled the sick man weakly. "This may not fit into a precise scientific theory. You may not be able to test it with your electronic microscope, but I know it here." He pointed to his chest. "The heart, my dear friend, feels everything and knows everything."

R' Aharonowitz did not give the brothers much time to recover. "But you didn't come here to look into the past," he said, very weakly. "What brought you to me?"

Yigal spoke succinctly. He was afraid that the rabbi would fall asleep in the middle because of his fragility and was as brief as possible. He succeeded in presenting the matter in several short and to-the-point sentences.

The rabbi thought a long time. "There is a directive to open the will, but it is gone. It is critical for the future of the Jewish people that it be read. What does your father say about it?" he asked suddenly.

"He called our sons to him and begged them to find the will. But they don't exactly understand his fears and doubts."

"Why didn't he summon you?"

Clear logic... but sometimes the more obvious things can create irreparable complications. How to explain to the sick rabbi that their father was able to communicate far better with his grandsons?

"Go and talk to him in person," R' Aharonowitz advised, tuning in to their very own thoughts. "Perhaps he will have something new to reveal to his sons."

44

Professor Eliad was a man with a split personality.

He was a brilliant scientist, one of the best researchers in the Weizmann Institute, one of the world's experts on genetic engineering. His studies appeared in the official publications of prestigious research institutions. He was a sought-after lecturer even in institutions that did not necessarily have any direct connection to his specific area of expertise. He appeared several times a year in the Harvard School of Law, for example, and all of his lectures were attended by the entire 'Who's Who' of the academic staff. Yale University, between whose walls the coming generation of leaders of the United States and the free world are being educated, honored him every year as their guest lecturer. He roamed the Oxford University campus feeling very much at home and in Princeton he was considered one of the elite, every appearance of his an exciting event.

Eliad's specialty was in D.N.A. research, and his discoveries in the area of the genetic code had excited the top echelon of the international scientific research community. He discovered a formula to crack the molecular chain which, due to its astronomical length, had been thought to be indivisible.

"What Einstein did to the atom, Eliad is doing to D.N.A.," quoted a columnist for the popular scientific magazine *Nature* in the name of

Professor Erwin Jefferson, head of the Institute of Strategic Studies in the U.S. "The process of splitting the atom is innocent child's play compared to what Eliad is doing in the infinite depths of the human cell."

Baruch Eliad began his career by working on dissembling and rebuilding the molecular foundations of plant seeds. Some inventions of the past — such as a yellow watermelon, an experiment which was not received enthusiastically by the public; a prickless prickly pear (sabra); a seedless watermelon, which was well received — were dwarfed by the direction in which Eliad was now aiming. He had been standing on the brink of a major breakthrough in the field of food improvement which needed another two or three years of further research, when the head of the Mossad came to the Negev University in Beersheba and heard a fascinating lecture by the young and brilliant scientist. A red light flashed in his brain. He targeted Eliad and began a thorough investigation of him. The information verified the Mossad chief's original theory: This young scientist was a rising star.

"If Eliad can crack the genetic code of several additional cells, cells from the animate world, for example, the entire country will benefit," the head of the Mossad endorsed him before the prime minister, and updated him on the vast importance of Professor Eliad's work. Two days later, a radical change took place in the life of the brilliant thirty-five-year-old scientist. Eliad almost disappeared from the scenery of the Negev University where he lectured and was added to a staff of researchers in the most highly classified department in the Weizmann Institute.

Actually, the department in which Baruch Eliad worked in the Weizmann Institute did not even officially exist. One cannot read about it in any official bulletin or publication of the scientific institute, and certainly not in the various tourist guidebooks.

In one of the wings of the Weizmann Institute, at the opening of a hallway painted a light cream, hangs a modest sign: Highly Advanced Technology — Research and Development. Anyone allowed to enter it will not see anything unusual. Even a visitor accompanying a professional in the field will not discover anything other than the usual technical equipment: sophisticated machinery with many flashing lights and digital beeps, catalyzers, advanced laser scanners, a staff of technicians in white lab coats and very strict security at the entrance.

But deep, deep inside, in a department within a department, behind many camouflages, is where the real action takes place. This is one of the best-guarded departments in the entire country, and the level of security approaches that of the nuclear reactor in Dimona. Here is where experiments in genetic engineering are being performed on living creatures, from the level of viruses, microbes and up. And the 'up' does not stop at animals and beasts, either...

A very tight security filter screens the list of candidates seeking to be accepted for work in the department, and one of the required data, aside from the ability to maintain a high level of secrecy, of course, is especially strong nerves. Anyone who cannot meet the stringent demands cannot be accepted here. The heads of the department shudder at the thought that patients who lost their sanity because of those tiny monsters, the miserable genetic hybrids and mutants which they produced, might circulate in mental hospitals and talk too much.

There are no waste baskets or disposal bins in the Weizmann Institute's genetic department. Everything is destroyed with carbolic acid contained in special chemical vats. All unsuccessful experiments are transformed within minutes from hair-raising hunks of flesh and bones to an unidentifiable chemical solution.

The workers of the department exhibit pronounced deference to Professor Eliad. His colleagues in the department know that he is the first among equals. In effect, no one challenges the fact that Professor Eliad is an indescribable asset to genetic engineering on a world-wide level.

That was one side of Baruch Eliad, the outside.

≈)⌒

Deep underneath the pleasant and self-assured facade of the prestigious scientist hid a frightened child, a little boy called Buki.

Buki Eliad, the *wunderkindt* of Yetzivim, the soloist who had the misfortune of having a father who caused the choir to go underground because of his violent objection and who forced the entire *moshav* to dance to his flute of obstinate caprice.

Buki Eliad, a warm, sensitive child, whose gentle soul had been woven of notes and chords, whose every limb and organ, every vessel in his body, had declaimed song and music.

Buki had grown in the shadow of a father who had lived through the compounded trauma of not only having lost his entire family in the death camp of Maidenek, but who had been tarred and feathered as a base renegade who had exploited his beautiful voice in order to survive, at the time that all of his acquaintances were being led to the gas chambers like so many sheep to slaughter.

Buki did not know that in some measure, he, himself, was another unfortunate victim of the Holocaust. Roman Spiegel had succeeded in ruining his life as well.

He loved music with every fiber in his body. Song was his very essence, but he had learned to suppress his deep love because of the angry, inexplicable look in the eyes of his father whenever he heard Buki sing. He himself was not aware of the fact, but before he reached the age of ten he had already composed over one hundred tunes! He had all of the qualities to become one of the major composers of our generation, and his rich, marvelous voice would certainly have placed him in the front line of popular singers.

He lost his ability to sing when the trauma affected the speech center in his brain and extinguished his talent for musical composition.

Buki never stopped mourning over his lost fountains of song. He had been cruelly uprooted from the world of music but longed for it all the time.

He and his wife Hadas named their firstborn son Aharon, after his father-in-law, Aharon Tzvieli, who died two days before the child's *bris*. Aharon soon turned into Roni, but the succeeding children were called names that emanated directly from the world of music. In a powerful yearning that knew no satisfaction, he called his second son Meitar (violin string) and his daughter Tzlil (note). After her came Shir (song), the merry child, and freckled Inbal (bell clapper), and his last child, Zemer (music).

Baruch created living memorials to the music which had been robbed from him. The future which had been erased in one fell swoop was immortalized through the names of his children.

Dassi had long since made peace with Baruch's idiosyncrasies. She understood that her husband was attempting to fill through his children the empty voids in his soul, the missing pieces of his puzzle.

He succeeded to a degree. Roni, his eldest, showed no musical inclination, but Meitar was a singer and composer from the cradle, like himself, like his great-grandfather, Baruch Horowitz, of blessed memory. Baruch encouraged Meitar's musical inclination and bought him musical instruments when he was still in diapers. Meitar enjoyed privileges that many singers lacked: His father built him a studio in the house complete with state-of-the-art equipment, the most expensive and modern on the market.

With unbridled joy Baruch used to tell his father of Meitar's tremendous progress, and when David's face would grimace with displeasure, he would softly explain, "Abba, that's how we are, we music lovers. You can't break the spirit of music in the third generation, as you did in the second."

He never forgave his father, David. He knew his father hadn't harmed him purposely, but to forgive him? Impossible. Not that David had ever asked his forgiveness. Baruch waited many years for him to get up one day, beat his breast with an *al chait* and ask forgiveness, but David had never done so. His complex emotions would not allow him. He had tried to appease the eleven-year-old Buki, but he was incapable of asking the forgiveness of the adult Baruch.

"Anyway, even if the old man lays himself out on the ground and begs my forgiveness, can he turn the wheel back?" Baruch would say to himself, the old resentment welling up in him again.

Later on he learned to love his father, as his father loved him. Even during the times when Baruch had begun straying and had abandoned his tradition, David did not cast him away. Baruch knew that whatever he did or however he looked — he could always come back home. David shuddered at the thought of expelling his son. He had experienced the taste of ostracism and estrangement. He himself had had his bout with secularism, of going off the track, and when he had returned to keep the Torah and its commandments through Odelia's influence he was the happiest man alive. Had his father stood over him with a whip and wrathful eyes, he probably would not have returned.

Precisely because of David's forgiving attitude, Baruch avoided any provocative acts, even after he had become a sworn secularist. He was careful not to stretch the rope too taut and kept *kashrus* and several other practices. "When Abba comes to visit, he should be able to eat everything in my house," he would explain to Dassi.

He knew that had it not been for the trauma he had experienced, the Jewish people would have gained a singer and composer and lost a front-line scientist who would project genetic science one generation forward. This is what his cold logical mind told him.

But his heart...

Baruch, the cold, nonchalant, self-possessed scientist hid his face in a cold mask and always maintained his distance and emotional control, while in the depths of his heart there lived a sensitive little boy, Buki, an innocent child who wished to shower his boundless love upon the entire world, a gifted child who sought recognition for his rare musical talents. Buki the soloist. •

Buki the composer...

≈)⌒

The silver Pontiac reached Yetzivim. It was almost midnight. David had retired for the night but Odelia was standing in the lighted yard, her eyes focused on the inner road of the *moshav*.

"Ima, how did you know we were coming?" asked Yigal in amazement.

"Your Avi called me," she replied. "He was with R' Aharonowitz and the *mashgiach* told him that you were on your way here."

Yigal was even more surprised. Avi did not like to serve as an information bureau. He kept his mouth shut as a general rule. What had caused him to volunteer the information to his grandmother so readily?

Odelia seemed to read his mind. "R' Aharonowitz asked that you return to him immediately after you speak with Abba. He has something urgent to tell you."

≈)⌒

"Roman Spiegel is alive? Certainly! I wish he had never been born, but he is alive and well, to my deep regret. He sends me painful reminders of his existence from time to time."

David had not been asleep. He lay awake and alert in bed, and as soon as he heard his two sons arriving, he leaped out and joined them for a midnight cup of coffee.

They sat in the living room around an old glass-topped coffee table. For the first time in their lives, Baruch and Yigal heard entire chapters in their father's life which he had never spoken about. He told them all about the strange packages, beginning with the dusty certificates hanging in his old office and ending with the Polish identification card that had belonged to Yechiel Horowitz, which had been sent the previous year from Vienna.

"Where is he?" asked Baruch. "How can he succeed in sowing his seeds of evil throughout the world?"

"I wish I knew," sighed David. "The question is gnawing at me. Who revealed my address and new name to him? When he left me in 5704 (1944) in Maidenek, I was Yechiel Horowitz."

"Abba," said Baruch daringly, "if we are already on the subject, I'd like to ask you a question." This had been disturbing him for thirty-five years and he was determined to get to the bottom of it. "What was the story that Meir Tzuriel told on that Purim? Did Roman Spiegel actually prevent the Germans from tattooing a blue number on your arm?"

David tried to reconstruct that unforgettable Purim night: a mute little boy sitting in a corner and listening to his father — who had persecuted him at every step and turn because of his hatred for music — singing away for several hours, playing a violin like a virtuoso. An innocent child who didn't know anything, suddenly hearing a horror story from Shalom Travitzky about his traitorous father. A great lump formed somewhere inside David's windpipe. He tried swallowing it but couldn't, and choked for breath.

Yigal and Baruch leaped forward to him in alarm, but David recovered on his own. He signaled to them with his finger that there was no need to get excited. He opened his left-sleeve button and revealed his arm.

"Look here," he said hoarsely, placing his arm under the strong halogen light bulb.

Yigal and Baruch drew near and stared.

Up along his arm, near David's shoulder, was a microscopic number, almost invisible to the eye: K-8729.

"Such a tiny number?" they both exclaimed in surprise. All Holocaust victims bore their stigma in much larger-sized figures.

"This is the handiwork of Roman Spiegel, master of micrography," said David, his eyes shooting sparks. "Shalom Travitzky was wrong. Roman tattooed my number in microscopic figures."

"But why is it so far up your arm?" asked Yigal. "Now I understand why we never saw your number all these years. You need a high-powered magnifying glass to distinguish it."

"I know you won't believe it, but it's the truth," said David. "Roman tattooed a blue number on his own arm as well. German soldiers and officers were also tattooed, as you know. He was a top-ranking officer and did whatever he pleased. He tattooed himself on the exact same spot as me."

"But why?" Yigal asked, raising his voice. He sensed that some weird, sick and perverted story was hiding here. He was not mistaken.

"Roman is not a person; he is an insane animal. In his opinion, we are twin brothers; both of us were born at the same hour, on the same day, and therefore, share the same horoscope. We are brothers, except for the fact that we were born in distant countries and to different parents. We are soulmates, sharing the same fate. He was the 'good brother' and I, the bad one, the Jew who stole the voice he should have gotten, and the musical talent that was his rightful birthright. That is why he made it a special point to persecute me.

"Roman gave me a different serial number than the other Jewish prisoners. He tattooed his own privileged officer's number on my arm: K-8729..."

The car swallowed up the few kilometers separating Yetzivim and Mesilot. Yigal was concerned. R' Aharonowitz's call in the middle of the night was uncharacteristic.

When they entered the sickroom, he relaxed. The old man did not look any worse than he had three hours before, when they had left him.

"Did the *mashgiach* summon us?" Yigal asked softly.

"Yes, indeed," replied the patient, nodding faintly. His weak voice sounded like the rustling of birds' wings. "I told Avi to summon you. What did your father tell you?"

Yigal told him of the latest revelations.

"I think you should send Avi to Vienna," he finally said.

"Vienna?" asked Yigal in alarm. "What's in Vienna? Whatever will Avi do there, alone and without means?"

"As for means," the rabbi turned his gaze to Baruch, "it will be all right. He will be helped…. Tell me, Baruch, do you have a son?"

"I have three sons," replied Baruch with satisfaction.

"I mean, do you have a son who can travel with Avi to Vienna?"

Baruch thought aloud. "Roni can't; he's in the army. Zemer is only two years old. Meitar could accompany Avi; he's the same age."

"Your two boys will go to Vienna a week after Pesach, or two weeks, at the latest. This is a question of *pikuach nefesh*, saving lives. My heart tells me that something extraordinary awaits in Vienna." The feeble voice which had evoked the fluttering of birds' wings became even weaker and now sounded like the rippling of water in a still pool. Baruch was afraid that the sick patient was about to lose consciousness.

"But why not us two, my brother and I? And why to Vienna, of all places? Roman Spiegel sent his fiendish packages from all over the globe," insisted Yigal. The rabbi's words were always like the oracles of the priestly breastplate, but his peace of mind was now disturbed by the fear that the patient was about to surrender his life forevermore. He tried to extract as much information as he could right now.

"The last package came from Vienna? Then we will go after that." The patient's tongue almost cleaved to his dry palate. Yigal brought a wet Q-tip to his lips and swathed them.

"Thank you, dear *talmid*," whispered R' Aharonowitz. "I will tell you the truth. As soon as you came to me, I began visualizing the city of Vienna in my mind and couldn't understand why. I was never in Vienna in my life, but the scenes of that lovely city kept appearing in my mind, colorful, clear and sharp, as if I were strolling there right now. Right after you left I decided that it was imperative for you to go and search there. That's why I asked Avi to call you. Now, after your father's story, I don't have the shadow of a doubt that you must send your sons there. It's a matter of life and death.

"You asked why you shouldn't go there yourselves," he concluded with his last reserves of strength. "Young boys have more acute senses and much more energy. They will be able to uncover what you might not see. Meitar can investigate places that Avi cannot or would not wish to enter..."

The rabbi's almost transparent, airy hand stretched out in farewell, its veins branching up into his thin arm like a geographic map drawn in with fine blue pen.

"The climax will take place in Vienna," he whispered in his dry voice to the two brothers standing stupefied before him. "Just wait and see."

45

"**I** refuse."

"But you have to go."

"Under no circumstances."

"Avi, are you arguing with Abba?"

"I never said 'No' to Abba," said Avi in a minor key, sadly. "But now I think that I cannot agree. Does Abba want me to consort with Meitar for several weeks? Abba doesn't know what a negative influence he can have on me!"

The genteel Avi had never spoken to his father in the familiar direct mode of address, 'you', but only in the third person: "Abba knows; Abba permits; does Abba agree?"

"On a general level you are right," agreed Yigal. "But you know what the Torah says about obeying our sages, even if they tell you that right is left and left is right. And this is what R' Aharonowitz ruled, so there is no arguing with me."

Avi was silent. After a few moments he slipped quietly out of the house and went to the home of R' Aharonowitz. When the *rebbetzin* opened the door he asked bashfully if he could enter.

"Forgive me, honored *rav*, but I fear that Meitar will be a bad influence on me," he said submissively when he stood by the bed. The patient's face could hardly be discerned from amidst the mass of tubing surrounding him.

"Why don't you think the other way?" suggested the rabbi. "Why aren't you sure of yourself? You see a secular person and panic. What is there to panic about? Perhaps he should be afraid of you! After all, his wagon is empty and yours is full. On the contrary, you must share your treasures, what you have to offer. A little bit of light dispels much darkness."

"'I am not a man of words,'" quoted Avi. "I am very weak in debating. Meitar will certainly try to get me involved in ideological arguments, as usual. Why we don't do this; why we do that. I am sure to lose the battle."

"How do you know?" the rabbi wondered. "Your approach is self-defeating. Instead of planning an offense, you are straightaway on the defensive."

Silence reigned in the room. Only the beeping of the electric I.V. monitor disturbed the silence every few moments, in rhythm to the flow of the infusion into the sick man's veins.

"Anyway, I don't think that Meitar is interested in discussions," whispered the rabbi again. "Your father told me that he is the soloist of some song group. I think that his dry soul is thirsty for something refreshing. It yearns for a spark of Jewishness. He will not argue with you. He will photograph you."

"Photograph?"

"Yes, everything you do will be registered by his curious eyes to be judged by his mind. He will wish to know if religious people are honest with themselves, if they are not phonies or cheats. Your deeds and your inner truth will speak to his heart a thousand times more than the most convincing argument. I think that there is some rule that newspaper men use: 'One picture is worth a thousand words...'" The rabbi smiled with slight irony. "That rule applies here too. Victory in theological arguments is not what makes true *baalei teshuvah;* personal examples do!"

In the following days Avi came to Yetzivim to help Savta Odelia clean the house for Pesach. His uncle, Baruch Eliad, had wasted no time. By the morning after the talk with R' Aharonowitz, he had ordered two open tickets for Meitar and Avi for Tel Aviv — Vienna — Tel Aviv. Avi felt butterflies in his stomach and he shared his apprehension with his grandfather. The old man laughed.

"Well, of course. *Reise fever.*"

"What?" asked Odelia and Avi simultaneously.

"*Reise fever,*" he repeated, enjoying himself. "The fever preceding a trip, the excitement before a maiden voyage especially."

"I will never learn Yiddish," said Odelia, vigorously rubbing a window with a clean rag. "I've been married to you almost fifty years and never heard you use that expression. For a moment I thought it was a woman's name."

David produced a sound of satisfaction and went off to the next room to study. His gaze locked into the page of *Gemara* in front of him and soon he was completely absorbed in what he was studying, having forgotten the world around him.

"Do you know, Savta," said Avi thoughtfully, tackling a huge pile of books, beating off the yellow desert dust off them, one by one. "It's not only the *reise fever*, like Saba calls it. I simply don't know what we are expected to do in Vienna. Where must we go? Abba said that he arranged lodgings for us through a good friend, somewhere in the religious community in Vienna. But what are we looking for there? Perhaps we should run through the streets and shout, 'Roman Spiegel, give back the will.' I am afraid that this whole trip is a wasted effort."

"You're getting a free ticket to go abroad," his grandmother answered. "Go and enjoy yourself. What difference does it make if you achieve your purpose or not?"

But Avi was made of different stuff. Years of *Gemara* study had trained him to separate the wheat from the chaff, to put prime things at the top of the ladder of priorities, and to ignore marginal, irrelevant things. Even if that marginal thing was a pleasure trip to Vienna.

"I heard that R' Aharonowitz gave his blessing, or, more accurately, he actually proposed the trip. If so, don't be afraid. I am certain you will succeed."

After a few hours of thorough cleaning, they sat down in the kitchen to eat. Over the years Odelia had not lost her vigor. She fried chicken shnitzel and french fries, cooked noodles and poured sauce over them from the previous day's dinner and lo, here was a delicious, quick meal.

They ate in silence. Odelia, usually so practical and down-to-earth, was now lost in thought.

"I want to tell you something," she finally began, to the surprise of David and Avi. "I think that perhaps it will strengthen Avi's morale on the eve of his trip.

"You know that I was born on the island of Djerba, Tunisia. This island was filled with Torah scholars and scribes. My father, of blessed memory, Chaniel Cohen, was a pedigreed *Kohen* whose parents had lived in the quarter of *Kohanim* on the island. It was called *Chara Zeira* to differentiate it from the larger quarter of non-*Kohanim*, *Chara Kabira*.

"Just imagine," she said, her eyes glowing, "my father told me that in his childhood he had prayed in a synagogue that was made up only of *kohanim*. And when they went to wash their hands before the priestly blessing, there was not a single *Levi* to perform the ablutions for them."

"So who did it?" wondered Avi. His grandmother hardly ever spoke about her childhood in Djerba, possibly because of the terrible memories that haunted her that were tied up with it. Her parents, Chaniel and Miriam, were murdered in a pogrom by Arabs two years after she and her twin brother, Shai, fled, with their parents' blessing, to *Eretz Yisrael*.

"The firstborn sons of all the *Kohanim* washed the hands of the entire congregation," she repeated what her father had told her. "But this was not the main problem. They didn't have anyone to bless for they were all *Kohanim*. This is why they did not bless facing the congregation, as is accepted in all synagogues, but turned around to face the walls and bless the entire city outside it."

Odelia's plate remained untouched. She was unable to eat the delicious food she had prepared. A flood of memories engulfed her...

⁌⁌

She sat in a small house in Djerba, on a low footstool by her father's side, playing with the fringes of his *tzitzis*. "Odelia, my daughter," Chaniel whispered affectionately, tousling her hair. "You are a big girl, already, you're all of eight years old. The time has come for you to know who your grandfather was, that is, my father, R' Yosef Matzliach Hakohen."

"Was he a *tzaddik*?" asked the young Odelia, her dark eyes gleaming. She loved stories about saintly people.

"A very great one, a hidden saint," said Chaniel longingly. "I only had the privilege of knowing him for a short while before he departed this world. I was a boy of six, but my mother told me about him. He was a great kabbalist and studied Kabbalah day and night. He even corresponded with the kabbalists in *Eretz Yisrael* and Poland."

"Poland?" the little Odelia asked with a start. "But that is so far away! Abba, tell me about Poland," she begged.

"What do I know about Poland?" said Chaniel. "All I know is what my mother told about my father's trip there."

"Saba traveled to Poland?" Odelia was astounded.

"Yes, he corresponded with some great *rav* from a Polish city, a kabbalist like himself. Only Hashem in Heaven knows how they discovered one another. After years of correspondence, Saba felt he must become acquainted with his pen friend and he traveled to Poland. He stayed there for two years."

"Why so long?" wondered the girl.

"Because he lost a whole year in Poland." Chaniel's voice expressed genuine commiseration with his father's plight as he wandered through foreign cities in Poland, seeking his friend. "He got off at the Danzig port..."

R' Yosef Matzliach Hakohen stood in the port of Gdansk perplexed, a huge bundle slung over his shoulder. He could not speak the local language and didn't know where to turn. He should have joined his fellow passengers but suddenly felt an inexplicable urge to stop. He stood for a long time transfixed, watching the sailors of the ship, the Maria Theresa, which had brought him to Poland. They were industriously engaged in securing the ship to the wharf. They wound the thick, coarse ropes that dangled down the sides of the ship through the rusty iron rings jutting out from the stone pillars of the dock and tied them with endless knots, one on top of the other.

"Those must be the sailor's knots discussed in Tractate *Shabbos* in the chapter on knots," thought R' Yosef.

Among the scurrying figures he discerned one worker who seemed to have Oriental features. "He will surely be able to tell me where to go."

He was both right and wrong. The sailor did speak Arabic but mistakenly, or perhaps on purpose, sent him in the wrong direction.

"Tell me," asked R' Yosef before he turned to go, pointing to the complex of knots. "Are those called sailor's knots?"

"I don't know, *hawaja*, the difference between sailor's knots and regular knots," he replied. "My shipmates taught me that they are called Gordian knots."

"Gordian knots?"

"A very complicated knot. One that can almost not be undone," explained the Arab.

"Ah, you're right," rejoiced R' Yosef. "Now I remember. Gordian must be connected with the ancient Greek King, Gordius of Phrygia." But the Arab knew nothing about that ancient city or about Alexander of Macedon...

≈⌒

"Do you understand, Odelia? The Arab sailor may have helped him to understand the words of the *Gemara* but he gave him the wrong directions. Grandfather wandered about for an entire year along strange roads which were unfamiliar even to the Jews of Poland. He was almost murdered by *goyim* thirsty for Jewish blood."

"And was he saved?" asked Odelia in alarm.

"Of course, silly girl," laughed Chaniel. "If he had not been saved, your father would not have been born. R' Yosef was young and strong, and he beat off his attackers. He returned to Djerba two years later, hale and hearty."

"Did he ever meet the Polish kabbalist?"

"Oh, yes. He stayed for an entire year in his home. They studied the secrets of the Torah together and became true friends. And after he returned to Tunisia he continued to correspond with him for several years, until his friend from Poland passed away."

"Abba," her voice took on a petulant edge. How she loved to sit by her father's side and feel his protective size and strength. The winter wind shrieked outside but inside it was warm and comfortable, a warmth that pervaded her heart. "Who was that Polish rabbi whom Grandfather visited? Was he an important man?"

"Most certainly, important. Saba described him as one of the great men of the generation. Saba told me that he could have lit up the entire world with the light of his Torah, but he chose to remain in the shadows."

"And what was his name?" asked the child, fawning upon her father like a baby.

"I don't know," replied Chaniel. "Saba never told us. His friend expressly told him not to reveal it. He always remained a mysterious person to us; only Saba knew who he was."

Savta Odelia's voice broke. She wept silently in longing for her father. She thought about her mother, Miriam, and about her murdered parents' bitter fate.

The silence lengthened until David finally asked, "Why did you tell all this now? What was it you wished to say to Avi?"

Odelia felt confused, in the grip of a strange emotion. She could not say why she had spoken those words, why this particular scene had suddenly floated up from the recesses of her childhood memories of Tunisia. So many years had passed since, and this particular story had long been forgotten. Now it had suddenly surfaced from the convoluted chambers of her memory, clear and alive, as if she had been sitting there this very day, in the heated room together with her father, Chaniel.

But why this particular episode?

She thought for a moment and found a plausible answer. "I wanted to tell Avi, er... er..." She was overcome with emotion. "Ummm... to convey the message that he should learn from my grandfather. That he should go to Vienna even if it involves difficulty and danger. Avi," she turned to him, her voice trembling with emotion, "even if you don't feel the ground secure under your feet, don't hold back. Go in peace and Hashem will grant you success!"

⇒)⇐

Meitar was annoyed. This strange episode had come precisely in the midst of a new recording he was making with Serenade. "I need this ridiculous trip to Vienna like a hole in the head," he grumbled to his father, Baruch. "All the members of the group are working round the clock, overtime plus. I simply can't pick myself up and run off right in the middle."

"What's the name of your new record?" asked Baruch with a wide yawn.

"Thanks for the interest, Abba," Meitar said sarcastically. Baruch was not particularly enthusiastic about the messages of the group's songs.

"Oh, by the way, what do you think about the new organ I bought you?" Baruch asked.

Meitar reddened. "Super, Abba. I haven't even thanked you for it."

The Japanese electronic organ was an expensive 'toy,' the last word in state-of-the-art modern music, a small but very sophisticated instrument that recorded tunes and adapted them to the chords and arrangements in its memory in an original type of mix. It was capable of storing many hundreds of familiar tunes in its memory in a few magnetic chips and then spouting them automatically as if it were a ten-piece orchestra. You only had to know which button to press in order to hear marvelous music being played all by itself.

Needless to say, the cost of this instrument surpassed the five-digit mark. In dollars.

"You didn't answer my question," Baruch reminded him.

"I know, Abba. The new record is called 'Weather Report.' How does that sound?"

"Fantastic," said Baruch. "I can't wait for the next one. You'll probably call it 'Purple Chocolate' or 'Ketchup Flowing in the Veins'."

"Abba, what's the matter? That's what goes today. Teenagers all over the world love to dance to an energetic, macho tempo. I can't market songs from the '60s today."

"Why don't you try producing something with values? Why all this nonsense? Those aren't songs, they're weeds. Have you ever seen a *kikayon*? It's a castor berry plant that springs up in the evening and wilts by morning. That's what your songs are like; they're sung in the morning and by evening they're already forgotten. Your song occupies the first place in the hit parade for a moment and a half, because by then it must move over to make room for the next all-time hit, which will not last more than thirty seconds either. You live in the immediate present, but I think that the present of today's youth can't even be called that. It is a terrible, frightening, confused disconnection from reality; it's floating in outer space. And you enjoy that?"

"Very much." Tears glistened in Meitar's eyes. "You're cutting us down for no reason. Today's youth also has its values. We're building a future, not only a present."

"Show me," said Baruch. "Are you prepared to invest in something with values?"

"For sure!"

"Then let's see you go to Vienna."

"But that's nonsense. What are we looking for in Vienna? For the legendary Roman Spiegel? I'm not even sure that he is a real person, that he ever existed. For all I know, he may be a figment of Saba David's imagination. But let us assume that he is real. Will he be waiting for us at the airport in Vienna? Will he bow deferentially and extend the will we are looking for on a silver platter? If he exists, he is surely living in some South American country, like all the other Nazi emigres, under some pseudonym."

Baruch looked at him with interest. "Aha! I finally detect some movement in those grey cells of yours. Meitar is thinking. Here's something new…"

Meitar did not react. He knew that anger, force and violence are ways to impose one's will on another; they are an extension of the love of power. But on the other hand, they sometimes can denote the very opposite and be an expression of weakness. If Abba was baiting him, it might be a sign that he felt incapable of forcing him to go to Vienna. Well, Meitar would surprise him.

"I'm going. Together with Avi," he said simply.

"Really?" Baruch's frosty countenance eased. "Very good. Even if you return emptyhanded, it will have been worth the effort. Avi is a companion from whose company you can well benefit."

"Don't get excited, Abba," replied Meitar cynically. "I'm rather afraid of him. Those *datiyim* stifle me. Everything is 'no,' everything is forbidden. No matter what I do, he'll find a reason to criticize. 'Don't drink that; don't eat this; don't breathe. You have to take *maaser* from the soap.' He will be constantly murmuring his secret spells from those books of his. It's going to be one big nightmare."

"So why are you going?"

"I am going to expand my musical horizons. There are some music groups in Vienna that I'd like to meet. That's all."

46

Avi settled himself into the padded seat of the airplane. He enjoyed being punctual and had arrived at the airport an hour and a half before the flight. The plane was scheduled to depart in twenty minutes; Meitar had not yet arrived. Most of the passengers already occupied their seats, waiting for takeoff.

Avi had hardly slept a wink the night before. His mother had suggested that he go to sleep early so as to be fresh for the trip, and he had obeyed by retiring at ten. But in a house like that of R' Yigal Eliad it was impossible to go to sleep early. Avi was the eldest, followed by ten brothers and sisters.

The house was noisy, as usual. Four-year-old Efraim came to pull his blanket off and see if he was really sleeping. "Ima," he reported, "he's lying in bed with his eyes closed. Does that mean he's sleeping?" Ima came on tiptoe and removed Efraim from the room. "Sweetie, don't shout. If he's sleeping, you might wake him up."

Lively discussions took place around his bed. The brothers and sisters discussed (in his room, of course,) how to take leave of him the following morning. They settled on large posters with bold lettering reading, "Avigdor, Travel Safely and Successfully." Avi did not move an inch; he didn't want to spoil their fun.

Later that night, when the entire household was truly asleep, he peeked at the clock. 2:30 it said. "Why waste my time?" he said to himself. "I can't sleep, anyway." He got up and dressed quietly, took out a *Gemara* from the bookcase, and sat down to study in the living room. He studied for about an hour until his eyes closed by themselves. Yigal found him there at 6 the next morning, fast asleep, his head sprawled on the *Gemara*.

The posters awaited him in the kitchen, bold and brightly colored. The nicest was that produced by six-year-old Avigail. "Avi, my swit brothr, Go in peece and gud luk," evoked a smile on his tired face.

"Were you excited last night, Avi?" Yigal asked with a sympathetic smile. "Don't worry; it's only natural. I would have been surprised if you hadn't been."

"I'm apprehensive," said Avi. "I don't know when I will be returning. What's going to be with all that time wasted from my Torah studies? The new *zman* just began a week ago and my *chavrusas* are waiting for me."

"You asked R' Aharonowitz about that aspect and he answered you in a very succinct sentence: 'Its [the Torah's] suspension is its survival.' We are talking about a life-threatening situation for the public and this waives aside any other consideration. Regarding your *chavrusas*, I arranged substitute partners for the interim. When you return, you can resume your studies with them."

Avi remained uneasy. "Throughout Pesach and the week following it, I thought about the trip and the words of R' Aharonowitz. I prayed that we succeed. Yesterday I went to the *Kosel*. I asked Hashem that my picture be successful."

"Picture?"

Avi told him about his talk with R' Aharonowitz and his warning that Meitar would 'photograph' him. One must look good in a photograph. Yigal was moved by the idea. "Don't worry. Meitar is a good kid at heart. I am sure that you will get along with him."

⇒⇐

He studied the ticket again. The flight was scheduled to depart at 8:45. Another ten minutes to go and Meitar had not yet shown up.

The stewardesses went up and down the aisles for a final check. One set of doors was already shut but the stairs had not yet been rolled away.

"He pulled a fast one on me," thought Avi angrily. "He promised to come but he made a fool of me." But this was followed by another thought. "No, Avi. You must judge everyone favorably. He must have a good reason for the delay. He will come."

All eyes were suddenly drawn to the windows. Something strange was going on below.

A shiny red open-topped sports car was approaching the plane with screeching tires, accompanied by an escort of two Airport Authority cars. These were followed by hundreds of teenagers in brightly colored T-shirts with the 'Serenade' logo splashed across the front, holding large signs, "Meitar — Don't Go," "Meitar — We're With You in Vienna." They burst out of the terminal building with rhythmic shouts of "Mei-tar! Mei-tar! Mei-tar!" A phalanx of policemen kept the heated crowd from bursting forward to the runway.

Meitar stood up in his car, a broad smile spread on his face. He waved to his fans. The car reached the runway and Meitar leaped over the side of the car and raced towards the plane.

When he entered, all eyes turned to him. A hum of pleasant surprise passed among the passengers. "Look who's here, Meitar Eliad, the soloist of the rock group Serenade!" Meitar stopped, bowed charmingly to the passengers and smiled from ear to ear in great satisfaction.

"How'd you like my show?" he asked, sitting down next to Avi. He was chewing gum and made a huge bubble. Many eyes were turned to watch the unlikely pair; no one understood how a close, familiar conversation had sprung up so quickly between such contrasting people.

"How did you stage such a spectacular farewell?" Avi couldn't help asking.

"Connections, my dear cousin, connections," Meitar said, walloping Avi on the back. "When you become a singing idol and have thousands of fans, you'll also be able to arrange such a smashing scene."

The plane left the ground and began its upward climb. Avi felt a sharp pang of remorse in his heart. "What have I done? I've wrenched myself away from *Eretz Yisrael!* Perhaps I am not worthy of it." A tear slid down his cheek.

"Attention all passengers," the pilot announced over the loudspeaker. "We are now beginning our flight to Vienna. Expected travel time is three hours and thirty minutes. We wish you a pleasant trip."

Meitar sprawled in his seat. The two youths stared out the window for a few moments, marveling at the sight of the receding ground and the familiar scenery growing smaller by the second, until they were up, high in the sky, flying over the sea. The water glistened and the waves' white froth could still be seen from their height. The view soon turned into a monotonous blue-green expanse.

"Avi," cried Meitar excitedly, "Listen, this is going to be the adventure of the century. The plane lands in Vienna and two minutes later the action begins. We storm our way into Roman Spiegel's home with a massive police coverage, shouting, 'Give back the will!' Roman wails and pleads, 'I can't; I'm emotionally attached to it.' We refuse to give in and, gun in hand, begin counting to three. Roman moans, limps off to bring the will, begs for his life, but we are adamant and drag him off for a Nazi criminal's trial in Israel."

Avi's eyes grew wet with laughter. "Tell me, how do you know that Roman Spiegel limps? And how will we reach his house within two minutes?"

"What? Don't you know?" Meitar assumed his clownish expression. "All thieves and pirates in the fairy tales limp. Roman lives near the airport. He is simply sitting and waiting for us."

"What do you mean?"

"Avi, let's cut this out," Meitar said, suddenly turning serious. "Did you buy that story about Roman Spiegel? We're only traveling to kill two or three weeks in Vienna. That's not so bad. We can visit the Burg Theatre and eat some of the famous Viennese *sacher torte*. We'll hop over to the Hapsburg palace of Kaiser Franz Josef and then we can return to Israel, tired and pleased with ourselves. We can tell them that we searched for Spiegel throughout Vienna but didn't find him."

"Meitar, you're a pessimist."

"I am not. I'm a realist. Roman Spiegel doesn't exist. Saba David dreamed up this demon and we, two innocent sheep, are going on a wild-goose chase to search for the villain of his nightmares."

"Meitar! How can you talk like that?"

"I am talking like a thinking young man," Meitar teased. "I may not be a *yeshivah bachur* but I have given this matter some thought. It just does-n't make any sense. Let us suppose that such a person does exist. So what? Is he sitting in Vienna, legs crossed, waiting for us to come and find him? Be logical!"

Avi was silent. He felt insulted for his grandfather's sake. How could one say that such a moving story as they had heard was a mere figment of his grandfather's imagination? He looked out the window again. The sky had turned a deep blue.

There was something festive about the expanse over which they were flying so peacefully. The clouds changed shapes all the time. They some-times resembled waves, sometimes snow and sometimes distant mountain peaks.

The crew was busily at work. In the narrow aisle between the seats a tea wagon stood laden with dinner trays which were handed out to the passengers.

Avi refused his tray. He leaned over and took a sandwich out of his traveling bag.

"What's wrong with this food?" Meitar was shocked. "Don't you rely on its *kashrut*? Here's the seal of rabbinical supervision."

"Oh, it's one hundred percent, but I rely on my mother more."

"I knew it!" Meitar fumed. "I told Abba that I'd have problems with you. Tell me, why must you be such a saint at every step of the way? Why must you stand out and be so different..."

Avi cringed under the attack. He went off to the far end of the plane to wash his hands and then chewed his sandwich in silence. Meitar felt a slight pang of conscience. Avi was so dignified, so princely in his actions. There was a certain charm, an aura to everything he did, an air of purity.

All true, but why did he have to be so holy? Why couldn't he let his hair down, so to speak, be normal, a *chevraman*. Why couldn't Meitar imagine his cousin singing and dancing in a pub until he was wiped out?

"D'you know, Avi, Saba always says that the yeshivah sharpens one's mind. I see the opposite. I'm the one doing the thinking here. I know that we're traveling for nothing, while you're certain that you're going to bring *Mashiach* back from Vienna on a white donkey. Come, show me your genius. Throw me a mental challenge and let's see who really thinks more clearly, a yeshivah student or a kid like me."

Avi accepted the challenge.

"Fine. Let me ask you a question: A small child and a cow are walking on a mountain road, along a narrow, dangerous path with a gaping abyss plunging all the way down. Which of them is more liable to fall?"

"What kind of a question. The child, of course."

"Why?"

Meitar thought a moment. "There are several reasons. The cow does not grasp the significance of the drop and is less frightened than the child. A person understands and the fear itself is liable to cause him fatal dizziness. There's another reason; the cow is more cautious; it has a sharper instinct of self-preservation."

"A very good answer," Avi praised him. "Now let me show you at what point a *yeshivish* way of thinking is sharper and deeper. Not for the sake of mental calisthenics but in its search for the truth. Why does a cow have a more developed mechanism of self-protection?"

Meitar was puzzled. He was not accustomed to thinking in the direction of cause and effect. "The question 'why' is irrelevant. It is a dry fact."

"On the contrary. The question 'why' is very relevant. The *mussar* thinkers have taught us that the difference is that a cow does not have free choice whereas a person does."

"I didn't get that."

"Let me explain. The cow cannot choose between good and evil. It was not commanded to 'choose life,' which happens to be a commandment in the Torah. This is why the cow is protected by its Creator, Who endowed it with certain tools, that is, a well-developed sense of self-protection and a highly acute instinct of preservation. This is why only animals, and not humans, were provided with such sharp senses and instincts.

"A child is different. As part of the human race, he has intelligence and free choice. Humans were given the choice to protect themselves over animals; therefore, one false step and — whoops — over they go. Our free choice enables us to mess more things up than a cow."

"That's a new concept for me. I need time to think it over." Meitar was deeply impressed by the acute logic, the wisdom in Avi's argument. Avi had defeated him in this first battle. Avi had not sought to show him up. He had merely stated what he had to say, quietly, informatively, intelligently.

In the background, the captain announced in a metallic voice that in another hour and ten minutes they would be landing in Vienna and that they were now crossing the border between Greece and Bulgaria. Their eyes closed.

≈≈

Baruch Eliad arrived at the laboratory with an uneasy feeling. He had accompanied Meitar to the airport and quickly fled at the sight of those hundreds of fans encircling him. "Who brought them here?" he fumed. It seemed to him as if from the moment Meitar saw them, he forgot his father entirely.

"Eliad, it isn't healthy," his colleague, Professor Manor, greeted him. He had arrived earlier that morning and was already busy taking notes.

"What's not healthy?"

"To eat a sour pickle on an empty stomach," replied Manor, a mischievous light dancing in his eyes. "Why are you so sour, so early in the morning?"

Eliad smiled. "Manor, my old friend, you are not only a talented scientist, but also an incorrigible humorist."

The two colleagues were certainly a study in contrasts. Baruch was stingy with his smiles; he went about with a severe look on his face. Manor considered it his solemn duty to make Baruch Eliad happy. To this end he would tell him a new joke each day from his bottomless source of witticisms. This morning he succeeded in squeezing a smile out of him.

"What's new here in the lab?" asked Baruch. A fresh sound had already crept into his somber voice. Manor rubbed his hands with glee.

"Everything's fine! The experiment with the baboons has succeeded beyond our expectations. Bobby is immune to heart attacks. His arteries are completely clear even after a half-year of dosing him with oxidized cholesterol and triglycerides directly into his veins."

"How big a dose did he receive?"

"Thirty cc a day. Even a full-grown Indian elephant would have collapsed with a heart attack from that long ago."

"But not Bobby," Eliad was beaming now. Bobby had undergone genetic engineering. This had been done at the point when Bobby was no more than an entity comprised of a few embryonic cells at their beginning of development. His mother gave birth to him several months later, an ostensibly normal baboon. But more. Bobby was different. His major arteries were completely immunized against blockages and fatty buildups since the makeup of his blood would never allow it to be affected by fats and cholesterol. They had begun the experiment on lab mice and proceeded to monkeys. If everything went as planned, they would be able to continue to the critical stage: experimentation on humans.

Perhaps this would be the breakthrough towards a healthy world, a world without heart disease... Hopefully. But Eliad and Manor would still sweat rivers before the hoped-for successful end.

A strong pressure on their eardrums woke them. The plane had begun its descent half an hour before and it was now plunging rapidly. They quickly buckled their safety belts. Vienna looked huge from the air; even from the sky they could see its unique beauty. The city looked like a an amazing conglomeration of geometric shapes fitting neatly next to one another, creating a magnificent mosaic of color.

The plane landed in the Schwacht Airport in Vienna. Meitar and Avi stretched themselves luxuriously. The flight had passed very quickly. They had to wait to retrieve their luggage from the conveyor belt and from there they hurried off to claim a place on the long line of people waiting to clear passport control.

A customs officer quickly and efficiently stamped their passports and punched their names on his computer keyboard. Something on the screen began flickering. The officer read the message but his impassive expression did not change.

After they had passed, he pressed some numbers on his cellular phone. He could hear ticking and then a long ring. When the receiver on the other end was picked up, he whispered, "Two young fellows from Israel bearing the name 'Eliad' have just passed through. What am I supposed to do?"

Someone on the other end whispered back, but the officer's face registered no expression. He rang up another person and whispered into the phone.

Meitar and Avi went out to the main street. A yellow cab slid up to them soundlessly and stopped in front of them.

"*Anschuldig, Herr,*" called out a polite cabby, "would you like me to take you into town?"

Except for the familiar *anschuldig,* they didn't understand a word he spoke, but they guessed the meaning of his offer.

"*Nein,*" answered Avi firmly.

"Why not?" asked Meitar in surprise.

"We have a bus every twenty minutes and the subway line No. 7 goes once an hour. It's only a question of fifteen kilometers to town. Why spend money on an expensive cab?"

"Aha, we are going to have to deal with misers, I see," grumbled Meitar. "I'll pay the difference."

The two climbed in. The driver revved into high speed and his left hand reached for the phone. "*Die yungendt befindt sich bamir.*" he said in German. "The young men are with me."

47

Professor Gideon Manor and Professor Baruch Eliad were jointly in charge of the Department of Genetic Engineering at the Weizmann Institute.

At least officially.

The elderly Manor had actually planned to retire many years before. But with his vast experience of accumulated research in the field of D.N.A. genetic coding, the directors of the institute would not hear of it. To retire and take home the tremendous reservoir of data which required years of study to amass? Unheard of! 'Old Manor' was almost forced to continue on.

"What are you going to do at home? Engineer the goldfish in your aquarium?" asked the head of the faculty, Professor Martin Shulman. This was the straw that broke the old camel's back. Professor Manor was truly incapable of imagining what he would do at home aside from spending his evening in a dopey trance before the flickering colored screen.

He remained in the underground department together with his friend and colleague, Baruch Eliad. There was no competitiveness between them. It was clear to both that Old Manor was not an active director, only an honorary president, so to speak, and his main responsibility expressed itself in training new students and novices.

≈⌒

Baruch Eliad was a lone wolf. Despite the vast trust and affection he bore for Manor, he did not include him in his new project.

Professor Eliad worked in the morning hours on developing various medical cures through genetic engineering. His lab was filled with animals that had undergone various mutations. Anyone accidentally entering Eliad and Manor's lab might lose his sanity or scream in fear at the strange monsters he beheld. There were six-legged animals, yellow furred rabbits, two-headed bats and the like. All these weird studies and experiments were designed only for peaceful use and the advancement of medicine.

This was the unappealing side of genetic engineering, but like all coins, experimentation on animals had its other side.

The reverse side was 'Baruch Eliad's zoo,' as the workers of the secret department termed it. A zoo of this kind was not to be found anywhere else in the world.

Through in-depth research, Baruch Eliad had succeeded in isolating twenty-two pairs of chromosomes responsible for the mechanism of growth and height in the genes of several animals. He engineered a change in this genetic code and the results surpassed all imagination...

In a special cage were housed a three-year-old lion and a Bengal tiger which had reached their full development as ferocious beasts of prey. They were no bigger than ordinary house cats. Two minuscule chimpanzees, so tiny that you had to handle them with care so as not to harm them, cavorted within a minijungle.

The star of them all was Lilliput.

Lilliput was a three-year-old elephant, descendant of two average African elephants, each approximately twelve feet high. Lilliput was the world's first test-tube elephant. He had emerged to the light of day in a zoo in the central part of the country. Eliad and Manor had to carefully sift through a pile of straw before they discovered him. The tiny elephant was all of four inches high. They quickly removed it from its mother before she inadvertently trampled it underfoot. She searched in vain for her baby and couldn't understand what had happened. Lilliput's height, after having reached its mature growth and development, was only two feet. Manor wondered if he could produce a dwarf Indian elephant no bigger than four inches.

There were experiments of the opposite kind as well: a gigantic butterfly; Gulliver-sized ants; and, swimming in a huge aquarium, an innocent carp which had been engineered to the monstrous size of a white whale.

The staff of scientists headed by Eliad and Manor constantly monitored the changes that might take place in the cells of these mutant creatures, in their attempt to affect and modify the future lives of all creatures on earth: their size, habits, health and life spans.

Yet, fascinating though it was, the 'zoo' was no more than a decoy, a camouflage. In reality, Eliad was working upon a different research project altogether. He had been mobilized by the Israeli security services, both the Mossad and the Shabak (*Sheirut Bitachon Klalli* — the General Security Service), to help develop bacteriological and chemical warfare for the country's defense.

Israel had experienced its first shock during the Gulf War. During those days, the entire country had been paralyzed with fear that the falling Scuds might be carrying chemical or biological warheads. The leaders of the country had learned that the direction of future battles would be completely different from everything they had known to date. Nonconventional warfare was slowly pushing aside the old method of fighting. Tanks and artillery were outmoded. The new threat was chemical, biological or atomic warheads. The ghastly scenes of the rebel Kurdish city of Halbazia in Iraq, which had been bombed from the air by the dictator's planes with clouds of gas and turned into a giant slaughterhouse, struck panic in everyone's hearts.

Professor Eliad did not underestimate the danger of chemical weapons. He, like every normal citizen, had heard enough about nerve gas and mustard gas to be afraid of them.

"The only thing that lay people don't understand," he explained excitedly in one of his testimonies before a secret U.S. Senate subcommittee on chemical and biological warfare, "is that five grams of bacteriological matter can sow total mass devastation no less frightful than any atomic or hydrogen bomb. The primary difference between these and conventional munitions is that chemical weapons effect only a relatively small area."

But Eliad did not reveal one important fact.

The State of Israel does not confirm or deny its possession of nuclear arms, but in any case, well-known defense experts have long thought that these weapons have lost their clout. Their use is considered 'Samson's Choice' — the victor goes down with the vanquished. Thus, even if Israel does possess nuclear arms, it knows that its hands are tied regarding their use. Biological weapons, on the other hand, can be just as destructive, but much more carefully targeted.

Baruch Eliad was trying to create Israel's first bacteriological bomb.

In the afternoon hours, after Professor Manor went home, Eliad would descend three flights to an underground lab. There, in the country's most secret and well-guarded set of rooms, Baruch and a select staff of loyal assistants worked on developing a weapon of mass destruction designed to be the most efficient in the world.

He began by dismantling bacteria, viruses and microbes and then reconstructing them. Through special methods which he had developed, using centrifuges controlled by supercomputers, he broke up the basic molecular structure of the viral or bacterial cell, then did whatever he liked with them.

In the course of his two years' work, Eliad had developed several strains of threatening bacteria and deadly viruses which were impervious to immunization.

But Eliad was still not satisfied. Virtually any breakout of a plague caused by biological warfare could still somehow be arrested. For years he had been looking for the most deadly virus, one that would truly be as powerful as a nuclear weapon, a virus that nothing would be able to suppress — but he had not found it. A big question mark still hung over his work in developing the 'devouring germ', the deadly streptococcus. Every missile has its antimissile, and every deadly germ or virus has its antivirus.

Eliad didn't know, at the beginning of the summer of 5755 (1995), that he was standing on the threshold of the biggest breakthrough of all ...

⋑⋐

Avi didn't speak Yiddish. In the home of R' Yigal Eliad, the spoken language was Hebrew, even though both parents spoke and understood Yiddish well.

But he did understand several words in that language, and Yiddish resembles its source language, German, very closely.

When he heard the driver speaking into the cellular phone say, *"Die yugendt befindt sich mitt mir,"* he immediately understood its significance. The word *'yugendt'* tickled his grey cells; from some corner in his brain a frightening phrase floated to the surface: 'Hitler Yugendt,' the Nazi youth movement.

He quickly scribbled a few words on a piece of paper and spread it on his palm for Meitar to see. The message read: "Danger — we've got to escape."

Meitar was busy looking out the window, transfixed by the Austrian scenery that preceded the capital city itself.

Avi coughed several times, trying to get Meitar's attention. But the only one who noticed was the driver.

"Bitte," said the cabbie, handing Avi a tissue.

Avi accepted the tissue politely and utilized the brief interlude when he turned his head to show the note to Meitar.

Meitar's eyes grew round with surprise. He studied Avi's face and scowled. "What danger are you talking about?" he whispered.

"We are being kidnaped by this driver," Avi whispered back. "Out!"

The driver, suspicious of the whispering behind him, pressed his foot down on the accelerator. The car doubled its speed. "Why in the world do you think so?" asked Meitar, bound to maintain his indifference.

"Don't you see that this driver is a gangster? Why is he driving at such speed?"

Meitar studied the driver's face in the mirror. Yes, he did have a sinister look. Meitar yawned and stretched. Then he settled back, put his arms down, and suddenly, with an unexpected lunge, punched the driver in the neck with a fist that had all of his strength behind it. The car careened wildly, but the driver was made of strong stuff. He increased the speed even more.

"Stop!" screamed Avi. He hoped the driver would understand that. He did, and pressed the pedal even harder.

"Avi, we have no choice. Out!" shouted Meitar. Simultaneously, as if choreographed, each one opened his door and shot out like a cannonshell. The cab shot onward, apparently ignoring this surprising turn of events.

They got up and quickly raced to the shoulder of the road, dusty and bruised. Avi was not accustomed to such activity and his ribs had gotten a hard blow. Meitar emerged with a slight bruise on his head. After they shook themselves off and brushed off their clothing, they scanned the highway. Some ten kilometers separated them from Vienna. They waved their hands and put out their thumbs for a ride but failed to stop a single car or cab. Their eyes locked in a long look that began with a question and ended with an answer that read resignation.

They began trudging to the city on foot.

"I don't believe it!" said Meitar, having recovered first from the shock. "I predicted it and didn't know how right I was. As soon as we reached Austria, the action already began. Someone spotted us the minute we landed at the airport. Who could it have been?"

"Really, who could it be?" Avi's question had a strong edge of sarcasm.

"Now, don't tell me it was Roman Sp … " Meitar's voice faded. He froze on the spot and stared into space. Suddenly, he faced Vienna and gave a shout. "Herr Spiegel, we are on our way to you. Just wait a minute!"

Avi studied Meitar for a long time. Then they both burst into rolling laughter. It felt good: finally, an emotional release.

"They say that there is no bad without some good," said Avi. "Look, if you doubted the necessity of this trip to Vienna, now you have your proof. We're on the right track."

"We have yet to see," grumbled Meitar. "We will yet see."

The long walk was relatively easy, to their surprise, especially because their hands were empty. Their suitcases were in the taxi's baggage compartment.

⇆

"W-w-what are y-y-you s-s-saying? It c-c-can't be! No, I'm not worried, b-b-but it's strange. They should have been there three hours ago."

That treacherous tongue of his! Always, in the most critical times, it chose to rebel against him and revert to its unfortunate stammer.

Baruch looked at his watch. He was sitting in his office next to the lab. Every five minutes he would leave his worktable, remove his sterile mask and run to the office to call. Under the dangerous conditions of his lab, any use of a cordless or cellular phone was unthinkable. The communications experts scrambled even the calls on conventional lines to safeguard against security breaches. In addition, cellular phones and similar devices could affect the laboratory's sensitive electronic equipment.

Baruch had begun calling his friend, Dr. Larry Pincus, a colleague living in Quaranterstrasse, one of the loveliest streets in Vienna, two hours ago. Before the boys' departure, he had asked Pincus to meet them at the airport, but Pincus had refused because of a very busy schedule. Now Pincus felt uneasy. He might be to blame that the two boys had gotten lost.

"Who kn-n-nows w-what c-could have h-happened to them," whispered Baruch to himself with growing fear. With trembling knees, he rose from his chair and went back to the lab.

⁀⁀

To the boys surprise, their walk was not an unpleasant excursion after all. The young mens' hearts drew closer on the extended march. The weather was pleasant; the sun slipped westward, shedding golden-orange rays. They spoke for a long time, and Avi felt R' Aharonowitz's blessing accompanying him. Meitar really did not want to tease or provoke him; he merely wished to understand. Avi showed him a whole host of practices, customs, and events in a new light. It was hard work; Meitar was steeped with prejudices against everything connected to religion.

They approached the city. "What do we do now?" asked Meitar. "Where do we go?"

"Where had you intended on going to begin with?"

"To my father's friend, Professor Larry Pincus."

"Why not go there?"

"I don't know where he lives," said Meitar, scratching his head. "His address is written down in a small notebook, but that's in the suitcase."

"Notepads should be kept in pockets," Avi chided him, taking a small pad from his own back pocket. "Come, let's go to the Orthodox community of Vienna, the *gemeinde*. I have an excellent address, a friend of my father's youth, from the days he learned in the Poneviezh yeshivah. He is awaiting me very eagerly."

"He's expecting you, not me," Meitar pointed out. "One guest cannot bring another. Saba once taught that to me."

"But you don't know what these people are like," said Avi enthusiastically. "Hospitality runs in their blood. He will be doubly happy to see us both."

"But see how I look," Meitar pointed to his green T-shirt and deliberately faded blue jeans. He had no need to add his bare head to the list.

"You're mistaken, Meitar. They don't judge people by their clothing."

The debate continued for a while, and Meitar finally capitulated, if only for the prosaic reason that he had no other place to go.

Their welcome was truly hearty. R' Shlomo Marcus and his wife spared no effort to make their guests feel at home and to set them up in their new surroundings. Mrs. Marcus didn't waste a moment. She disappeared for a few hours but returned with a full wardrobe. "This is to replace the clothing in your stolen suitcases," she explained. "A pity I couldn't find more. Tomorrow, I'll go out and buy you some more things you may be need."

They rested a bit. Avi felt very much at home but Meitar kept on pacing the room. His distress was transparent. Avi suggested that they go out for a breather, and Meitar jumped at the idea.

The two went out for a walk with their host's son, Yoel, an intelligent and alert child of eleven. He took his guests on the A tram to the Prater, Vienna's huge amusement park.

"The Prater is in Vienna," explained Yoel, "but it is actually on a small island surrounded by the waters of the Danube."

They laughed heartily in the room of Crazy Mirrors and screamed in fright on the Devil's Train but the icing on the cake was the largest Ferris Wheel they had ever seen. Yoel didn't say a thing when they suggested going all the way up. They paid their shilling and sat expectantly in one of the swinging compartments. But soon their hearts were in their throats, as the wheel rose higher and higher until it reached a height of two hundred feet, the height of an eighteen-story building!

The view was breathtaking. "What a sight!" Meitar exclaimed. Night had already fallen and the big city, bathed in a lovely light, winked and beckoned to them with its millions of orange lights.

They returned to their host's home at midnight. Rabbi Marcus had found out Professor Pincus' address and phone number. "He must be worried about me," Meitar explained as he dialed. "He was supposed to have been my host."

The answering machine spoke in German. After the beep, he began conveying his message: "This is Meitar Eliad. I couldn't come. I am staying at the ... "

"Hey, why'd you pinch me?" he whispered in annoyance to Avi, rubbing his cheek.

"Don't offer any information. Just a brief message."

"I will be in touch with you."

"They're already on our tracks," Avi apologized after Meitar had put down the receiver. "Who knows what will happen to any information you volunteer."

⁓)⁓

The yellow taxi had arrived at the huge estate on Wolffgasse.

It honked in front of the locked gate, and after a few minutes an infrared beam scanned the license plate for a fraction of a second. The gate parted on its narrow track and opened wide, revealing a grove of chestnut and cypress trees. A narrow path wound between the ancient trees, leading to the three-story Gothic mansion with the sharply peaked roof which lay beyond. The building had been built in the mid-seventeenth century and little of its exterior had changed since.

The last beams of sunlight lit up the narrow arched windows with a reddish glow, lending a frighteningly bewitched look to the ancient building with its convex towers and turrets. The lengthening evening shadows emphasized the threatening look of the majestic edifice.

The driver approached a wide door. It was locked, of course, and he pressed the intercom button.

"Who's there?"

"You already saw me on the closed circuit system at the gate."

"Who's there?" The voice was metallic and cold to the freezing point.

"Siegfried."

The door buzzed and the man opened it. He climbed to the second floor on a wide stone staircase. Each step was a foot and a half high and six feet wide. The climb was always exhausting, all the more so now that he was not the bearer of good tidings.

The room was dimly lit, and the figure with whom he had spoken was hidden, as always, among the shadows. He had never seen his mysterious employer and toyed with wild guesses at his appearance. All he knew was that every mission accomplished was always rewarded with a very handsome fee indeed!

"You've come alone." It wasn't a question, only a statement.

"They ran away in the middle. They jumped out like monkeys. I wasn't prepared and couldn't turn around."

"What are you blathering about? You failed."

"Only partially, Herr. The suitcases are still in my baggage compartment."

"Bring them up immediately."

The suitcases were brought up. Two thousand shillings awaited him on the table. "But we had agreed on ten thousand," fumed Siegfried.

"Take the money and leave," said the faceless voice. "When you bring the boys, you'll get the remaining eight thousand."

After the driver left, the man sprang out of his niche. With a deft hand he opened the small locks with a smooth, all-purpose skeleton key. A brief search through one of the suitcases brought Meitar's notebook to light.

"They're supposed to be staying with Professor Larry Pincus on

Quaranterstrasse. Very interesting." His hand shot to the phone. He spoke in his usual curt manner and gave precise orders.

⇒)⇐

The telephone rang in a nearby office. Baruch Eliad leapt up and with large strides spanned the short hallway separating the lab and the office.

"Yes?" His voice shook.

"Baruch? Everything's all right. Meitar called me." It was Dassi, his wife.

"When?"

"Just now. Don't ask. They lost their suitcases and he is staying with Avi in the Orthodox community."

Baruch frowned. Something about the story sounded fishy. He smelled danger.

"Tell the truth; did Meitar really call?"

"Of course."

"Why didn't he call me?"

"Because you were in the lab and he lost your unlisted number."

"So then everything's all right," said Baruch, relieved. His mask of nonchalance reappeared as he headed back to the lab. When he was out in the hall, the phone rang again. "That must be Meitar, himself," a wishful thought crossed his mind.

He picked up the receiver.

"Eliad?" the sound reached him from across thousands of kilometers, a dull buzzing in the background told him. "I think that your object has been found. You've got to come here within two days."

He identified the voice clearly even though the speaker had not bothered to state his name. It was one of his many friends from the Weizmann Institute, now scattered throughout the world — Dr. Simon Kaplan.

Dr. Kaplan was in Zaire.

48

Professor Larry Pincus was fast asleep; he was alone at home. His wife, Dr. Elsa Pincus, a top economics analyst in the Austrian Department of Commerce, had traveled to the United States for a year of advanced studies at M.I.T. She had been working feverishly for the past two years on a major computerized project involving Austrian food consumption, and she needed the help of M.I.T. to finish it up. Larry and Elsa were childless.

It was 2:30 a.m. when the door of the house swung silently open and two black-masked men in sneakers, one short and one tall, slipped in.

They tiptoed from room to room, the short one cursing under his breath. "Those stinking Jews. They're not here."

"Maybe we should take care of Pincus. He surely knows something," suggested the tall one.

"But we were warned not to leave any traces. That was pretty clear."

They passed the phone. The answering machine's light was flashing, a sign that there were recorded messages. They ripped out the small tape. The tall one took out a strange electronic device from a small kit he carried and put the tape in it.

"What are you doing?"

"Can't you see, stupid? I'm copying the tape. I'd bet a hundred to one that the Jews left a message with some important information. *He* will be very happy to hear it."

The tiny tape was copied within a short time and returned to its place. In his haste, the tall one did not notice that he had replaced it on the reverse side. Nor did he see the small slip of paper fall out of his pocket and land on the floor beside the telephone table. They left the house as noiselessly as they had entered.

⁂

Five hundred green monkeys had been sent from Central Africa, from the forests surrounding Lake Victoria, to the Bering pharmaceutical plant in the pastoral city of Marburg in northern Germany. It was a normal shipment for a plant that produced all kinds of serum from the blood of monkeys.

Had the workers known of the virus being carried in the blood of these particular monkeys, they would have employed the strictest precautions: Special air tunnels, the type used in laboratories dealing with high-risk material; disinfecting chemical showers; biological sterilization, and so on.

But the workers didn't know, and they took no precautions whatsoever.

The first to be stricken was Klaus Ferr, the worker who fed the monkeys and cleaned their cages. He was attacked by fierce headaches, then hemorrhaging that finally led to shock. All of his fellow lab workers caught the disease, one by one. Seven died.

This is how the Marburg Virus was first discovered and categorized as 'a biological threat of the fourth degree,' — the most dangerous classification.

That was the beginning. The damage done by Marburg Virus did not, however, nearly approach the monstrous scope of the Ebola epidemic which broke out in Nazara, South Sudan, in 1976, and turned the local hospital into a slaughterhouse. The medical staff, it turned out, had injected patients with infected needles. The Sudan Ebola virus killed off hundreds of people, but it stopped suddenly. It was so 'hot' that its victims died out before they had the chance to infect others.

The next epidemic erupted two months later in northern Zaire, in the Bombe district, a tropical rain forest on the banks of the Ebola River. It is here that Public Enemy No. 1 got its name. Again, it was spread in a hospital — the Yamboko Hospital, run by Belgian nuns. They injected hundreds of people using the same needles without sterilizing the needles between patients.

The virus erupted simultaneously in fifty-five villages and killed hundreds of people who had been treated in the hospital. Nine of ten people who contracted the disease died in days. Zaire's President Mobutu, declared a state of emergency. The entire area was sealed off; army units encircled it and shot at anyone who attempted to leave.

The quarantine helped. The Zaire Ebola virus ended as suddenly as it had appeared.

In Kikwit, Zaire, the Ebola hit again nineteen years later, in May 1995. The epidemic broke out in a deadly manner. At first authorities tried to hide it, but the virus ran rampant. It jumped from one person to another, from neighborhood to neighborhood. The shadow of a major disaster hovered on the horizon.

⌒)⌒

"Baruch, when are you going to come to work with a smile on your face?"

This was the introduction to the daily joke. Professor Gideon Manor was not prepared to forego this daily custom. Baruch could have sworn that he had come to work in a good mood that morning.

"Listen ... " This was the customary opening. "Napoleon Bonaparte was sitting with the members of his war cabinet when he suddenly slapped the minister on his right in full view of all the other ministers. The man was taken aback. What had he done? How should he react? Return the blow with the knowledge that he would surely be hanged? Keep quiet? Everyone had seen his shame; he would become a laughingstock."

"Well, what he did do?" asked Eliad.

"Something very clever. He slapped the person on his right and said, 'The emperor asked to pass this on.' "

Manor almost fell off the chair with laughter. Baruch gave a restrained smile.

He was disturbed this morning and was in no mood for Manor's jokes. Kaplan's message had been too brief. He knew that he could rely on Simon, but what in Heaven's name was going on in Zaire? What was so urgent that he had to go there on such short notice?

The phone rang.

"Eliad?" It was the head of the Mossad.

"Yes?"

"Are you alone?"

"No."

"Ah, Manor's with you. Go to the phone in the next room. I'll call you back in five minutes."

"Who was that?" Manor asked casually. "Oh, a friend," replied Eliad offhandedly. He hurried off to the other room to get the phone there.

"They called us from the World Health Organization in Geneva. Have you ever heard of the city of Kikwit in Zaire?"

"No."

"Well, you're going to be hearing a lot about it from now on. Meanwhile it's confidential, but in a few days the whole world is going to hear about the Ebola."

"Ebola? The Judgment Day virus!" Baruch cried out in surprise. "I've been following it for years but I haven't succeeded in locating it."

"Well, this is your chance." The head of the Mossad spoke softly, but the urgency was pronounced. "You're going to Zaire today. The official purpose of your trip is to isolate the virus and try to create an inoculation against it. This is of universal interest, a project of the first order. This is the deadliest virus in the world. Everyone is waiting for you to find the antidote against it. The real purpose of your trip is, of course, different."

"Is the breakout very severe?"

"I think that it will run itself down soon, despite the fact that WHO believes that this is the end of the world. At least this virus is not carried through the air."

Baruch opened the door and thought he heard the sound of footsteps receding down the corridor. "Nonsense," he said to himself. "My lack of sleep is catching up with me. There's no one here."

⇌

They brought their loot, a single item: a tiny cassette.

"You went to kidnap two boys and this is what you came up with?"

"They weren't there," said the tall one. "Perhaps this can give you a clue as to where they are, though."

"*Danke schoene*," said the faceless man sarcastically. "Siegfried brings me suitcases and you bring me a tape. Who needs all of you, anyway?"

They grew alarmed. When the Boss talked like that, one had to be prepared for unpleasant surprises.

"What do you want us to do?" asked the short one defensively.

"Give me a moment to think." He had already gone through everything in the suitcases. One of the boys was an Orthodox Jew; he had *tefillin*. He must surely be staying somewhere in the *Gemeinde*. Perhaps the second one had gone along.

"Your next assignment is to sniff things out in the Jewish quarter of Vienna. Walk through its streets, alleys and pathways and inquire about two youths, one religious and another not, who arrived yesterday in Vienna."

"Yes, sir." They retreated fearfully, before he got any ideas about punishing them. The Boss was very unpredictable and capricious. Half-substantiated rumors had it that people he found inefficient were shot or expediently involved in fatal traffic accidents.

"One minute," he stopped them with a loud whisper just as they reached the door. "Why are you running away before being dismissed? Remember the names: Avigdor and Meitar Eliad."

⇌

Professor Larry Pincus woke up early the next morning, as usual. He had a big workload and sleeping late was an undreamed-of luxury. On his way to the bathroom he glanced at the answering machine. It was not lit.

"Strange," he mused. "I heard it beeping several times last night." He flicked the machine on and was shocked to hear messages that had been recorded about a year ago.

"What's going on?" He bent down and then noticed the slip of paper on the rug.

∽⌒

"I hear that you're involved with music," Shlomo Marcus said to Meitar at breakfast the next morning. "You've certainly come to the right place."

Meitar munched a toast sandwich with gusto. The Viennese fare was not bad at all. "Is that what Avi told you about me?"

Marcus blushed slightly. The Viennese approach is indirect and filled with affected mannerisms and courtesies. Meitar's forthright style threw him off somewhat.

"Vienna is the cradle of music," said Marcus, again talking circuitously. "The world's most famous composers lived and produced their great works here. There was Mozart, Haydn, Schubert, Strauss, Beethoven and others. They found an especially conducive and inspirational atmosphere here. To this very day, the city is bursting with good music, culture and art."

"I heard that there are forty museums here," said Meitar. "Such a significant collection in one city!"

"If you like music, you must not miss the Opera House," said Mrs. Marcus. "Hearing 'Carmen' by Bizet is an unforgettable musical experience."

"He should visit the Schoenbrunn castle," interjected their nine-year-old daughter, Malka. "I'm sure that Israel doesn't have a magnificent palace like that of the Hapsburg royal house."

"She's right," concurred her mother. "The Schoenbrunn castle is one of the most beautiful palaces in all of Europe. It has 1441 rooms!"

Avi returned from *Shacharis*. R' Shlomo Marcus had made the rounds among his acquaintances to obtain a pair of good *tefillin* to replace those that had been stolen. He hadn't dared say anything on the subject to Meitar. "I hear that you're planning some sightseeing trips for us," said Avi lightly. "What's this Shumbrum thing?"

Everyone laughed. "Not Shumbrum, Schoenbrunn. The place breathes history," explained Mrs. Marcus, a history buff. "As a boy Mozart played there before the Empress Maria Theresa. Napoleon lived there after he conquered Austria, and this is where the Emperor Franz Josef was born. The 640 years of the Hapsburg dynasty came to an end in this palace when King Karl signed his resignation in 1918. You must visit there!"

Meitar waited for Avi to finish his breakfast. He sat on the bed in his room, staring into space.

"Avi, I can't stand this! I don't have anything here, not even a tissue of my own to wipe my nose. Our thoughtful driver didn't leave me with a thing and I can't go on like this."

"Well, what do you have in mind, then?"

"I can't stand it," Meitar repeated. "I'm going to move in with Larry Pincus, in an enlightened secular home where they won't look strangely at me when I don't put on *tefillin* and don't go to the synagogue to pray. I can't stand this Orthodox Viennese ghetto here."

"No one looks at you strangely; you're only imagining it." Avi defended his hosts.

Meitar shrugged, unconvinced. "Anyway, I didn't come to Vienna to stay in a ghetto."

"No," Avi said dryly. "You came to find Roman Spiegel."

"That's right," Meitar nodded. "And what have we accomplished? Stuck here, without money. I'm calling Pincus." His fingers punched the numbers on the phone.

"Hello?"

"Is Professor Pincus home?" Meitar asked.

"Meitar? Meitar Eliad! I'm breaking my head trying to locate you and here you are, calling me yourself. Is everything all right?"

"Yes, why do you ask?"

Pincus gave an audible sigh of relief. "Someone visited me here in the middle of the night and played around with my answering machine." He panted like a steam engine. "Did you leave a message where you were staying?"

"No." Thanks to Avi. "But how do you know they were interested in me?"

Pincus hesitated for a moment. "The person who broke in here dropped a piece of paper with your name and description on it."

Meitar's face took on a greenish tinge that reminded Avi of a slightly underripe cucumber. Pincus had not yet finished. "It also had a description of another man, whom I presume is your cousin."

"Professor Pincus, are you sure?"

"You tell me: Answer yes or no to the following description: color of eyes — blue, glasses. Your cousin has brown eyes and no glasses. You have a snub nose and Avigdor has earlocks behind his ears. You're 1.8 meter tall and Avigdor is 1.75. Is this accurate?"

"Totally." Meitar's fingers were white.

"I reported the break-in to the police but if you listen to me, you won't put too much faith in the Austrian police."

"What should we do?" Meitar was at a loss.

"Be careful. Don't come anywhere near here. He must be a very dangerous person, the one who knows all this information in such detail. Watch out. I'm cutting this short; you never know who might be listening in."

The receiver was slammed down. "Meitar, you're changing colors like a chameleon. Now you've turned grey. What's the matter?" Avi was alarmed.

"What's the matter?" Meitar could hardly breathe. "This is beginning to be dangerous. I don't know if it's Roman Spiegel, but there's a very efficient person involved here. He's very thorough. He's trying to track us down from the clues in our baggage, each one respectively. He knows our exact description and where to look for us. I'm sure he will track us down to this place, too."

Without a moment's hesitation, Avi called home. He told his father, R' Yigal, all the developments, without omitting anything. His father was panic stricken. It sounded so much more threatening from a distance.

"I'm going to consult with R' Aharonowitz immediately," he told Avi. " I'll call back in half an hour."

He raced off to the ailing rabbi, whose condition was worsening from day to day. The doctors had prepared the family for the imminent end of the battle. Only relatives and the closest friends were admitted to his sickroom. R' Yigal Eliad belonged to the latter category.

"Don't talk to him. His condition is very serious," R' Aharonowitz's son warned at the doorway to the bedroom.

As Yigal stood by the bedside and saw the hue of his face, he was certain R' Aharonowitz had already passed on to the other world. His eyes were closed and his breathing imperceptible. Yigal studied the elderly rabbi with tear-filled eyes until he noticed his chest rising by a millimeter. R' Aharonowitz was flickering out like a candle. The family stood by the doorway, letting him commune silently with his Rav and mentor.

"R' Yigal?" He spoke without opening his eyes. His lips didn't move. "What is new in Vienna?"

"How is the Rav feeling?" Yigal was overwhelmed by the rabbi's concern for his student even as his own end drew near.

"May Hashem have mercy on me. What's happening in Vienna?"

Yigal told him briefly.

"They're in danger?" The rabbi's hoarse voice was barely audible. "I was afraid of that but there was no choice. They must persevere. Tell them to go underground, to be prepared for risks."

"What about the will and Roman Spiegel?"

"Let them search among the tiny letters."

"Where?"

"In the tiny letters," the rabbi repeated painstakingly. These were his last words. "The answer lies there. In the combination of letters, the combination of letters..."

"Where are there tiny letters?" Yigal pressed him. The mercury in the blood pressure monitor hanging above the rabbi's bed suddenly plummeted. The rabbi gurgled; the death throes had commenced. His doctor warned the family not to leave the patient alone for a moment. "Be prepared for the worst in the coming hours."

Yigal remained in the rabbi's home for several hours together with dozens of students from the yeshivah, reciting *tehillim*, and awaiting the dreaded and awesome moment of the departure of the soul so as to recite the *Shema*. After three hours of an exhausting wait, the doctor was again summoned. He gave the patient several more hours.

Yigal returned home, his face tearful. He paced his room with heavy heart. He had a parting message from the dying rabbi, an inscrutable message dealing with the ancient will. Who was clever enough to decipher the riddle?

Suddenly he remembered that Avi was awaiting his reply. He dialed the number on his antiquated black phone.

"This is the Marcus family," answered a little girl.

He asked for the father or one of the visitors from Israel. The girl replied that her parents had left and the visitors had given up waiting and had gone off too, 'to visit the Shumbrum palace.' She laughed with a clear voice that rang all the way to Mesilot. Yigal wondered what was so funny.

⇀⇀

Baruch arrived in Zaire three days after the phone call. He had flown via Switzerland and arrived in the African country together with several experts from the United Nations World Health Organization in Vienna.

In the country, panic reigned. An entire area comprising half a million people living in the remote city of Kikwit, some five hundred kilometers east of the capital, Kinshasa, where the first cases had been discovered, had been quarantined off to all incoming and outgoing traffic.

After receiving special government permission, Baruch arrived in Kikwit in a small executive plane.

"Professor Eliad?" Simon Kaplan was already waiting for him. "It's good to see you, though a pity it's under such unfortunate circumstances."

Simon introduced him to the others on the staff: the head of the WHO delegation, Dr. David Heiman; Dr. Phinehas Osborne from the American Center for Contagious Disease in Atlanta; Dr. Andre Gage from the Pasteur Institute in Paris and several other famous personalities who had made the effort to come in order to help prevent an international catastrophe.

"Where are all the patients?" asked Baruch, looking around at the deserted hospital.

"They've died," replied Osborne. "Nine out of ten who contract the disease die within a week; their suffering is excruciating. The medical staff simply fled."

A Zairian doctor arrived at the hospital, grim faced. "Help! An outbreak has been reported in Monsanago. We don't know what to do!"

Two small planes took them to Monsanago. When they landed, they were taken into a sealed car, dressed in rubber suits which they had put on in the plane, with gas masks on their faces.

Monsanago was a ghost town. The streets were deserted. The frightened population cringed in their homes, waiting for the danger to pass.

The team reached the hospital where dozens of victims lay. The scene was shocking. The patients had lost all resemblance to human beings. They writhed in indescribable, unbearable pain, bleeding from all the apertures in their bodies.

The team stood around one patient's bed as a doctor described the course of the disease:

"The incubation period is about 21 days. This is a critical period during which the affected person can infect others through contact with his bodily secretions. The initial symptoms of the disease are high fever (every person present instinctively put a hand to his forehead, which was covered by a gas mask), sore throat (hands stroked their throats), headaches, and muscular aches and pains."

"What happens next?" asked the dull voice of Jean Claude Amaier, a senior physician from the Pasteur Institute.

"The patient then begins bleeding from all the openings in his body: his eyes, ears, mouth. Red blisters form all over his body and head, and burst. His skin grows dark and within several hours all the tissues in his body and head begin to disintegrate and turn into a sticky, oozy substance. His body turns into a mass of viruses while he is still alive — if you can call it living."

They looked at the patient writhing in his bed and tried to guess at which stage he was and when his tissues would turn into a putrescent mass.

"This is the apocalypse incarnate," murmured Jean Claude Amaier in Baruch's ears. "A miracle that this virus is not carried through the air, but only by direct contact. Otherwise you could say good-bye to all life forms on this planet."

"Precisely," said Baruch, an inscrutable expression on his face. "You've pinpointed the situation exactly."

He opened up his attache case and took out a sterile package containing a syringe and needle. He pricked the patient with it and without removing the packaging, drew up some of the infected blood into the syringe.

"Please note," said the head of the team, "at this very moment you are witness to an attempt at finding a cure for the Ebola. Professor Eliad from Israel is taking a blood sample containing the Ebola virus."

"Dear colleagues," intoned Dr. David Heiman somewhat pompously, "Professor Eliad, one of the chief researchers of the genetic code, will take this sample to Israel. We hope that he will succeed in cracking the Ebola's code and creating a genetic mutation within the basic cells of the virus in order to develop an antidote to this terrible disease — a disease threatening the entire world which, at this point, has no cure."

The members of the team stared in silent admiration at Eliad's deft hands, carefully packing the syringe in a mobile cylindrical freezing unit.

"If you knew what I was really planning to do with the Ebola, Dr. Heiman, you would not sound as smug," thought Dr. Eliad, his expression remaining impassive.

≈)(≈

At that very moment the epidemic also hit Kanga, two hundred kilometers away from Kinshasa.

Two dark-skinned scientists arrived at the hospital in Kanga. They had no need to identify themselves to anyone; the hospital was deserted. They put on protective rubber suits and gas masks.

Like Eliad in Monsanago one of the scientists drew up a syringe of infected blood from the arm of one of the patients, who was at a stage of semi-consciousness.

Like Eliad, he also had no real intention of developing a serum against the Ebola. He wanted to be the first one to reach the goal that the Israeli, Eliad, had set for himself. It was a race for survival, a question of life and death. The question was: Who would get there first?

They knew that they would have to work very hard in their gigantic laboratory in Iran in mutating the virus. The Boss wanted results in the coming days. And if Roman Spiegel wanted results, he would get them.

49

Meitar and Avi roamed through the spacious halls of the immense Schoenbrunn castle for hours. They saw only part of the wonders which the lavish palace of the Hapsburg dynasty had to offer. They were in the Hofburg, which was a city within a city. There they gazed upon the *Schatzkammer*, the national treasury which represented the glorious Austrian past: the imperial crown which had been made to the measurements of Otto the Great; a goblet made of agate to which miraculous powers were attributed; and the cradle of Napoleon's only son born to his Austrian queen, Marie Louise. They rambled through kilometers of museums until they were exhausted.

"What next?" asked Meitar, as he slumped down on a bench in a nearby public park.

"You've taken the words out of my mouth," Avi smiled. "We've been, we've seen. What now?"

"I think we should find out what's doing at home," suggested Meitar. "Let's hear what the elderly rabbi had to say to your father."

Avi felt a flutter of excitement. Meitar wanted to know what the rabbi had said? Was this the first sign of a turning point?

Don't let yourself be caught up in false illusions, Avi. This is a secular kid down to his very roots; he has no real interest in Judaism.

Avi called the Marcuses. In brief words Mrs. Marcus told Avi that R' Aharonowitz was in his death throes and that hundreds of yeshivah students were hovering near his bedside. Meitar looked with astonishment at the tears streaming down Avi's cheeks. "Your father was the last person to talk to him before the final stage. He ordered you to go underground and be prepared to sacrifice your lives. What's this?" she asked herself, studying a note her husband had written. "It says here that he told you to look for tiny letters."

"What?" Avi was completely thrown off. "What does that mean? Which tiny letters? What does he mean that we should go underground? And be prepared to sacrifice our lives? Does any of this make sense to you?"

"I can't explain, but the rabbi said you were in danger. I suggest that you stay away from our home."

"Where should we go?"

"Wait where you are, in the park. I'll send my husband to you soon."

Avi sank into deep thought. Small letters. What did that signify? In Jewish jargon, when one wanted to note that a person was well versed in Torah, especially in its mystic secrets, he was described as knowing the tiny print. *So what should we do? Should we begin searching through the entire Torah or the works of Kabbalah? That makes no sense.*

He repeated the conversation to his cousin. Meitar had an original solution to the enigma.

"Sometimes newspapers have ads in very small print, notices about unclaimed inheritances and so forth, people who died during the war and left estates. Perhaps R' Aharonowitz meant that this might be the thread of a clue."

"Meitar, you're a genius!" Avi exclaimed.

They rushed off to buy a newspaper and began scanning it with the help of a local resident sitting on a park bench, who seemed not to have anything particular to do, and who was happy to translate the assorted ads in small print put in by government agencies.

"This is idiotic, a wild-goose chase," they both sighed hopelessly, after a long and fruitless search.

They sat on the white park bench, physically and emotional wrung out. "The prognosis is shining," Meitar summed up sarcastically. "We're dealing with an invisible enemy who is several steps ahead of us. The Marcuses are shaking off all responsibility and want to have nothing to do with us. We are told to go underground and haven't the faintest idea of how to solve the whole riddle."

"What is this all leading to?" sighed Avi.

"To the cemetery," said a voice behind them. They turned around to see the smiling face of Shlomo Marcus, who had sneaked up on them from behind.

"Don't be angry at my eavesdropping," he laughed. "We haven't dropped you as quickly as you feared. I truly think that the best thing for us is to go to the cemetery and to pray at the graveside of the many *tzaddikim* buried here. It is the most effective thing I can think of at this stage."

"The cemetery?" Meitar made a face. "For this I flew to Europe? Just to visit some old graves?"

Marcus and Avi looked at one another but said nothing. "Go and pray at those graves, if that's what you enjoy doing. I have more exciting hobbies. I'm going to the Royal Opera House."

"When you're finished, go to the home of..." Marcus looked all around, fearing someone listening in on them, then he whispered something in Meitar's ear. A smile spread across the face of Serenade's chief soloist. The idea was brilliant.

The secretary in the office of the *Gemeinde* was short tempered. "I've already told you," he said angrily to the two visitors, "I have no idea if two youths came here from Israel or not, or where they might possibly be staying. Our community is filled with visitors."

"You must make inquiries," said the tall one.

The secretary's suspicion was aroused. "What's so urgent about it?" he demanded to know. He studied the two men before him; he didn't particularly care for what he saw.

"We have an important message for them," explained the short one.

The secretary stretched out a hand to the phone. "Either you leave this office at once or I call the police," he said authoritatively.

The two almost ran out of the room. The secretary chuckled to himself with satisfaction. Had he subsequently seen them interrogating several innocent Jewish passers-by until they extracted the information they sought, his smile would have quickly disappeared.

They split up. Meitar went to Quaranterstrasse, to the most beautiful opera house in the world, while Marcus and Avi went to pray at the graves of *tzaddikim* buried in the ancient Viennese Jewish cemetery.

They entered the Friedhoff cemetery. Avi shed tears by the grave of R' Shmuel Engel for the recovery of R' Aharonowitz, and prayed for the success of his trip at the graves of the revered chassidic leaders, R' Yisrael of Chortkov and R' Yitzchak Meir of Kopishnitz. R' Moshe, son of the Kopishnitzer Rebbe, was buried near his holy father.

"His ashes are buried here," explained Shlomo Marcus. "The Nazis killed and cremated R' Moshe and then sent his ashes to his wife in a vial..."

"Just like Roman Spiegel," thought Avi bitterly. "Roman also sent either a bone or the ashes of Saba's first wife, Ita, to him." He threw himself upon the tombstone and prayed from the depths of his heart.

"Help me, Father in Heaven, to destroy the wicked empire of Roman Spiegel. Protect us from his murderous hands. Give us the wisdom to know what to do."

At that very moment Meitar pressed himself into a long line at the entrance of the opera house, thoroughly overwhelmed by the pomp and majesty of this magnificent structure, the likes of which he had never seen in his entire life. "Which ticket will you have? Sitting or standing?" asked the man in the ticket box.

"What's the difference?" asked Meitar.

"A big difference." The polite clerk rattled off the information he must have repeated thousands of times. "The opera house has over 1600 seats and five hundred standing places. A seat is very expensive, while a standing place is quite cheap."

Meitar did not hesitate for a moment. He bought a seat for $150, like a rich man, rather than joining the many teenagers who only bought standing-room places. *I don't intend standing for three and a half hours after roaming around museums for the past six hours,* Meitar said to himself. The exorbitant price meant little to him; his father had never stinted on anything.

The auditorium was constructed entirely of marble and gilding. Meitar felt himself uplifted as the gigantic curtain rose, revealing the breathtaking scenery and props of 'Don Giovanni' by Mozart as the orchestra led into the opening chords.

He had gotten his hands on a pair of opera glasses, but hardly used them at first since he sat up front, in the middle of the seventh row. Aside from this, Meitar had eagle eyes. The impression of shortsightedness lent by his eyeglasses was entirely false. The lenses were made of plain glass. He only wore his elliptical glasses as a fashion fad.

He took them off and studied the stage, orchestra, musicians, choir and conductor.

The opera began. The auditorium lights were extinguished and the immense stage was bathed with multicolored spotlights. All eyes were riveted on the opera stars as it began.

∾⌒

The head of the Mossad waited for him in the V.I.P. waiting room of Ben Gurion Airport when he returned from Zaire.

"Do you have the Ebola?"

Eliad pointed to his small attache case. "Israel's next atom bomb is right here."

"'Let not the one who girds himself for battle boast like the one who ungirds himself,'" teased the head of the Mossad goodnaturedly. "You haven't made any changes in the makeup of the virus. At this stage it is only contagious through direct contact."

"I don't think it should be a problem to crack the code of this particular virus," said Eliad.

"Well, then, off to the lab with you," said the top man, slapping him on the shoulder. "Go to Rehovot and let's hear from you in a few days."

⌒⌒

Over two thousand people attended 'Don Giovanni,' and despite the fact that the play took three and a half hours, the audience maintained absolute quiet and decorum. The usual coughing reserved for philharmonic concerts were completely lacking in this opera house.

The elderly conductor was a virtuoso. He waved his baton without stop, turning alternately to the opera singers and the orchestra musicians. Meitar's attention focused on him. He studied the program: "Don Giovanni by Mozart. Conducted by Dr. Yoachim von Krautemburg."

He put the opera glasses to his eyes. The conductor was thin and tall; despite his advanced age, his back was not bowed. A full white mane of hair topped off his commanding stature. "An interesting person," thought Meitar to himself. "I could swear that he's at least eighty, but look how energetic and supple he is, what youth and vitality he exudes."

He adjusted the binoculars and studied the conductor's face. "Look at that! An old man like him without glasses!"

And those eyes! Such a clear blue gaze. They were the eyes of a young boy; the eyes of a person upon whom life had smiled from the day of his birth.

Meitar tried to contrast those eyes with the ones of his grandfather, Saba David, whose look was so tired and extinguished. What a difference!

They say that if someone stares at you for a long time, you eventually become aware of it, and even if it's one among two thousand, you'll be able to pinpoint him.

The conductor felt eyes on him. Dr. Yoachim von Krautemburg waved to the first tenor with his baton, signaling him to burst forth in a resounding roar. Then, suddenly, he turned around and looked at the audience, his gaze falling directly on Meitar, separated from him by seven rows.

Meitar removed the glasses from his eyes and their eyes locked. Meitar suddenly felt as if a frozen millipede were crawling down his back.

That man was very familiar, but he didn't know from where. Until he grasped it.

He had seen such eyes before!

He had seen pictures from the Holocaust of Nazi officers with the same coldblooded look in their eyes. How he despised the evil those eyes conveyed.

Many pairs of such satanic eyes instinctively rose up in his mind, eyes full of cold, evil malice and mockery.

He was sure of it. The eyes of the opera house conductor were such eyes, bearing that evil, arrogant Aryan look. Only Nazi officers had eyes like those.

That was the very look!

≈⊂

The tall man and the short one reached the street and stationed themselves on the roof of a nearby building, from where they watched the house of the Marcus family with powerful binoculars.

≈⊂

Meitar wanted to get up and flee. A choking sensation gripped his throat. He had never come across eyes boding such evil. The blue icebergs had pinpointed him and studied him intensely, identifying him. He was sure of it.

Meitar had lost all interest in the opera. *If he has identified me, I know who he is, as well. You're Roman Spiegel, that's who!* The thought suddenly struck him, and its aftermath: *You're headed for the gallows, you fiend!*

He got up, whispered, "*Entschuldigung,*" dozens of times, and made his way out. When he was near the exit, he turned his head in order to see the conductor, Dr. Yoachim von Krautemburg, gazing at him with a look as cold as the grave.

Perhaps I am mistaken, he suddenly thought. *To suspect a person I never saw in my life, just like that? But on the other hand, if it wasn't him, why did he stare at me with such eyes? I saw that he identified me. Why not? He has my passport and all my other documents.*

≈⌒

He went out to the dark street and ran to Larry Pincus' house at the other end of Quaranterstrasse. It had been Shlomo Marcus' idea. "They tell that in the First World War soldiers used to hide in the ditches created by falling shells. Statistics showed that two shells very rarely fell in the same spot. The safest place for you, now, is Professor Pincus' house, since they've already looked for you there."

Dr. Elsa Pincus, the mistress of the house, opened the door for him, to his great surprise. "I've just returned from Massachusetts today," she explained to Meitar with a tired smile. "I've already heard everything from Larry. Please come in."

Everyone awaited him in the spacious living room: Professor Pincus, Shlomo Marcus and Avi.

"Meitar, you look beat," said Avi with concern.

"I've found him," he said tersely.

"Who?"

"Roman Spiegel!" He tried to sound indifferent but his excitement filtered into his voice. Everyone jumped up. "What?" "What do you have to tell us?" He told them about the opera house conductor. The Pincuses looked at him with a strange expression and shook their heads.

"Why are you staring at me like that?"

"Because you don't know what you're saying," said Elsa angrily. "Are you mad? Dr. Yoachim von Krautemburg — a former Nazi? Why, he is considered one of the greatest conductors in Europe. He is one of the most distinguished figures in Vienna, a very pillar of our culture! Who doesn't know him?"

"Exactly so!" her husband agreed. "The conductor of the opera house is one of the most revered people in Viennese society! You've made a base accusation!"

Meitar was taken aback. *Perhaps I really did make a mistake. When a person is looking for something, he generally finds it. Perhaps this was a figment of auto-suggestion?*

Avi was not ready to dismiss Meitar's hunch so quickly. He attacked the problem with cold logic and asked, "Do you have a photo of this famous conductor?"

≈)(≈

"We're wasting our time." said the short man angrily, having remained at his rooftop watch across from the Marcus house for hours. "Only one elderly Jew has entered and a child of eleven. Certainly not two teenagers."

"You're right, but we mustn't give up so quickly. Nothing good will come of it."

"Well, let's follow the older man. Perhaps he can lead us to them," suggested the short one.

≈)(≈

Things began happening quickly by the following morning. Shlomo Marcus left his house without noticing the two men tailing him like a shadow. After making the rounds of several book stores, he found what he was looking for: "Who's Who in Vienna / Important People and Figures." He located the picture he was looking for immediately. When he arrived at the Pincus house with it, Dr. Elsa Pincus decided to enter the picture into the computer with her professional expertise and analytical powers. "I only want to prove to you how wrong you are," she explained to Meitar teasingly.

She called up the Yad Vashem Museum in Jerusalem and stated her request. After a brief explanation, the director referred her to the Museum's computer expert.

"Roman Spiegel? I have no such person," said the voice on the other end of the line doubtfully.

"Try again," ordered Elsa with authority.

"I'm running the name through the program," the expert said. "Ah, wait, here. Of course. You should have given me his full name and title:

Obersturmbannfuehrer Roman Wilhelm Karl Spiegel, Maidenek Death Camp, born in Dusseldorf, Germany, 1915. Displayed a psychopathic sadism in killing prisoners en masse to the sound of music. His main hobby was micrography. He disappeared after the war... Any other details you would like?"

"Thank you, there's no need for more information. Please send me the picture immediately through the Internet."

"Hats off to you!" exclaimed the man. "We got hooked up to the Internet just last week. The director of the museum approved it. You'll receive the picture on your computer screen right away."

They waited in suspense while the computer man got the request approved by the museum administration. A short while later, the desired picture appeared on Elsa's computer screen. After punching a few keys, Elsa succeeded in getting the printer to produce a photo of Obersturmbannfuehrer Roman Spiegel as a young Nazi officer in the Maidenek death camp.

Dr. Pincus was full of energy. She worked with the expertise and agility of a magician, leaving everyone openmouthed at her ideas and their masterful execution. It was evident that the connections that she had established over the years of her work were extensive. She called up Interpol headquarters in Paris and spoke briefly with one of the men in charge. A few moments later she received a criminal identification master program through her computer modem with the strict warning that she erase the program immediately after its one-time use.

"And now," she announced ceremoniously, in a voice that bore just a tinge of snobbism, "watch and see the marvels of the computer. I first have to adapt the program to our specific requirements."

"Elsa," wondered Larry, "that must be the work of several days."

"Not in these times." Elsa's fingers danced across the keyboard. "Today, my dear husband, there are shortcuts."

Elsa Pincus was a computer genius. This became clear to everyone in the next hour. Her fingers sped so fast as to be almost invisible. She stopped every once in a while and frowned, a sign she was thinking, then resumed her speedy key punching. "Finished!" she finally declared with satisfaction an hour later. "Now bring me Roman Spiegel's picture."

The phone rang. It was one of Elsa's friends calling to welcome her back. She left the computer for a moment.

Dr. Pincus' equipment included an optical scanner which scanned the picture they had gotten from Jerusalem and fed it into the computer's memory. The program began with the face of the young Nazi and ended up with the face of an eighty-year-old man.

Meitar and Avi stared agape at the screen. Pictures changed rapidly, appearing and disintegrating until it settled on one solid picture.

They stood in disappointment. Dr. Elsa did not hide her joy. The face that emerged in the end did not have the faintest resemblance to that of Dr. Yoachim von Krautemburg.

⇌

"What makes you think they're here? We searched the first night and there was no trace of them."

"Let's give it a try. At least for half a day."

They approached the windows.

⇌

The phone rang. A hand stretched out to the receiver.

"Father." It was Eric, the son who lived in a nearby neighborhood, an Internet buff. "You better watch out. I saw your picture on my screen about half an hour ago, on the Internet. Yad Vashem in Jerusalem sent it. It was a picture dating back to the war."

"Don't worry, Eric. The mouse has entered the hole, just like his grandfather. Thanks."

⇌

The air in the room was heavy and taut. Larry Pincus chain-smoked, the others were also visibly nervous.

"What happened?" said Meitar, chewing his nails. "I was certain it was Roman Spiegel."

"Perhaps something is missing in the program?" suggested Shlomo Marcus gently. He was the only who succeeded in keeping his cool. "Even without the computer I can detect lines of similarity between Roman Spiegel and Yoachim von Krautemburg."

"Superficial resemblance doesn't mean a thing. John Demanjuk is the proof," stated Elsa authoritatively. "The Israeli Supreme Court had already passed his death sentence before the entire world and then they had to free him, since they could not positively prove that John Demanjuk was actually Ivan the Terrible. It was —?

Elsa broke off. She gazed at the blinking lights of her monitor, then suddenly attacked her keyboard with such ferocity that the others could only stare.

"I forgot to save the file in the computer because of the phone call that interrupted me," she managed to say, as her fingers flew. "Half the program went down the drain because of my stupidity."

Once again, the screen produced the face of Roman Spiegel as a young man. Four heads huddled around the monitor.

Roman Spiegel grew older before their wondering eyes. Dozens of years were added to the young face. After five minutes, the familiar face of Dr. Von Krautemburg, conductor of the Opera House, smiled at them.

Another two pair of eyes saw the picture on the screen. The two men in the garden looked into the window with the help of binoculars, not understanding what the picture of the famous conductor was doing on the screen.

It made no impression on them. The faceless Boss in the Gothic tower on Wolfegasse was not paying them to think, only to track down and kidnap the two youths.

And they saw them with their very eyes, there in the room. When the young men next left the house they would be in for a surprise — not a very pleasant one.

50

Roman Spiegel had fled for his life.

Like other Nazi war criminals, he was a fugitive at the end of the war, wanted for the crime of murder and genocide. The gallows at Nuremburg was waiting for him, too. There was plentiful testimony to the fact that he had killed thousands of Jews in Lublin and Maidenek with his own hands, or had sent them to the gas chambers and crematoria.

He did not wait for the noose to tighten around his neck. He had confiscated much Jewish property during the war and had accumulated great wealth in gold, silver, gems and valuable works of art. With the end of the war, he hid in Italy and converted his treasures to gold ingots with the willing help of the Sicilian Mafia. Then, when he became more mobile, he fled to Argentina and acquired a new identity with the help of a passport forged with his own hands, with characteristic skill. He now went under the name of Yoachim von Krautemburg, an innocent immigrant from Schleswig-Holstein in Germany.

With the vast fortune at his disposal, he began his first steps in the world of heavy industry. He successfully managed two plants for tractors and industrial machinery. His astute financial skills catapulted him to the top of the industrial business world of Argentina. Not content with this, he continued to climb higher. Ten years after his arrival in Argentina, Yoachim von Krautemburg was considered one of the major magnates of South America.

As a wealthy and powerful tycoon, he controlled a chain of factories. An army of accountants kept his books and the scope of his wealth was estimated in the hundreds of millions. But he was gripped by a constant unrest. The Jews had escaped the fate designed for them by the Fuehrer; they had slipped out of the Final Solution which the Germans of the Superior Race had envisioned.

Roman Spiegel did not stop dreaming.

Baruch Eliad sat frustrated in his lab. Several days of exhausting work on the deadly Ebola virus had produced no results. For the first time in two years, he and his practiced staff members were at a perplexing stand-still. Baruch had succeeded in isolating the virus from the infected blood sample he had brought from Zaire. It was a member of the family called Filo viruses, which looked like ring-shaped filaments. Up till this point, all went according to plan. The difficulty arose when they tried to isolate the chromosomes of the virus itself in order to identify the internal com-mand which caused it to spread only through direct contact rather than from air exposure.

"What's happening here?" asked Baruch, vexed.

His genetic laboratory was equipped with the most updated com-puter available, supplied directly by the Pentagon. Its circuits were the fastest in the world. He ran the virus' infinite code through the pro-gram but failed to bring up the specific cell responsible for the desired command.

"The virus is playing games with us," he grumbled, shrugging his shoulders. He stared at the screen and began running the code with its as-tronomical numbers through the program again.

After three fruitless days, the head of the Mossad called up, asking if he had made any progress. Baruch exploded in anger. "Maybe if you did-n't stand on my head I would get somewhere. I can't work with a stop watch ticking in my ear."

"Baruch, is that you?" The quiet voice of the head of the Mossad expressed astonishment.

Baruch calmed down. "I'm sorry for that outburst. I don't know what happened to me. The stubborn virus is sealed like the walls of Jericho."

"Maybe you can tell me how you're going about it?" the Mossad chief asked pleasantly.

Baruch lectured fluently on the subject. "You're familiar with the beginning. I brought a test tube full of infected blood from Zaire in a liquid hydrogen container. That much you know. Each drop of blood has millions of viruses. I isolated some of the strong ones and am now trying to crack their DNA. Incidentally, what do you know about DNA in general?"

"Almost nil," his boss said candidly.

"O.K. Then I have to start from scratch. Every living thing is built up from DNA. These are the building blocks of life, the basic cells of every living entity. The cells contain our entire genetic heritage. These cells determine our intelligence, the color of our eyes, our musical inclinations, whether you are going to enjoy the saxophone and whether you are going to be a melancholy type or a happy-go-lucky person.

"Now listen carefully. Inside each drop of blood of any living creature there are billions of strings of the genetic code called DNA. Each such string contains three billion genetic codes!"

"Incredible!" His bellow reverberated to the lab beyond. The team members smiled. This was how all laymen reacted when they heard a description of DNA for the first time.

"Yes, exactly that. If you were to write out the genetic code of one single string of DNA on a computer screen and look at it every second for eight hours straight, it would take you two whole years to scan its full length!"

"That's why you have your super computer that can read the entire material in five minutes," commented the head of the Mossad.

"Very true," agreed Eliad. "But still, we are now at a standstill. Something in this virus refuses to cooperate and we don't know what it is."

⋑⋐

When Avi phoned Mesilot, he heard the news and wept like a baby. R' Aharonowitz had passed away and at that very moment his funeral was taking place, attended by tens of thousands. And he, Avi, was away in Vienna!

For the first time in his life he understood the significance of the verse, "Would that I had a wing like a dove." How he would have loved to spread wings and fly to Israel in order to participate in the funeral of that *tzaddik*. But those were wishful dreams. Now that he had definitely determined that Yoachim von Krautemburg was Roman Spiegel, there was work to do. They had to plan their next step.

"He must be kidnaped and brought to Israel, just like Eichmann," suggested Meitar.

"How?" asked Avi. "You may watch the man for two weeks to find his weak spot and then in the end you'll find out that he doesn't have the will on him."

"If you have a better idea, out with it."

"Yes," said Avi with uncharacteristic daring. "Let's break into his house."

"You're not serious. We would never get out alive."

"That's our only chance to find the will," explained Avi. "Do you have a different explanation for R' Aharonowitz's message that we must be prepared to risk our lives?"

"Avi, do you really intend for us to enter the lion's den?"

"Exactly so."

"He'll shoot us down like dogs. He knows who we are."

"He know us," Avi grinned, "but he also knows the power of the press."

Meitar was the first one to finish his makeup. He looked just like a television reporter. Dr. Elsa Pincus called the home of Von Krautemburg and asked if the famous conductor would be gracious enough to give her station, CNN, an interview.

Then Avi's turn came. Meitar did a marvelous job and even succeeded in camouflaging his *payos*. The two looked like Americans born and bred. The costumes were perfect.

≈)⌒

Roman Spiegel had sworn to finish off what the Fuehrer had begun. The Jewish nation had, meanwhile, acquired its own country, established a strong army and a flourishing economy, and had absorbed millions of immigrants. It was doing very well for itself in its homeland.

"They're all concentrated in one area, Palestine. That will make it all the easier to liquidate them," he comforted himself as he watched the Jewish people's amazing comeback after the Holocaust's devastation.

He had found the way to implement the second, decisive stage of the Final Solution which the Fuehrer had formulated, and was prepared to invest his entire fortune towards that end.

It all began when he'd read the will written by the ancient Jewish kabbalist, grandfather of Yechiel Horowitz. The lines had stared at him from memory all those years:

"And I hereby seek to divulge an awesome secret, a secret which you can use to bring balm and healing to all people on earth in a time of terrible danger. This selfsame secret can also bring ruin and destruction upon all of mankind, G-d forbid. 'And you shall choose life'!"

This was followed by several lines which Roman could not understand. He knew, however, that they embodied a real secret.

At the age of sixty, right after his wife, Claudia, was killed in a plane crash, Roman decided to leave Argentina. His huge mansion in one of the most luxurious and beautiful suburbs in Buenos Aires suddenly took on a deserted air. He began longing for Vienna, his city. He left his oldest son, Franz, in charge of the economic edifice which he had built, and went to Vienna. Thanks to his ties with the Nazi underground, which dominated all kinds of key positions, his entrance into the famous opera house was assured. Aside from a good singing voice which he lacked, because "Yechiel Horowitz, his astrological twin, had stolen it from him," as he firmly believed, Roman was gifted with a wide range of musical talents, and the fine art of conducting an opera house choir had been absorbed into his very blood from the times he had stood by his father's side as a child. Even Yechiel Horowitz could bear witness to that.

But neither his loneliness nor his music were the main reasons for his return home. The primary and foremost reason was quite different: From Vienna it would be easier for him to maintain his many contacts with the scientists whom he had mobilized to carry out his plan to bring destruction down upon the Jewish people in its homeland.

At first he forged ties with Iraq, but after the Gulf War he despaired of the Iraqi scientists and the biological weapons which Saddaam Hussein had developed. The suffocating blockade imposed by U.N. inspectors made their biological research ineffective.

He was looking for something efficient, something at least as powerful as an atom bomb; he found exactly what he wanted in Iran.

He led a double life. Two days each week, in his Gothic mansion on Wolfegasse, he wove his ties with the Iranian scientists and operated his vast network of messengers. He paid out large sums and bribed employees and managers in every possible place. He was thus able to command a wide range of sources of information, and his influence reached out and dominated many areas. He always sat in a hidden niche, surrounded by a blind of slats which enabled him to see and remain invisible. This earned him the name of 'the faceless one.' He was also 'the nameless one.'

During the rest of the week he was Dr. Yoachim von Krautemburg, the famous opera conductor. During those days he resided in a luxurious home in one of the main *Ringe*, ring road, from which he went forth to conduct the choir and orchestra of the Viennese Opera house.

The Iranian scientists with whom he worked could not decipher a word from the strange formula he presented to them. After he revealed to them the source, they tried their luck with Iranian Jews, but they, too, were unable to shed any light on the enigmatic words. The secret remained too difficult to crack.

"You need a combination of a scientist and a kabbalist," the experts told him. "Perhaps you should kidnap a religious Jewish scientist."

The Iranian secret service went into action. After gathering the necessary information, they found their object. And they didn't even have to coerce him to cooperate; he did so willingly.

It was a foremost scientist working in one of the most highly classified institutions in Israel! None of his colleagues knew that his love for money had driven this scientist to sell secret information of the first degree to the enemy for dozens of years. He loved money and this craving knew no bounds. Russia had received from him a staggering amount of top-secret information. This data streamed through secret channels for many years until the Soviet regime fell apart. Then Iran discovered him; Khomeini's successors leaped at the opportunity to explore this gold mine. They succeeded in putting pressure on him by threatening to reveal his treachery. That was the stick; the tens of thousands of dollars which he received in exchange for his efficient espionage was the sweet carrot.

"He isn't well versed in Jewish lore, but he works together with a world-famous Jewish scientist," the undercover agents reported to Roman Spiegel. "If you can manage to lay your hands on him, you are very close to achieving your goal."

≈)⌒

Repeated blasts of the car horn broke the silence. The CNN car, driven by a cheerful, blue-jeaned young American by the name of Randy, awaited Avi and Meitar by the entrance of the house. Again, it had been Dr. Elsa Pincus, with her wide-ranging contacts, who had arranged the entire matter through a single phone call to New York.

The pair of men on the opposite sidewalk entered into a state of high alert but the disguises threw them completely off. They lost several precious moments in a whispered argument over the identity of the two television reporters; meanwhile, the van slipped out of sight.

Ten minutes later Meitar and Avi arrived at a luxurious mansion. They came with heavy equipment, cameras and lighting apparatus, long electrical cables and microphones. Randy, the CNN driver, had been chosen to serve as the interviewing reporter because of his accent. Meitar was the cameraman and Avi acted as light man.

Meitar rang the bell. "Who's there?" asked a voice over the intercom. "We're from CNN," replied Randy with a distinctly American accent.

Yoachim studied his visitors on the screen. A fixed camera over the door covered the entire grounds around the house in a closed circuit system. He saw three typical American youths.

These can't be Israelis. But in case you do happen to be the grandsons of Yechiel Horowitz, I have a little surprise in store for you...

The door buzzed and they pushed it open. They were inside.

"Baruch, Baruch, it can't continue on this way!"

"What can't?"

"Your dour Tishah B'Av face. When are you going to begin smiling?"

Eliad sighed. Old Manor was turning into a downright nuisance. He danced about him all day long, not leaving him alone for a minute. All the efforts that he and his team members had invested so far had met with no success. The Ebola refused to be cracked. It seemed that ever since the Ebola had arrived in the lab, Manor was staying later and later, causing unnecessary delays. So long as the old man was amongst them, they were unable to descend to their underground lab and work on the real project, their primary goal. Perhaps he sensed something. They said he was the king of nosybodies.

"You're going to smile now," he said, prefacing his routine morning joke. He spoonfed Baruch jokes three times a day, a tonic against the doldrums. "Seventy years ago, when they finished building Pinchas Guttenberg's power station in Nahariya..."

"Pinchas Rottenberg, not Guttenberg," Eliad corrected him. "Guttenberg invented the printing press."

"What difference does it make? It can be Krautemburg, for all I care," said Manor. He stopped and then continued. "Anyway, they invited King Abdullah of Jordan to visit the new station. He looked all around him at the gigantic machinery and was given a full explanation from Rottenberg. 'This is a very powerful station,' said Rottenberg. 'It has an eighty thousand horsepower capacity.'

"Abdullah looked all around him, as if searching for something. His head turned from side to side. 'What are you looking for?' asked Rottenberg. 'For the stables!' said Abdullah."

Baruch laughed politely and left the room, excusing himself, "I'm in a hurry." This old man had become impossible of late. He left Manor laughing aloud to the four walls.

≈)⊂

They sank comfortably into the deep leather armchairs. Randy asked questions and Dr. Yoachim replied. It was a routine interview for all purposes. Still waters, but deep beneath the surface underground streams and whirlpools rushed and raged. They knew very well who he was and 'he' instinctively felt that they knew, and they suddenly knew that he knew...

The atmosphere became artificial and unreal; a kinetic tension hung in the air. Avi toyed with his hands under the table, pulling his knuckles nervously. *My goodness, if we ever leave this snake's lair in one piece, I vow to study three hundred pages of Gemara in the coming year.* He did not even think about salvaging the will...

The movie camera scanned the large room paneled in expensive teak. A contained opulence reigned everywhere. The camera captured every item to create a background atmosphere suited to the commentary. It roved among metal statuettes, Picasso originals, distinguished awards and diplomas from the government of Argentina and so on. Suddenly, Meitar's sharp eye focused on some small glass boxes standing on an Italian mantelpiece. Inside the boxes, on small stands, stood several eggs inscribed with lovely pictures. From the egg in the center there smiled up at him the bearded face of his older brother, Roni.

The lens froze. Meitar felt his heart stop beating. Was Roman Spiegel an omnipotent fiend? How had he gotten hold of a likeness of his brother, Roni?

Then he understood.

Not in vain did the entire family repeatedly aver that Roni was a spitting image of Saba David.

It wasn't Roni, then; it was Saba David Eliad, alias Yechiel Horowitz. This was the famous egg that Roman had decorated in Vienna sixty years before, the egg that R' Avrumele had ordered to be destroyed, the egg that had given him away and landed Yechiel Horowitz into the hands of Roman Spiegel.

The circle was now closed. *This egg will deliver you into my hands. This is the proof that you are not Yoachim von Krautemburg but Roman Spiegel, the escaped Nazi war criminal!*

He filmed the egg in the center and the ones surrounding it in their glass cases for a long time.

Yoachim stole a side glance at the cameraman. Randy took note and looked that way. Then he whistled in astonishment. "*Entschuldigung,* Herr Von Krautemburg, but I happen to be an art buff. What are those eggs, there?"

"The eggs? Ah, that's one of my hobbies. In my spare time I enjoy painting miniature pictures on eggs."

"How do you do that?" Randy asked in candid amazement.

Yoachim got up; his visitors followed close behind. They approached the glass cases. Meitar filmed the eggs from all possible angles. His hands shook like autumn leaves when he focused on the center one with his grandfather's likeness. Yoachim's sharp eyes noticed the camera's trembling.

"First I empty the eggs of their contents. I pierce them with two tiny holes and blow out the liquid to the last drop so that there should be no foul odor. Then I sit down by my worktable and under a high-powered light I begin drawing with a graphic stylus."

"Is there any special secret to this?" Randy asked innocently.

Yoachim looked at the three youths long and meaningfully. Avi and Meitar exchanged glances and the color drained from their faces.

"Yes, there are several professional secrets to the process," his voice intoned slowly. "The first secret is patience. Ironclad patience."

"And the second?" asked Meitar.

"The second secret is here in the cupboard," said Yoachim, opening the drawer. An old, long-barreled Colt revolver suddenly leaped into his hands as if by magic. He held it firmly, leveling the barrel straight at them.

"This is the second secret," he laughed in a metallic voice. He spoke in Hebrew with a heavy German accent. "It's time we stopped playing this game. You didn't fool me for a moment, Meitar and Avigdor Eliad, you pair of fools. I identified you immediately. Now sit down, all three of you."

The three sank again into the armchairs. There was a soft buzzing in the air as the abandoned movie camera continued filming automatically, its lens focused on Yoachim.

⤙⤚

"I've been waiting for you for a long time," said Yoachim, his finger resting on the trigger, sure and firm. The mouth of the long barrel stared at them, grey and threatening. "Actually, it is not you that I've been waiting for but your father, Baruch Eliad the scientist."

Meitar and Avi smiled. So he thought them to be brothers. Never mind. The less he knew, the better.

"Why are you smiling? Big heroes! I've had you followed from the moment you landed in Vienna."

"Who told you that we were coming?" Avi dared ask.

"I have my men everywhere," Yoachim boasted. "If an octopus has eight arms, I have a hundred."

"You're Roman Spiegel, aren't you?" asked Meitar.

"Correct. I don't mind revealing that because you will never get out of here alive unless your father comes in exchange."

"What are you talking about?"

"About this," said Yoachim, becoming Roman again, as he pointed to one of the eggs in the glass case. "Why have you come here?" he suddenly inquired.

"Have pity," wailed Randy. "I have nothing to do with this. I only work for CNN. Let me out of here. Let me go home."

The round barrel was aimed at Randy's head. "If you utter another word, this will talk," Roman whispered threateningly. "I asked why you came."

"We came to look for our great-grandfather's will," said Avi. The words sounded unreal in the strange atmosphere that pervaded the room.

Roman burst into peals of unbridled laughter. "You came to search for the will?" he heaved with pleasure. "By my life! The very same numbskulls as your grandfather, not a whit smarter! That was Yechiel Horowitz and that's you two, all over again. Transparent and predictable, lacking any sense of vision to the point of boredom. You are no fitting opponents for me. Well, never mind. Soon your father will come here. Baruch Eliad — now there's a suitable rival of stature."

"Why do you need him?"

Roman breathed heavily. Then he spoke slowly and deliberately, as if to savor the full flavor of the moment.

"He will solve the mystery for me." He pointed towards the egg. "Baruch Eliad Horowitz will finally solve the secret of the will of his great-grandfather, Avigdor Horowitz."

51

Avi was filled with a helpless fury. "You opened the will? You... you grave robber!"

Roman gave a little smile. "Grave robber? Hardly." His grin broadened. "We didn't leave much to be robbed."

"You sent my grandfather a container of zyklon gas containing the bones of his first wife!" Avi continued, hardly noticing the interruption.

Roman laughed again, a laugh full of satisfaction and enjoyment. "Ita's bones?" he said, with a wild guffaw. "That's a good one!" He gave Avi a long look, as if trying to come to a decision. Finally, his pistol aimed squarely at Avi's head, he gave the grandsons of his greatest enemy their orders.

"W-w-where are y-y-you? W-w-what's happened?" Baruch stammered. It was his nephew on the line, his nephew calling him 'Abba' and asking him to come. Danger signs. He pulled at his right ear lobe, a clear sign of stress.

"Abba, you must help us," murmured Avi, the cold barrel pressing on the nape of his neck. The phone was slammed down.

"Sit, *bitte*," said Roman with surprising courtesy. A tall young man descended from the upper story, smiling pleasantly. "Please make the acquaintance of Hans, my bodyguard. Watch out for him. Despite his pleasant appearance, he is as swift and deadly as a cobra. He will enable me to explain certain points to you with my hands free."

"What do you know about your great-grandfather, Avigdor Horowitz?"

"Don't mention my pure and saintly great-grandfather's name with your foul lips!" said Avi angrily.

"Let's pretend that I didn't hear you," said Roman lightly. "You are a pair of boors, searching for an ancient piece of writing without even knowing what it's about. Do you know that Horowitz the kabbalist was also a brilliant scientist?"

Silence. They were surprised. They knew that Zeide Avigdor had been a hidden saint, but a scientist?

Roman removed the eggs from their glass case. He brought one egg close to Avi's eyes. "Read!"

Avi shrugged his shoulders. "I don't want to."

"Read, you fool! It's your grandfather's will."

Avi squinted and read the Hebrew words with difficulty, "In those days we discovered the secret of the tiny creatures, my friend and I. This secret is known only to a select few and hidden from all others."

Roman pulled back the egg. "What is it talking about?" asked Avi.

"Ah, so it's beginning to interest you," chuckled Roman. "That's only a small excerpt from the will."

"But how can that be?" asked Meitar. "Zeide did not write his will on an egg."

"Of course not. It was written on parchment; I copied it over on the egg. It's my hobby, you know, to write all kinds of things on eggs. Besides, the ancient parchment was beginning to disintegrate from contact with the air. Your grandfather said not to open it for one hundred years, remember?" The open ridicule was pronounced in every single word he uttered.

"Listen, here, you scoundrel," said Avi, leaping up with clenched fists. "It's our property. Give us back the will!"

"Hans," Roman said quietly. The bodyguard waved the pistol. Avi turned silent.

"Let me tell you a story," said Roman. "Many things will become clear to you. After the war I went to Argentina, taking the will with me. In the first few months I was busy reestablishing myself in Buenos Aires. After half a year, I had some free time on my hands and wanted to know what was hidden in the wooden tube which Yechiel Horowitz had guarded with his life. I broke the seal... No, the sky did not fall on me and I wasn't struck by lightning as a punishment for having violated the will of the Jewish kabbalist. On the contrary, I discovered some very interesting things written there. It appeared from the will that your great-grandfather, together with another kabbalist colleague, had cracked the secret of the genetic code some one hundred years ago. And all this only through his knowledge of Kabbalah!

"Can you imagine how I blessed myself for knowing Hebrew? As an average German citizen, I could not possibly have understood a single word of the will. To tell the truth, at first I was sure that it was all nonsense and gibberish. A few years ago, when the science of genetics became more popular, I realized that your great-grandfather had preceded modern science by almost a century. I consulted with my scientists and showed them several formulas which Rabbi Horowitz had written, and they unanimously agreed that he had known what he was talking about.

"And now we get to the crux of the matter. Those formulas were culled from kabbalistic works. In order to complete what is missing in the will, it is necessary to fill in information contained in those mystic texts. This is why I need the combination of a brilliant genetic scientist who is also familiar with kabbalistic lore. Only such a person can solve our problem.

"A few months ago my people in Iran discovered — I won't tell you how — that there was such a person. He was the world-famous genetic scientist, Baruch Eliad: none other than the son of Yechiel Horowitz! And he is the very one who will help me decipher his own great-grandfather's will. We've come full circle!" Roman was so ecstatic that he almost danced with joy.

"Why is the will so important to you?" wondered Meitar.

"Don't you understand yet? The will almost certainly contains a special secret showing how to crack the genetic code of deadly microbes — and how to be inoculated against them as well.

"My scientists in Iran are now working around the clock in developing a bacteriological bomb that will destroy all the people of Israel. Eliad is one step ahead of us. All we are missing is one small but crucial fact without which we are back at square one. But that missing link will open the door for us.

"Just imagine," Roman's eyes flashed sparks, "the Fuehrer began and I will finish up! I will wipe out the Jewish people in its very homeland. And how? Through an Israeli scientist, no less! Marvelous! The sword that will sever the throats of the Jewish people and remove this scourge from this world once and for all will be one of Jewish origin. The father, Yechiel Horowitz, began the treason against his people and his son will complete the process. How do you Jews put it? The power of the son surpasses that of the father... The father only did something small and symbolic whereas the son will bring total destruction upon his people!"

Roman's eyes shot ice-blue bolts of electricity. He looked mesmerized, in a deep hypnotic trance. "From the times of Nebuchadnezzar and Titus, no inventor has arisen like myself. Had I lived in Egypt in Biblical times, I could have spared Pharaoh much headache. Unlike my predecessors, Pharaoh, Haman, Amalek and Hadrian, who failed, I will succeed!"

"And what will you do with the Jews of America?" mocked Meitar.

"Ah, they pose no problem. They are self-destructing through assimilation. They'll take care of themselves. They'll be totally wiped off the demographic map within fifty years."

"G-d forbid!" breathed Avi.

"You're insane!" said Meitar, leaping up. "You should be hospitalized in a mental institution."

Hans gnashed his teeth. He shot glances at Roman, begging permission to be let loose on them, but Roman seemed to be enjoying every minute.

"Why harm the kid? Better let him see how his father helps me develop the bacteriological atom bomb that will turn Israel into one huge cemetery."

"But there are close to two million Arabs in Israel as well, Israeli and

Palestinian Arabs. Don't forget that they will also be killed along with the Jews," Meitar pointed out with cold logic.

"So what?" Roman dismissed the argument with a wave of his hand. "A nation that cannot make sacrifices is not a nation. The Arab people will sacrifice two million people for the sake of getting rid of the accursed Jews, once and for all. The president of Egypt, Anwar Sadat, was prepared to sacrifice a million Egyptian soldiers in order to destroy Israel. And he was right. Admit it, yourselves, isn't it worth it? This was the Fuehrer's dream! This is the final solution! If Hitler were alive now, he would be proud of me!"

We must gain more time, thought Meitar helplessly. *How can we get the old man to keep on prattling?*

"Is it true that our grandfather, David Eliad, that is, Yechiel Horowitz, collaborated with you during the Holocaust?"

Roman gave him a significant look. "Who told you that?"

"Meir Tzuriel."

"Meir Tzuriel?" Roman frowned and combed his white mane with his fingers. "Ah, you mean Shalom Travitzky, the watchdog I put on your grandfather. Travitzky did a good job, too. He slandered him and besmirched his name everywhere. It was worth keeping him alive. He revealed to me that he had always been jealous of your grandfather and despised him, though Yechiel saved his life in Maidenek. I would surely have killed him had it not been for your grandfather."

"And what is the truth? Did Yechiel Horowitz collaborate with you? Was he a kapo?"

Roman burst into laughter. "If I am an altar, your grandfather is the sacrifice. And you still ask? Don't you know that your grandfather is a proud Jew? Even I must grant him that. He was the best tenor the world had; no power in the world could have forced him to utter a note while his brothers were being killed. But he had one weakness; he loved his family too much. One should never be that soft. You must be strong enough to be able to sacrifice those who are nearest to you, too, for your own interests. This is how we Aryans are built. I took advantage of his weakness to the fullest. I turned his wife and children into my hostages; I blackmailed him for four years."

"Our Saba stopped singing after the Holocaust. He swore that he would never sing again," said Meitar, in a rush of emotion. Only now was he beginning to see into the profound depths of his grandfather's soul.

They all sank into silence. Everything had apparently been said for the time being. This wasn't good. Hans was now busy unwinding some rubber fetters. He was going to truss them up.

"Could I see the egg again?"

"Which one?"

"The one with Grandfather's will."

"*Bitte, bitte,*" said Roman generously. "Come and see what a genius your grandfather was. Too bad you haven't inherited his cleverness."

"Dear offspring, be wise in utilizing the power which I am transmitting in your hands only for building up, not for destruction, G-d forbid. This secret will save you from terribly difficult diseases. But if you use its power for destruction, it is liable to rise up against you, like a *golem* rebelling against its maker, and bring terrible ruin and devastation."

"I don't understand," said Meitar, shrugging his shoulders. He looked at the elliptic point of the egg. "What's the secret? It doesn't say here."

They studied the decorated egg with its tiny letters fashioned in exquisite calligraphy and felt that an esoteric secret remained buried in the cryptic writing.

"You are right. This egg is only the second half of the will. I wrote the first half on another egg."

"Where is it?"

Roman burst into a peal of satanic laughter, a laughter full of smug enjoyment. "Wait for 'Abba.' He will be coming in a day or two. You will await him at the airport and then we will all come here."

Roman went over to the sideboard and poured himself a large shot of brandy.

As he watched his grandfather's nemesis calmly drink from the thin, gleaming crystal goblet held in exquisitely manicured fingers, Meitar felt a wave of fury engulf him.

"You... you Nazi," he hissed, forgetting in his rage that the epithet was, in some circles, considered a compliment. "You live with luxury and honor, while my grandfather is a ruin...

Roman chuckled at the boy's wrath. "A walking corpse," he agreed cheerfully.

Now it was Avi's turn to feel a rush of overpowering emotion. "No!" he cried, lifting his arm, the fragile egg still clutched between his fingers. "A ruin! No! My grandfather lives, a Jew, in a Jewish land, farming Jewish soil, learning Jewish Torah. G-d's land, G-d's Torah. He lives in his children and in his grandchildren. He even sings through them!"

Meitar watched his usually reserved and controlled cousin in wonder. His eyes turned towards their captor. Avi's last words seemed, somehow, to have diminished him: He looked like an old man.

Avi wasn't finished yet. His voice grew quiet, dangerously quiet. "You thought you could destroy him, as your wretched leader thought he could destroy our people. But you failed, Nazi, you and your leader both. He is dead and you are the walking corpse. You can't destroy G-d's people — you couldn't even destroy my grandfather. And you come with your stupid schemes of mass murder. The Jews live, their spirit is unbroken — and you are worth nothing!"

Avi's hands came down swiftly — and suddenly the egg was on the floor, cracked into hundreds of fragments.

"*Was war das?*" Roman leaped forward as if bitten by a snake. He stared at the cracked eggshell that lay on the floor and at the youth who had dared address him so. He hurled the crystal tumbler in his hand forcefully against the opposite wall; the yellow liquid slithered down the wall together with thousands of tiny crystals.

"Filthy Jew!" he screeched at Avi like a witch.

Fifty years disappeared; Spiegel was again an S.S. officer in Maidenek. The young Nazi officer Roman Spiegel had one weakness — he enjoyed shooting his victims from close range.

"Roman," his friends used to laugh at him, "your pistol can shoot from fifty meters also."

"But I like to see how the hard bullet pierces through soft tissue,"

Roman would explain, a typical explanation for a human fiend. But his friends knew the true reason: He was a poor marksman.

Spiegel lunged at Avi and released the trigger. Randy, who'd sat quietly, not understanding a word of the Hebrew conversation going on around him, suddenly burst into life: His long foot shot out and tripped the old Nazi. Spiegel sprawled on the floor and his gun fired wildly. The bullet hit the forehead of his gigantic bodyguard, Hans.

Spiegel stared in horror at the dead man. He tried to aim his gun at those... those filthy Jewish swine, grandsons of his foe, the thief who'd stolen his voice and his very identity. His hands — hands that had wielded a conductor's baton, a paintbrush, and a machine gun with equal dexterity — would not stop trembling. Adrenalin was pulsing through his blood.

He suddenly remembered his last conversation with Horowitz, on the eve of the liberation of Maidenek. "The day will come when I will avenge myself on you, Roman... my sons and my daughters.. will avenge..."

That was all it took. He felt a sudden, stabbing pain course through his body. The room swam before his eyes. Everything became cloudy and confused. Through a fog he saw a face staring at him. It was Henry Horowitz, but it couldn't be Henry Horowitz. This was his children, his grandchildren; they had come to seek vengeance, just as the Jew had promised fifty years before. That cursed Jew had offspring who loved him, grandchildren who followed in his footsteps. Roman knew he was dying. His whole life passed before him like a motion picture. And he saw it was all worthless. It was all nothing. In all his years, he had accomplished nothing but evil.

With a groan he feebly lifted his head. Then he fell face down onto the smooth marble floor. Roman Spiegel lay there, still and silent, silent as the grave.

≈)⊂

Baruch left the campus building. He stopped by a public phone booth and punched the secret number of the head of the Mossad. In brief words he relayed the contents of the message he had received and concluded, "I am leaving for Vienna on the next flight."

"No!"

"W-w-why not?" stammered Baruch in anger.

"You're not going to Vienna. It's a trap. Go back to your lab. Call up their hosts and find out where they went. My men in Vienna will reach them within a few minutes."

⋑⋐

"Meitar, are you all right?"

"Yes, Avi. How about Randy?"

"I'm O.K.," whispered Randy in the dark. "But my foot hurts a lot. What happened to the old man?"

Meitar stared at the two recumbent figures. Hans lay sprawled on the ground, a red splotch spread between his eyes and his head askew at a strange angle. The old man looked at them with glassy eyes. Meitar felt his pulse. There was none.

"He's dead," Meitar announced.

"The shock of killing his bodyguard must have killed him," Randy theorized.

"No, it was the shock of your words, Avi," Meitar said slowly, giving his cousin a look fraught with meaning.

"Hey, what's that?" Avi interrupted. A rising and falling sound was issuing from the electric fuse box.

"It's an alarm," shouted Randy. "The old man must have been wired to some emergency service or neo-Nazi underground movement in the vicinity. Let's get out of here quickly."

They raced feverishly towards the entrance of the house. Randy insisted they drag along the camera and equipment. "We mustn't involve CNN in this business," he shouted. "They'd fire me. It would cause an international scandal."

"What are you afraid of more?" quipped Avi.

"To tell the truth? Of being fired."

Meitar lingered behind. He reached them a few moments later.

"Look what we left behind in the room," Meitar smiled. He held a transparent plastic bag filled with white fragments. "Grandfather Avigdor's will is all here."

"It's not worth a cent," said Avi, pained. "We would never be able to put this Humpty Dumpty together again."

"Well, at least that monster won't be able to do it either," said Meitar with satisfaction.

They went outside. The cool night air greeted them in a rush, pure and refreshing. A car approached them and ground to a stop. A young man leaped out and ran towards the house. He opened the door and let out a terrible cry, "Father!"

The three began running with a speed that would not have put experienced marathon runners to shame. A white car suddenly appeared from nowhere and stopped.

"Are you the Eliads from Israel?" someone shouted from inside. They were confused for a moment, fearing another trap.

"Climb in!" ordered the driver. "Don't be afraid. Welcome to Israeli territory."

They hesitated for a fraction of a moment, but the driver flicked an identification card. "I'm Shlomo Carmon of the Mossad. It's all right. I've come to rescue you. Hurry up!"

A volley of shots from the street corner convinced them. The young man had his gun aimed at them and was shouting in German.

They didn't wait a moment longer. Shlomo pressed on the accelerator and the car shot out of the range of fire.

They landed in Israel the following day. Spiegel, it seemed, had not gone entirely unnoticed: The Mossad supplied Austria's intelligence service with a thick dossier on their opera house conductor. The embarrassment in high places was profuse. The Austrian media suppressed the story while the European press did not allow it to leak out either. A short notice in the papers announced that *Yoachim von Krautemburg, the renowned conductor of the Royal Opera House, died from a sudden heart attack in his house at the age of eighty.* A few days later, an article appeared commemorating Yoachim's great contribution to the world of music and opera: The chapter was closed.

Baruch and Yigal awaited their boys with tense anticipation. Black circles under their eyes testified to anxious days and sleepless nights.

"Where are we headed?" They sat comfortably in Baruch's large car, retelling their experiences, relieving themselves of accumulated stress. The car sped southward.

"To Yetzivim, of course," said Yigal. "Saba can't wait to see you! Be prepared for the first and foremost question: Have you brought the will?"

Avi and Meitar looked at one another in silence. Meitar uttered a short but meaningful sentence. Baruch and Yigal burst out in surprise at his words. They couldn't believe it. Avi verified the statement. Yigal dialed R' Calfon's home from his brother's cellular phone and spoke succinctly.

❦

Gindush Avivi, the acting *moshav* secretary, was up to his neck in work. At R' Calfon's request he had called up all of the members of Yetzivim and invited them to a gathering at David Eliad's home.

"I have no idea what it's about either," Gindush repeated for the umpteenth time. "R' Calfon just said that a big surprise would be awaiting one and all."

When the car reached Saba Eliad's home, it was accorded a royal welcome. Gindush's calls had brought almost all of the members of the *moshav*. The elderly Yoni Avivi, leaning on his cane, arrived supported by his son. R' Calfon was as vigorous as ever, his youthful eyes smiling merrily despite his advanced age. There was Moishe the onetime redhead, who was always looking for witnesses who remembered his ruddy beard, and Hillel Weiss, Shmuel Kastel, Dani Morelli... almost everyone, except for a few who had passed away over the years.

Meir Tzuriel did not come. He boycotted the gathering, and had good cause to do so.

❦

The grass in front of David's house was bathed in a strong light. Rumors about Avi and Meitar's marvelous trip and the secret of the ancient will had swept through the *moshav*, and everyone was anxious to hear about it in detail.

"Friends, I don't really know where to begin," said Meitar, somewhat helplessly. His hands were thrust in his pants pockets. "I'm inviting my cousin, Avi, to report instead."

Avi stood before the large audience, moved and afraid. He, too, was unable to speak.

"What's all the dramatics!" thundered Yoni. "We were promised a surprise. Did you bring the will or not?"

Meitar held a small leather bag. He removed a transparent plastic bag from inside and held it close to his grandfather's eyes.

"What's this?" David stared uncomprehendingly.

"I'm sorry, Saba, but these are the remains of Zeide Avigdor's will. It was shattered in Vienna, in Roman Spiegel's home."

A peal of laughter burst forth from the crowd. "You went all the way to Vienna and came back with broken eggshells? A pair of worthless comedians, Abbot and Costello. Eggshells!"

52

Meitar ignored the shouting. He pounded the table with his fist and silence fell. He had a lot of experience hushing wild audiences from his Serenade performances.

"Where's Meir Tzuriel?" Meitar asked. "Why hasn't he come?"

"Hey, where is he? Let's go and bring him!" a few shouted.

A minor uproar broke out. The residents of Yetzivim would never have arrived at David Eliad's home had it not been for R' Calfon's express wish. They could not forgive the idol of Polish song who had been a traitor to his people, not even in his waning days. But they revered R' Calfon and having come, expected it to be worth their while. Had the rabbi not promised a great surprise? A battle between the two old-timers, along the lines of a cockfight? Eliad and Tzuriel were the symbol of archenemies; they had avoided one another for the past many decades.

"There he is," a whisper swept through the crowd. "Gindush Avivi brought him."

His eyes shooting sparks, Meir Tzuriel sat down heavily on a chair. David Eliad's lifetime enemy resented his having been brought here by force. "He ruined my entire life, that traitor. I don't want to have to participate in any celebration of his," he grumbled aloud.

"Abba, calm down," his son, Shevach, said, laying a restraining hand on his shoulder. "We can go home soon and you can lie down to rest."

Meitar ran about frantically. While the others had been escorting Tzuriel he had brought over a movie projector and screen from Yetzivim's cultural center and placed it in front of a wall. Suddenly, without warning, the figure of an elderly man appeared, a flickering image on the screen.

David Eliad shuddered. Roman Spiegel himself! He recognized him even from the distance of fifty long years, without any help from Interpol or sophisticated computer identity software. Yes, that was him without a doubt! So Roman Spiegel really had been in Vienna!

David grabbed hold of Meitar's hand. "You filmed this?"

"Yes, Saba," smiled Meitar cryptically. "Wait, wait. Soon you'll understand why."

The people watched the screen, mesmerized. Those who knew English translated the interview for the rest who didn't. It seemed to be a routine interview on the surface, for the underlying currents of emotion on the parts of the interviewing team could not be seen. And yet a discerning eye could easily have seen Avi's pale face and dry lips, and Roman's nervous eye twitches.

The camera focused on some eggs. The audience could clearly see the tiny writing on them. Avi explained the background to the fascinated viewers.

Suddenly the placid interview changed: The Nazi had pulled a gun. Emotional cries erupted from the audience. "You were captives!" people breathed in admiration. "It may have been no great feat to overcome the old Nazi officer, but how did you deal with his gorilla bodyguard, Hans? What a giant!"

The pictures flashed by on the screen. The audience was completely swept up in the drama of the events. It watched breathlessly as Roman gave his fearsome monologue. "That's not a man, it's a monster! It's Satan in the flesh!" murmured Odelia, gripped by terror.

"And to think that Krautemburg was considered the greatest conductor in Europe!" Yoni Avivi sighed in dismay. His whole world of culture had suddenly collapsed and shattered to shards before his elderly eyes.

And then came the bombshell of the evening: Roman Spiegel told the truth about Yechiel Horowitz.

෨෬

David Eliad had suffered throughout this strange evening. All his old wounds were suddenly laid bare, wounds still raw under the scab of years which had only covered them up but not healed them. Roman Spiegel pursued him day after day; he had never succeeded in forgetting Ita, Avigdor, Shaul Yitzchak and Blumele...

When he had parted from Roman after the war, he had vowed to avenge himself within the decade. This had turned into five; for fifty years he had dreamed of wreaking vengeance upon the murderous beast and repaying him in kind. But today he had learned the meaning of the verse, "Hashem is a G-d of vengeance." The Creator had planned His revenge, a sweet, perfect retaliation which no mortal could have concocted. David stared at the screen, his eyes two glassy marbles. His archenemy, the man who had ruined his life, was admitting the truth. "Your grandfather is a proud Jew." The words exploded like shells in the emotionally laden air. "No power in the world would have forced him to utter a note while his brothers were being killed... I turned his wife and children into my hostages... I blackmailed him for four years!"

He felt like crying. Oh, how he wished he could give release to his emotions, to feel the relief of sweet tears, the liberation of shaking shoulders and a hoarse throat and purifying tears.

In vain. His spring of tears had become sealed back in Maidenek.

David Eliad stared at the screen like a stone Sphinx. The victory was too big for him; the revenge too sweet for him to absorb.

A loving hand was laid on his shoulder. Yigal spoke with a restrained voice."Abba, it's all right."

David covered his face with his hands for a moment but his head shot up immediately afterwards. He continued to study the screen. This film surpassed anything that his imagination could have conjured up.

Meir Tzuriel felt all eyes turned on him. He wanted to run away, but his old legs rebelled against him.

"...Meir Tzuriel?" Roman asked on the screen. "You mean Shalom Travitzky, the watchdog I put on your grandfather... He revealed to me that he had always been jealous of your grandfather and despised him... Yechiel saved his life in Maidenek. I would surely have killed him had it not been for your grandfather!"

430 / *The Gordian Knot*

Meir Tzuriel blinked rapidly. He looked all around him as if seeking an escape.

Hundreds of eyes looked at him with an accusing look, as if to say, "You sold us your story that David Eliad was a traitor to his people, a kapo, a Nazi collaborator, saved by virtue of his legendary voice... That he should have committed suicide rather than turn against his people..."

Hundreds of gigantic boulders crashed against one another inside his brain. He felt an excruciating pressure inside him. A gigantic hand grabbed him and flung him into a catapult of hell. The entire structure of his world had come crashing down before his eyes. The best years of his life had been dedicated to a personal vendetta against Yechiel Horowitz, and now had come the moment of truth. *Truth rises up from the earth, and if you deny it, it will strike you in the face.*

The terrible truth was closing in on him from all sides.

Tzuriel rose from his seat and walked over ponderously to David Eliad. He stopped in front of him and gave a terrible shout. Later, people argued whether he had screamed, "*Gevald,*" or, "*Oy vey.*"

He burst into stormy, hysterical tears. "Forgive me, Yechiel. Forgive me, Yechiel," he wept. "You are the righteous one and I, the sinner. I tortured you for no good reason; I persecuted you for no fault of yours. You were right all these years; I was jealous of you. I hated you. I sinned in suspecting the innocent. I was ungrateful."

He turned to face the crowd. "My friends," he shouted in a strange voice, "look at me. Stare at me and learn from my mistake. Don't be like me." He beat his chest with his fist, as on Yom Kippur, and called himself a string of harsh guilty names.

The movie was over and colored lines danced wildly across the screen. No one paid any attention. The real and painful drama was now taking place before their eyes.

"I want to confess," groaned Meir Tzuriel. "David, tell us, did you ever receive reparations from Germany?"

"No!"

David had violently objected to the idea of reparations, even when his financial situation had been very difficult. "You can't buy pardon through money," he had explained to Odelia in those years. "Genocide is unforgivable, and accepting reparations will only give the Germans a feeling of a clear conscience. Better that they should choke upon their reminders of genocide for the coming generations."

"I claimed that you didn't get German reparations all these years because you were a kapo and collaborator. I'd like to tell you a secret. I did fill out a form for reparations right after Ben Gurion signed the agreement with Germany. Two weeks later I received a registered letter signed by Roman Spiegel which read, 'My colleagues are everywhere: in the committee handling the reparations monies, and in Israel as well. Write and tell me at once: Where is Yechiel Horowitz and what does he call himself today?'

"The envelope contained a check with an enormous sum made out to a Swiss bank. 'Send me details on Yechiel and you can cash this check. And if you don't, you will soon be smelling flowers from the root side.' I was afraid, deathly afraid... and I was also greedy. I sent Spiegel the information he wanted and since then, I haven't heard a word from him."

He turned to Eliad again, "Yechiel, forgive me." He bawled like a baby. "Please, I beg of you, judge me favorably. I have been enchained by a foolish spirit all these years, since my childhood. I came from a deprived home; we were so poor and despised... Most of your friends were poor, while you were born with a silver spoon in your mouth. You were well born, high up on the social ladder, and you were born with your marvelous voice besides. When you sang, you had everyone in tears. People imagined they heard the singing of angels. R' Avrumele told me once, at a Friday night *tish*, while you were singing a particularly moving passage, that '*Yechiel hatt a hoicher neshamah*,' an exalted soul. We were all jealous of you. All of your friends in Lublin consumed you with their eyes, but I was the worst of all. Envy gnawed away at me, it sucked up all of my energies. I could have been happy with my lot; I could have become a truly great Torah scholar, a *rosh yeshivah*. I gave a lecture in a yeshivah before the war, but what became of me in the end? A country lout, a simple farmer. A tiller of the ground. I've wasted my entire life. Seventy years gone down the drain, consumed in envy, bitterness and frustration."

Meir turned to the people of the *moshav* and shouted with all his might,

"Friends, I am a living *mussar* lesson! See how jealousy can reduce a person to nothing, take him to the bottomless pit of hell! Learn from my example and never repeat what I did."

He threw himself at David's feet and struck his head on the ground. "Forgive me, Yechiel. Like you, I also lost a wife and children in the war."

The entire *moshav* was on its feet, waiting to hear what David would say.

"You don't see a drama like this even in the movies," whispered Yoni to his wife Berta, who sat at his side in a wheelchair. She was partially paralyzed from a stroke, but her brain was as lucid as ever, as alert as the next person's. And she had been avidly following the developments along with the others.

David shook his head from side to side, as if trying to shake off a nightmare. He murmured something quietly to himself and then suddenly arose, grabbed hold of Meir's jacket lapels and dragged him up to his feet. He stared at him, his eyes like white-hot skewers. Meir shut his eyes in fear.

"So now it has all come out! Shalom, your father, Shevach, was the one who started the shameful slander and you finished it up. You delivered me over to my monstrous enemy a second time, after the war, when all I wanted from life was to dwell in peace and forget the *gehinnom* I had left behind. So it was you who informed Roman where to send all of his parcels!" he roared from the depths of a wounded heart.

"And do you know what? *I forgive you!* I forgive you utterly and completely. I don't even bear the slightest grudge against you. Divine Providence chose you to be the whip. I was punished because I disobeyed R' Avrumele's words, his explicit warning on the eve of my *bar mitzvah*. I forgive you…"

A round of thunderous applause drowned out the end of his words. Hillel Weiss wept aloud, unashamed. "I always knew you were okay, David. I believed in your innocence all along."

R' Calfon approached the two men. "My friends," he announced ceremoniously, so that the entire gathering could hear, "now you all understand which surprise I was referring to.

"If my humble memory does not serve me wrong, I predicted that the truth would yet come out. It was at the Purim festivity that took place in my home in 5720. I knew David was no traitor. I said that when the time came,

I would reveal my sources. It was R' Goldberg who told me the truth."

"How did R' Goldberg know?" asked Yoni Avivi.

"A sage is better than a prophet. R' Goldberg had spoken to David on the eve of his engagement to Odelia and had heard the full story from him. At the time he had said to me, 'The truth can be recognized'."

"And you relied on that, on that Purim in 5720, when you said you had authentic information and true witnesses that David was no traitor?"

"Yes," said R' Calfon emphatically. He pointed to the movie projector. "These are the best witnesses in the world. What could be more convincing than an admission from the litigant himself? Roman Spiegel in person admitted the truth; such a confession is equal to a hundred witnesses. Know that when a sage as great as R' Goldberg uses the phrase 'my heart tells me,' it is a supposition coming straight from Above; it is a spark of Divine intuition. Such a statement can be relied on implicitly. This evening you saw that I was right."

Meir Tzuriel was only the first on line. A wide circle formed around David; almost all the members of the *moshav* wished to ask his forgiveness personally. It was an absolute absolvement of guilt, a full exoneration and a reinstatement into *moshav* society.

"If you had gone to Vienna only for this video film, it would have been sufficient, *dayeinu*," said David to his grandsons later that night. It was long after the celebration was over and the last members had returned to their homes. "What you did for me today cannot be measured by any yardstick whatsoever. Only the Creator can repay you for your deeds. It's a pity that you did not succeed in saving the will but I feel I did whatever I could."

"David, what are you trying to say?" said Odelia, alarmed.

"The will warned of a catastrophe," David reminded those present. "The Guardian of Israel will continue to watch over us, will or no will."

"The ancient will," said Meitar, waving his little plastic bag. "We can put this together again with the help of experts and decipher the writing."

"You might as well sign up for the next flight to the stars," David laughed bitterly. "You'll reach Jupiter sooner. How do you expect to put together these tiny, tiny letters?"

"To join tiny letters; to join tiny letters…" murmured Yigal quietly.

"What did you say?" asked Baruch.

"To search among the small letters, the fine print… Isn't that what R' Aharonowitz said right before his death? Is this what he was referring to?"

Meitar held the video cassette in his hand. "The close-up shots of the egg are right here. If we use that as our guide, we can put the egg together and complete our puzzle."

To join, to put together, to connect tiny letters one to the other…

It was work which proceeded at a snail's pace. Baruch secretly invited a micrography expert to his home, who worked at pasting together the egg for an entire week. When it was over, the egg looked almost like before. Only a few pieces were missing but they were filled in by the video close-up.

Baruch devoted an additional day to copying the text into his computer. He read the words again and again, and slowly he began to understand the gist of it. Lacking some sources from the texts, he went to Mesilot and sat with Yigal over it all night. Yigal whipped out one volume after another. They discussed the meaning of the words. Each one was significant; each word was critical and fateful. The matter became clearer and clearer. Baruch felt he was very close to the solution of the mystery.

"You know what?" he laughed. "I have been running the code of a certain microbe through my computer for a whole month and coming up with a blank. It's become a question of professional pride, you understand. DNA scientists consider themselves deputies of the Creator. They fiddle around with the raw stuff of creation and change it at will. Their swelled heads burst with pride and arrogance. Sometimes I think I am omnipotent. The things I was able to do with the genetic code surpasses all imagination. So we reach the point where we think something along these lines: I am the master to decide if our descendants will have three eyes, a much higher I.Q. and so on. I can determine that the next generation will be only white haired and that people will live to be two hundred, that we will be healthy, thin and beautiful. To say nothing of curing genetic diseases like Tay-Sachs, cystic fibrosis, muscular dystrophy and sickle cell anemia. And then comes the blow. You see that you can't break any code, unless Someone Up There gives you permission to do so. The proof — I have now found the formula I have been searching for all this time in your sacred books, thanks to the will."

"At what stage are you?"

"I am very close to actually cracking it. I have a very important lead."

But on the following day it became clear to Baruch that the Ebola was as elusive as ever. He went back to the starting point. A tiny fragment of the formula was still missing. This must have been in the first part of the will, the part they didn't have.

⁀⁀

Baruch called an emergency meeting in Yetzivim. This time the family gathering was kept secret. Yigal and Avi came from Mesilot. Baruch and Meitar came from Rehovot; Roni, Meitar's brother, was given special army leave.

Baruch threw the problem into the family court. "We've only found part of the will. Where is the first half? Zeide Avigdor's warning is still very real and imminent!"

"What can we do?" sighed David heavily. "We've done everything we could. The Nazi hid the first half."

"Let's run the film once more," suggested Avi. "Perhaps the first half is there, somewhere, on one of the eggs."

The video was turned on and the family studied it from every angle, even playing the film backwards.

Meitar was enthusiastic. "Saba, there's the egg with your picture. This was the drawing that helped deliver Roman into my hands."

"That egg delivered me into Roman's hands," murmured David, his hands shaking. "It was measure for measure, because that same egg gave Roman away and delivered him into my grandson's hands."

"You should have brought it back with you. It's a slice of history," interjected Odelia.

"Destroy the egg!" shouted David.

"Excuse me?"

"Never mind. Better that it should remain in Vienna."

Roman was on the screen. "I wrote the first half on another egg," he said, and Meitar asked, "Where is it?" Roman answered with a satanic laugh.

David leaped up. When had he heard that laughter before?

On the night of the Krampitz massacre! When he had sung while his own wife and children were being murdered along with thousands of other Jews. Roman had stood laughing to himself in smug satisfaction, smiling a secret smile whose significance was known to him alone.

"Run the film backwards again," ordered David, and Meitar brought the cassette to the moment when Roman removed the mask of Yoachim von Krautemburg, the opera conductor, from his face. "Why have you come here?" he asked. "We came to look for our great-grandfather's will," answered Avi. Roman burst out into fiendish laughter. It was that same laughter again.

David paced the room, a lit cigarette in his hand. "The key to the mystery is in my hand! Roman laughed because he had a secret." He paused. Things were growing clearer. "He was mocking our stupidity. He had sent the will a long time before, hidden inside something.

"The precious will is here, in *Eretz Yisrael*, in Yetzivim itself. Very near to us. Avi, go to my office and bring me the two diplomas."

Baruch took apart the old frames with sure hands. The dusty wood creaked and groaned in protest at the disturbance of a decades long peace.

"Don't you understand?" asked David, excitedly. "Roman wrote me at the time that he would return all of my stolen effects to me. He kept his word. He must have hidden the will behind the diplomas."

The Viennese diploma was opened first. The old cardboard was carefully removed. Two cards fell out. Baruch turned them over.

Two charming Jewish children smiled up at them, dressed in the typical caps of Polish and Galician Jews. They had curly *payos* and round cheeks and a mischievous look in their eyes.

"Avigdor and Shaulke," roared David like a wounded animal, hugging the pictures to his heart. "If I only had known that your pictures were in my possession all these years..." He froze for a moment and devoured the photos with a longing look. David had returned to the Lublin of yore, Lublin before the Flood... He kissed the pictures gently and then shook himself out of his trance with superhuman effort. "Baruch, open up the second diploma, the one from Maidenek."

The second frame held another photo, Ita holding six-month-old Blumele.

These were difficult moments for David. He rushed around the room like a wounded bear, spouting unintelligible phrases and words. Yigal rushed to bring him some water but David rejected the offered glass.

"Many waters cannot quench the love," he quoted. "You are trying to put out an eternal fire with a glass of water? The entire Atlantic Ocean cannot extinguish the fire in my heart!"

Baruch stepped aside with Odelia. They considered calling a doctor but David stopped them. "I'm all right."

"From where do you get such strength, Abba?"

"Hashem gives strength," he said in a cracked voice. "R' Saadya Gaon says, 'The Blessed One decrees and executes.' Hashem passes a certain decree upon a person but at the same time that He executes it, He endows him with the strength to endure.

"Now I understand why, whenever I saw the diplomas, I could not help seeing the faces of Ita and the children in my mind. Their spirit hovered in my office all these years. Odelia, didn't you take those diplomas secretly and go off to Beersheba to have them translated? I guessed as much when I met you on the road. I was driving an army jeep, remember? And that night, when I was sitting in the garden with Yoni and Hillel, you ran off to replace them in my office by the barn. But you switched them around... I know everything. But it didn't matter to me. I had hidden the diplomas from you because I wanted to protect you. I was concerned for you and I didn't want you to become involved in the tragedy I had experienced. I suffered enough."

"And what now? Should we give up?" asked Yigal in a broken voice.

Everyone sank into his own thoughts. Odelia broke the heavy silence. "We'll talk about it this coming Shabbos. Together."

❦

It was a most uplifting Shabbos; crowded and noisy but full of joy. Twenty of them crowded into the small house and enjoyed every moment of it. Since the families had expanded, with the two brothers living such different lives, they had not gotten together like this in the parents' home. But now it was different. The recent events had brought hearts closer. Baruch, Dassi and the children were trying to draw nearer. Odelia wept secretly several times at the sight of Baruch's children joining the Shabbos singing together with their religious cousins, Yigal's children, as if they had never been worlds apart.

On Shabbos afternoon, Yigal studied with his son, four-year-old Efraim. The little boy's voice rang out with Jewish sweetness and filled the entire house. "And wash your feet and rest under the tree..." he repeated the familiar words from *Parashas Vayeria* over and over, and all smiled with pleasure.

Only David refused to smile. "Under the tree..." The words tickled something in his grey cells. What was the significance of those words? To him, personally?

"Under the tree..." A hint from Heaven. Sweet Efraim was the messenger to hand him the solution.

After Shabbos, as soon as he had downed the *havdalah* wine, David got to his feet and raced out with youthful vigor to the shed, his eyes glowing. He came out with the old spade and went off to the garden, his sons hot on his heels.

"What's going on?"

"You'll see very soon. Someone bring a flashlight."

David dug feverishly under the peach tree by the light of the flashlight. The spade hit something metal and clanged loudly.

"Here it is," he said, drawing up, from its burial place, a cylindrical metal tin wrapped up in a plastic covering.

"Let's take this home," he said to the family. They all followed behind, surprised.

Twenty pairs of eyes watched as David's eyes freed the round box from its plastic prison. The evil label 'poison gas' with its skull and crossbones was exposed to the fluorescent light.

"My goodness, David, what are you doing?" moaned Odelia weakly. "Are you removing Ita's bones from their grave?"

"That's what Roman wanted me to think," David replied hoarsely. He pried up the lid with a sharp knife and they heard the click of air entering the vacuum as the lid flew off into the air.

There were neither bones nor ashes...

It lay inside, wrapped up in a skein of soft, loose cotton wool, reposing on a spongy padding, whole and shining — a designed egg with tiny precise lettering covering it from end to end. A work of art.

There was a small envelope on the side. With semiparalyzed hands David opened it up and read:

"Greetings to you, Henry Horowitz. I knew you as Henry, and for me, you will always remain Henry. Not Yechiel and not David Eliad. I am sending you a copy of your grandfather Avigdor Horowitz's will. Remember? Roman Spiegel, master of micrography, enthusiast of miniature writing on eggs, on pages only half a centimeter big, on grains of wheat.

"This is only one half — the less important one — of your grandfather's will. The second, more significant half remains with me. I assume that you will not have the emotional strength to open this box. But if ever you do, you will see that I was right. What Roman promises, Roman fulfills. I am returning everything to you. The original will has long disintegrated and no longer exists. Your grandfather knew what he was doing. The paper upon which he wrote the will was apparently treated with a special chemical solution, and it disintegrated very rapidly when it came into contact with air. The air in the original tube was sucked out through a sophisticated technique not known in those days to create a vacuum. These two facts show that Avigdor Horowitz was well versed in scientific knowledge.

"Read the words well and when you finish the first half of the text and become curious about the second half, look for me. I am here, in a safe place. I've sent you several clues already. I am waiting for you or for your son, Baruch.

"*Danke schoen und auf wiedersehn*, Roman."

53

reetings to you, my dear grandsons:

> *I am writing to you without knowing your names or how you look. I estimate that you are five generations removed from me, and hopefully assume that you are Torah-observant Jews living in Eretz Yisrael.*

I am writing this on Monday evening, the middle of Teves, 5695. I received an important letter today via the French consulate with an answer to my question from my dear friend, the kabbalist, and I am hastening to write this will since I feel my strength ebbing quickly. My end is approaching and no man knows when it will overtake him.

I commanded my sons, who received the will, not to open it before a hundred years pass from the day of my death. I did not explain to them why, because they cannot begin to understand.

Know that several years ago I received a letter from Tunisia, from the city of Kohanim on the island of Djerba, written to me by my dear friend, R' Yosef Matzliach Hakohen...

"My grandfather!" cried Odelia in astonishment.

Yigal held up a high-powered magnifying glass to the egg and continued to read:

Despite his young age, R' Matzliach Hakohen is a veteran kabbalist, an astute expert in the mystic secrets of Torah, but he had many questions on the Zohar and the works of R' Chaim Vital. He sent his questions to several addresses in cities and countries throughout Europe, asking the rabbis there for names of known kabbalists. I don't know who provided him with my name since I have always been careful not to publicize my knowledge of the subject. At any rate, my name became known to him and since then we have been corresponding regularly.

A few years ago our mutual longings overcame us. Because of my weak state of health, I was unable to travel such a great distance, all the way to Tunisia. But R' Matzliach came here to Lublin and remained in my home for an entire year. This is after he had wandered about, lost, throughout Poland for an entire year."

"That must be Saba," Odelia wept. "Avi, don't you remember what I told you on *erev* Pesach? It was no mere coincidence that that particular episode sprang into my conscious memory."

We studied together that entire year. Many obscure matters concerning the fate of Jewry became clarified to us but I am not at liberty to reveal them. There is only one thing that I may disclose, regarding the tiny creatures that fill up the entire world. I will come back to this later. My friend returned home and we kept up our correspondence.

A few months ago I had a dream from which I awoke agitated. I dreamt I was walking along the seashore in Danzig and saw a ship in the water. I looked at the side of the ship and saw 'Israel' painted across it. The ship was anchored to the shore and throngs of Jews were getting on to go to Eretz Yisrael, I amongst them.

The sailors tied the ship firmly to the pier with heavy ropes, knotting them with innumerable sailor's knots, one on top of the other.

I stared at the rope and it suddenly turned into a thick branch, a myrtle branch blooming with the smell of fragrant haddasim filling the air. The myrtle-rope continued to grow before my eyes until it reached the sky. Branches grew out from it on all sides, and these lengthened rapidly and became knotted, one knot on top of the other, until they reached the number of one hundred.

The sailors now untied the knots of this myrtle-rope that bound the ship to the shore and the ship began sailing all over the world to gather Jews from their lands and bring them to the land of their ancestors. When the ship arrived in Tunisia, my good friend, R' Matzliach, came on board. And we took one of the myrtle branches, he tying one end to his hand and me, to mine, to symbolize a covenant of true friendship. When the ship arrived in Eretz Yisrael we took the thick rope of one hundred knots and we all went to the Kosel Hamaaravi to pour out our hearts in prayer and to ask for the rebuilding of the Beis Hamikdash. Then, from the mosque on the Temple Mount, thousands of Ishmaelites suddenly descended with drawn swords, seeking to kill us and to cut the thick rope. Then on the top of the myrtle branch which R' Matzliach and I had tied between us there sprouted a small leaf. An Arab boy with a sharp sword sought to cut it off. Tiny creatures flew all around him, biting and stinging, and killing people. I wept bitterly, and suddenly I awoke to see that it had all been a dream.

"What then, it should be true?" Roni and Meitar joked together and burst into laughter. "Who ever invented such a fantastic thing? It must have been Roman Spiegel."

Avi grasped Meitar's shoulder and said, "Take it easy, Meitar. Wait a bit and see. Don't be so hasty in judging."

Yigal held the powerful magnifying glass in his right hand and the egg in his left, and continued to read the miniature text.

I sent a letter to Tunisia asking my friend for his opinion. Today I plowed my way to the French consulate, since Tunisia is under its rule, through thick snow-drifts, and this is what R' Matzliach answered:

"I duly received your dear letter with the description of the dream. I was immediately reminded of the teaching of our Sages that the feet of a person are his surety that he will get to the place where he is destined to be.

"Several years ago, when I arrived in Poland, I saw sailors in the Danzig port tying a ship to the dock with heavy ropes. I suddenly felt a strong urge to find out what they called such a knotted rope. The Arabic sailor told me that it was called a Gordian knot, after a mythical knot that was almost impossible to untie.

"I am not an impetuous person. I am far from one who does things on wild impulse, and therefore I could not understand what strange spirit compelled me to find out if this was the very knot mentioned in Tractate Shabbos. Now it all becomes clear to me; not in vain did I chance to see those sailors and their knots, rather, it was the Creator Who had known the future and directed me to the right place. I never told you what I saw there at Danzig, but you saw it yourself in your dream.

"I know that every dream has its irrelevancies. Only one part in sixty of a dream is prophetic, and I fear that this dream has even more than that share. I therefore fasted for three consecutive days and immersed myself in a mikveh

dozens of times. Finally, I began to understand the significance of the dream, and this is the solution:

"The ship 'Israel' represents the Land of Israel. The myrtle represents the Jewish people who are likened to the fragrant myrtle. This leads me to hope that the dream is a good omen, for 'whoever sees a myrtle in his dream is assured of success in his affairs,' as we are taught in Tractate Brachos. The myrtle-rope which binds the ship to the shore is the destiny of the people and the promise of the Almighty to give it to the Jewish people. The Gordian knot is the knot which no man can untie. It is the strong bond tying the Jewish people to one another, to Hashem, and to their homeland.

"The hundred knots are one hundred years. In one hundred years' time a great danger will threaten the Jewish people in their homeland from the barbaric Ishmaelites. The danger will come from the Temple Mount. The branch that ties us together probably signifies mutual offspring in the future. It seems that in Eretz Yisrael our descendants will marry. The Arabs will seek to murder our grandson through the tiny creatures which swarm through the air, and together with him, to wipe out the entire Jewish people.

"Let us pray that it will not come to pass. Hashem, in His infinite mercy, will foil the scheme of the evil ones and ruin the plans of the enemy.

"Inform your future generations of the secret which we discovered, of the power hidden in these tiny creatures and how to be cured of their danger. Let their power be used only for the good, and by the knowledge overturn the evil schemes.

"Your friend, Yosef Matzliach Hakohen, City of Kohanim on the Isle of Djerba, Tunisia."

The room looked like the aftermath of a gas attack. The Eliad family panted for breath, faint from the impact of the revelation. No one was able to utter a word. If this was not prophecy, what was?

Their forebears had lived in distant lands, under different cultures and with different mentalities. And yet the Gordian knot, the fate of the Jewish people, had brought them together, the one from Poland and the other from Tunisia, and made close friends of them. And after many years these two friends had become family and their mutual grandsons, mutual against so many odds, knew nothing of the close relationship their grandfathers had enjoyed until a century had elapsed since the death of the one — R' Avigdor...

"I told you not to be so hasty about passing judgment, Meitar," said Avi hoarsely. "Let me ask you a logic problem: Could Roman Spiegel have known that your grandmother was a Tunisian and that her grandfather was a Kabbalist who had once visited Poland and wandered about, lost, for a year? He thought we were brothers..."

"Can I finish?" asked Yigal, holding the egg. "I am getting to the end."

Know, my dear grandsons, that you are descendants of the Horowitz family. Our family stems from a line of Levites who sang in the Beis Hamikdash. Song and music has never ceased in our family. May the Beis Hamikdash be speedily rebuilt so that we will return to stand and sing upon the special duchan platform. The power of music is mighty and exalted. It is capable of raising a person to the highest levels. "And it was when the musician played that the spirit of Hashem rested upon him."

The Gaon of Vilna said that most of the secrets of the Torah and the secrets hidden in the songs of the Levites cannot be fathomed without knowledge of music. Music can bring people to the point of expiration from its sweet pleasantness, and it can similarly revive the dead through the secrets hidden in the Torah. He also said that some of our melodies originate straight and pure, directly from Moshe Rabbeinu, who brought them from Mount Sinai. The rest are composite creations.

And you, my dear Levite grandsons, you are all gifted with the talent of music and song, some more and others less. Some of you are a single unit with music, while others may think they have no connection or inclination to it, but this is a mistake! The power exists dormant in their souls; it needs only to be awoken.

Use this power only for the good, for it is a tool given to you by the Creator to use in serving Him.

If you are not true to its trust and use it for profane things, it will bring great troubles upon you, but even then, the door is always open for returnees; even one who was scalded should "return unto Hashem and He will show him mercy, and unto his G-d Who is plentiful in pardoning."

Know, too, that our family is tied and bound to the Torah like to the flame in a glowing coal. I am preceded by thirty-six generations of rabbis and great sages, mighty geniuses, cedars of Lebanon.

The brilliant cerebral talents and the power of music are the seal identifying the Horowitz family of Levites. Just as one can mend souls through the power of music, so one can cause ruin, G-d forbid. Your talents, a gift from G-d, can be used for the good, to grow in Torah, to innovate, to fulfill the will of the Creator, but it can also lead to ruin and create evil. Don't misuse it!

I am asking all this, for I am about to reveal a hidden secret which became known to us and with which the Creator preceded the remedy to the blow, a terrible catastrophe which is liable to happen. Know to utilize it only for the good and not, G-d forbid, for evil.

In the second letter I will write the secret, and with this I am concluding, Avigdor Halevi Horowitz, Lublin.

"Does anyone know today's date?" asked Yigal.

"Today? It's *motzaei* Shabbos, the eve of the twentieth of Sivan," they answered in a chorus.

"Abba, when did Zeide Avigdor pass away?"

David shut his eyes in concentration. He was somewhat confused. "What's the question? The twentieth of Sivan, 5655 (1895). My father gave me a sign to remember it by. This is the day known as 'the fast of *tzaddikim.'*

"Tonight, *motzaei* Shabbos, on this eve of the twentieth of Sivan, 5755, exactly one hundred years have elapsed since the death of Zeide Avigdor. He asked that we open the will on the one hundredth anniversary of his death, and so has it come to pass. This is what we did, unknowingly," said Baruch, his eyes glowing.

"Meitar, was this a coincidence?" Avi teased good-naturedly.

"Leave me alone; I'm not into dates," Meitar squirmed. A small hammer was pounding away inside his head. *Where are you trying to run? You are escaping from reality, you ostrich!*

It was an overwhelming experience, too much to handle at once. Weeks and months would yet pass before everything fell into place in his brain. But seeds had been sown.

Later that night everyone left the home of Saba and Savta. The ancient warnings imposed a fear upon them all, but the words were too obscure.

A normal person tends to fear only clear-cut, specific things. On Sunday, everyone would be going back to their normal routine.

But not Yigal and Baruch.

Yigal was a *rosh yeshivah*, a scholar and delver to his very marrow. He absorbed and interpreted the words differently than the others, in depth and with clarity. The scenario that his imagination conjured up was blacker than black.

Baruch did not return to Rehovot with Dassi and the children. At first, he sat with Yigal to clarify the last, missing part of the secret. They groped futilely until Yigal summoned his student, Shimon Eliasyan, from his bed in the dark of night. "His father is a kabbalist," he explained to Baruch, who resented his involving a young student into the thick of the problem. But Yigal was right; Shimon Eliasyan gave a new direction to their search and the picture began to clarify. Baruch returned to Rehovot towards morning and knew that a grueling day awaited him in a few hours time. The puzzle had been completed. At his request, Yigal had skipped several significant sentences in the family reading of the will. Baruch only understood these lines that night.

Tomorrow or the next day he would crack the Ebola's genetic code.

While the rest of the family returned to Rehovot, Roni went to Jaffa. Roni was a very clever, thoughtful young man who had begun keeping *mitzvos* as a high school student, bringing much joy to the hearts of the second half of his family. When he finished his army service, he was offered a position in the Shabak, Israel's General Security Service. He fulfilled the expectations pinned on him and climbed very quickly up the service's ladder of success. He was an active operative and made many visits to Arab villages throughout Judea and Samaria and in Arab population centers in Israel. Aside from his parents, no one quite knew what Roni did.

The G.S.S. had lately been sniffing around Israeli-Arab centers, and their findings drew a very dismal picture indeed. Israeli Arabs were showing superchauvinism for Arab interests. Precisely in the Israeli-Arab sector there were disturbing attempts to set up underground organizations.

Several secret cells had set off red lights that spelled danger, cells so extreme that Hamas seemed like a Boy Scout movement in comparison. They belonged to the most virulent fundamentalist stream, more extreme than the Islamic Jihad and the Hizbullah. The new organization was called 'The Sword of Mohammed.' Its aim was clear and razor sharp. It rejected any diplomatic connections with Israel, and refused to be satisfied with less than an immediate and absolute dissolution of the State of Israel and the murder of its Jewish inhabitants! Its activists received their orders through a hidden channel connected directly to Iran.

≈)⌒

The lines raced along the monitor at a dizzying pace. Yigal studied the text to see if he had loaded the code in the proper sequence.

In those days we discovered the secret of the tiny creatures, my friend and I. This secret is known only to a select few and hidden from all others. Avi and Meitar had already seen those lines in Vienna. Baruch read further: *We understood from our study that the atmosphere of the world was filled with tiny flying creatures, so small as to be invisible to the naked eye. These are of several degrees, some smaller than others; the smaller, the more dangerous. In order to neutralize the danger of these smallest ones, it is necessary to change their natural makeup from the very foundation, and the new order shall be like the addition of the holy names, and their reverse in the subtraction of its signs.*

The last cryptic words left Baruch and Yigal baffled; it was Shimon Eliasyan who suggested the simple but brilliant solution. Shimon had occasionally peeked into his father's *siddur*, which was filled with holy names, thought-concentrations, holy combinations and codes. "Kabbalah focuses upon the Names of Hashem according to a certain internal order," he explained to Yigal and Baruch. "At first, only the first letter, *yud*; then the first two letters, *yud* and *hey*; then *yud, hey, vav*; and finally, they add the last letter of His Name, *hey*."

Baruch leaped up as if stung. "Shimon, do you know what you just said?" he cried excitedly. The youth blushed in confusion. "What did I say? Everyone knows that."

"R' Aharonowitz foretold this... What did he say a moment before his death? *Search among the small letters.* This statement had a double meaning.

In the miniature writing, and also to what the study of mysticism is commonly referred to...

"What else did he say? '*The combination of letters.*' He was not only referring to the will on the broken egg; he was also speaking of the changing of the genetic code!"

≈≈

Baruch sat in his lab, changing the inner sequence of the virus' genetic code. He had not bothered to deal with the "addition of names," only with their subtraction, with the negative aspect. This was what Zeide Avigdor had implied in the words, "And in reverse in the subtraction of its signs."

If he would write the code in a rising sequence, he would find the antidote to the virus; if he subtracted it or loaded it in descending order, he would turn it into a powerful weapon. How easy; how elementary...

After he called up the infinite genetic formula on the screen, he entered his own formula according to a descending order. When the equation was complete he ran it through a quick search-and-find command.

The main computer blipped and winked as billions of numbers and letters flitted across the screen at a speed millions of times quicker than the grasp of the eye.

After a ten-minute wait, the desired beep was heard. Baruch leaped forward and read the line familiar from previous attempts:

"An equation for a new genetic sequence. Yes or No?"

He punched the 'Y'. The computer whirred for several moments and then beeped again, "The equation for the new genetic sequence has been tried and passed successfully."

Baruch heaved a deep breath. The computer would take care of the rest. He would only have to examine what happened in the test tubes.

And also to be careful of the new Ebola virus. The mutated Ebola could be Israel's next atom bomb. The most deadly virus in the world...

≈≈

Roni sat in an apartment in a private house in Jaffa, together with

Halad, one his informers, and listened in deep concentration. "There are suspicious signs of organization in Rahat."

"Rahat? In the south, among the Bedouin tribes?" Roni could hardly believe his ears. His contact stuck to his story. He was one of the G.S.S.'s best informers and his information had never disappointed.

The next day Roni traveled to Rahat. This time he looked like the perfect Bedouin. He stayed the night in a friendly Bedouin camp and at midnight went out to a desolate place for an encounter with a local informer.

He waited for ten minutes before he became accustomed to the thick darkness and realized that he was not alone. Dozens of camels surrounded him, watching him with interest without making the slightest noise. Abu Snina arrived two minutes later.

Roni told him about the camels and he laughed. "One who does not live in the desert cannot know. The camel can be very quiet at night. You can stand two centimeters away and not be aware of it."

The information which Abu Snina brought was up to date. "The orders come from Rahat. A visitor was here from Lebanon; he's enlisting young men for something new."

"Suicide bus bombers?" guessed Roni. Abu Snina laughed out loud at his naivete, revealing white teeth that gleamed in the darkness. "You're behind the times. That's small-time business, kindergarten games of the type Yichye Ayash, the Engineer, used to do. They're planning big things here, far more serious than that kid stuff."

"Like what?"

"I really don't know. They're very secretive. But I was told this evening that the target is not here. It's in Jerusalem."

"Thanks a lot for your precise information," mocked Roni. "Where in Jerusalem?"

"In the Old City. Go there quickly. It's going to be something big, something on a very major scale!"

⋙⋘

Two rats munched hungrily on some cabbage leaves. They were indifferent to all the action going on around them. Baruch and his team of three select assistants were dressed in sealed protective suits from head to toe. A veil of heavy secrecy shrouded this first experiment with Ebola II. The cage with the rats had undergone massive sterilization beforehand to rule out death from any other cause. The test tube was opened inside the cage by an automatic device. Right before zero hour, the cage had been transferred to a sealed room. Baruch and his team watched what was happening through closed circuit television.

The distance between the open test tube and the rats was big. They had no direct contact with it. But after two minutes, the rats began writhing in pain and twitching violently on their sawdust-covered floor. They bled from their eyes, noses and ears and, after five minutes, froze in their final convulsion of death.

Baruch repeated the experiment a second and third time to verify their findings. At the second stage it was tried on dogs and at the third, on chimpanzees. The results were identical each time. The unfortunate creatures bled and died after excruciating suffering within four or five minutes. The post-mortem showed all the symptoms of the Ebola.

The experiment had succeeded. The virus was contagious through air contact.

Baruch was a white as a sheet. "Something's wrong," he whispered in panic. "The Ebola is not that quick."

After testing the new genetic formula for the Ebola, Baruch learned that the mutation it had undergone had turned it into a much more lethal virus. Not only was it contagious through air contact, it was a thousand times quicker and more deadly.

"We got it!" shouted Tzviki Lachover, Baruch's assistant. He jumped up into the air from sheer joy. "We did it! We have the quickest, most deadly virus in the whole world. The bacteriological atom bomb is in our hands!"

Baruch measured his assistant with a severe look. "Don't rejoice like that, Tzviki. This Frankenstein-golem is liable to rebel against its maker. This virus is so dangerous that I am deathly afraid of it. It is as quick as cyanide, but while cyanide is very limited in its scope, this spreads like the flu. It's worse than a hydrogen bomb. If you fly over Iran and spread only one spoonful of Ebola II in the air, life there will cease to exist within hours!"

"So be glad. Isn't that what we wanted?" cried Giora Cohen. "What's wrong with you? I don't understand you. Wait and see what a party we're going to make tomorrow! Everyone's going to be here: the prime minister, the head of the Mossad, the top echelon of Israel's security forces. We've developed the atom bomb of the twenty-first century!"

He broke out into a lively dance. "Tra, la, la! Five grams of Ebola II and all of Iran is going to sleep."

"And what happens after Iran? Did you stop to think about that? What's going to stop the virus? There is no antidote against it." Red lights went on in Baruch's head. He had ignored the major request of Zeide Avigdor, to develop an antidote to the disease. Instead, he had concentrated upon developing the death machine. *Tomorrow I'll work on changing the genetic sequence in the opposite direction,* he promised himself.

But the following day brought no further search for the antidote. The potency of Ebola II terrified him. If an irresponsible person laid his hands upon the test tube with the transparent liquid, he could put an end to all life forms on earth. And all this rested on the shoulders of Baruch Eliad!

He searched for a way of mitigating the deadly virus. He reviewed all the equations and ran through the program from scratch. He drew diagrams and compared results. After a week's arduous work, he had made tremendous advances. The Ebola III had a much more limited life span; in open air it did not last longer than ten minutes.

"This way I can have some measure of control over the virus," he explained to the head of the Mossad when the latter visited the lab and saw the results of the research from close up. "The virus will only be effective locally. It will be so hot that whoever is there will die immediately and will not have time to infect others in a wider area."

"Let us assume that we throw it down from an airplane into a busy marketplace or mall with a thousand people present. What effect will it have?" asked the Mossad chief.

"A thousand or one hundred thousand; it's all the same," explained Baruch. "Whoever is exposed to the virus within its immediate radius will be destroyed immediately. At a larger range its effect will diminish to a minimum."

"So what have we accomplished?" the Mossad chief wondered. "This is no more than a regular bomb."

"Not quite," smiled Eliad dryly. "It is a smart bomb which does not operate on a scorched-earth principle. It does not destroy houses and vegetation, and, most important, does not leave a residue of radioactive radiation for dozens of years to come. It's clean and efficient. And besides," he pointed to the safe, "we still have the previous version, the Ebola II. The deadliest weapon in the world."

The information was immediately transmitted to Iran. "Ebola II acts like an atomic weapon in every way. Ebola III, on the other hand, is only effective locally, and its life span in open air is no more than ten minutes."

54

The car slid along silently, its headlights extinguished, and stopped in front of a well-lit house. Perhaps a luxurious villa would better describe the structure, though its humble owner preferred to call it home.

A man in evening suit got out of the car and rang the intercom bell. He identified himself as Shaul and the door opened immediately. He ran up the stairs and entered an opulent living room.

"Do you have it?" He didn't like going about in circles.

"Not yet."

"Why?"

"It's in his safe."

"What is a safe for: to be broken into? We've invested millions in you, this villa is really ours; you want to play around? Go right ahead, if you like, but don't be surprised if you're soon summoned for questioning by the Mossad people. We'll expose you and the whole country will be turned upside down and you'll rot in prison until you die."

"Why are you so upset?" said the host in alarm. "I can't just go and ask him politely to give me the test tube. We spoke about your organizing something for me. What about his son? I gave you all the information on him. We agreed that you would pull him into a trap."

"Fine. Perhaps by tomorrow we'll have the son in our hands. After that the father will surely sing. But remember, if you don't bring that test tube to us within forty-eight hours, you're finished."

The liaison man left the house as quietly as he had come, leaving the host shaking with fear. Trembling, but hungry for money. The Iranian intelligence service had promised him a seven-digit figure for the test tube in the safe. A deposit of one hundred thousand dollars was already warming another safe and had been deposited in a Swiss bank account in his name.

An old hunchbacked woman made her way through the teeming market in the Old City. She was leaning heavily upon a cane in one hand and carrying a heavy basket in the other. No one gave her a second glance. She sighed hoarsely and begged for help, but even the dogs ran away from her because of the heavy stench she exuded. She waddled along Rechov Hashalshelet and continued along Rechov El Wad towards Maale Chalidiya, stopping finally by the courtyard of an ancient house near the "Cotton Sellers' Market." She slowly dragged her heavy basket inside, sighed and sank upon a filthy couch.

"Very touching," said a young man, studying her with laughing eyes. He spoke Hebrew without a trace of an Arabic accent.

"Hard times, Chalil," Roni sighed. He got up from the couch and began shedding his old woman's disguise, layer by layer. "In these modern times you can't expect even a little help, a little consideration."

"With a smell like that you still expect help?" Chalil held his nostrils together and made an ugly face. "What did you put on yourself, Chanel No. 5?"

"Nina Ricci," laughed Roni, and took out a green bottle from his pants pocket. "Want some?"

Chalil ran off to a corner. "What's that?" he cried, making a face.

"Good stuff," said Roni. "It's extracted from a skunk's glands, very effective against nosybodies, cockroaches and other nasty things. Just one drop and you stink for the rest of the day."

"The Secret Service doesn't have better methods? Very well, let's get down to business."

They talked in undertones for a few minutes. "Are you sure?"

"A hundred percent," promised Chalil.

Roni trusted him. Chalil was considered a reliable source. Until now he had not disappointed them. He contacted his controllers from a public phone booth. "There's a Moslem holiday this Friday. Tens of thousands of Palestinians armed with knives are expected to visit the Mosque of Omar on the Temple Mount. After prayers there's going to be a rousing sermon which will galvanize the tens of thousands to go down to the Kosel square and carry out a mass massacre on the Jews."

"Bring some more details," was the reply. "Go to the nearest site you can to verify."

He walked to another liaison apartment which was also situated deep in the heart of the danger zone, in the midst of the Moslem quarter. This time he was disguised as an old peddler dragging his cart with wares behind him on Rechov Sallah a Din.

Surrounded by throngs of Arabs, Roni felt a twinge of fear. *What if one of them realizes I'm an impostor?*

But no one suspected him. He reached the place and waited for another contact to appear. He never arrived. Roni grew tense. Impatient, he went over to the arched window and studied the traffic of pedestrians below.

Someone called up to him from below — using his real name. "This is the end," thought Roni. He didn't even hear the catlike padding of footsteps behind his back. His eyes bulged like marbles when the terrible blow fell upon his head. After that he didn't feel a thing.

Professor Manor cavorted around Eliad and did not leave him alone for a moment. The two had arrived at the labs of the Weizmann Institute early that morning and Baruch had felt a suppressed anger at the pest who knew where to be at the exact moment he was least wanted. The old man was unbearable. Baruch suddenly felt an urge to give him a shove and roll him down all the stairs. There was a limit to what one could take.

"Manor, ever since you came this morning, you haven't given me a moment's respite. Perhaps you can let me work in peace."

"Just one more joke," begged the old man. "Something I heard only yesterday." He told his joke in one breath. "A group of crazy people were transferred to a new building. The crazies were discussing a plan to escape the new wing and couldn't decide whether to dig a tunnel underneath or to climb over the fence. 'Listen,' said one. 'We're in real trouble. There's no fence.' Ho, ho, ho! That's a good one, isn't it?"

There was a beep from the pocket in Manor's white lab coat. "You have a cellular phone, Manor? That's against regulations, you know," Baruch said sternly. Manor ignored him. He took out the phone from his pocket and as he listened, a smile spread over his face. He didn't say a word. He didn't turn the phone off but put it back, still on, into his pocket. When he withdrew his hand, he was holding a gun with a silencer on it. The blue steel gleamed before Baruch's surprised gaze. Manor aimed the gun between Baruch's eyes. "Now it's not the crazy ones who are in trouble, but you. Get a move on. Give me the code to the safe."

"Manor, have you gone mad? What are you doing with that gun?"

"I'm not mad. I'm very serious. The game is over. Forward march, my friend. Give me your magnetic card and a drop of your blood. I've discovered your secret, haven't I?"

What had R' Aharonowitz said? "Check those who are close to you. Perhaps there are some dangerous elements among them."

He had not checked, not asked. He had placed his trust in traitors. He felt pain in his chest. Another heart attack in the offing? Perhaps.

Manor pressed him. "There's no time. Give me a sample of blood. I'm going downstairs to your real lab. This is only a front. Did you think I didn't know?"

"What else do you know?" whispered Baruch, clutching at his chest. "I-I-I'm h-h-having a h-h-heart attack."

Manor handed him the phone. "Wait until you hear what he has to say." Baruch put his ear to the receiver. "Abba, it's me, Roni. I'm sorry."

"Sorry?"

"For having been captured. Abba, meanwhile I'm okay. They haven't done anything to me yet, but if you don't give them what they want, they're going to kill me."

"Where are you?" shouted Baruch. Manor grabbed the phone away. He held out a needle. "Give me your finger."

"What do you want from my finger?" asked Baruch, clutching his chest again.

"Don't be a fool. To open up the safe downstairs."

"Open it yourself."

"Idiot. I've already tried. I didn't know that you built a mechanism that is activated by your nerve-wracking genetic inventions."

Baruch Eliad suffered each time he had to open the secret safe. It hurt him physically. He had to prick his finger with a needle, just like a diabetic taking his daily insulin shot, and smear the drop of blood on a magnetic card. The safe's activating device was built according to his specific genetic code. No one else could open it.

Each time he gave his blood for inspection, the scanner would read his genetic code to the central terminal and it would, in turn, verify and open the door, or refuse to admit a stranger to the secret lab.

"What's in the safe that so interests you?"

"Enough!" roared Manor. "Do you think that I am a complete idiot? I want the Ebola II. I've been watching you since the day you began working on bacteriological weapons."

This was a bad business. How could he get himself out of it? He thought of several possibilities. The old man was weaker than he. He could knock him out with one punch aimed at the center of his face. He had been taught this trick once in an army survival course; the principle was to concentrate all of your strength in one blow and knock your enemy out of commission.

Manor read his thoughts. "If something happens to me, they're going to kill your son Roni."

Baruch leaned weakly against the wall. The big wall clock continued ticking as if nothing had happened. He had still to recover from the shock. Old Manor, the nudge, the bore, a spy? "Who are you working for?"

"It's a secret. But what do I care? You won't see any more of me. I used to sell information to Russia; now I work for Iran."

"You low-down traitor! You sold yourself to our worst enemy! Iran is even worse than Iraq!"

"I'm not the traitor; you are. In a few hours they'll discover that you've disappeared. Then they'll see that the Ebola II has also disappeared and they'll connect the two together and conclude that the top Israeli scientist, Professor Baruch Eliad, was an Iranian spy!"

"And where will I be?" whispered Baruch. His voice refused to obey him. His mouth was dry and his tongue thick and sticky.

"In the disposal unit," Manor said gleefully. "Your own chemical disposal device. Soon you'll be able to feel what all those miserable creatures, your unsuccessful genetic experiments, felt like two seconds before they were liquidated in a chemical bath and their flesh consumed in carbolic acid."

"And what will you do?" Baruch was talking to buy time.

"I already notified the administration of my imminent leave a month ago. I'll stay on for another month or two and then I'll go to the Hawaiian Islands. There I'll spend the next twenty years having a good time and laughing at the entire world."

≈)(≈

"You're a murderer! A traitor! Who's behind you?" Baruch shouted.

"You're yelling at me? What does the name Yoachim von Krautemburg say to you? Your son and nephew killed him. He was the head of the network."

Roman Spiegel, the octopus with the thousand arms, closed in on him from all sides. The handwriting had been on the wall, clear and sharp. Manor had made a slip of the tongue that day when he had told the flat joke about Rottenberg's electric station and had said Guttenberg by mistake, and then blurted the name Krautemburg as well. Baruch had heard that unusual name for the second time in a week, when Meitar and Avi had returned from Vienna, but he had made no connection between the two. How could he have been so careless?

He suddenly felt a dizzy spell coming on. The room swirled around in a lively hora and he collapsed to the ground. As in a dream, he felt his finger being pricked with a needle. Manor squeezed a few drops of blood into a plastic test tube and dragged him towards the chemical disposal system. He pushed a button and the cover rose up. A sharp odor hit their noses.

"Get in."

"No," moaned Baruch weakly. "Don't you have an ounce of pity?"

"Climb in!" Manor pushed him inside and put the lid back on, ignoring Baruch's desperate screams.

Gideon Manor put his ear to the disposal unit. He didn't hear a thing. "Excellent!" he thought with satisfaction. "Baruch Eliad has disintegrated into acid." He had planned his actions very carefully. He was built similarly to Baruch. Having gotten rid of his colleague forever, he put on his protective suit, knowing that none of the lab guards would be able to identify him through the plastic mask.

He went down three flights underground in the elevator used only by staff members. When he approached the first checkpoint, his gloves stuck clammily to his palms. He was bathed in a cold sweat. The square metal box which he carried almost slipped from his shaking hands.

The guard looked at his identification tag, which read "Professor Baruch Eliad," and bowed slightly with deference as he let Manor in the main entrance.

Manor was still full of trepidation as he approached the second checkpoint, the one just before the lab. He identified four armed guards in their booths and his heart plunged downwards, but a moment later he learned with what reverence they regarded his name tag.

Two guards scanned the card while two others passed his magnetic card through the slit.

"Have a good day," one of the guards called. "Do only good things for the Jewish people." Manor nodded lightly.

"What's the matter today, Professor Eliad?" asked the guard. "You seem so distant."

"Leave him alone," his friend chided him. "If you worked like he did, you'd be laid out on the floor long ago."

The door of the sealed lab closed behind him. His body was bathed in another wave of cold sweat. He would have gladly sat down to rest for a few moments but time was short. He approached the huge safe with awed trepidation. Here was where the Ebola II reposed, a small test tube worth a million dollars in crisp green bills.

He opened the test tube with Baruch Eliad's blood in it, carefully smeared a drop upon the special area and passed the magnetic card through the slot. There was a light humming as the mechanism scanned the sample. "Approved." The safe door slid smoothly open.

Manor whistled in amazement. The door was half a meter thick. Its sides were reinforced and built to withstand a nuclear attack. In a tiny frozen container, in a long metal tube containing liquid hydrogen, lay two test tubes, and not one, as he had thought up till now. He took a quick look at the label of the first one. "Ebola II." "That's the one," he whispered to himself. He took the tube with its two vials and put them into a metal box. After three minutes, he returned to the checkpoint.

"You finished quickly today," noted one guard.

And so he had. Two hours later Manor had already reached the meeting point where he would hand over the vials to his controllers and receive two million dollars in exchange.

The chemical purification vat, or disposal unit, in the genetic lab was a huge affair. It had been Baruch's idea. Manor had suggested building a much smaller one but Baruch had won out. "We are going to work on a broad scale. You can't think small, like in the past," he had argued. The device that had been built was a huge vat filled with carbolic acid into which were thrown all the failures of his genetic experiments.

There were three meters between the entrance of the device and the vat itself. These three meters were also permeated with poisonous fumes.

He held on to the metal handle of the lid from inside with all his might, thanking the maintenance workers in his heart for having insisted upon these handles being welded on.

How much longer would he be able to last, grasping on to the handles with both hands and feet?

When Manor had pushed him inside, he had suddenly felt the will to live revive within him. The terrible dizziness that had gripped him simply melted away into nothingness and he clutched instinctively to the first thing his fingers latched on to. Then he found the footholds. He was prepared for a desperate fight for his life. He had been saved from falling into the deadly acid below, but the fumes were liable to kill him as well, even without direct contact with the thick green caustic liquid.

Eliad began to slip into semiconsciousness. The dizziness again threatened to overcome him. He shook his head stubbornly from side to side. "I intend to fight with all my might," he promised himself. And with a superhuman effort, he banished away all the defeatist thoughts for as long as he could hold out.

Thirty-five years of his life passed before his eyes like grains of sand in an hourglass. He saw himself sitting as a boy on the wide lawns surrounding Yetzivim. He loved to stare at the yellow sand rising in the wind, revealing the whitish desert boulders beneath.

He became the little Buki once again, a frightened child of ten, like then, in the Arab house in Beersheba, in the dark cellar.

"This can't be happening to me. I must be dreaming."

His shoulders that were being torn from their sockets and the pain in his legs disproved that premise.

"*Elokim*, I shall sing a new song to You; on a ten-stringed lyre shall I play for you. Deliver and rescue me from the many waters, from the hands of the gentiles." From the treacherous waters of the poisonous acid which can consume my entire body within five minutes, to the very last bone.

"Deliver and rescue me…" The words floated up to him from the abyss of his soul. The dust of years which covered them had suddenly vanished into nothingness. The passing years had lost all reality; they were only imaginary, nothing but a dream. Only the words of the verse were real.

I was once a religious boy. I sang the verses of Tehillim. This was the song I was supposed to sing as soloist in the choir, in the ten-year celebration of Yetzivim. But in the end, I never sang them… I shall sing that song now. But how does the tune go? The tune that I, myself, composed?

The tune floated up by itself, just like then, on Rosh Hashanah eve, when he had first composed it. He had not sung for thirty-five years, but now that gift of music had suddenly returned to him! He hummed the old tune. He sang and wept, wept and sang. He remembered the lecture of the famous psychologist who had spoken of "melodies and the soul of man."

"Melodies are like a record," he had said in his gripping lecture, before the era of the compact disk. "When they make a new record, a needle engraves the song into the plastic disk, so to speak. The phonograph needle passes along these grooves and reproduces the sounds that were imprinted on it in the studio, even after fifty years.

"The soul of a person has such a phonograph. If you hear a new song upon a certain background, you can be sure that whenever you hear it played again, you will always reconstruct the setting and atmosphere of the first hearing. That song will be imprinted in your memory with the special atmosphere of that time and place, and each subsequent hearing will evoke the same old memories."

This is what the psychologist claimed. He compared songs to the smells and tastes that evoke certain forgotten memories. Yigal had told Baruch that to this very day, whenever he heard the familiar song "*Shifchi kamayim libeich*," he relived his first days in *yeshivah ketanah*, since it had become very popular just then and had been on all lips.

That atmosphere of Yetzivim 5720, with all of the flavor of yore, returned to him now as fresh and vivid as new. He remembered those panicky moments in the Beersheba basement and how he had not lost his wits then, either, even as a boy of ten.

And what about now? I'm crying like a baby. Stop it, Baruch; calm down!

"Rescue and save me from the many waters, from the hands of the gentiles."

Manor was prepared to sell out the entire country to pander to his greed. He was walking about with deadly weapons. Who knew if he hadn't opened one of the vials yet?

And I'm to blame. The will spoke about utilizing the power for good, and instead of developing a serum against the Ebola, as I promised to Dr. David Heiman and Phinehas Osborne, I turned the virus into a monster, a relentless, unstoppable Angel of Death.

Just like Abba, Yechiel Horowitz, who utilized the power of song for profane purposes. But what comparison can there be between a killer virus and an opera performance?

The pain in his chest increased and his heart started beating erratically. The automatic emergency button attached to his heart went into action. The sensitive electrodes identified the signs of an eminent heart attack and being activated, began sending emergency signals to the nearest medical headquarters under whose care Baruch was. The men at the headquarters arrived within moments. A tornado would have been mild in comparison to the speed of the medical team that burst into the Weizmann Institute.

"Where's Eliad? He's about to have a heart attack."

The department was in a turmoil. Eliad on the verge of a heart attack? Where was he?

The medical team searched the department with a sophisticated device, and when they approached the disposal unit, the beeps increased to piercing whistles.

"He's inside the vat!" screamed Carmi, Baruch's assistant, and pressed the button. The lid rose and Carmi peered inside. He looked and immediately thrust his hands in and grabbed hold of Eliad, drawing him out.

Dozens of people stood there, not believing their eyes. The senior director of the department had been thrown into the chemical disposal unit? Eliad had been taken out of the vat at the last moment and he looked nearly dead.

"Move aside," shouted the senior medic. He laid Baruch down on a stretcher and wheeled him into the waiting ambulance. The heart attack took place on the way to the hospital.

The country rocked. Events streamed at a dizzying pace. The media transmitted data in rapid succession. "A Secret Service man, Roni Eliad, has been kidnaped by a fanatic Arab organization identifying with Iran. The organization has spread a video cassette in which the Secret Service man, Roni Eliad, is seen being kidnaped and held in a secret hideout. The security forces are making intensive investigations.

"The terrorist organization, Sword of Mohammed, has announced that it stands behind Eliad's abduction. The Sword of Mohammed is an unknown organization to date and its activists are thought to be Iranian.

"The Sword of Mohammed has presented its demands in a statement circulated in Judea and Samaria. They demand: 1. the immediate dissolution of the Israeli Knesset 2. an announcement by the Prime Minister that he is nullifying the sovereignty of the State of Israel 3. transfer of the military command to authorized representatives of the Sword of Mohammed.

"The Israeli government has announced that it does not intend to negotiate with the kidnapers because of what they define as their 'crazy demands.' In response, the spokesman of the organization has said that if negotiations do not begin, Roni Eliad will be executed within 48 hours. He also threatens that the people of the Sword of Mohammed will carry out a series of mass attacks."

⇒⇐

Meitar stood next to Baruch's bed in the hospital. Baruch lay in the Cardiac Intensive Care Unit under strict surveillance. Meitar's eyes were red and swollen. He loved his brother Roni with all his heart. Baruch tried to sit up in bed but Meitar restrained him.

"I feel much better," protested Baruch weakly. "But Roni…"

"What are they going to do to him?" Meitar sobbed. "My Roni. Don't let those rats hurt you!" His voice echoed through the entire department. The patients and staff understood what he was going through. The entire country sympathized with him. The kidnaping of a Secret Service operative had shaken everyone up. The terrorist organizations had again struck at the heart of the military apparatus and reduced the high and mighty *Shabak* to ineffectual nakedness.

They don't talk about Manor. That's good. If they had, the entire country would be upside down. What would happen if the secret leaked out about the scientist-spy and the Ebola II which was in his possession? These were only thoughts; secret reflections which Baruch did not share with Meitar.

His skin burned. He longed to do something, but his weakness overcame him and he fell asleep.

⇒⇐

Professor Manor reached the meeting point, smiling broadly. The test tubes warmed his heart. Yes, two, not one. Two million dollars! The vials had been carefully checked in a sealed lab he had in his villa. The unfortunate creatures died within minutes.

"You did the job!" said Imar, alias Shaul, slapping him on the back with effusive friendliness. "Bravo!"

"I don't need any bravos. Give me the money," Manor rasped impatiently. "You owe me one million nine hundred thousand dollars."

"Of course, you'll get it all," laughed Imar. But his laugh sounded off key to Manor. *He's scheming something. Watch out!*

"The check is waiting for you on the table," said Imar, gesturing. Manor turned his head carefully. There, on a low coffee table to his left, lay a check. He saw a lot of zeros and his heart welled up with pleasure. They had honored their promise. He had suspected them in vain. They were decent people, after all. He turned to the table to check if the amount was correct.

Imar shot him in the back three times. Professor Gideon Manor died with a happy smile on his face and the check between his fingers.

The news items followed one another rapidly. Wild rumors about an anticipated mass mob of incited Arabs attacking the worshipers at the Kosel on an upcoming Friday. Security forces went into a state of high alert but there was no real substance to the rumors. The Sword of Mohammed had circulated a cassette and then another one. They reiterated their demands but they made no dent on the government's position. The information they had might cause a general state of panic if it leaked out, so the Israeli government maintained a poker-face silence.

The religious concentrations of the population prepared for a prayer day for the welfare of the kidnaped soldier. The public rallied. All the rabbinical organizations, the various councils of Torah leaders, chassidic rebbes and elder kabbalists joined in calling for a mass day of prayers at the Kosel for the welfare of Aharon ben Hadas. The public was tense. It would converge upon the Kosel en masse, in forces that no incited Arab mob would be able to stop or harm. A kinetic excitement was felt. This time, people felt, the prayers would rend all the heavens. This time there would be a change.

55

A mass of people streamed through the streets of Jerusalem, towards the Old City. The large fleet of buses could not contain even a fraction of the pulsating flood of humanity. Thousands made their way in private cars, despite the strictures of the security forces to refrain from doing so. Traffic on Jaffa Street came to a standstill as thousands of pedestrians headed for Jaffa Gate. At the same time, a huge throng of walkers swarmed the streets of Meah Shearim in the direction of Damascus Gate.

It was a gigantic crowd of hundreds of thousands, all streaming towards the Kosel to pray for the welfare of Aharon ben Hadas. The story of the young security agent, Roni Eliad, had shaken people up and plucked at hidden strings in everyone's heart. The picture that was publicized throughout the media touched everyone. The smiling face of a young man, hardly more than a boy, looked out with big eyes reflecting all the good in the world; it was the expression of a pure, innocent soul.

Jewish solidarity did its part. The Kosel square had been prepared for the event. Huge batteries of loudspeakers had been hooked up to transmit the voices of those leading the prayers.

Children passed among the people distributing special flyers with select psalms and *slichos* printed on them to be said at this monumental event.

The crowd broke all records. "A crowd as large as this has not seen since the eve of the Gulf War," declared the old-timers. It may have been exaggeration, but not by much. The police officers who sat in a hovering helicopter had trouble estimating its size. Both the upper and lower levels were packed. It was an especially hot summer's day and the Magen David Adom station set up was already busy dealing with people who had fainted. The roads leading to the area were closed to traffic along both directions. Police helicopters circled above. The police command level was afraid of a major incident taking place if the congestion became any more acute. At five in the afternoon, all the roads leading to the Old City were closed to pedestrian traffic as well.

꒤꒤

The bus from Yetzivim reached the police barrier at the Jaffa Gate. "No entry," the signs announced. The driver ignored them and continued on.

A young policeman drew up to the driver. "Hey, mister, can't you read?"

The windows were opened and heads popped out. "You should be ashamed of yourself!" "Don't you know who's here? This is David Eliad, the grandfather of the kidnaped soldier!"

The officer was not prepared for such an onslaught. He drew back but then decided to get on the bus to check.

David Eliad sat in the front seat. A collapsible wheelchair stood ready at his service. When he had heard the terrible news of Roni's kidnaping, he had suddenly become too weak to stand. But neither was he prepared to forego the mass prayer rally at the Kosel under any circumstances. At the last moment, Gindush Avivi found a sturdy wheelchair and the old man joined the passengers.

Odelia sat next to him, covering her face with a large *Tehillim*, already soaked with her tears, the tears of a Jewish mother, a courageous woman whose entire life had been one solid block of suffering and strength. She ignored everything around her and concentrated upon the comforting words, her lips moving slowly, intently, verse after verse.

꒤꒤

The nurses hovered around Baruch's bed. He lay on his side, a small *Tehillim* in his hand from which he murmured a few verses from time to time. *The irony of fate,* he thought. *The small letters have been pursuing our family all these years. Will there be an end to the chase?*

Yes, Baruch, another thought followed. *The end will come. You surely admit that your life will never return to what it once was. How many times must Divine Providence send you signs and signals and shout, 'Open up for me,' without you opening the door?*

◈

Yigal sat across the aisle from his grim-faced father. An expression of abysmal agony was stretched taut across the face of the *rosh yeshivah* of *Amal HaTorah* in Mesilot. Avi and Meitar sat behind him, drawn and silent.

Stormy sessions had preceded this trip.

"I'm not going and I'm not praying," shouted Meitar angrily. "Roni was the religious one, the good guy. And he should be the victim? What did our family do to deserve all this suffering?"

"You're quarreling with the Almighty?" asked Avi. "Don't you see the hand of Providence navigating the course of events at every step?

"Besides," he continued, "where is your brotherly solidarity? If the entire country is going to the Kosel to pray for Aharon ben Hadas, how can you, his younger brother, exclude yourself and boycott the event?"

Meitar had no answers for Avi's questions. His shouts emanated from the suffering of his soul and the pangs of his own conscience. Ever since he had been a child, life had streamed along one channel, towards a single goal. He had become a famous singer, the idol of Israeli youth who reaped thunderous applause at each public performance and raked in a fortune from the sales of his group's records, which were the most popular on the market.

And suddenly, this blow in the face. An invisible hand had been holding him by the nape of his neck and shaking him about for the past three months. An inaudible voice was heard screaming inside him. But he had shut his ears, plugged them up to still the voices through his raucous jazzy rhythms. But one cannot drown out the voice of the heart. It pierces and penetrates at all times.

Meitar could not understand what had come over him lately. Even his compositions had undergone a metamorphosis. They were no longer the energetic screaming that revved up the base emotions. His last songs had already gotten critical flak from his fans. "What's happened to the soloist of 'Serenade'?" the media asked. "Is he about to join the *Teshuvah* movement?" His latest compositions were quiet, moving songs, and his particular audience could not appreciate the language of the soul.

Many people from Yetzivim occupied the rear seats of the bus, especially the younger generation. No one was surprised to see Meir Tzuriel, the old man who was beside himself with regret. "If only I could mend something of what I ruined with the few years still left to me on earth," he would occasionally sigh, sending sad looks towards David Eliad.

"Abba, don't eat your heart out; it's not good for your health," his son, Shevach Tzuriel, told him.

"Health, health," his father parroted. "I'm already as old as Terach, what difference does it make? The only important thing now is that they get Roni back in one piece."

The policeman got off the bus. "Move on," he waved to the driver. He gave some orders into his cellular phone so that the bus would encounter no trouble along the way. "Let the bus with license number 398-598 pass. It has the close family of the kidnaped security agent."

Two people stared out of a tiny window overlooking the Kosel square with high-powered field glasses.

"This is it, Massoud," the man on the right smiled with pleasure. "Our plans are proceeding like clockwork, just like we wanted. This gigantic crowd. The *yahud* did not disappoint us. Jewish solidarity is at work: one for all and all for one. You need only tickle them a bit and right away they turn out en masse. Boy, soon this is going to turn into the biggest cemetery the world has even seen."

"Can we take the soldier to the square?" asked Massoud.

"We've received clear orders," said Fahad. "At exactly six o'clock, we're to take him down to the square. We still have ten minutes to go."

They looked at the soldier. Roni stared at them with expressionless eyes. His kidnapers wondered if they had not injected too strong a dose of the narcotic. He looked as if he were about to lose consciousness. His head lolled back on the wheelchair where he sat, a dark blanket covering his legs, concealing the time mechanism on his lap.

If he could have seen clearly, it is doubtful if he would have identified himself. A professional makeup man had worked on him in the morning. This Secret Service man and camouflage artist who had been able to change his disguise seven times a day, from one type of Arab figure to another, in order to circulate among them, would not have dreamed that the day would come when a hostile Arab would dress him against his will, with a Jewish disguise, of all things, so that he could mix in a Jewish crowd. His face had been smeared with layers of superior makeup and his wrinkles were very convincing. A long white beard had been pasted on his cheeks and chin and he looked the epitome of an elderly rabbi.

"Is the time clock working?" asked Fahad. "Check it," said Massoud.

∽⌒

Fahad lifted the blanket. Roni's legs were fastened together with a flexible rubber strap, strong enough to hold a heavy tractor in place.

The time clock was connected to his bound legs. A fuse was hooked up to a plastic test tube containing a transparent liquid. The bomb's digital clock was already activated and the countdown had already begun half an hour ago. The red numbers changed rapidly. At seven p.m., the climax of the mass rally, the fuse would be activated and the twenty grams of Ebola II would be released into the open air.

In ten minutes they would take the soldier in the wheelchair down to the Kosel area and "Project: The End of the State of Israel" would be launched.

The plan was perfect. The Sword of Mohammed had learned the lessons from all the mistakes of its predecessors. This time there would be no room for error. Massoud looked the part of a young *chareidi* from head to foot, with a long dark suit and a round chassidic plush hat upon his head. His features were Western enough that his chassidic outfit would not look ridiculous. His beard was glued on tightly.

Massoud began to roll Roni's wheelchair forward. No one would suspect an old man in a wheelchair to be carrying a powerful bacteriological bomb on his body. No one would dream that the soldier for whose sake they had all gathered in the tens of thousands was actually in their midst and was about to inflict the biggest, most unprecedented catastrophe that mankind had ever known, a mass destruction that might even surpass Hiroshima and Nagasaki.

≈)≈

Avi pushed Saba Eliad's wheelchair along. David felt very weak. He had tried to walk on his own, but had immediately sunk down on the padded chair. He turned back to Avi. "The time comes when a man must surrender to the limitations of age."

"It's O.K., Saba. You needn't apologize. With Hashem's help, they're going to find Roni safe and sound and then you'll regain your strength, too."

"Make way," people cried on all sides. "That's the grandfather of the kidnaped soldier." And despite the crushing congestion, the crowd moved to make way for the wheelchair.

It was a moving scene. "Splitting a sea of humanity," whispered Avi to Meitar. A wide swath was created in the sea of people and Avi and Meitar pushed the wheelchair forward towards the level below.

≈)≈

Massoud took down the wheelchair with Roni slumped in it and left the house. He passed through one of the alleys leading towards the Kosel where he and his 'old man' were swallowed up in the bustling crowd. Thousands of people moved along in the crush, inching their way through the narrow roads between the Damascus Gate and the tunnel leading towards the Kosel at the upper level.

Roni had no idea of what was happening. He was completely under the effect of the narcotic. All around him were thousands of Jews reciting *Tehillim* in unison.

Suddenly, a voice boomed out deafeningly, drowning out the sound of the prayers down by the Kosel. Echoes rang out and bounded off the Judean hills in the background. Talaas, like Massoud, spoke a perfect Hebrew. "Listen, all Jews at the Kosel. Listen carefully. This is the Sword of Mohammed speaking to you. If your lives are dear to you, don't make a move. Don't push and don't do anything foolish. In the midst of this large crowd at the Kosel is one person carrying a bacteriological bomb on his body. It's a small bomb and no one can possibly detect it. But our might is very great. If you try to do anything, no one is going to get out of here alive. We have several demands to make of the Israeli government. If the Zionist government accepts them, you will be able to go home in peace. If the Zionist government does not begin negotiations with us within the hour, the bacteriological bomb will explode and destroy you all immediately. It is as strong as the atom bomb that wiped out Hiroshima and Nagasaki."

There was silence for a moment, a terrifying silence. People looked at one another in panicked disbelief. This was the moment everyone had dreaded. The black scenario that existed in the collective imagination could not be real. How could it, with so many rabbis, Jewish leaders, chassidic *admorim*, saintly figures… All in the same place. Here, at the Kosel, by the Holy of Holies. It was inconceivable!

After the first moment, the stunned crowd recovered from the initial shock. The threat sounded very close and very real. People could talk about being strong and courageous in the face of danger and crisis, but when the threat of mass extinction stared you in the eye, you couldn't help screaming hysterically…

Cries of panic rose up from the crowd. "*Oy vey!*" "Help!" from the women's section. "*Shema Yisrael!*"

Massoud whispered into his sleeve. "This is great! They're panicking. Carry on."

Talaas continued. "We demand that the prime minister come here at once to negotiate with us. An authorized representative of the security forces shall inform us immediately if the prime minister is on his way here. We demand the dissolution of the Zionist state, the abolition of the Knesset and the government, and the transfer of all military installations to the hands of our own authorized representatives, who will be arriving from Iran within the half hour.

"I repeat, there is a man in your midst carrying on his person a bacteriological bomb. If you try to touch him, he will explode. His whole body is wired with explosives. We can bring a second Holocaust upon you. If you don't want to die here, every last one of you, you had better bring the prime minister here, immediately."

⧼⧽

The hysteria at the Kosel swelled to frightening proportions. The Sword of Mohammed had planned its actions carefully. It had prepared snipers along several rooftops overlooking the Kosel square. They picked off anyone who tried to flee from the place with murderous precision. Their purpose was clear: to block off all exits of escape. Dozens of people had fainted and shouts for help could be heard from all sides.

The government ministers received an immediate report on the developments. The prime minister's face had lost all color. No Israeli head of state had ever received such a threat. A group of madmen had turned three hundred thousand Jews into hostages, a bargaining card with no parallel. And their demands were no less than the voluntary dismantling of the Jewish state, at once.

"Tell the madmen that I'm on my way to the Kosel, and stall for as much time as possible," he commanded the Chief of Staff.

He knew that the threat was real. He had just received a disturbing report of several fleets of Iranian battlecraft making their way towards Israel. The Israeli Air Force had mobilized its best pilots and planes into the air to meet them but the fears in his heart increased. Threats streamed in from all sides. Only four days had passed since Gideon Manor had stolen the two test tubes, one containing the Ebola II, the other Ebola III.

The prime minister received urgent calls on his hot line. Heads of state from all over the world offered their help. The U.S. president put it this way: "Time is short. The world has never stood under such a threat. Either we succeed in solving this immediate problem, or we all perish together!"

This was no empty figure of speech. The prime minister trembled, for the second possibility seemed far more likely!

⧼⧽

Shevach Tzuriel fell and got up several times. The satanic voice on the loudspeaker continued to sow panic within the crowd. People went wild, screamed and wept, and continued to push on all sides in an attempt to flee. Some fled towards the Kosel tunnel in the hope that the bomb would not reach them there. The tunnels were sealed off and the screams reached up to the skies. Some tried to run out and ran towards the Dung Gate and the Old City market. People trampled one another down indiscriminately. Security forces had closed off all streets leading to the Kosel, imprisoning hundreds of thousand inside the Kosel square, playing right into the hands of the Sword of Mohammed.

"Abba, where are you?" shouted Shevach. He knew that there was no chance in the world of finding his father among the hundreds of thousands, all the less so since when he had lost hold of him, he had been near the Kosel and now he had been pushed to the upper square. He futilely continued to shout and search, mindlessly, helpless: a lost son looking for his father.

Suddenly he spied David Eliad in a wheelchair. "Hey, what's he doing here?" he whispered to himself in surprise. "The old man was together with Abba before, only thirty yards below me. Perhaps both of them were swept to the upper level."

He studied the old man's face and then realized that it wasn't David Eliad at all. It was someone who resembled him very closely. What was this? A coincidence? Two old men in wheelchairs looking like one another?

He studied the eyes. Yes, those were Eliad's eyes. Eyes of blue-grey steel. But there was something strange about those eyes; they were dull and unfocused.

He thought he saw a flash of consciousness for a moment. A flicker of life in those dead eyes, as if he was trying to hint something, to convey some message. He studied the face of the young *chassid* pushing the wheelchair and their looks met. Shevach felt a sinking feeling in his guts. The young man looked very strange.

The television crews from all over the world which had been sent to cover the mass prayer rally had chanced upon an incomparable drama. An entire country under the threat of death was being broadcast in real time — hundreds of thousands of people facing total annihilation in the next few moments.

The reporters filmed like crazy. Hundreds of millions of viewers throughout the world watched these unforgettable reports. Faces petrified with fear, eyes gaping wide with terror, women fainting, young yeshivah boys reciting *Tehillim* with bitter tears, rabbis encouraging the people around them.

"Tell me," one American yeshivah student asked a reporter, "are you crazy? How can you film this with such fervor when your own life is being threatened just like the rest of us."

"You're right," said the cameraman, his finger pressing the zoom button, "but what do I have to lose? I'll go up to heaven with the biggest scoop I've ever had in my life!"

≈)(≈

Shevach Tzuriel knew Roni Eliad well. He studied the face of the old man once more and suddenly felt sure: It was Roni. It was a gut feeling, but he was certain he was right. He leaped towards the wheelchair and shouted at the top of his voice. "Roni Eliad is right here! This is him!"

The young '*charedi*' Arab whipped out his gun with its silencer. There was a soft noise, like a cork being pulled out of a bottle, and Shevach felt a sharp pain in his shoulder. He ignored it and threw himself upon the young '*chassid.*'

There was a riot on the spot. Some people fled as quickly as they could. Others rallied and threw themselves upon the young man in his innocent-looking disguise. The gun coughed again and Shevach Tzuriel fell to the ground, lifeless. Massoud continued to shoot until his bullets were spent. A violent fight took place around the wheelchair. Massoud threw his disguise aside and lifted up the blanket from Roni's legs.

"Stay away!" he shouted in a fiendish voice, his eyes shooting deadly sparks. "The biological bomb is here. Don't dare touch me or you'll all die. This is the Ebola II. It kills within minutes."

He ended with a shout of "*Itbach el Yahud*" (death to the Jews) and laid his hands upon the fragile glass test tube. His fingers grasped the delicate glass vial threateningly and the crowd drew back instinctively.

No one knew how it happened, but when it did, it took place in a flash...

Gindush Avivi suddenly leaped forward from behind. His hand clutched the Arab's throat. The young Arab let go of the vial and fought for his life with superhuman strength, but Gindush overpowered him and pinned him to the ground, unconscious.

He bent over Roni's legs. "No one's getting close here," he shouted. "I know about these things. I was in the army engineering corps."

He studied the wires connected to the time mechanism. Blue, red and yellow. Which should he sever? The red? It wasn't always positive. If he pulled the wrong wire, the fuse would blow on the spot.

"Oh, *Ribono Shel Olam!*" he prayed softly, his eyes tearing with the effort of concentration and the weight of the responsibility, "I don't know what to do. Guide me. Lead my fingers to the right wire. Don't let me get this wrong. Three hundred thousand of Your beloved sons are trusting in me."

He felt an alien power taking over and guiding his fingers. They pulled the yellow wire and disconnected it. The red numbers on the digital clock stopped their swift motion and froze.

It was one minute to seven.

≈)⪕

A collective sigh of relief burst out from the excited crowd. "He did it! He neutralized the bomb!" People wept with relief. Now the first aid and emergency services went into action.

A volley of shots could be heard from the Temple Mount and afterwards, another volley. The security forces stormed the Mosque of Omar with battalions of reinforcements and killed Talaas and the dozens of young revolutionaries who surrounded him. Another war broke out on the rooftops. Crack units gave chase to the groups of sharpshooters and encircled them on all sides.

U.S. AWACS planes which had been launched into the air were the first to note on their radar the about-face of the fleet of Iranian planes headed for Jerusalem. The warplanes simply turned around and headed back in the direction they had come. The Sword of Mohammed command headquarters in Iran had learned of the failure of 'Project: End of the State of Israel' and had ordered the planes back home.

Yigal Eliad made his way through the teeming crowd. "They didn't hurt you?" he asked his nephew, who was still sitting in this wheelchair, hardly moving. Roni shook his head. "They didn't get the chance," he murmured with dry lips. The influence of the drug was just beginning to wear off and his eyes slowly regained their usual luster.

"Where is the second test tube?"

The head of the Mossad spoke to Baruch on the phone. Professor Zimmerman, head of the department, had not been too happy to allow this call to his patient, who still had a long way to go until complete recovery. But the tone of urgency on the other end had convinced him more than any threat. "The Ebola II has disappeared. The terrorists of the Sword of Mohammed made the mistake of their life. Instead of using the Ebola III with its local effect upon the crowd at the Kosel and saving the Ebola II with its aerial potency for blackmail, they wasted the Ebola II and were left with a much weaker weapon."

Baruch shrugged his shoulders. The Ebola III was no inconsequential weapon either. The threat still hovered over the heads of Israeli citizens.

"We must protect the Kinneret and the sources of the national water carrier," he said softly. "They might try to empty the vial there and poison our drinking water."

A crack patrol unit leapt from the helicopter. Trained soldiers surrounded the central water reservoir of the national water carrier. Low flying helicopters circled around every strategic site, beginning with the Kinneret and flying northward to the sources of the Jordan to report every suspicious movement. The terrible vial had disappeared. Intelligence sources had discovered that the test tube had made its way to Iran.

This threat now joined the other dangers that were forever hovering over the heads of Israeli citizens. People would learn to live with it and would forget about it in time, just as they had forgotten its predecessors. No one lost sleep over the nuclear stockpiles of the former Soviet Union. Soviet missiles were being transferred to hostile powers but everyone slept well at night. Only the true Guardian of Israel did not slumber or sleep.

≈)⊂

It was late at night. Most of the crowd had already left and there was hardly a trace of the bloodcurdling drama which had taken place such a short time before. David, Avi and Meitar were still there, in the Kosel square. The entire Eliad family was there, refusing to leave. They lingered by the warm, loving, secure stones, praying quietly from overflowing hearts. They knew that nothing would ever be the same again. This day had changed things for them all. David sat in his wheelchair, weakened to the point of fainting. But a strange feeling suddenly welled up in him. He felt like singing! To thank his G-d for all the kindness He had shown him. How could he sing when the fountains of song had been stopped up for fifty years? How could he sing when his new friend, Meir Tzuriel, had lost his only son that very day? Shevach Tzuriel had sacrificed his life to save David's grandson. Shevach Travitzky and Shevach Tzuriel... The circle had been closed. And another circle: Gindush Avivi, Yoni's son, had saved Roni at the very last minute. Only Roni? Three hundred thousand people! Hundreds of thousands of circles of life would continue to open and close, to stream and froth like an endless river.

How marvelous are the circuits of the Creator of Worlds as they come full circle.